The Paris Ripper

First published by 280 Steps Publishing 2016

This edition first published 2017 by Fahrenheit Press

10 9 8 7 6 5 4 3 2 1

www.Fahrenheit-Press.com

F 4 E

The Paris Ripper

By

Seth Lynch

The 3rd Republic Novels

Fahrenheit Press

To Minty and Karuna, Scarlet K

Saturday, November 7th, Night

The shrieks and calls of Left Bank drunks were absorbed by the city long before they could reach the river. Only the sound of a speeding automobile on the Quai de Montebello broke the silence on the place du Parvis-Notre-Dame. Then the beat of footsteps followed by an inarticulate shout from behind Charlemagne's statue.

Two dark figures were silhouetted between the trees alongside the embankment wall. They came together then one fell to his knees as the other broke away and ran. He spluttered as he went, left a trail of spittle on his unshaven chin. A hand swept aside a stray branch, his feet pounded through dirty iced over puddles. Bruises had already formed on his throat.

The running man wore a short grizzled beard, black with shards of grey. His thin overcoat was held together with a safety pin. Held together until ten minutes earlier when the pin had snapped. His cloth cap had fallen somewhere near the statue. Further off, on the other side of the river, lay an old burlap potato sack. The man's scant belongings, which had been carried around inside it, were strewn across the embankment.

Having broken free, the man ran towards a middle-aged couple. They were on their way back from the Deux Magots on the boulevard Saint-Germain and contemplating cocktails at the Ritz bar. It was late but this was Paris. They watched the man run, filled with dread as they realised he was heading in their direction. Between gasping breaths this stranger shouted a frantic garbled message which, being English, they didn't understand.

The man gave up, changed tack and veered across the square towards the cathedral. Wet cobblestones sent him sprawling. Back on his feet, he reached the cathedral doors.

The other figure had appeared and glared over at the English couple. The first man stumbled and fell again. He hadn't gathered himself back up before he was kicked in the ribs. He collapsed face first to the floor. The pain of a broken rib merged with the sensation of having his head jerked back and a rope flipped around his neck. His fingernails broke trying to release the rope's grip. A knee pushed so hard into his back it felt as if his spine would snap. The doors of the cathedral turned blood red.

The pursuer stood up as the other man's body fell limp at his feet. He wiped the back of his hand across his mouth then stuffed the rope into his coat pocket. Without a moment's pause to get his breath back he pulled out a lock knife and cut off his victim's ears. He repeatedly stabbed him in the hole where the right ear had once been.

The English couple were already across the pont d'Arcole and out of sight. Once again the square in front of Notre Dame fell silent, save for another speeding automobile on the Quai de Montebello.

Sunday, November 8th, Morning

Chief Inspector Belmont sparked up a self-rolled cigarette and coughed. The morning, barely light, was damp and cold. Belmont's head span from lack of sleep and the bottles of red he'd hidden behind at last night's gallery opening. He didn't hate modern art, something his wife had accused him of as he made in-roads into the second bottle. Some of it was really rather lovely, amusing even. Far too much of it, however, and every piece from last night, displayed a distinct lack of discipline. Still, given the choice, he'd prefer to be back at the gallery, even without the shield of wine, than here, sploshing about in puddles, watching the technical boys line up another photograph of the murdered tramp.

Sergeant Galabert detached himself from the melee of technicians around the corpse when he noticed the Chief Inspector.

'Morning, Chef.'

'Morning, Galabert, isn't it?'

'Yes, Chef.'

'Are you the one who went to university?'

'Yes, Chef. Are you a university man?'

'Four years at the University of Flanders taught me more than I ever wanted to know. You were at Versailles before the Quai, that right? Worked on the Marcotte murder?'

'I was at Versailles and I helped on the Marcotte murder. It was on my patch but it wasn't my case. They wouldn't let us local boys handle it.'

'So, let's have it, what have we got over there?'

'A dead vagrant.'

'Beyond what I can see, please, Galabert.'

Galabert blushed.

'A male of about thirty years. Probably strangled, I could see markings on his neck. His ears have been cut off and one side of his head's been repeatedly stabbed. There's all sorts of brain matter on the floor near his head. That bit of rain we had washed away most of the blood and cleaned him up a touch. The technical guys from The Bureau have taken all his measurements and should be finishing with their photographs presently.'

'Any idea as to the time?'

'I think he was killed sometime between midnight and two.'

'Why's that?' Belmont asked.

'It was called in at two and the cess pit cleaners pass through here a bit before twelve, they'd have reported it.'

'Are you so sure they're that public spirited?'

'I don't know if they're public spirited, but they're always calling things in when I'm on night duty. I think they do it out of boredom.'

'You're probably right, Galabert. If you spend all night pumping shit then a dead tramp's as good a distraction as any.'

How many people, Belmont thought, had walked past that poor sap, afraid to catch his eye lest he should hold out his palm for a few sou? Even the guy who'd called it in hadn't realised he was dead. He'd simply been doing a public service by reporting a dirty oaf asleep at the doors of Notre Dame. It was only when the local flic tapped him with his boot that anyone had realised he was dead.

People bustled each other beyond the police cordon, strained their grubby necks to gain a glimpse of death on the pavement. It was a cold damp morning, seeing the tramp in a heap, dirty and lifeless, left them feeling a bit better about their own miserable lives. And it would make for an interesting story at the dinner table.

A motor-car spluttered to a halt out beyond the onlookers. It coughed out a middle-aged man in tweeds with a homburg hat. The motor, a dark-green 1922 Citroën Cloverleaf, always looked as if it'd never start again but somehow the doctor managed to drive it to every crime scene he was called out to. And that vehicle, like the student doctors on the front steps with cigarettes dangling from their lips, was a permanent feature at the médico-légal institute. The man in tweeds, the doctor, placed his hand on his hat and pushed it down as he manoeuvred through the police cordon.

'Fine start to my Sunday this is, Belmont. What have you got for me?'

The doctor lit a cigarette and regarded The Bureau's photographers at work.

'Another dead vagrant, Doc.'

'Nasty business. And the ears?'

'Both cut off and they've had a go at one of the holes. That and the bruising around the neck makes me think we're looking at the same killer.'

'Any suspects?'

'Nothing doing.'

'What, nothing at all? We've got a lunatic going about mutilating people and you've got nothing?'

'Until this morning it was person rather than people. And that person, not being a tax payer, didn't raise much interest back at the Quai.'

'Whoever's been doing this is a lunatic, Belmont. You'll have your dead tax payer soon enough.'

'Don't put this on me, Doc. It was Superintendent Péraud who talked of tax payers and a general lack of resources.'

'Péraud, that imbecile! What's he been saying?'

'Forget about Péraud. Besides, why are you getting so worked up? I thought doctors were inured to death.'

'Death that can't be prevented. But this…' He waved his hands in the general direction of the dead body.

'I don't deny that this killing is horrendous, but we can't afford to take any of it personally. You're going to poke and prod his mutilated body without puking into your hat. You'll do it because you're a professional and you wouldn't be able to if you took it personally.'

'Does none of it get to you, Belmont?'

'It'd all get to me if I let it. But don't worry, even Péraud can't argue against two killings. I'll get a squad together and we'll soon take this maniac off the streets. Then everyone can sleep safe and sound in their beds, until the next murderous lunatic comes along.'

The doctor ground his cigarette into the cobblestones, 'You going to this soiree on Thursday?'

'Think so, work permitting. I know the wife's pencilled me in for something.' Belmont rolled himself another cigarette.

'It's at Allard's place. Cocktails followed by who knows what.'

'Allard, he has that wonderful Gauguin. I'd go just to see the painting.'

'Each to his own, I go for the wine. He has the best cellar in Paris.'

'From what I remember, he mixes a pretty fine Martini too,' Belmont said. 'By the way, I didn't see you at that god-awful opening last night, you dodged a bullet there, Doc. Absolutely dreadful rot. I sometimes fear the future of art is in the hands of empty-headed wastrels. Can it be that all the talent was destroyed in the war, that our future Géricault's, Monet's, Rodin's and Pissarro's all perished at Verdun?'

'No, Belmont, you're just getting old. New talent always appears to be less substantial than its predecessors, just as the summers of our youth were always warmer than the summers of our dotage. Not that we're either of us in our dotage.' The doctor nodded at the corpse and the technicians who were packing away their equipment.

'Anyway,' Belmont said, his mind drawn back from the gallery walls and once more facing the canvas he had to work with.

Sergeant Galabert waited for the doctor to set to work before retreating back to Belmont's side.

'Anything else you'd like me to do before I knock off, Chef? I mean I can stay on longer if you wish but I'm on nights again tonight.'

Belmont flicked his half-smoked cigarette away and watched it settle between two dog turds. Then he turned his attention to the sergeant.

Galabert's eyes kept flicking back to the body. He'd watched the technicians as he now watched the doctor. His eyes were alert, his body seemed to be constantly moving. Not twitching but ready for action.

'You can forget about nights for a while, Galabert, I want you to work this case with me.'

Galabert almost leapt up and down in excitement.

'Stop bouncing around like a damn puppy dog and listen to me. When the doctor's finished there'll be a bit of time before they cart the body to the morgue. Use it to go through the victim's pockets. See if you can find some identification. If not, go home and grab some sleep. You can have three hours. After that I want you down at the médico-légal institute pestering Doc. When he's had enough and throws you out, get upstairs at the Quai and bug The Bureau boys. See what they've got. They'll have had time to turn up a fingerprint match, if there is one. If not they'll have to use the anthropometric measurements which could take a day or two and then, again, only if he's on record.'

'Will do, Chef.'

'If you don't get any luck with the prints you'll need to circulate a description to the regional police and the Sûreté. Give it to the press but don't let them know how he died. They won't push it once they hear he was a vagabond. And once you've made an identification, you'll need to draw up a list of everyone he knew, any friends, associates, family. They'll all need to be interviewed. He's the second man to have been killed in this manner, which means this isn't a normal murder investigation. Still, we cover the basics, do the interviews as if it were any other killing. Then we broaden the scope.'

'Will there be anybody else on the case?'

'I'll bring in Tabaraut and Caillou and anyone else who's free. But it'll be you and me in the main, Galabert, which means you're going to be doing a hell of a lot of tedious basic stuff.'

'Suits me?'

Belmont raised an eyebrow.

'I mean it suits me better than night duty.'

'It's going to be dull. Routine and dull. But take another look,' Belmont pointed at the body. 'Just a couple of hours ago we had a mad man sat over there sticking his pocket knife into that poor bastard's brain. We mustn't let that happen again.'

Sunday, November 8th, Night

There was hardly enough room to stand let alone stretch out a leg. Maddie fiddled with her stockings, tried to pin together a ladder which she'd caught on her motorbike.

'Does it show?'

'Course it shows, that's why they pay us.'

Laughter. There was always laughter in the dressing room. Took their minds off the fact they weren't at the Folies Bergère. There they might get noticed by a film producer or a banker who'd set them up with an apartment. Make them his cinq à sept. No more working this flea pit each night. And no more finishing the night at Madame Roscoe's, turning tricks to cover the rent.

'Don't show too bad and it's dark out there, no-one will notice, my dear.'

'Thanks, Leonie.'

The room was hot, the air thick with cigarette smoke and cheap scent. Someone propped the door open a touch to get that stale air circulating. Renée, a dark-haired girl of about twenty-five, sat near the door and fanned herself with an old copy of *La Coquette*. Leonie checked herself in a broken mirror and applied a smudge more makeup to cover her bruised eye.

A whisper went round: he's watching. Renée pulled her top down and jiggled her breasts at the door. Their laughter became shrieks. More girls joined Renée's show. A shadow flicked past the door, and then: he's gone.

'Don't know why 'e comes peeping,' Renée said. 'Gets the whole show for free each night anyway.'

'Thinks he'll get to see something extra.'

'He can 'ave something extra if 'e stumps up the cash.'

More laughter. Someone produced a bottle of rough ersatz absinthe. It got passed round as they each took a slug without bothering about niceties like glasses and water.

'Give us a smoke, Leonie.'

Leonie tossed Renée a cigarette.

The door burst open. 'Get moving you lazy bitches, I don't pay you to loaf about gassing and drinking.' The Boss, forty years of cigarettes, resentment and venom, held the door open as the girls trooped out.

Philippe paid scant attention to the punter leant against the bar, a war cripple with a missing left arm and scarred up face.

'She couldn't get enough of me, Phil, I tell you.'

'Yeah.'

'You'd never know it to look at her. Looked all sweet and innocent but she was a fiend. Sex mad. Big tits, biggest I've ever seen.'

'Good for you.'

The same stories repeated each night or each week depending on who was doing the telling. But if they were so good at attracting women why did they come to this sleazy decrepit dive with its overpriced, watered down drinks and enough stink to make a pig sick. Philippe turned to the stage. There they were, tits out and high kicking away.

Philippe discreetly helped himself to a drink. The punter returned to his table. Over by the stage, the accordionist raced through another can-can while the girls struggled to keep their legs up. Sweat cascaded down their backs. Smiles melted on their faces. Philippe reckoned this was dance five but couldn't be sure. If it was there'd be mingle time next. A break from the dancing where the girls came and sat on the punter's laps. They got five percent on any drink the poor fool bought. They get more, on the quiet, if they let him stick a hand up their short skirts.

Philippe thought about earlier and spat on the floor

behind the bar. That Renée is a slovenly whore. Where did she get off flashing her tits at him like he was some drunk punter? If he wanted to watch them change then that was his business. Besides, he wasn't eyeing that ugly trollop. He was looking at Maddie.

Mingle time. Cigar ash fell on Maddie's lap. The man brushed it away, let his hand linger on her thigh. She pretended not to notice that he was still brushing though the ash was gone.

'You gonna buy me a drink, sweetheart?'

'Sure, darling, what d'ya want?'

'Gin.'

He called out to Philippe who brought over a gin. Philippe lingered longer than needed, let his eyes rest on the fat fella's hand as it caressed Maddie's thigh. She was perched on the man's lap with one arm draped around his neck. Maddie took a sip of her drink and winked at Philippe who retreated back to the bar.

Maddie whispered, 'if you're leaving your hand down there you're gonna have to pay some rent.' He was no sap, he knew the drill, he pulled out a note and stuck it down her cleavage. The hand crept up between her legs. She sighed in his ear and pretended to enjoy being touched.

A bell rang and the girls scuttled back to the dressing room. The accordionist stopped playing and lit a cigarette. He only got a ten minute break. Philippe brought him over a glass of wine.

Philippe poured two gins. The last of the punters had been manhandled out the door. He wasn't supposed to do that. The rule was simple: if they're paying they're staying. Not likely. If he let them, they'd stay all night. The last of the girls had gone too. Gone to Roscoe's to earn a few more francs on their backs. Maddie hadn't though. She'd stayed on for a nightcap.

'Just a small one, Phil. A friend of mine had three large gins and ended up wrapping her motorbike round a street lamp at 70kph.'

'What happened?'

'They buried her in the Saint-Vincent Cemetery.'

'Shame.'

'Yeah, and that street lamp's never been the same since.'

They both laughed and took a sip of gin. Phillip's eyes never left Maddie. He looked her up and down, mostly gazed into her eyes and hoped she didn't think him a pushover.

'I had a friend who died,' he said.

'That's sad, how?'

'Jumped from a tree. He had a notion that if you landed on your feet you wouldn't get hurt. Climbed up nice and high then jumped.'

'His theory didn't hold water then?'

'I don't know. His foot hit a branch on the way down and he landed on his head.'

They both laughed again.

'I gotta get going, Phil. Do you want a ride home?'

He was about to say yes when he pictured himself on the back of her bike. Liked the idea of holding her tight, holding her close. Not so keen on the idea of other people seeing him. They'd think he was a cissy being driven by a girl.

'Thanks but no, I've gotta lock up.'

'Suit yourself, Phil, I'll see you next Friday.'

Philippe poured himself another gin. Drained it in two gulps. Kicked the bar hard then wiped it down.

Monday, November 9th

Belmont's office was uncomfortably hot. All the windows shut while a stove roared away. Belmont didn't seem to notice. He sat at his desk and rolled a cigarette, waited to hear what Galabert had to say.

Galabert had just entered the room and the heat had gotten to him straight off. It was like walking into an oven. Sweat trickled down from his temples. The seat Belmont had offered was in direct line of sight of the furnace. Would the Chef mind if he took off his jacket? He didn't dare to ask.

This was Galabert's first case at the judiciary police. He'd been there two months and in all that time they'd used him as a dogsbody. Stuck him on nights to watch the telephone. He'd get called out to drunken rapes and hang around the scene until an inspector arrived to take over. Then it'd be back to the Quai des Orfèvres to watch the telephone some more. That was until Belmont had asked him to work this investigation. The resentment he'd felt at not being utilised melted away. His old enthusiasm was back and kicking him in the stomach. He didn't want to blow it by complaining about the heat.

'We found a fingerprint match, Chef. Got it yesterday afternoon. It took a while longer than expected as some of the files had been misplaced.'

'Good work, Galabert. So who was he and what crimes had he committed?'

Galabert flipped open his notebook.

'His name was Hervé Ferrand, thirty-five years of age. Last known address was an apartment at 27 bis, rue de la

Reine-Blanche. Convicted in January 1930 for stealing from a former employer. Sentenced to six months – served at La Santé. Good prison record. I went and spoke to his former concierge.'

'So what did they say?'

Sweat crept down Galabert's back. Couldn't concentrate. Felt as if he might faint. He had to say something.

'May I remove my jacket, Chef?'

'If you wish.' Belmont stubbed out his cigarette and poured himself a glass of cognac, 'care for a glass?'

Galabert wasn't sure what to say. All the others drank but he avoided it during the day, it made him sleepy and it was early.

'Put it this way, Galabert, a flic's gotta drink.'

Belmont poured another glass and passed it across the desk.

'The concierge gave me Ferrand's life story,' Galabert said. 'Some fifty men, including Ferrand, were laid off from the local box factory. They virtually closed down operations, keeping on a skeleton staff of ten. Ferrand and the others were owed two months wages. After six months of dispute the company said they weren't going to pay up. If they'd had money to employ an advocate then Ferrand and his work mates could have sued. They didn't so Ferrand went it alone and climbed over the factory fence to steal some tools. They were valued at about half the money he was owed. The night watchman caught him and he was charged with theft.'

'Tough break,' Belmont said. It wasn't the first story of this kind he'd heard and, in the current economic climate, it wouldn't be the last.

'There was no money for the rent and once the sentence was passed his wife left him and moved back to parental home in Tours. The Ferrands were childless so the wife's move severed all ties with her husband. When he got out he had no home, no wife and no work. He ended up living on the street.'

'Good work, Galabert. Now take a drink before it

evaporates.'

Galabert took a small sip and kept hold of the glass to show willing.

'I want you to get a list of everyone this Ferrand knew,' Belmont said. 'All the frequent visitors to his old apartment. Even his cell mate from La Santé, if he's out yet. Do we know if the wife is still in Tours? Contact the local boys and get them to send someone round to question her. It's extremely doubtful she played any part in this but I want all the basics done and dusted. Give the boys in Tours a bell and I'll meet you in the briefing room. We're going to get things moving. And, Galabert...'

'Yes, Chef?'

'Put your jacket back on, I don't want you wondering around the building half-naked.'

Sergeant Gracianette rested his bulk on a chair beside Sergeant Caillou. He held a small plate of sandwiches in one hand and a bottle of beer in the other. Caillou just had a beer. The seating was arranged in a semi-circle in front of the far wall. A table had been pushed to the side of the room and used to hold a rough buffet. Two inspectors, Riquet and Tabaraut, were stood at the table. They helped themselves to beer while eyeing the sandwiches uncertain if they contained anything edible. Riquet was the longest serving among them having served in the judiciary through the war. The other three had fought before joining the police shortly after de-mob.

Sergeant Jouvin slouched against the wall near the doorway. He smoked a cigarette and let the ash drop to the floor. He was a little too young for the Great War. Did most of his eighteen months national service in the French Protectorate in Morocco. Saw the occasional skirmish but he was out the army and a police recruit by the time French forces became embroiled in the Rif War. Right now he looked bored, he wasn't much of an indoors man.

Galabert ate a sandwich over by the inspectors. They all

waited for Belmont.

'What's this all about, Bébé?' Jouvin said.

The name calling needled Galabert. Some people called him Dédé, short for André. Jouvin always made a big deal of calling him Bébé, baby. He decided to ignore him and took another bite of his sandwich.

'I said what's this all about, Bébé?'

The two seated sergeants, Caillou and Gracianette, shifted in their seats to look pointedly at Jouvin. They did it to make him shut up but he took no notice. And Galabert took no notice of him. The inspectors gave up on the sandwiches and carried their beers over to the chairs. This left Galabert alone at the table.

Jouvin sauntered over, took a long drag on his cigarette before stubbing it out in Galabert's sandwich. He glared at Galabert daring him to do something about it. Galabert continued to ignore him. Put his plate down on the table and went and took a seat with the others. Tabaraut shook his head and muttered to himself. Jouvin followed after Galabert as the door opened and Belmont walked in.

'Good, you're all here,' Belmont said taking a look at the table. 'Even better, the beer's arrived.' He opened a bottle, poured it into a glass and took a long swig. Looked around at the others. 'Sandwiches look to be of the usual standard, I see. Can I get anyone a beer?'

'No, but Galabert might want a glass of milk,' Jouvin said.

'Shut your mouth, Jouvin,' Belmont said, 'we'll have none of your playground bullshit today.' He made the men wait as he rolled a cigarette, then walked around in front of them and said, 'we've got two men dead, both murdered. Same M.O. Long and short, there's a lunatic out there and we need to catch him.'

'What kind of a lunatic?' Caillou asked.

'The kind that cuts your ears off then sticks a knife in your ear hole.'

'Do we know who it is?'

'Ever the optimist, Caillou, I like that, but we've got no

idea who it is.'

'Probably a North African wog,' Jouvin said. 'They're always sticking knives in things.'

Belmont fumbled in his jacket pocket and pulled out a lock knife. Short blade, wooden handle. 'Any of you got one of these?'

Galabert and Tabaraut didn't, the rest of them did.

'Well, Jouvin, this is the sort of knife he used. It's the sort of knife a lot of white French men carry with them. Anyway, before using the knife he strangled his victims.'

'Bare hands or garrotte?' Caillou asked.

'Doc is pretty certain it was a knotted rope. He said it's because of the bruises on the throat. That and the damage done to the windpipe matched what you might get when pressure is applied unevenly. Plus there were friction burns on the neck.'

'What's the motive? Did the victims know each other? Were they robbed?'

'Motive, who knows? Both the victims were vagrants. We don't know if they knew each other. It is possible they were robbed of the little they had. Certainly there wasn't much on them when they were found. Galabert is drawing up a list of family and known associates for the second victim. We already have a similar list for the first chump. Caillou, you and Gracianette can work through those lists looking for any overlaps. We're going to question them all but we'll focus on anyone who knew both victims. You'll all have to do your share of interviews. Galabert's going to contact the regional police to see if they've had any similar murders. We've already sent enquires to the International Criminal Police Commission in Vienna. The killer could have come from anywhere and there's always a chance someone's got something on him.'

'I'm willing to bet it's a North African.'

'Don't be such a fart-knuckle, Jouvin,' Gracianette said.

The Scarlet K café was busy. Packed with flics, all ranks. A medley of conversations bounced off the walls which were adorned with photographs of flics from previous generations. Belmont drank cognac, talked to another chief inspector, gave him the lowdown on his murdered tramps. In return he got a woman smothered as she slept. For money. By her nephew. And an old pawn broker beaten to death round the back of his shop. For money. Perpetrator as yet unknown.

Caillou, Tabaraut and Galabert sat together. Tabaraut finished off a sandwich he'd managed to sweet-talk the waiter into fixing for him.

'Where's Riquet?' Galabert asked.

'Riquet?' Tabaraut said. 'He'll be at home listening to jazz on his gramophone, drinking wine and masturbating over the film starlets in those Hollywood magazines his cousin posts him.'

'Tabaraut! That's a brother officer you're talking about,' Caillou said. 'And Galabert here doesn't know what Riquet's like.'

Tabaraut put his arm around Galabert's shoulder. 'Galabert, my son, our brother officer, Riquet, has got a thing about America. He spends his spare time in the black American jazz clubs around Montmartre and he watches every American movie that ever gets shown over here. He used to have pictures of Garbo up around the inspector's office until an uncouth sergeant started making untoward and lewd comments about her.'

'*He* claims they were untoward and lewd comments,' Caillou said, 'I merely told him what I'd like to do if the real Greta Garbo happened by the office. I think Riquet actually blushed as I got to the nitty-gritty.'

Jouvin was sat with Inspector Cruchon and Superintendent Péraud. The same superintendent who'd not afforded Belmont extra resources after the murder of the first tramp. The three of them drank red wine.

'Damn right, Jouvin. Sooner we drive out the coloureds the better. Get at them from every angle, we need to keep the pressure on the Arabs. If it wasn't a wog it'll have been a wop communist. The red bastards are always sticking knives in people.' The superintendent took a swig of wine. 'Keep an eye on Belmont for me, that man's been a stone in my shoe for years. He gets a bee in his bonnet you let me know about it. I don't want any surprises. And if the case doesn't move on I'll have every *bougnoule* in this city dragged in for questioning.'

'Yes, Sir, you know me. I'd love to get the whole lot of them in the interrogation room. They might not have committed this crime but the filthy buggers will have done something I can have them for. And it's always good to keep the pressure up, make them remember whose country this is.'

'Good man, Jouvin.' Péraud drained off his wine. 'Come on, Eric, we have a meeting to attend.'

Inspector Cruchon finished his wine, grabbed his hat, shook Jouvin's hand and followed Péraud out the door. Jouvin, now alone, ambled over to Galabert's table.

'Mind if I join you, Bébé?'

Galabert clenched his fist under the table. Resisted the urge to stand and challenge him. Decided it'd be best to keep ignoring Jouvin.

'Sit down, Jouvin, and stop getting at Galabert,' Caillou said. 'Calling him Bébé when he's not much younger than you are.'

Jouvin took a seat and glared at Galabert. Galabert stared back at him. They locked eyes and stayed locked until Gracianette slapped Jouvin on the back.

'You two knock it off,' Gracianette said. 'You're worse than the stray cats in my neighbour's yard. If you've got nothing better to do, Jouvin, you can fuck off to your own table. We were having a pleasant drink until you came along.'

'I'll drink where I like, Gracianette, this is my country and I don't take orders from you.'

Caillou nodded at Gracianette. The two men got up and stood either side of Jouvin. 'You want to test out that theory,

Jouvin, about where you can and can't drink?'

Jouvin looked up at them. Gracianette was big. Could be twice the weight of Jouvin. If he got some of that mass behind him he could lift Jouvin up and toss him across the room. Caillou was lean and mean. Older, not too many years of service left in him. Hard. Could take a kick in the face from a mule. And Jouvin had seen Caillou in action, watched him take out three men in less than five minutes.

'Sit down why don't you?' Jouvin said, 'can't any of you chaps take a joke?'

Caillou and Gracianette sat back down.

'That's better, Jouvin. So what were you and the superintendent getting all cosy about?' Gracianette said. 'You and Cruchon looked like a pair of fartleberries dangling from the hairs of Péraud's arse.'

'Nothing to do with any of you,' Jouvin said. 'We belong to the same club, that's all.'

'What sort of a club?'

'I can guess,' Caillou said. 'One of those France for the French clubs. Or is it a Bring Back the Monarchy club?'

'You can't deny that France needs a powerful ruler,' Jouvin said. 'We're dying on our feet and infested with foreigners.'

'So you put a king on the throne and hey presto! we're back in the glorious golden age.'

'Not a king but a strong leader, a man with vision who'd be given the authority of a king. The democratic experiment has failed. It's failed here, failed in Italy and it's failing in Germany. We are in desperate need of a dictator who'll put France back on track, make her prosperous once more, before handing the reins of power back to a governing body. We are crying out for a man with vision, someone who'll kick out the communists and the Jews. They're ruining the economy, bankrupting our nation, while trying to strong-arm us into another war. Two more years and the country will be on its knees.'

At Belmont's table the talk had turned to the Body in the

Trunk murders. They both laughed. Belmont had been a sergeant when someone had cut up a body and stuck it in a wicker basket. They were caught trying to pay a rail porter to help dump the basket in the Seine. The time before a woman had posted her dead husband to Nancy. The trunk sat in lost property until the stink got too much. Both Belmont and his drinking partner had been new recruits for that one. New but not fresh faced. The trenches had seen to that.

Midnight. Belmont told the taxi-cab to pull over on the street outside his apartment. After the Scarlet K he'd lost hours talking to his informers. He rolled a cigarette and watched the rain trickle down the windscreen. Paid the driver. Pulled his hat on and made a dash for the front door of the apartment building.

The Belmonts lived posh, boulevard Delessert, Passy. The concierge was more like a doorman from a plush hotel. He wore a dark green livery fronted with golden braids. Saluted residents when they entered the building. Having spotted the taxi-cab, he'd already summoned the elevator in anticipation of Belmont's arrival.

Belmont fumbled for his key. The apartment was quiet. It was getting late but his wife would be out. She rarely went to bed before one or two in the morning unless…

On opening the door Belmont was confronted with a distorted part-bird part-human face which leered out from a Max Ernst etching. Didn't like the picture and hated it greeting him every time he got home. Marginally better was the de Chirico which hung at the far end of the hall. In the three metres of hall space between Ernst and de Chirico there hung a crowd of African masks. Each one held some meaning, apparently. Fertility for the most part but some were worn to help the dead pass over to wherever it is the dead pass over to. Belmont placed his coat and hat on the stand. He needed a drink of water and thought he might as well drop some whiskey in it.

Belmont opened the kitchen door. There by the sink was

a Clara Bow look-a-like with a straight black bob, like she wore in Wings, dark eyes and thick red lipstick. Her symmetrical face was pretty close to perfect. A green pendant necklace dangled down to her cleavage. She wore a long scarf which caressed the line of her back. Then there was the red and black garter belt which hugged her thigh. Other than that, naked. She drew on a cigarette and blew the smoke out in a long stream as she gave Belmont the once over.

He was speechless. Lost for words. Reverted to a primitive form. Wanted to lay this woman on the kitchen table. That'd take too long. Up against the wall near the basin in the corner by the cupboard. Fought to control his primordial urges. Couldn't control the swelling in his trousers.

'Howdy, sweetheart,' she said. 'You must be the flic husband.'

'Pleased to meet you.'

Belmont held out his hand and felt like a school kid being presented to the mayoress. She drifted over, preceded by a musky perfume. Took his right hand with her left and went up on her tip-toes to kiss him on the cheek. Very close to the mouth. Belmont could feel her hard nipples through his sweaty shirt. She kept hold of his hand.

'Pleased to meet you too, Chief Inspector.'

Belmont stood dumbstruck as she pointedly stared at his crotch. There was no hiding the bulge. Naked women who looked like Clara Bow had that effect on him.

'Adrienne's waiting, I only popped out for a glass of water,' she giggled, 'and look what I found.' She still held his hand and turned her gaze up to meet his eyes.

'Well, I, I mean, I better get going,' Belmont said.

'Going? But, silly, this is your home.'

'I know, it's late, I should get ready for bed.'

'Oh, goodie. Adrienne will be pleased. She says you never join her when she's got company but you will tonight, won't you, darling?' She fluttered her eyelashes and again Belmont thought of the kitchen table.

'Best not.'

Belmont almost ran for the spare room. His room, as it was most nights. All his stuff was in there. Pyjamas, spare tobacco and a good lighter. He sat on the bed and listened to his heartbeat. Then she, that girl, walked across the hall from the kitchen. She said 'night, night' to his door and it sounded as if she blew a kiss. Moments later he heard the door to the master bedroom open and close. His wife and her talking. Laughter.

Belmont undressed and climbed into bed. Lit a cigarette. He could hear them again, low moans and groans. Two distinct sounds. His wife and Clara Bow. In the darkness he could see them as if they were all in the same room. Her more frequent groans, his wife speaking, the words indistinct. Belmont couldn't think. Long after the room fell silent he could still hear them in his mind, over and over. He'd never sleep. Finally he slipped his hand down his pyjamas and eased the tension. Then came sleep.

Tuesday, November 10th

The wall was decorated with photographs. Unpleasant photographs of the two victims. Dead bodies laid out on the ground. The darkness of the cobblestones made darker by blood. Contorted faces, bulbous eyes. Bloody lumps of cartilage where ears had once been. Photographs too of the area around the corpses: the imposing main entrance to Notre Dame and a corner of the embankment by the pont de l'Archevêché. Also on the wall, a map of Paris with two red tacks indicating the locations of the crimes.

Belmont rolled a cigarette and squinted at the images. His squad, minus Inspector Riquet and Sergeant Gracianette, waited. They occupied the semi-circle of chairs. All had a glass of beer in hand, yet all looked fed up. The last two days had been spent questioning relatives and associates of the dead men. Nothing. Normally someone would have a hunch or an interviewee would crack. There'd be something.

'Well,' Belmont said, 'you may have heard about the post office that was robbed on the rue Vauvenargues last night. They broke in and went at the safe with an oxyhydrogen blowpipe, got away with nearly a million francs worth of bonds and cash. I've let Riquet and Gracianette help on that one, hence the empty seats.'

'Lucky bastards,' Caillou said. 'I bet they've got something to go on. Fingerprints even, witnesses!'

'We do seem to be up against a brick wall,' Belmont said. 'Anyone had any luck with informers?'

'Been through mine and got nothing,' Tabaraut said. 'They didn't even know there'd been any killings.'

A chorus of 'same here' echoed through the rest of the men. Belmont too. He'd wasted hours in sleazy bars and run down cafés. Informers wheedled drinks out of him giving nothing in return. This was the driest case he'd ever worked on. With his two previous unsolved murders he'd known who the perpetrator was but the examining magistrate had dropped each one claiming the evidence was circumstantial. What he wouldn't do for a bit of circumstantial now.

'Galabert, how'd it go with the cess pit cleaners?'

'Nothing, Chef, and Christ they stink. I thought the vagrants were bad until I got two of them in a room. You'd really think they'd just crapped their pants.'

'What about the two witnesses, Tabaraut, how'd that go?'

'They were English. Useless, the pair of them. They heard a shout from behind Charlemagne's statue. Ignored it as they couldn't see anyone about and it wasn't repeated. That's where we found the cap, the one with the hairs inside which matched the victim's, just behind Charlemagne. We got little else of any use from them except to say that they thought the killer was of a low type, was male and,' he turned to look at Jouvin, 'white.'

'What was their exact description?' Jouvin asked.

Tabaraut pulled out his notebook and flicked through the pages. 'Dark hair, average height, medium build. Dressed scruffily. Obviously disreputable and of low character. No hat or collar. White faced.' He put his notebook away.

'To my mind,' Jouvin said, 'they might be wrong about him being white. It was dark and they've provided no details about what this killer looked like. Besides, the English aren't used to seeing Arabs, they might not realise how pale some of them can be.'

'They said he was white, not pale,' Tabaraut said.

'Before we get into an argument about it,' Belmont said, 'I think we should consider what Jouvin is saying.'

Jouvin and Tabaraut stopped eyeballing each other to look at Belmont. Both of them surprised. It was rare Belmont ever sided with Jouvin.

'Not about him being an Arab but about us not reading too much into their description. If you look a man in the face, as they did, but still can't describe any of his features then you aren't a reliable witness. We can take the height and build as approximate. I think we're safe saying it was a man. We can probably rule out his being black, they would have noticed that. We can't rule out Arabs, for now anyway.'

Jouvin looked pleased, saw himself rounding up Arabs and beating shit out of them.

'It's all immaterial now though. I can't keep you all on this case without any leads to follow up. The remaining interviews will keep you busy until Friday. Come Saturday, if we've got nothing new, you'll all be assigned other work. Except Galabert. You can have another week at it and I'll help out if needed.'

'If you don't mind, Chef,' Jouvin said, 'I'd like to stay on the case too.'

'I'm sure we all would, Jouvin, but there isn't any work for you on this one.'

'Like I said before, we could round up the darkies. What we got to lose?'

'We aren't rounding up anyone without evidence.'

'Let me round up a few and I'll soon have some evidence.'

'No doubt you would. And the next day it would all be retracted. And after that every Arab in the city will have it in for us. More than they do now. We aren't a big enough force to police without co-operation.'

'If I got some evidence beforehand?'

'We aren't going to blanket question a whole section of society. You get some evidence and then you can bring in specific individuals. And you get this evidence through proper investigative work. I'm not having you trawling the North African community just because you've got it in for them. If you start causing trouble there I'll have you working the night desk until retirement.'

Belmont made his way to an address on rue de Rivoli.

Parquet flooring with thick Turkish rugs. Mahogany panelling. Tapestries on the walls. The waiting room was discreet, patients entered and left through different doors so as not to encounter one another. When Belmont arrived this discreet waiting room was empty. The doctor would be with his final patient of the day. And that was the way Belmont had planned it.

'I'm sorry, sir, but the doctor requires an appointment.'

'Oh, he'll see me,' Belmont said, 'I'm practically a friend of the family.'

The secretary did not look convinced. In fact she looked disgusted. Her reaction surprised Belmont but he took no notice. Made himself comfortable on one of the waiting room's chrome-plated steel and leather Marcel Breuer chairs. A Monet hung on the wall facing him. Large enough to fill most of the space. Framed in gold. Belmont left his chair to take a closer look. The secretary kept him in her sights and he in turn kept his eye on her. The moment she glanced away he pressed a thumbnail into the frame. Decided it was real gold leaf, not just paint. Also decided the painting was a fake. Doubted the doctor knew it and that amused him. Amused him enough to start whistling as he paced the waiting room floor.

A door opened in the corridor and Belmont heard voices. The day's final patient departing. The secretary jumped up and shot to the doctor's door. Belmont followed close behind. She opened the door and Belmont side-stepped past her and into the doctor's consulting room.

The dead polar bear momentarily distracted him. He'd known it would be there but was surprised by its size. The thing was spread-eagled flat on the floor, open mouthed, giving him a dead-eyed stare. The secretary dodged in front of Belmont and tried to bar his way further into the office by holding out an arm.

'Chief Inspector Belmont, Paris Police.' Belmont lifted his hat.

'It's OK, Sylvie,' the doctor said, 'I'll deal with this.'

The secretary huffed once or twice before leaving. The doctor tried to guide Belmont out the office, 'I'm afraid it's late, Chief Inspector, and I really must be home on time this evening. Tuesday is my bridge night. Perhaps if you could speak with my secretary, Sylvie, she'll make an appointment for you.'

'Come, come, doctor, I know you can always make time for a Belmont. Or is it only my wife you can accommodate at short notice?'

The doctor blanched, 'if you've come to cause trouble I must warn you-'

'Shut-up, Frappier. If I'd come to cause trouble you'd be wiping the blood from your shirt by now.'

'Well, then I don't see-'

'You don't need to see, doctor, as I'm going to explain.'

The doctor edged slowly backward. Belmont moved forward to maintain the short distance between them.

'I know you've been sleeping with my wife. In here, on that disgusting polar bear.'

'What preposterous lies, who gave you that idea?'

'You've been seeing her as a patient for a couple of months now. I believe you've been lovers for most of that time. If you actually knew anything about her you'd know she doesn't keep secrets from me.'

For a moment Belmont could see them, his wife and Frappier. Two bodies becoming one on that mangy polar bear. His wife's face was clear to him, he knew the low moans she'd be emitting as she pretended he was pleasuring her. And the doctor, sweating, unable to contain himself, grunting on top of her. Then it was no longer his wife but her, the Clara Bow look-a-like, and Belmont. He was on top of her, drowning in her. He could…

Frappier spoke, his voice brought Belmont back to the here and now.

'I never, I mean, it's not that…'

'I don't care who my wife takes to bed. That's her choice. I am concerned about a doctor sleeping with his patients. I believe the medical board would describe it as unethical.'

'Please, Chief Inspector, tell me what it is you want, my heart can't stand the anxiety.'

'Actually, Doctor, I want your expert opinion on something.'

Once Frappier realised Belmont wasn't going to hit him he began to relax. Now he was able to revert to his role as psychiatrist, a role he'd been playing these last twenty years. He sat behind his desk and waved a hand for Belmont to take a seat.

Belmont rolled a cigarette and pulled over a carved ivory ashtray. Looked around for the place where the doctor might keep his drink. Couldn't see anywhere obvious. Eyed the doctor for a clue. For a second the doctor's eyes flicked towards the bottom right-hand side of his desk.

'If you've got booze in that drawer you'd better get it out. I always think better with a drink in my hand.'

'Really, why do you think that is?'

'Don't play the psychiatrist with me, Doctor. Just pour the booze and listen to what I've got to say.'

Frappier produced a bottle of scotch and a pair of glasses. His hands trembled as he poured Belmont a generous measure and matched it for himself. Belmont, after wetting his lips, proceeded to give the doctor a run through of the murders.

'Well, from what you have described, I would say we are dealing with a very dangerous individual.'

'Thank you, Doctor. One sentence and you've blown the case wide open.'

'There's no need for sarcasm, Chief Inspector.'

'Then tell me something I didn't already know when I walked in here. Something to make me forget you've been fucking your patients.'

Belmont enjoyed watching the doctor squirm and almost didn't care if he got nothing useful out of him. Any other doctor and Belmont would have been drumming his fingers on the desk or pacing the room. But today he didn't feel impatient, he felt satisfied. It made him realise that there was an underlying jealousy. He'd never felt it before, he'd met many of her lovers and not felt the least pang of jealousy. But why else would he enjoy watching this man squirm?

However, along with filling him in on the details of their sexual exploits, his wife had attributed to the doctor a brilliant mind.

'Anything I say is bound, by the very nature of the situation, to be speculative. After all, I have never met the patient.' The doctor gesticulated as he spoke and stroked his goatee beard in the pauses between sentences.

'Come along, Doctor. There must be wheels turning in that great brain of yours. Little sparks flying. What are they saying to you?'

The doctor re-charged their glasses then produced a pair of cigars.

'Leave the cigars. I don't want you using them to delay talking. Save them for later.'

'Very well. I have some ideas I just don't feel comfortable...'

'OK, I'll tell you what we'll do. We'll go to a café where you can pretend we're two friends discussing a story from the newspapers.'

The café was half empty. It looked out towards the river. Through the evening fog could be seen the Hôtel de Ville on the left. The Louvre on the right. Straight ahead, towering above a cover of trees, Notre Dame de Paris formed a penumbra against the darkened sky.

'Well, Chief Inspector, the first thing that came to mind was an inferiority complex and sexual repression. The two combined have created a pent up aggression. One aspect, which I find particularly disturbing, is the way in which he persisted even after he'd been spotted. Most criminals would baulk after being witnessed. And he could easily have turned tail but instead he continued with his killing ritual. All of which says to me that he had to find release right there and right then. If the English couple had interfered, rather than walking away, you might have been dealing with their dead bodies too. Else he'd have gone and found some other poor soul to take. I'm absolutely convinced that your man was compelled to kill that night.'

Belmont scribbled as the doctor talked. All his amusement at baiting the man was gone. This was as close as he'd gotten to a lead since the case began. But even as he wrote he knew it wasn't enough. He continued because it's never enough in one go. He just needed some other detail to crop up, something insignificant on its own but combined with the doctor's testimony it could set Belmont and his men on the killer's track.

'How would someone like that go about their everyday life without drawing attention to themselves? I mean this guy is nuts, completely lit up, yet he must be going about his business without anybody noticing.'

'Remember, Chief Inspector, I said it was a pent up anger. The killing acts as a release. Then, over time, the anger builds again. He may appear perfectly normal day to day. The fellow could even be polite and courteous, especially so in the days following a killing.'

'I see. And what sort of work would he do?'

'Well, I'm moving into the realms of pure speculation here, but I'd say he is employed in a servile position. He might very well be a servant in a large household where the employers treat him badly. This is someone who's likely to be put on by a number of other people. For example, an army private. Someone at the bottom of a chain of command.

'They must be older than other people in their position. Younger people, at work, expect to lie bottom of the pecking order. This fellow is at the bottom despite his age. And I'd say despite his intelligence. I don't claim him to be a genius but a simpleton would also accept a place on the bottom rung.'

The doctor relaxed, he enjoyed pontificating. He'd noticed too, that Belmont had stopped provoking him and was busy making notes.

'Can you think of any reason why he might be in that position?'

'I can, but perhaps it's your turn to speculate. I could light this cigar and listen to your ideas.'

Belmont nodded his consent. They lit their cigars and took in the surroundings. Belmont, when absorbed, blocked out all other stimuli. Until this point he hadn't been aware of the people around them or that he was cold. He certainly hadn't noticed the dreadfully shoddy reproductions of Georges de La Tour adorning the walls. The blacks were charcoal grey and the candle flames were nothing more than white triangles with absolutely no sense of burn. If he'd noticed this earlier he would have insisted on them going elsewhere. Instead he decided to throw himself back into it and hope those insults to seventeenth century art could be blocked, once more, from his mind.

'A foreigner. New to the country, maybe he can't speak the language.'

'Fits the bill, Chief Inspector, but let's not forget this is Paris. Anything beyond the Île-de-France is foreign. We could be dealing with a provincial drawn to the bright city lights.'

'OK, foreign or provincial. What else?'

'What did you say about the man he killed?'

'He was a tramp.'

'A tramp who'd lost his job. An ex-convict. Either of those circumstances could see you back at the bottom of the ladder. Maybe the killer had been destitute himself. He attacks tramps to expunge himself of the memory of that past humiliation.'

'Foreign or non-Parisian French. Lost his job. Perhaps a convict. That's a pretty wide net but, none the less, we do now have a net, and for that I thank you, Dr Frappier.'

Belmont stood on the street outside the café and watched a tram stop to pick up passengers. Saw them climbing on and off and heard the bell ring as the tram departed. He'd go through the interview notes tomorrow, see if anyone matched the psychiatrist's description. For now though he had something else to attend to. For now he'd spend half an hour with a cognac in a bar that didn't feel the need to desecrate art. And he'd spend that half an hour thinking about her, naked, on a polar bear rug.

Wednesday, November 11th

They sweated like stokers on a fast train to nowhere. Filthy like stokers too. The stench of their stale sweat pervaded everything. And the hot stoves kept it coming. As the day wore on, food smells mingled with the sweat. Not the salivating odour of food in the pot. Léon's hands, red raw from the hot water, ran a rag over a dirty spoon. At the next basin an older woman washed the cream pots they sent up with the coffee. It all dragged on for endless hours.

Outside, people had stopped to remember the war dead, they stood together like civilised beings. In this shit-hole the staff were allowed to stop work for a minute at 11. The hotel had barely fallen silent when the washroom rang out with the cry, 'back to work, you lazy bastards.'

The noise was like a prison at lights out. Waiters crashed about, swore. Some kicked out at Léon if he moved too far back. Kicked at his ankles. Made it hard to stand at the sink for hours on end.

'You need to keep in,' she said. 'They always kick you if you step back, even me and I'm a woman.'

'That's different, you're an old whore. Old whores should be kicked.'

'Your good mood didn't last.'

Léon spat in the sink and went on scrubbing the cutlery.

Break. Ten minutes. Squat for a shit and a smoke. Four days of this and then two more at another hotel filling breakfast orders and coffee pots. Different waiters, different cooks, same bastard ignorant attitude.

Léon found some plates from the lunch serving. Chop fat

with teeth marks beside a stubbed out cigarette in a sludge of gravy. There were ashtrays on the tables but the slobs here liked to use their plates. Another plate had potatoes and peas which, along with the fatty chop bone, he took and wrapped in a handkerchief. He stashed it all in his coat pocket. You couldn't leave money in your coat but no-one would swipe left over food from your pockets.

Hours more washing. Another cigarette smoked in the toilet. A swig of wine from a half-finished glass. Not a bad day for wine and he'd even had a nip of brandy. He rarely got spirits, the waiters always got there first.

The day ground on. Léon dreamt of a flood filling the hotel. Drowning them all, guests and workers alike. He'd survive, slip out before the water level rose too high. Then he'd drop a wooden prop against the door and listen to them banging on the other side trying to get out. Not a flood - a fire. Banging and screaming.

He grinned as he plunged his hands back into the water. Didn't care about the noise or that his hands stung. Kept seeing the hotel in flames and hearing them pounding at the door, knowing all the while that he could open it but never would. He looked over at the woman at the next sink. The two of them spent thirteen hours a day together in this room. He'd let her escape. No, no he couldn't just in case someone else got out too. She was way too slow. She wouldn't slip through as he held open the door. She'd want to go back for something, ask if he could keep it open a minute while she went to fetch her handbag. She'd tell him not to be so impatient. He spat in the water again. She could burn with the rest, couldn't let her out if it meant one single bastard got out too.

After work, a café bar. Léon sat with Pavel. They'd been ploungers together in a different hotel. Given half a chance Pavel would steal from people's coats or the stores, anywhere. Pavel liked it best if he could steal from the cooks. And he always gave ten percent to Léon for covering for him. Cover meant washing a dish or two from Pavel's basin and making excuses if anyone came looking. Léon enjoyed covering because he always wanted to know how long you could leave your post before someone came looking. He liked it too because he'd invent stories to explain Pavel's absence but didn't give a shit if Pavel got fired. And he did get fired. And so did Léon.

'We live like rats,' Léon said.

'We are rats,' Pavel replied.

'I'm no rat, I'm a man. And I won't eat this shit forever.'

'Not forever, we've all got to die sometime. But if you've got somewhere better to be, go. Else you've just got to put up with it and make the most of it. That's what I do. Help myself to a bit extra here and there. A bottle of brandy from the cellar, a few coins left in a coat pocket. It's all a game. Anyway, you're French, there must be better places for you out there.'

'Not for me, I'm on a blacklist.'

'For what?'

'I had a job in a factory down in Toulouse. We went on strike and when the gendarmes came to cause trouble I gave them some back. After that they had me pegged as a red.'

'Are you a red?'

'Red enough. After all, they're the only ones who care about the common man. To the rest we're just dirt on their shoes.'

'What makes you say you're blacklisted?'

'Whenever I got a job it wouldn't be long before the gendarmes turned up to tell the boss I was trouble. The foreman would call me in for a word and I'd be let go. Everywhere I went the bastard flics would follow, snitching me out. Then the flics stopped coming but I'd still get laid off. Blacklisted. When I came to Paris that bloody list followed me. They send it round, factory boss to factory boss. Only the hotels don't give a fuck. They'll take anyone on and work them like dogs. One day, though, to show them how grateful I am, I'll take a bomb and walk straight into the dining room. Right in the middle of the fish course. Put a few of them fuckers on my own blacklist.'

'Léon, my friend, thoughts like that are poison. They'll eat you up. Anyway, a bomb in the dining room of some crummy hotel won't change a thing.'

'That's the point, Pavel. There is nothing we can do to change a thing. All we have is the grand gesture. A bomb. Firing a revolver into a crowd. How I'd love to take out a president or a king.'

Léon grinned. Saw himself being given a hero's funeral. Crowds carrying his photograph pasted on placards. A black flag draped over his coffin. Once he'd been lowered into the ground, the funeral would turn into a riot which would itself transform into a revolution. By the time the sun sets that black flag flies high above the Élysée Palace.

'No, Léon, all your gesture does is add to the killing. One more, two more, three more deaths. Cemeteries are running out of space. Your name will become one of the many forgotten names. Your life one of the forgotten lives.'

'No, Pavel, my name will not be forgotten. It will be a name mothers whisper to their children to keep them quiet at night.'

'Léon my friend, you must find a cure for cancer. Else it's oblivion.'

'The way I feel about the world I'd rather invent a new cancer.'

Belmont looked a little smarter than usual, all the men did. They'd been out to the tomb of the Unknown Soldier for the remembrance ceremony. Every last one of them had lost someone. Belmont had thought of the war dead and of the hundreds of thousands of others who'd died of the Spanish Flu. There were no memorials to them, no national remembrance, yet their deaths touched nearly as many as the war. These were the dead who would be forgotten, but not by Belmont or those around him who'd lost loved ones to that modern plague.

Belmont scooped coal from the scuttle and fed it to the

stove. Galabert wished he hadn't. The room was too hot and Galabert had already removed his jacket. He hadn't delayed this time, asked to remove it as soon as he'd crossed the threshold. Then, begrudgingly, he'd said yes to a cognac. He tipped some on the floor while Belmont tended to the stove. Took a small sip and put the glass on the desk. It would look like he'd drunk half of it. Now he feared he'd emptied too much and it would encourage Belmont to recharge the glasses.

'Where were we, Galabert?'

'You'd been going through the witness statements, to see if they matched the psychiatrist's description.'

'And did they?'

'You said they didn't, Chef.'

'That's right, they didn't. The others will be finishing the last round of interviews presently. I'll skim their notes when they've finished. I hold no hope that I'll find anything of use. So what do we do next?'

'You were going to take the others off the case and leave me on it.'

'That's right.'

Belmont pulled out his tobacco pouch and rolled a cigarette while staring at the ceiling. He'd already blocked Galabert from his mind. Blocked the room and the ceiling itself. He stared into the void and let his mind run blank. Somewhere, out there, was the killer. He felt the analysis Frappier had given him was a golden thread snaking through Paris, he needed to extricate it. Belmont could almost see the thread weave through the streets to his man. Held it in his hand and gave it an ever so gentle tug.

The thread led from the Quai des Orfèvres along the river to Notre Dame de Paris. About 500 metres. That's how far the killer had been from the headquarters of the Paris Police when he'd committed his second murder. And the first murder, 750 metres, just over the river. In fact, if you picked the point behind the statue of Charlemagne, where a shout had been heard, to the site of the first murder there was a distance of about 350 metres. Maybe less.

There was a sudden pang in Belmont's chest. It felt like he'd forgotten something it was important not to forget. What the hell was it? Intangible. This wouldn't be grasped by force, he had to let his mind empty. Relax. He concentrated on his breathing, took long deep breaths and held the air in for a count of ten before exhaling for another count of ten. It hit him again and this time there was no mistake. It was her. Standing by the kitchen basin, reaching up to kiss his cheek, holding his hand. Those deep dark eyes, a mouth he longed to possess. The pang became an ache and it was as if the floor and walls had been swept away and Belmont had fallen to the street outside.

Belmont cast a furtive glance at Galabert. He'd forgotten his sergeant was still there. Should he send him away? No, the young fellow looked like he was wrapped up in something. Belmont needed to wrap himself up in something too, push the image of *her* out of his head.

He'd been onto something. The distance between the two murders. Within sight of each other – save for the odd wall obscuring the view.

Belmont played over the testimony from the English couple. They'd heard a shout from behind the statue. It probably came from the Promenade Maurice-Carême. He pictured himself standing at the statue and looked around. No, they couldn't have been on the Promenade. That's down by the river. To get to the statue they'd have had to scale the embankment wall.

The English couple had been walking from rue de La Cité, taken short a diversion to see the cathedral at night. There were only a few trees down there and they provided pretty scant cover this time of year. Belmont guessed the killer and his victim were moving East-West while the English couple were moving West-East. At the moment their paths crossed the statue was sat between them. Then the shout. The victim broke away and ran, saw the couple and turned to them for help. They shunned him and a minute later he's dead.

'Hmm,' Belmont said.
'Chef?'
Galabert had switched off. Belmont had fallen into a reverie and the heat had almost put Galabert to sleep. The heat and the long days and nights he was putting in to try and get somewhere on this case. To impress Belmont. To impress the others too.
'The first victim was found dead very near the pont de l'Archevêché on the Left Bank, not much more than 300 metres from where we found the second body. We know the second victim had been trying to escape. I suspect he'd been running from the east – from the direction of the pont de l'Archevêché.'
'You could be on to something, Chef. I knew the sites were close but I hadn't reckoned on them starting out from the same spot.'
'Still leaves us nowhere, Galabert. We're talking about the centre of Paris. How many people walk along by the river or cross that bridge each night?'
'Many, Chef.'
'We've got a killer who might have picked his victims from the same spot. And, based on Dr. Frappier's description, we've got an idea of what sort of person he might be. A foreigner or someone from outside Paris. How many people originating from outside of Paris live in this city? Probably half the population. The psychiatrist said it might be someone in a low level job who might normally expect to be higher on the ladder. We live in a time where men are finding it hard to get any work at all. People are losing jobs they've worked at for years. They'd be happy to jump back on the ladder, top or bottom. It's frustrating, Galabert. I feel like we only require one more something and we'd be onto him. Yet we're as far away from that one blasted something as when we started.'
'No, we must be getting closer.'
'This Saturday night, Galabert, I'm going to let you lead a squad. You're going to get some waggons, get some

uniforms and get down to the pont de l'Archevêché. Pick up every vagrant you see and bring them in. I doubt there'll be many more than ten under that one bridge. No rough stuff. Get them back here and serve them coffee and rolls, treat them kind. Hand out cigarettes. It'll be a real treat for tramps. Keep them in the cells for the night, let them sleep somewhere warm for a change. Sunday morning we'll feed them breakfast and coffee, more cigarettes. Then, early afternoon, we'll all come in and interview them. Nice and friendly. The way I see it, if they're sleeping under the bridge this Saturday night at least one of them must have been sleeping under it last Saturday night. And that one person might have seen something – any bloody thing.'

Galabert nearly burst with excitement.

'Yes, Chef, I'll get right on it.'

Saturday, November 14th

The Belmonts climbed into a taxi-cab. Then they were away, through the Trocadéro following a straight line towards the boulevard Haussmann. Their destination: a soirée on the rue Pierre Fontaine.

Madame Belmont pulled her husband close. Engulfed him in her perfume. Her gloved hand rested on his knee. She was excited. It wasn't often that she got to go out with him. Most evenings he was stuck in that silly office or out investigating. Tonight the police could go to hell and she would show him off. And she had a surprise in store for him.

The party was already underway. You could hear the music out in the street. Madame Belmont, satisfied that they were suitably late, sent the taxi-cab away. The doorman took their coats while a waiter offered them a glass of marc to combat the cold.

Although this was an apartment it took up most of the building. The basement was owned by an old widow who was, considerately, deaf. She would often pop up for the first half hour of any party, meet the early arrivals then declare herself away to bed.

A band played in the living room. Flappers danced and Madame Belmont, if she was anything, was a flapper at heart. She knocked back the marc, encouraged her husband to do the same, then made straight for the dance floor. The last thing she said before the music drowned their conversation was, 'goody, I adore the Charleston.'

Twenty bodies occupied the dance floor. The men were wearing a mix of formal evening wear and bohemian costume. Artists mixed with bankers and diplomats and, of course, one chief inspector. Belmont wore his monocle, an affectation he'd adopted then dropped in the early '20s and resurrected for parties. He also wore a green shirt with a black bow-tie. He hated the shirt but his wife had told him to wear it. Said it matched her dress, which matched her eyes, and 'don't you like my eyes anymore?' A flutter of eyelashes. Of course he liked her eyes and he kissed her eyelids to prove it. Kissed her eyelids and pulled on the green shirt.

Philippe walked to work. All uphill from the river. Past a couple of early evening drunks. Past the 'want to come with me?' girls and their pimps who played cards in a nearby café. Towards the dope pushers, the con artists and the pickpockets. Along rue Fontaine where some posh types were turning up for a party.

The streets were dirty from a recent rain. A muddy sludge ran over the pavements and filled the gutters. Some scrawny cat had tried to befriend him. Got a kick in the ribs for its trouble. Philippe wasn't out to be friendly.

At this hour the club would be preparing to open. The Breton cleaning woman would be putting away her mop and lighting a cigarette. Albert, the doorman, knocking back a glass of something then cracking his knuckles. The punters would be drinking elsewhere. Downing cheap gin and trying it on with any tart who happened to cross their paths. If they got lucky they'd give the club a miss. But they wouldn't get lucky because the club's clientèle weren't the lucky kind.

He stopped for a Canadian whiskey. Stood at the bar and swilled the booze around his mouth. He wasn't in the mood for today. Hated the idea of being stuck in a room full of lecherous drunks. Listening to their bullshit stories. Nodding and smiling and trying to look impressed. What he wanted to do was smash someone's face in.

The bad mood had ridden him all day. A fitful sleep left him grumpy. Grumpy became pissed off when he found there was no coffee. His lousy brother had the last of it before taking off for work. That set the tone for the day and nothing had come along to change it.

'One more for the road.'

He took the second glass and drained it in one. Then he left the café and walked past the Moulin Rouge and the tourists queueing up to get inside. Here the route got steep. Up rue Lepic where gangsters peered out through the darkened windows of lowlife cafés. Past a couple of Bals Musettes where working-class boys and girls came to drink, fight and fuck. He climbed up rue Tholozé until it met rue Lepic again, almost under the sales of the Moulin Galette, where the nightclub could be found. He nodded at Albert on the door and went in to set up the bar.

Two old men sat in the window. They played backgammon, smoked Turkish cigarettes and complained about the cold. They both wore jumpers under their jackets and had scarves wrapped around their necks. The stove, which sat only a metre away, had just been lit and wasn't yet giving out any heat.

An hour ago the old men had been fine. The place was packed. Hannachi, fresh from Algeria, sang. Drew in a decent crowd and warmed the joint up. Now Hannachi was gone. While the old men played their game he ate a light meal and prepared for his nightclub spot. Only back in Paris two days and he already had a full schedule of bookings.

Ferhat sipped the sweet black coffee. He waited for his brother who'd gone with Hannachi. The two of them had become friends during Hannachi's visits to Paris. It wasn't a purely social catch up for Ahmed, Ferhat was expecting a letter from a friend in Oran. Not the sort of letter you want travelling through the French postal system. It had been too public to pass it over earlier so Ferhat had sent Ahmed off to retrieve it some place discreet.

Ferhat stroked his moustache with his finger and watched the backgammon players. Not so many years ago he'd watched his grandfather play. He used to sit at his feet and listen to the gentle chatter of dice and breathe in the fragrant smell of tobacco. He couldn't remember his grandfather ever playing backgammon without the old man having some shisha on the go. He thought of those bright eyes in his ageing face. Ferhat looked at his nicotine stained fingers and the fragments of a serviette he'd been absentmindedly tearing to shreds. Life had been simple back then.

Belmont left his wife and took a seat at the side of the room. There was a time when he could have danced for hours. These days he felt his age, became conscious of the sweat on his brow, thought his movements awkward.

Halfway into a glass of red he noticed his wife dancing with a cravat-wearing young man. This man, Belmont knew, was a rising star on the Avant-Garde art scene. A surrealist fellow traveller who spent his time making statues and drinking with Giacometti.

The young man's luck would be out tonight. Belmont's wife might bring men back to the apartment but she'd never ditch her husband at a party for one. Not without Belmont's agreement. And tonight Belmont felt more like crushing desire. In fact the idea appealed to him.

He relaxed and enjoyed the show. His wife in her green chiffon dress. The neck embroidered with silk flowers. Her garter just visible when the dress bounced up above her knee. On her head was a thick black and silver band with two feathers stuck in the front. The sculptor moved around her like a love-struck sap. It was almost cruel.

She'd stop soon for a drink. Then she'd drag Belmont on a tour of introductions. Faces he remembered with names he'd forgotten. And each of them would look at him and wonder if he knew what his wife got up to. Belmont would smile, size them up and make a small joke before being hauled off to the next introduction. Occasionally there'd be someone worth meeting. An artist whose work he respected. Or an artist whose work his wife had purchased and he'd now be able to put a face to the signature. But best of all would be the occasional wit, someone Belmont could trade one liners, puns, and laughter with. Because in a joke you could forget yourself.

Philippe was in such a funk he didn't bother trying to spy on the girls. Didn't want to see them at all. He re-checked the float in the cash register. Gave the bar top another wipe. Then he went into the small room at the back of the bar.

Wasn't really a room. It was a cupboard he'd cleared out and started to use. He hung his jacket up in there when he put on his white barman's coat. The room stank of floor polish. A persistent smell as nobody had polished the floor this side of the war.

He kept a bottle of whiskey in there. He kept this bottle because it had proper booze in it, not the watered down stuff they sold. And he didn't want to be accused of stealing and was sure the boss marked the bottles and measured them against the takings.

Philippe took a large hit, let the drink go down and re-corked the bottle. Then he heard the miserable caterwaul of his boss. Some days the sound of that woman made his skin crawl. One day his luck would change, he'd make it big and quit this dump. When that day came she was going to get a slap she'd never forget.

The boss was a miserable hag. Made some money flashing her tits and fucking until she grew so ugly no-one wanted her. Took what she'd saved and added it to what she'd extorted and bought the club. Sat on it now like a miser on his pile of gold.

'Philippe, get your arse out here and give me some wine.'

'Yes, your majesty,' he said, but not so loud that she could hear.

'Red or white, boss?'

'Do I look like I'm eating a steak? Give me white, from the good bottle. I don't want that swill we feed to the pigs.'

Philippe poured her a glass and was grateful that she took

it to her office to drink. He didn't need her hanging around giving him ear-ache. The mood he was in he might have ended up losing his job. He wasn't sure that would be such a bad thing.

Ferhat signalled for a pair of coffees. His brother had just returned, bringing in the cold and the letter. After the waiter had left, Ahmed placed the short note on the table and they both leant over it.

'What will you say?' Ahmed asked.

'I'll say yes.'

Ahmed looked his brother in the eye, 'is that wise? What'll happen if we get caught? There could be repercussions.'

'Sometimes we have to do what is right and not what is wise. If this man needs our help we must give it. His aims are the same as ours and if he falls into the wrong hands it won't just be his life in jeopardy.'

Ahmed stared at the letter, chewed his lower lip and tried to think. They could make space for him, Ahmed could give up his cot and use a mat on the floor. That wasn't the point. If they let this man stay at the apartment they'd be aiding and abetting a known criminal. If he was caught they would torture him. If he was caught at their apartment they might torture them too, might think they were a party to the events in Oran.

'If they catch him,' Ahmed said, 'they'll think we were with him.'

'We are with him, brother. Remember we have cousins in Oran, men who played their own part. If they torture him he'll give them up. Nobody likes to think about this but there aren't many who won't talk under torture.'

'How can you say we are with him? I don't live in Algeria, I live in France. I have nothing against the French.'

'I have nothing against the French either. I only have something against the French in Algeria. If they want to live in our cities as we do in theirs, then I say welcome. But if they want to stand as masters in our homes, then we must do all we can to overthrow them.'

'We should forget all that. It's the past. Algeria is nothing but a memory for me. Home is Paris and no-one stands as master in my home here.'

'You are young, Ahmed. Too young to remember our grandfather. His broken spectacles, the mournful wails of grandma when they carried his body home. When I think of the French in Algeria, it's his bloodied face I see. I don't consider them to be brothers or friends.'

Ahmed knew they would do as his brother wished and put this man up. He didn't like it, didn't see why his new life should be jeopardised by events which had occurred when he could barely walk.

'Don't worry,' Ferhat said, 'it will only be for a few days and then we can rest easy.'

Belmont was pleased to find a few people he knew and liked. An art dealer who specialised in the Impressionists. Out of fashion but Belmont loved them. A banker who had the decency never to talk about this work. And a film director, always ready to dish the dirt on his cast.

'Caught any murderers lately, Chief Inspector?' the banker asked.

'Me? No! I'm strictly traffic duty.' Belmont did an impersonation of a flic directing traffic. Held up one hand while beckoning with the other.

'You don't get to be chief inspector directing traffic.'

'I've been at it for ten years and not caused a single accident. Service like that doesn't go unrewarded. How about you, Lambert, got any new Monets in?'

'There are no new Monets, Belmont. The man's been dead these last five years. I'm sure I saw you at the funeral.'

'You did, I travelled up to Giverny on the same train as Clemenceau. I watched them lay dear old Monet straight in his grave.'

'There you are then.'

'But I didn't see them lay all the forgers in there with him.'

'Hey, Belmont! That's like me saying you executed the wrong man.'

'But we don't execute people for traffic violations. I just wave my fist at them and jump up and down on the spot.'

'What made you bring up all this Monet business up anyway, you looking to expand your collection?'

'I'm always on the lookout for a good painting, Lambert. I only brought it up because I'm sure I saw a fake the other day.'

'Oh Christ, where was that?'

'Dr. Frappier's waiting room. Was in a lovely gold leafed frame.'

'Well, I didn't sell him it. The old fool probably bought it off some sly dog in a bric-a-brac shop off the place du Tertre. They always have unnoticed masters tucked away for simpletons to discover. Anyway, I have two paintings by Courbet which you ought to come cast an eye over.'

'You didn't find them in a bric-a-brac store?' said the banker.

'You'd better check the paint's dry, Belmont,' said the director.

Belmont's wife returned, 'you gentlemen don't mind if I steal my husband, do you?'

'You'd know all about stealing husbands,' the banker said, but only when the Belmonts were out of earshot.

The night dragged as he knew it would. One of the girls slipped over during her solo spot. Possibly because the floor was wet, possibly because she was drunk. The punters loved it, she wasn't wearing any underwear and they got an eyeful. It sickened Philippe who saw the fall as a cynical ploy to earn a few more francs when it came to mingle time. He found himself more and more in the back cupboard with the bottle to his lips.

Philippe wasn't a pretty sight come closing. Nor was the nightclub. One of the punters had thrown up in the corridor just outside the lavatory. It fell on Philippe to mop it up.

Then two of them had a fight over the girl with no knickers, like she wouldn't have let them both stroke her crotch. Albert had to step in and clean that one up. Then the booze and the re-occurring thought of the puke he'd mopped left him feeling sick.

The bar was closed, the takings in the boss' safe and Philippe was about to leave. He wanted to go on drinking, make a night of it. Only work had already used up most of the night and around here only the serious dives were still open at this hour, only the club's punters would drink in those shit holes. Maybe he'd head towards Les Halles and drink in one of the market cafés. Or one of the bars in Montparnasse which stayed open all night. No, he couldn't stomach the English and Americans you got drinking in Montparnasse.

Maddie appeared. She'd been slow getting changed and thought she'd have a chat and a gin with Phil before going home. She wanted the gin more than the chat.

'Hi, sweetheart,' she said. 'You got time for a quick drink with me?'

'Not tonight.'

'What's the matter with you, Phil?'

Philippe couldn't think what the matter was. The bad mood he'd been in all day, could it really stem from a lack of coffee when he woke up? It had gotten worse as the day wore on. He wanted to fight, to bite into something and rip it to pieces. Seeing Maddie being groped each Friday, Saturday and Sunday didn't help. Tonight it was the man who'd puked. Spent most of mingle time with a hand up her skirt and his dirty fingers up inside her. The image of the man's tongue popping in and out of Maddie's ears haunted him. Some days he could switch off to it, other days it ate away at it him.

'I don't feel like drinking with whores tonight, that's all,' he turned his back on her and went to get his coat.

She wasn't going to cry, she'd been called worse than that. Never by Phil though. She'd thought he was different, that he might be alright, that they might be friends. A lot of crazy thoughts had passed through her head, no need to get too hung up on this one. She marched out the back, kickstarted the bike, revved the engine until noise flooded the alleyway and drove home like she was possessed by a demon.

Philippe walked half-a-mile before he stopped to use a pissoir. Noticed some one duck up an alley. Looked like he might be casing the joint. Philippe didn't care. Buttoned up his flies and went up the alley too. The guy was standing on a dustbin trying to reach up to a window ledge.

The bin made a hell of a racket. The man fell and didn't land too good. Next thing he knew he got a boot in the head. Then another. Someone grabbed the front of his jacket, lifted him slightly and punched him in the face. Kept on punching until he passed out. All he could think was that he must have disturbed someone, that the householder was having a go.

Philippe left the guy in a heap by the dustbins, alive but Philippe didn't care one way or the other. Almost wanted him to be dead. His fist throbbed and there was a chance he'd broken a knuckle. If he had it'd have to mend itself. Didn't have the time, money or inclination for doctors. He decided to skip Les Halles and head straight home. The fight had lifted his spirits, got the pulse going. There was wine back at the apartment. He'd drink that to ease the pain.

Jouvin sat in the back of a baker's van, a cigarette dangled from the corner of his mouth. There were three other men with him and one up front in the driver's seat. They wore neckerchiefs like cowboys and played cards. Despite the front window being opened a crack, the van was full of cigarette smoke.

A large man, mean, looked like an old boxer, broken nose and cauliflower ear, known as Delfour, sat opposite Jouvin. Sweat ran down the side of his face. He wiped his forehead with his neckerchief and said: 'I don't see why they want this specific guy. If we didn't have to have him we could have had someone else and this would be over by now. This is dull.'

'They want to teach this guy a lesson,' Jouvin said. 'That's what this is all about. You teach lessons, you keep control. You don't teach lessons, you lose France.'

'What do they want to teach him a lesson for?'

'None of our business. All we need to know is what we need to do,' Jouvin said. 'It's like being a flic. We each do our bit, the bit we're trained to do.'

'You don't need to train me to kick in darkies,' the fat man said. They all laughed. 'Besides, all *bougnoules* look pretty much the same. What happens if I beat shit out of the wrong one?'

'Nothing happens so long as one of us gets the right one.'

A motor-car pulled up and parked about a hundred metres up the road. There were four men inside. The front-seat passenger was Superintendent Péraud. Cruchon sat behind him. All of them, except Péraud, wore neckerchiefs.

Someone cycled towards them. Stopped outside the café and used its light to take a look at his brakes. He glanced at the motor-car, then got on the bike and cycled back the way he came.

The motor-car flashed its lights three times. The driver of the van said, 'now'. Jouvin and the others pulled the neckerchiefs up over their noses and piled out the van. The men in the motor-car did the same. Péraud didn't move, kept his eyes fixed on the front of the café.

Two of the men from the van barged in through the café door. Silence broken by shouts. They reappeared with Ferhat who was being dragged between them. He writhed and struggled to get free. They dropped him in the middle of the road and started kicking. Jouvin and the van driver joined in. The men had their hats pulled down almost over their eyes. Their neckerchiefs covered most of the rest of their faces.

There was a screaming yell from the café. Ahmed came running at them, leapt on the nearest man and pulled him off his brother. Ferhat lay still as the other men turned their attention to Ahmed. Delfour swung at him but Ahmed, fast, stepped back and the punch swung through empty air. Jouvin moved in and stuck Ahmed on the nose. In return, Ahmed hit him on the cheek twice with two quick jabs. Jouvin rocked back and Delfour came forward once more. Ahmed side-stepped his punch, moved in and hit Delfour on the side of the face. Delfour went down cracking his head open on the curb as he went.

Delfour hitting the ground was the last Ahmed saw of the fight. Someone hit him over the back of the head with a life-preserver. His legs crumpled and as he collapsed he felt a kick in the back. He rolled over and tried to curl into a ball. The sole of a boot came towards his face, broke his nose. One of the next kicks put out his right eye. He wasn't conscious for the rest.

Belmont's wife led him upstairs where the other guests were working their way through the buffet. Waiters glided about with trays of champagne while a nephew of the host stood behind a small bar and mixed cocktails. Up here the music was provided by a gramophone and not a live band. It played Jazz direct from the States.

The music grated. Belmont could tolerate Jazz when dancing. Jazz while eating gave him indigestion.

Irritated by the music, Belmont piled as many vol-au-vents as he could onto a plate. Didn't care that people were watching him and tutting. He didn't care if they thought him greedy. The more he felt their eyes upon him the more inclined he was towards balancing just one more pastry atop the pile.

'You've been in a funny mood these last few days.'

'How so?' Belmont said.

His wife sized him up. She did that at times. It meant she was up to something. He had a vision of himself taking down his two Pissarros and replacing them with something by that new Spanish artist. Dali. He grimaced.

'Don't worry,' she said, 'it's nothing bad.'

'What is it then? I've told you I'm not moving any more of my paintings to make way for yours. If you need more wall space you'll have to take down one of your own.'

'I haven't bought anymore art. Well, not big pieces anyway. I did promise Séraphin I'd buy one of his statuettes. He's modelled it on me. He's called it *nude reclining by a window* – although you only get the nude, there is no window. It's not finished yet. You could buy it for me, for my birthday.' She paused to smile and clutch her husband's arm.

'Why not, after all your birthday's only eleven months away. Tell this Séraphin to send me the bill, but only when it's complete. Last time I bought a work in progress it remained a work in progress. We'll stick it by the window in the front room where it can recline to its heart's content.'

'That's smashing.' She planted a kiss on his cheek. 'Anyway, I've noticed you've been distracted these last few days.'

'I've been working on a case with very few leads. It'll be that.'

'It'll be that my hat! It all started when I had my friend to visit. She told me the pair of you had a little tête-à-tête in the kitchen. I don't know what she said but it obviously made a lasting impression.'

'I don't remember her.'

Blast his wife. How had she picked up on that? He'd not mentioned her once. Yet he was thinking of her all the time. Her face bursting through as he contemplated a murder scene. Giving orders to a sergeant he'd become aware of how she'd felt against him.

'She's here, darling, downstairs. I'm going to take you to her and then I'm going to have Séraphin take me to Bricktop's nightclub. I'll stay at his studio tonight so he can finish the statue. He'd have finished it weeks ago if he kept his hands on the clay instead of my breasts.' She laughed, took Belmont by the hand and led him downstairs.

He saw her before they'd reached the last step. The band played and she swayed in time to the music. Although she wore a blue satin dress, Belmont saw her as she'd been in his kitchen - naked but for a necklace and scarf. In the background he heard his wife introduce them. Didn't catch her name, just stared like a damn puppy dog. She moved next to him, stood on her tip-toes and whispered in his ear, 'take me away from here.' Then she gave his ear a small lick. Electricity shot through Belmont's body, it killed his ability to speak.

'Don't wait up, my darling,' Mme. Belmont said. 'I'll see you tomorrow.'

Belmont heard himself say, 'no, I'm in work late morning.' He was vaguely aware of his wife disappearing back up the stairs. Listened to his heart pounding above the sound of the crowd around him and the band playing in the next room. Then he felt her holding his hand.

'Come on, Chief Inspector, let's grab our coats. I want *you* somewhere private.'

Belmont followed her out into the cold dark night. The iciness of outside brought him to his senses. He noticed her coat was too thin for the time of year, more for show than warmth. Her eyes were overly blacked up, dark kohl styled like Cleopatra. And she'd put bits of sparkling gold on her face too, around the eyes and on her cheeks. Her lips were bright red. Her dark hair in a neat bob escaped from the sides of her hat. He wanted to lick the gold off her face. Instead he rolled a cigarette.

'I would have pegged you as a man who smokes American cigarettes,' she said.

'I've gotten used to these. I took them up during the war. Rolling them first meant they seemed to last longer.'

'Ah.' She smiled and got closer, looped her arm through his, 'You're a man who savours anticipation.'

They walked towards the Blanche Métro stop on the boulevard de Clichy. Didn't know where they were going but guessed it was to his place.

'We'll have to change,' he said. 'At Étoile. Then we can head straight down to Passay. From there it's just a two minute walk to the apartment. Or we could get a tram from Étoile–'

His talk ended as she'd reached up and kissed him on the mouth. Her tongue ran over his lips. He pulled her tight towards him, she broke away.

'Save if for later, Chief Inspector, it's far too cold out here.'

'I could warm you.'

She put her finger to his lips, silenced him, then led him to the Métro. They arrived in time to hop straight on a train. The Métro was nearly empty, too late for people to be going out and too early for them to be returning home. They and two others shared the entire compartment. One was an old lady who'd probably been visiting a friend. The other was a middle-aged man who'd likely been with his mistress and was now on his way home to the wife.

She kissed him again and worked her hand slowly up his leg from the knee. He was getting too excited. Belmont thought of the old lady, wondered if she owned a cat. He tried to count the checks on the man's coat but he was too far up the carriage and Belmont couldn't make them out. Belmont returned her kisses and tried to picture all those checks on that man's coat. She rubbed him through his trousers.

They reached a stop and Belmont moved to break away but she didn't let him. The old lady got off. No-one got on. She pressed herself closer and rubbed a little faster. Her tongue reached deep into his mouth, Belmont couldn't hold it back any longer.

'Oh! Chief inspector!' she said in mock surprise. She left her hand on the wet patch for a moment and licked her lips.

Belmont didn't know what to do. The excitement was over, for now, and they still had to change trains at Passay. He'd have to cover his trousers with his coat. She laughed and he joined her. He decided that when they reached the apartment he was going to carry her up to the bedroom, rip that dress off and devour her.

Saturday, November 14th, Night

They came in blue waves across the embankment. Galabert watched from up on the road beside the van they had ready to carry the transients away. The tramps, for the most part, accepted their fate. Spotted flics closing in from both directions and resigned themselves to whatever came next. Two made a break for it, dodged past the flics and ran up the stairs to the road, which saved someone the job of dragging them up there.

One, however, was not so keen on a chat with the boys in blue. He went to run, saw the law in his path, turned back and moved for the stairs. After taking a single step he looked up and saw Galabert looking back down at him. Thought better of the climb, ran to the water's edge and dived into the river.

Whether he'd never been able to swim or the shock of the cold overwhelmed him wasn't clear. Either way he started to drown a few metres from the edge. The current dragged him further from the quayside. Two of the flics watched him, neither man willing to follow him in.

The tramp waved his arms, spat and spluttered. His shouts were extinguished by the water pouring into his mouth whenever it opened. He went under for a moment and popped up another metre downstream. One of the flics looked about for something to throw, a rope, a ring. He looked at a small row boat moored nearby and decided to go for it.

There was a confusion of shouts. Some tramps kicked up a fuss, 'you can't do this!' The flics answered back, 'we can and we are.' Belmont's order of no rough stuff was being adhered to. These flics didn't count a clip round the ear or a prod with a club to be rough. Rough would be a good kicking or use of brass knuckles. A simple blow to the head didn't count.

The tramp in the river was gone, out of sight. His clothes, heavy with water, pulled him under. A flic clambered down an iron ladder to the row boat. His colleague shouted, 'he's there, no, there,' and pointed at shapes under the surface of the water.

They were both shocked by the sudden splash. Another man was in and swam double quick out into the river. The flic in the boat stared on in amazement. The one on the bank shouted, 'get after him, man, get rowing.'

The vagabond and the sergeant warmed their hands on their cups of coffee and stuck their feet up in front of Belmont's stove. Galabert knew the thing would soon have the room up to an intolerable temperature and for once he welcomed the prospect. Wet clothes were strewn over chairs and arranged around the stove. Galabert sneezed. The tramp sneezed. What a way to spend a Saturday night.

'Are you going to tell me why you jumped in the river?'

If it hadn't been for Belmont's instruction to be nice this clown would be freezing his arse off in the cells by now.

'Fancied a swim.'

'The way I see it, I saved your life. You owe me honest answers to my questions.'

'You ought to check the terms of the contract before you sign, friend, I don't remember agreeing to anything like that. I fancied a swim and the river looked inviting in the moonlight. That's the only answer you're getting from me.'

'If you fancied a swim so much, why did you give up? By the time I got there you'd spent more time under the water than above it.'

'I said I fancied a swim. I never claimed to be any good at it.' He chuckled to himself.

'Fair enough. You got me there. Put your clothes on and I'll have an officer escort you down to the holding cells.'

The tramp looked over at his clothes, drops of water formed puddles on the linoleum floor. 'Hold on a minute, friend. Perhaps you could put a nip of brandy in this coffee and I'll answer your questions for you.'

Galabert fetched his boss' cognac bottle. 'Just so you know the terms of *this* contract,' he said. 'If you get clever, I'll get nasty. You'll be sent down to the cells in your wet clobber and I'll have someone douse you in ice water every 30 minutes until morning.'

'I won't get clever, friend.'

'Good. Now that we understand each other, I'll begin. Why would anyone pick a cold night in November to jump in the Seine?'

'I panicked.'

'And?'

'And I jumped in. I was half-asleep. Been up since four am this morning because some bastard was banging trash cans together and woke me up. Then I had to piss and it started to rain. By the time I'd got my head back down I was awake. That's why I'm so ratty, I've not had more than ten minutes kip in the last twenty hours. Anyway, like I was saying, I was half-asleep. I heard shouting and ran for it. Saw people coming from both directions and went for the stairs. Saw someone looking down at me so I turned to the river.'

'In total we brought in thirteen people. You were the only one to jump in the river. The other twelve must have been equally confused but they all managed to stay dry.'

'Don't lumber me in with that lot, friend. Most of them are sheep. One man and his dog could have rounded them up.'

'But not you?'

'I'm a man and I'll keep my dignity, thank you very much.'

'You think this is dignified?'

Galabert indicated the fact they were sitting in their underwear with water dripping from their slightly blue bodies. The tramp had a towel draped over his shoulders.

'Dignified in its way. I'm sure you have the sheep penned in downstairs. Whereas I am in a hot room drinking coffee laced with brandy.'

He smiled a black-toothed smile and took a sip of coffee.

'I can see how you panicked in the first instance. By the time you went for the stairs that panic must have worn off. You'd have noticed it was the police after you.'

'I didn't. I thought it was thugs or someone else. You get them now and then, especially on a Saturday night. They come along the river causing trouble. Provoking, snarling, kicking out, starting fights.'

'Thugs or someone else?'

'Yes.'

'Who else?'

'You know, ruffians, hard nut drunks looking for a scrap or someone to take their frustrations out on. I reckon most of them know they'll be on the street within a year and have a go at us because we represent a feared future.'

'You're an insightful chap, aren't you.'

'I wasn't born on the street, friend. I went to school. I can read and write. I was an N.C.O. during the war. Led my lads to hell and back many times before I got captured. Came home to Paris and worked hard at my job. Did well until last year when I got laid off 'cos the company relied on orders from America. Wall Street crashed and so did we. The equation's simple: no job no money, no money no home. Me and many others are testament to that.'

'How long have you been on the street?'

'Nigh on a year.'

'Nearly a year and you still got spooked?'

The tramp looked away from Galabert and over at the stove instead.

'I also had a schooling,' Galabert said. 'And I've been a flic for three years. Long enough to know when someone's holding out on me. So spill it or you're down with the sheep.'

'OK. I really didn't notice you were flics. Like I said, I was half-asleep. Then I heard a shout, then another. I get up and see someone coming towards me. There was no shouting but I happened to wake up and see something. You sleep on the streets and you spend half the night waking up. I saw two men fighting. I recognised one of them, Hervé, a dirty bugger who'd try to grope you when you slept. I told him, "you do that again, and I'll cut your eyes out." He didn't try it with me no more but he kept on with the others.

'They were fighting and I figured Hervé had been caught with his hands down the other guy's pants. I didn't recognise the other guy but his clothes looked alright so he must be fresh to the street. I go back to sleep but keep one eye on the commotion. Hervé runs and the other guy goes after him. I saw Hervé drop his sack of belongings so I wandered over to see what was happening. They'd crossed the river so I picked up some of Hervé's stuff and figured I'd keep them.

'I didn't think any more of it until someone told me Hervé had been murdered. I felt bad about having taken his stuff.

'That's who I thought you were, not flics but the murderer come back. I realised after I was going under for the fifth time that there was too many of you. The killer had been on his own.'

Galabert tried to hide his excitement. By pure luck he had landed himself a witness. Well, maybe not luck. Maybe it was something to do with his Chef's idea of going back to the scene of the crime and rounding everybody up. But it was luck that he'd ended up in this room with him. He hoped the vagabond would be of greater use than the English couple.

The situation would have to be handled with care. If the tramp knew his worth he'd play them. Spin out and exaggerate his story for booze, cigarettes and food. Galabert winced. Remembered what the tramp had said about payments for groping.

'You said you thought the killer was new to the streets. His clothes were alright. What does that mean?'

'Means they were alright. Mine are OK but they aren't alright.' He picked at his trousers. 'They've got holes in and are wearing through in places but they'll do for a while yet. Still, now we're getting into winter I could do with another pullover. My coat's not bad. It'll see me through 'til next autumn. Then I'll start looking for a new one. I've had-'

'I'm not interested in the state of your clothes. I want to know what the killer was wearing.'

'Why?'

'Because I'm a flic, it's my job.'

And Galabert realised there was no handling this with care. Any fool would know how important this information was. He decided to get in a pre-emptive strike.

'It seems to me that you had evidence about a murder and decided to withhold it. That makes you an accessory.'

'A what? I didn't kill anyone. It's none of my business, that's all.'

'None of your business! It's everyone's business. That's why you jumped in the river, you idiot. You thought he'd come back to kill you. And so long as he's on the loose he might do just that. For one week you've been sitting on this. I'm going to call the magistrate, he'll have you charged.'

Galabert walked over to the telephone. The tramp watched him. Galabert picked up the receiver. The tramp watched him. Was he calling Galabert's bluff? Didn't he care if he got charged as an accessory to murder?

'I'll tell you what,' Galabert said. 'I won't make the call if you tell me all that you saw.'

'And another nip of brandy?'

'You'll get brandy when I'm satisfied you've told me everything. What did this guy look like?'

'He was about my height, I reckon.'

'And?'

'It was dark and he was fighting with Hervé. He wore a cloth cap, herringbone. And his coat matched it, herringbone too. He had dark trousers and dark shoes. Like I was saying, I don't reckon he'd been on the street long. His coat was alright, couldn't see any holes in it. But then I wasn't really looking at his clothes. I was watching the fight. I wanted to see him land one on Hervé but he didn't, he just tried to choke him with a bit of rope.'

Knowing that there had been a murder, and they would have all known not long after it happened, it wouldn't be difficult to work out that the police would be interested. Galabert felt his stomach twist like a hand had reached in and grabbed his intestine. This guy might not have seen anything. The whole thing could be a yarn from start to finish. On the other hand, he had been sleeping under the same bridge. There was every chance he was there on the night of the murder. Galabert couldn't decide if he was mining gold or iron pyrite. He paced the room, left the tramp to fill the silence with waffle about wearing old newspaper for a vest.

The lies might not be for direct reward. This man tried to escape by jumping in the river, a pretty desperate measure even in summer. Galabert picked up a large leather bound book which had been discarded on Belmont's desk. He walked up behind the tramp, who was busying himself lighting a cigarette from a packet Galabert had gotten for him, and slammed the book down.

The tramp turned around and said 'swatting flies?'

Not the least bit skittish, Galabert thought. Most likely he'd committed a crime. The sort of crime he'd risk a swim for. Either thieving or perving.

Galabert continued pacing, his coat flapped open and closed as he went. The tramp smoked his cigarette, enjoyed the warmth of the room, sat in his dirty underwear with a towel over his shoulders. An inspector knocked on the door and entered.

'Sergeant,' he nodded at Galabert and took a look around the room. 'I heard about your heroics, well done.'

'Thank you, sir.'

'Why are you marching about near naked?'

'My clothes are wet.'

'After all this time?' The inspector walked over to the clothes drying near the stove. Picked up Galabert's trousers.

'Dry as a bone. You'd best get dressed, or you'll gain a reputation.'

Galabert scuttled over to the stove and dressed.

'And you, sunshine,' the inspector said to the tramp. 'Anyway, Galabert, I'm sending out for some food. Want anything?'

'Beef sandwiches and a bottle of beer. Perhaps a -'

'Not you, sunshine. You can have soup downstairs with the others.'

The inspector took Galabert's order and left.

'I see,' said the tramp, 'you get sandwiches and beer and I get soup. I like that.'

'If you'd rather we could always put you back out on the street,' Galabert said and took a look out the window, 'it's starting to rain again.'

All bluff but Galabert felt like going through with it. Only a sense of decorum stopped him snatching the pack of cigarettes out of the tramp's pocket. The ungratefulness irked him so much the case lost its significance. It was the heat, which was beginning to get to him, that stopped him. Reminded him of Belmont and that this case could establish him.

'Talk and talk fast,' Galabert said. 'The man you saw was wearing a cloth cap, herringbone. And a coat to match. Dark trousers and dark shoes. About your height. What else?'

'That's about it.'

'Did he speak?'

'He might have said something but I didn't hear him.'

He was less use than the English pair. Galabert recommenced his pacing. Felt a prickly heat, his skin itched. Maybe the heat or could be the river water had irritated his skin. Whatever the cause, it wasn't helping. Made him irritable and now he wanted the tramp out. Then it occurred to him. It might not have been thieving or perving. He might have been trying to avoid a murder rap, after-all, an appointment with Monsieur de Paris and his guillotine could inspire a getaway swim across the Seine. Galabert stopped pacing. Tried to remember what had been found in the man's pockets.

An officer entered with sandwiches and a bottle of beer for Galabert.

'There's soup for him downstairs,' he said.

The tramp stood up to leave.

'Not so fast. Before you go I want you to think for a moment. What impression did you get of the killer?'

'I got the impression he wanted to give Hervé a good thumping.'

'You said you thought he'd been on the street a short time. What made you think he'd been on the street at all?'

'I don't know, I just assumed.'

'Close your eyes and try to see the scene once more. I want any impression you get. This time don't assume. Let it come to you.'

'I can picture them fighting but nothing's coming.'

'Do you still think he's a vagrant?'

'Maybe not.'

'What do you think then?'

'He wasn't in the right clobber for a factory worker or a railway man. The clothes were cheap and grubby but not blue collar. Better than mine now but not better than they were new.'

'Anything else?'

'He was a swarthy type.'

'Dark skinned?'

'Yeah.'

As opposed to white which is how the English couple had described him. Galabert could see Jouvin jumping all over this piece of news.

'An Arab?'

'Christ no, I know what Arabs look like. He was swarthy like he came from down south or worked as a miner. But we don't get miners in Paris.'

'Alright, off you go.'

'Will you need him back after he's eaten, Sergeant?'

'No, let him get some sleep.'

Galabert couldn't rule out the possibility that the tramp was the killer. He pulled on his hat, went and had a word with the duty inspector before heading back out.

First he took his torch and searched under the bridge. Despite the round up there were three more dossers sleeping there. They grunted at him but shut up once he'd identified himself. He even made them move so he could search where they slept. Then he went to the embankment stairway and had a look around. Then along the river's edge. The only place he didn't search was the river bed. So either the tramp didn't carry a knotted rope or he'd dumped it in the water.

Galabert went back to the station to take his leave, had a word with the desk-sergeant to see what else was going on. An Arab had been run over and died in the ambulance on the way to hospital. There'd been a knife fight which ended with one man seriously wounded. An Italian woman claimed she'd been raped near the Tuileries. A dead woman, suspected suicide, had been fished from the Seine near the pont de Sully. All-in-all, pretty quiet for a Saturday night.

Sunday, November 15th

Belmont faced the semi-circle of chairs and the tired faces which stared back at his own tired face. Galabert looked ill. Jouvin had bruising on his right cheek. The day had been spent interviewing tramps. For that they'd gained nothing more than Galabert had ascertained the night before. That was, however, all Belmont had expected to come of it. The raid on the bridge was about plumbing the depths before chucking in the towel.

'By the way, Galabert,' Belmont said, 'my office stinks. I've had to open the window which lets all the heat out.'

'You should smell it downstairs, Boss. It's disgusting,' Tabaraut said. 'They've got a cleaner with a double dose of carbolic trying to neutralise it. Lord knows what else they've left behind, I've been scratching non-stop since interview one.'

'Thanks for that, Tabaraut, you've got me at it now,' Belmont scratched at his chest then head. 'Anyway, Galabert. I've recommended you for a bravery commendation. You saved that man's life last night and I note that two other officers refused to stick their toes in the water. Not sure I would have either, it's far too cold for me.'

'Thank you, Chef. I didn't really think about it. I spotted him floundering about and dived in.'

'Well, although we didn't catch the killer, your heroics mean we ended on a positive note. Much happier than a fishing trip with a grappling hook. But we've now done all we can do. Galabert will remain on the case to tidy up the paper work. The rest of you will join Riquet and Gracianette on the Post Office break in. At least they've got some leads. Gracianette is sunning himself down in Marseille, following up the origins of the oxyhydrogen blowpipe. Seems there was a manufacturer's mark on the inside.'

Jouvin shifted in his seat, arms folded. Belmont noticed and ignored him. He had a pretty good idea what Jouvin wanted to say and he didn't want to hear it.

'Thank you all for the time and effort you've put in here. Tomorrow, the rest of you can report to Inspector Riquet, he'll brief you as to what's been going on and take it from there.'

'We're just going to ignore what the tramp said, then?' Jouvin asked.

Belmont rolled his eyes and sighed. Knew this was coming from the moment he read the word "swarthy" in Galabert's witness statement.

'The tramps didn't say anything of any import,' Belmont replied.

'One did and he said the killer was swarthy, not white.'

'Look, Jouvin,' Belmont said, 'we all know you've got a thing about Arabs. Unless you have some evidence that points to a particular person we have nothing to go on, just as we had nothing to go on when the killer was described as white.'

'I specifically asked if he could have been an Arab,' Galabert said, 'and the answer was no.'

'And the English couple specifically said he was white. We all know witnesses can miss details in the heat of the moment. We ought to look into it. Send a squad down to the Grand Mosque when they're at prayers and round them all up.'

'That mosque was built as a thank you to the North Africans for helping us during the Great War. You think it's appropriate to go down there and start a battle?'

'What else is there to go on?' Jouvin said.

'There's nothing to go on, Jouvin, that's why we're dropping the case. Now it's time for you to channel your enthusiasm into the Post Office robbery.'

'I just think-'

'Button it, Jouvin, and that's an order. You do still remember what orders are, don't you?'

Jouvin huffed loudly but said no more.

Monday, November 16

Monday evening. Galabert and Belmont together in the Scarlet K. Belmont ordered a cognac. Galabert ordered the same but felt self-conscious about it. Didn't want to look like he was aping his boss. In fact, after drinking all the glasses Belmont had pushed on him, Galabert had acquired a taste for cognac.

'You got much more to do, Galabert?'

'Not really, Chef. I've collated and filed everything. Just tying up the loose ends before I take the files up to archives.'

'It was good thinking, going down to the river to look for the rope. I know it didn't pay off but it was good flic thinking.'

'Thank you.'

'This case won't stay closed for long. There will be a third murder. When that happens the little we've gleaned here will be of some use.'

'And I've been thinking, about the assessment from Dr. Frappier. I worked in a hotel for a short time after my National Service. They have pretty strict hierarchies in hotels and tempers get fraught. If you're low enough down the chain then you'll be working long hard hours and getting plenty of stick with no-one to take it out on.'

'Well, Galabert, make a note of that and stick it in the file. Unfortunately, we can no more round up all the hotel workers than we can the Arabs.'

'Speaking of Arabs, Chef, have you seen this morning's L'Humanité?'

'I tend not to read the newspapers, Galabert, and the

communist ones would be bottom of the pile if I chose to start.'

'There's an article in there about an incident on Saturday night. An Algerian kid was run down in the street and taken to hospital. Dead on arrival.'

'Yes, I read the report. Shame.'

'The newspaper contends that he wasn't run over, that his brother was dragged from a café by a group of thugs. The victim came to his aid and those thugs set upon him, kicked him to death.'

'Were there any other witnesses?'

'The café owner was out back when it happened. Two old men had been playing backgammon earlier but they'd packed up and left ten minutes before the attack.'

'No witnesses then.'

'Yes, the brother. And, according to the article, he was covered in bruises.'

'You have read the report on the case? The investigating officer gave the opinion that the two brothers got into a fight with each other. One of them, unfortunately, fell into the path of an oncoming vehicle. The surviving brother can't face his guilt so he's looking for someone to pin the blame on.'

'I have read the report, Chef, and to my mind it adds credence to the newspaper article.'

'How so?'

'Because the only verifiable fact that report contains is the fact that one Ahmed Djaout is dead. The brother's testimony is missing, in fact there's no testimony in there! Not one deposition. There is a short note stating that the brother is an unreliable witness because he was, in part, responsible for the tragedy. All this is the investigating officer's conjecture, based on what? It's as if he plucked the story out of thin air. What's more, he's made no attempt to instigate a search for the vehicle. Why? Because we have no description of any vehicle. The case is being brushed under the carpet and we are failing in our duty as officers of the law by allowing that to happen.'

'The report is scant, I'll grant you that, but the magistrate is happy with it.'

'But I'm not. The newspaper points out that there have been other attacks. Each victim had connections with the North African Star Party. In this case the victim's brother was a member.'

'I thought the North African Star Party was dissolved a couple of years ago.'

'It was but the old membership still exists, and some of them are still pushing for Algerian independence. Then there's Jouvin.'

'What about Jouvin?'

'He had all those bruises on his face, like he'd been in a fight.'

'Don't let your prejudice against Jouvin colour your assessment of the facts. Otherwise you'll end up just like him.'

'I won't, but we do have a man who says he was attacked. We ought to hear what he has to say.'

'And are you're angling for that job?'

'Yes, Chef.'

'Then go see him, decide if he's credible. First look into his past, make sure he hasn't got a record. If he has, drop it. We can't push this if the man has previous. I know it sounds harsh but you're going to be swimming against the tide with this one and you won't get anywhere with an ex-con on your side. If he's clean, report back to me. Right, I must dash.'

Belmont dropped some cash on the table to cover their drinks, shook Galabert's hand and left the café. Galabert finished his drink before leaving. As he passed through the tables he heard a voice say, 'goodnight, Bébé.' Galabert didn't turn to look. He knew what he'd see. Could picture the smug face, head tilted to one side, crooked smile, a glass of red wine held up as if offering a toast. One of these days, Galabert thought, I'm going to smash that bastard's face in.

Outside he thought about the Arab and Jouvin's bruises.

If he could pin that on him he'd be rid of Jouvin once and for all.

The café was more refined than the Scarlet K. Which wasn't difficult. A violinist played in the corner, the chatter was gentle as opposed to raucous. Even so, Belmont didn't like meeting her here. It'd been her idea but Belmont's dormant puritanical side didn't think it was right that women should be in cafés at all. In his younger days he'd taken his lady friends for drinks in patisseries or English style tea shops. His papa and maman had drummed it into him that women in cafés were wanton. It had never occurred to them that their son might wish to meet a wanton woman.

She was sat at a table on her own. Alone except for the glances of other men. Some eyed her discreetly in the vain hope that they might be able to arrange a secret rendezvous. Others were more open, expecting her to invite them over. She did nothing to encourage them and refused any drinks bought for her. Normally she'd have accepted but today she didn't want any complications. Any complications, that is, beyond Chief Inspector Belmont who was complicated enough.

Galabert walked home. He wasn't in the mood for the Métro. Wanted a bit of solitude and the walk was only a couple of miles. The cool air allowed him to think of the case he'd been given. How should he approach it? The Arab was obviously a troublemaker. That didn't mean he was lying. Could it be true that he'd fought with his brother and accidentally pushed him in front of the vehicle? It was possible, especially if they'd both been drinking.

The concierge took his time opening the door. Galabert bade him good evening and climbed the dirty stone stairs to his apartment. Half-way up the four flights he could hear her. His daughter. Screaming. She was three years old and had, what his wife called, frequent temper tantrums. Screaming fits the neighbours called them and there wasn't a neighbour in the block who hadn't complained about it.

This was the first time his wife had seen him awake since Saturday and she had a real go when she heard that he'd jumped in the river. 'You risked your life for some vagrant… Leave me to bring up your daughter on my own... How am I to get by on a police widow's pension? I'll have to work and that'll mean getting maman in to look after our baby.' Then she cried and said she'd miss him terribly. He had to promise not to do it again. He'd made the promise and they both knew it was a lie.

Tuesday, November 17th

Jouvin collared Galabert in the corridors of the Quai des Orfèvres.

'What's this I hear about you investigating the hit and run?'

Galabert shrugged Jouvin's hand from his shoulder.

'That is what I'm doing. The victim's brother says there was no hit and run, that they were set on by a gang of mindless, ignorant, thugs.'

'He's a liar. This is a waste of police time.'

'Even if he is, we still need to find the driver who ran the kid over. Killing someone while driving is called involuntary homicide, look it up in the penal code. That is if it was an accident. If you consider it a waste of time, take it up with Belmont.'

Jouvin prodded Galabert in the chest, 'you watch yourself, smart arse. Just because you've been to university don't make you someone special. Belmont's got money and connections. You've got nothing. Think about that when you're out investigating involuntary homicides.'

Galabert strode off, Jouvin's words played over in his head. His anger was exacerbated because he knew Jouvin was right. With Chiappe as the Prefect of Police it was the right wingers in ascendancy. You had more chance of promotion being a member of Action Française than being a good flic.

A bitter wind ran along the Seine, it set the tricolours flapping wildly along the front of HQ and tore into Galabert as he stepped outside. If Jouvin was a part of the conspiracy he'd tell whoever instigated the cover up that Galabert was re-opening the case. The conspirators would watch him, make things difficult. And the magistrate would give Belmont a dressing down. Did he need the trouble? For a moment he considered giving it up. Jouvin's warning was true, there was no-one on his side. There were no powerful allies keeping an eye on his progression, ready to step in if needed. Maybe Belmont, but Belmont was not high enough up the ladder and his own boss, Superintendent Péraud, could neutralise him.

To Galabert, policing only had meaning if he could look himself in the mirror each morning. Without that, why not take a job as a teacher? Shoulders hunched, he kicked a few stones against the embankment wall and strolled towards the station. Jouvin and his kind needed to be stopped. By the time Galabert entered the Métro his whole body was shaking.

Ferhat had been in a fight, there was no doubt about that but it tied in with the official line of the two brothers fighting. Like Belmont had said that very morning, it's the only story that could fit both brothers being injured. It didn't prove a conspiracy but neither did it exclude one. At least Ferhat Djaout had no criminal record.

'You police?'

Galabert pulled out his identification. Ferhat blocked the apartment doorway, he wore a black arm band in mourning for his brother. From inside could be heard the sound of a child screaming.

'What do you want?'

'I'd like to ask you a few questions. May I come inside?'

Ferhat stood aside and let Galabert enter the hallway between the apartment's two rooms. The sound of crying came from the room on the left. Over the crying could be heard the sound of a woman singing. She sang in Arabic, not French but the tone and the pitch were so soothing that Galabert wanted to stay and listen at the door. Ferhat led him through to the apartment's other room. This was a drawing room which also made do as dining room, living room and, judging by the cot bed in the corner, a spare bedroom. There was a sideboard with photographs on it. One, which showed a young Arab lad, had black crepe draped over the frame. Ferhat signalled for Galabert to sit at the table. Ferhat sat opposite and lit a cigarette.

'I have already talked to the police. They said I was fighting with my brother and that I pushed him. Where did these ideas come from? They call me a liar but it is they who lie. They said that we'd been drinking but we don't drink. Look what they did to me.' He showed Galabert the gap where his front teeth ought to have been. 'Two teeth kicked out. And look at my face.'

Galabert looked. The right eye was swollen closed. The left was bruised. His nose broken. The right ear mangled and abrasions covered his face.

'Do you think my brother could have done this?' Ferhat reached across to the dresser and picked up the photograph. 'Look at him. I always took care of him since our grandfather was killed. Beaten to death with clubs because he walked past a demonstration and the police decided he must be a protester. My father was killed in the war, fighting for this country, fighting for France. My brother didn't even know his father and hardly remembers his grandfather. I raised him.'

His words were drowned in sobs. Galabert wanted to do something but didn't know what. He pulled a crumpled copy of L'Humanité from his coat pocket, 'this newspaper claims you were beaten by a gang of thugs, is that correct?'

'Yes, it's correct. It's like I said, some men dragged me from the café. When we got outside they dumped me in the road and started kicking. There were more of them outside, maybe four, maybe six. They joined in so I was being kicked all over. Ahmed came to help. I couldn't see. I heard him shout and the men shout back. They left me and went for my brother. I tried to get up but someone knocked me back down. You see my face? The rest of my body is like this. I have cracked ribs. My legs are bruised and swollen. Each time I tried to stand I either fell or was knocked back down. Then it stopped. The men ran off towards a baker's van. I crawled to Ahmed's side. His face. It was horrible. An eye rested on his cheek. There was blood everywhere. Eventually an ambulance came but my brother was already dead.'

Ferhat cried. Galabert couldn't help looking at the photograph. A young lad, unblemished face, with a big smile for the camera. He'd seen his other photographs, the one's taken at the morgue. The mangled face and missing eye. He scanned the line of pictures on the sideboard, a man in army fatigues, must be the father. An older man, grey hair and grey moustache, the grandfather. Three generations of men. All dead before their time.

'Were you ever a member of the North African Star Party?'

Ferhat's eyes flicked to the cot bed.

'Look, I know there have been other attacks reported. The victims had been members of the North African Star Party or associated with the independence movement in Algeria. It says as much in this newspaper. I want to know if it's true, were you tied in with that in anyway?'

'I was a member, it wasn't illegal. It was only treated as if it was.'

'They did try to lead a revolt against French rule.'

'Wouldn't you do the same if some foreign power came and occupied your country?'

'This isn't about me, it's about you and I'm looking to see if there could be a link between your attack and the others. And we have now established that there is.'

'Someone killed my brother, he wasn't a member of anything.'

'It was you they targeted. It was you they dragged from the café. It was unfortunate that your brother got involved.'

It certainly was unfortunate that Ahmed had interceded. None of the other victims came away with anything worse than broken bones. When the brother joined in the attackers panicked, wanted him out the way in case the fight escalated further, in case someone called the police.

'My brother is beaten to death and you call it unfortunate.'

'I'm sorry, I didn't mean to be callous. I meant they targeted you and not your brother, he just happened to be there. The key to finding them will be through you, not him. And the link between you and all the other beatings is the Party.'

'Find them, please, for my brother.' Once again Ferhat held the photograph up for Galabert to see.

Galabert would file a report for Belmont in the morning. If Belmont gave him the nod, good. If not he'd take the case on anyway, investigate in his own time. A France where crimes like this went unpunished was not a France in which Galabert could feel any pride. Men a little older than him had fought their battles in the trenches of Northern France. Galabert would fight his in the back streets of Paris. No less filthy, no less deadly.

Friday, November 20th

Galabert had been blocked at each turn. Belmont, distracted, gave him half his attention as he smoked self-rolled cigarettes and loaded more coal into that infernal stove. The Notre Dame murder case was over. Galabert pressed the Arab murder which Belmont would not even accept as a murder. He'd given Galabert a week. 'Give me something to go on or else shut it down.' All he'd been able to do was circulate a description of the Baker's van. In the meantime, Galabert would follow up his hunch.

Since the day Galabert had joined the Judicial Police, Jouvin had needled him at every opportunity. So far Galabert had been able to walk away, but each snide comment hit the same spot. A spot already sore and festering from all the previous jibes. There was no hint that Jouvin planned to back off. Calling him Bébé in the café, in front of their colleagues. Stubbing a cigarette out in his sandwich. They'd all think Jouvin was an arsehole but they'd also start to think that Galabert was weak. If Galabert could prove Jouvin had something to do with the Arab boy's death then that would be an end to him. If not he was going to have to fight him.

Galabert had tried to look at the case objectively. At the simplest level someone had run the Arab kid down and killed him. He doubted the driver was Jouvin. He doubted it was a hit and run. What else did he have? Jouvin's racism? Jouvin was not alone in his hatred of Arabs. It wasn't enough on its own but the day after the attack he'd arrived at work with bruising on his face. Most damming of all, Jouvin had warned him off the case. Why would he do that if it was a genuine hit and run?

Against that Galabert weighed opposing considerations. There were plenty of right-wing groups in Paris. Many of them violent, for example, Action Française were always beating up socialists in the Latin Quarter. No reason to think they wouldn't go further afield to attack Arabs. Would Action Française bother to target ex-members of the defunct North African Star Party? Whoever carried out the attacks had a list of party members. The sort of someone who might work for the police. Jouvin had already admitted he was a member of some group like AF. Superintendent Péraud was a member too. Were they a group of unpleasant yet harmless gas-bags or one of the more dangerous organisations who trafficked arms and conspired to over-throw the government?

Then there was the warning to drop the case, which might have meant nothing as Jouvin loved to issue threats. It helped make a pathetic man feel important. Same with his hatred of Arabs, he saw them as an inferior race so as not to deal with his own inferiorities.

Galabert spat into the gutter. Fuck Jouvin's inferiorities.

Belmont waited upstairs at the Café Flore. It was busy. The wait meant cigarettes and coffee. He'd switch to booze later but for now coffee was fine. The wait also meant thinking about Galabert.

For most of the week his young sergeant had been on about the dead Arab. Belmont understood his officer's keenness. One murder enquiry had closed so he wanted to open another. But something about this one stank. It was a rock best left unturned.

Belmont didn't fancy being drawn into the battle. And that's the way this one would go. If it wasn't a hit and run then it was a cover up. And cover ups took power. Favours called in. Interfering chief inspectors transferred to Corsica. And young sergeants?

Belmont could face Corsica. He could face the threat of it.

He would never leave Paris. If it came to the crunch he'd use his connections and move to the Sûreté. The bottom line, he'd tell them to stick Corsica where Corsica belonged and spend his days collecting art. He could probably protect Galabert too. Maybe the lad would end up walking a provincial beat for a year or two. Belmont would have him recalled to Paris at the first opportunity. What Belmont couldn't do, what nobody could do, was prevent another hit and run with Galabert stood in the road blinded by the headlights.

Philippe didn't stop for a drink on the way into work. Last weekend had been a wash out, in a funk from Friday until Monday. Today things felt OK. The last couple of days hadn't been too bad either. In fact he could almost say he was enjoying life.

By the time he reached the club Albert was already at his post making sure only the riff-raff and the dregs got in. Although at this hour nobody would get in as the club wasn't open. Philippe shook Albert's hand, 'evening.'

'Evening, Philippe, looks like a good one.'

'What you doing out here so early? We aren't open for another hour.'

'Well, I like to get my eye in, size up the Montmartre crowds. I can tell from the hour before we open what sort of a night we're in for. I'm never wrong. You get to read the street, see the signs. It's in the air, like telling the weather forecast. People are affected by atmospheric conditions more than they think. Tonight we'll be OK, no trouble, a quiet one.'

'That's good news at least. How's The Bitch?'

'Seems calm but hasn't had her early evening wine. You'd best get in there as she'll be at the bar *tout de suite*.'

Philippe pushed open the nightclub door and glanced around. She couldn't be seen, that was a blessing. The last thing he wanted was to ready the bar with that hideous gorgon perched on the counter. He went to his room, pulled on his white coat and sparked up a cigarette. Then he took a seat and puffed away.

Tonight he was going to make a move on Maddie. Offer her a drink and this time he'd accept if she offered him a lift on her bike. If not he'd see if she fancied going for a drink somewhere else, perhaps getting some Welsh rarebit at a café in Montparnasse.

Could he take her back to the apartment? The concierge was no problem. Léon had given her so much stick over the years that she didn't bother them anymore. The problem would be Léon himself. Most nights he'd be sound asleep by the time Philippe got home but he didn't always work on a Saturday, which meant he might be up with a bottle of cheap wine.

Philippe wouldn't risk it. Could he persuade Maddie to go for a knee trembler round the back of the apartment? There was only one way to find out. Philippe closed his eyes and started to think about Maddie, running his hand up the side of her thigh, reaching up through her skirt. He was about to go and take a quick look into their dressing room when he heard The Bitch calling him.

Philippe poured wine and listened to his boss complain. First she berated him for not being behind the bar. Then for looking slovenly, although he looked exactly the same as he always did. Then she had a short rant about the girls costing too much. If, Philippe thought, I hit her over the head with this wine bottle would anybody care? We could dump her body down in the cellar.

Galabert found a corner where he could keep an eye on the restaurant. He'd have preferred a higher vantage point, a place to see straight in through the windows. This would have to do. At least a clear view of the door meant he could see anybody arriving or leaving.

Jouvin, who was inside, could never afford to eat in a place like that on his police salary, even with kickbacks and bribes. Someone had to be treating him. Galabert didn't know who was inside already but he'd witnessed Cruchon arrive. Cruchon, Péraud and Jouvin were always drinking together at the Scarlet K, as if superintendents usually drank with sergeants. Chief Inspector Belmont only drank with Galabert because they were on a case. Normally the sergeants stuck to their own tables while the senior officers stuck to theirs. There were, of course, some cross-overs. Personal friends among the ranks, colleagues who'd worked together for years. Jouvin and Péraud didn't fit that bill.

Galabert's hands ached. He pushed them deep inside his pockets, where, even in gloves, the cold gnawed away at them. Inside the restaurant, Jouvin and his friends would be warm and cosy. He shuffled his feet to keep them warm. Another hour passed which meant Galabert had been standing around for two hours now.

The last few days had been spent tailing Jouvin. It wasn't easy. Jouvin had his own cases to work – the Post Office robbery and the Tuileries rape. There was little point following him while he actually worked. As such, Galabert came into work later and started his tail from the moment Jouvin finished his post-work drinks at the Scarlet K. Two nights Jouvin had played cards with a tall man and a couple of non-descript workers in a seedy café near Les Halles. The whole area stank of rotting food from the market. Galabert had been tempted to start smoking – it'd give him something to do and mask the smell. Instead he ate bonbons.

Each night Jouvin got through a bottle of wine while Galabert sat across the street on a bench and watched frost crystals form on his knees. Any other surveillance and he could have gotten someone else involved. Sat a uniformed flic on the bench and gone and gotten himself a drink. With Jouvin as the target he couldn't risk bringing in anyone else.

Tonight, as Jouvin got up to leave the Scarlet K, Galabert heard the superintendent say, 'see you at eight.' Didn't say where so Galabert stayed on Jouvin's tail. Jouvin didn't go to the market café to play cards. Instead he went straight back to his apartment. An hour later he reappeared looking spruced up in formal evening wear. Then he flagged down a taxi-cab. Galabert was lucky and managed to flag down one of his own with Jouvin still in sight. They ended up at this fancy restaurant on the rue de Boulainvilliers in the 16th arrondissement.

She arrived in a new dress purchased that very week from Schiaparelli. Belmont pictured her in the fitting rooms, assistants fussing around with pins in their mouths or producing glasses of champagne for their valued customer. He'd sat in those same rooms himself, sipped their champagne and waited while his wife looked at dress after dress following some show or another. He could smell the perfumes of the place as he rose to kiss her cheek. Eyes were upon him, those artists who'd smugly thought him a cuckolded fool stood open mouthed. She was stunning at her worst and tonight she was at her best.

'Take me to the Ritz,' she said, 'I want American bourbon and they've got the good stuff there.'

Belmont dropped some cash on the table and escorted her out. It was too cold to walk so he hailed a taxi and she pressed up against him the whole way. Belmont thought of their Métro ride, of her hand. Had to stop himself and stared out the window. She had other ideas and pulled his mouth to hers. Her hand crept along his leg. The taxi reached the Ritz. Too quickly.

'Drive round the block,' Belmont said, 'we'll make the Ritz later.'

Maddie looked divine, covered in sweat, stockings torn. She was always tearing them on her bike. Philippe couldn't take his eyes off her. Before she'd gone on stage he'd managed a small wave but she'd ignored him. Maybe she hadn't noticed. The music reached its climax. Acidic bile filled his mouth. Next up, mingle time. She'd be sat on their laps getting pawed and drooled over. All for a few francs.

They were dirty stinking bastards. Philippe had turned his

attention to the customers. If he thought he could get away with it he'd poison every bottle behind the bar. Wouldn't mind them throwing up then, if it were their last act on this rotten planet. The good mood was gone, slipped through his fingers in a slick coating of nerves and jealousy. Maybe he'd pay a few francs and take Maddie to his room behind the bar, let his own hands run up and down her legs. She wouldn't be able to say anything about that, not if he were paying. No! He'd have her but there'd be no cash involved.

The music stopped. Philippe took a drink over to the accordionist. Smiled at Maddie as she stepped down from the stage. She saw him, that was certain, then she'd pointedly turned her head away and walked off. When did she become such a stuck-up bitch?

Back behind the bar. Punters leant their fat bellies over the zinc, pointed at spirit bottles and breathed their foul breath in his face. Others sat at tables and clicked their fingers. Maddie was with some factory grunt, fifty years if not older. Philippe caught her eye and when he did she put her tongue in the man's ear. Kept her eyes locked with his for a moment then turned her attention to the punter. Bitch. The pair of them could click their fingers all night long, he wouldn't be waiting that table.

Jouvin appeared in the doorway, laughing, cheeks flushed red from the warmth inside. A group of six men formed around him, including Péraud and Cruchon. Cruchon raised a hand and hailed a taxi-cab.

'Shit!' Galabert's breath formed ice clouds around his face as he made off quick time to catch a taxi of his own. He couldn't beckon one from where he was, they'd notice it pulling up and see him getting in.

Soon as he rounded the corner he flat out sprinted to a taxi rank. The driver, a Russian, took a moment to understand Galabert's panted instructions.

'Drive to rue de Boulainvilliers and wait. I'll point out a group for you to follow. When they get in a taxi you tail them.'

The taxi-cab swung into rue de Boulainvilliers. Galabert jittered about on the back seat. They were gone. No, two of the group were stood outside the restaurant as another vehicle headed up the road. They flagged it down and got in.

'Follow them,' Galabert said.

The driver's French was poor but his driving superb. Kept the other motor in sight the whole time. Galabert's heart picked up the pace. Tonight would be make or break. If he didn't turn something up on Jouvin, Belmont would take him off the case. He'd resolved to carry on regardless but he knew that was a bust. Couldn't put in a day shift then spend his nights in the cold watching Jouvin.

They drove west, out to the edge of the city up against the Bois de Boulogne. Traffic thinned out so they laid off from hugging the other motor. Kept it just in sight until it parked up in front of a Louis XIV mansion house. The two men climbed out their taxi and entered through a pair of wrought iron gates.

Galabert paid off his driver and took cover behind a tree. The warm from the taxi was gone and he clapped his hands together to beat the cold out of them. He stared at the wall and the iron gates. Looked at the large house beyond and wondered if Jouvin was even in there.

Another motor arrived. Galabert scampered along the opposite side of the road, hiding behind the plane trees, keeping his eyes on the vehicle. Three men got out and went through the gates. Galabert heard them talking. They said they were late.

Galabert crossed the road about 100 metres from the gates. Overly conscious of the street lighting. Afraid they'd posted a look out. He had to know if Jouvin was inside. Had to know what they were doing in there. Crept along by the wall to the entrance. No other vehicles arrived. Gates locked. Blast!

Through the gates he could see a large courtyard. An English motor was parked near the door. Looked like a

Rolls-Royce. The house was lit up. Plenty of windows. Anyone in there would see him if he attempted to climb the gates.

The Rolls-Royce stuck in his head as he attempted to scale the wall. If Jouvin and his crowd were such patriots, why did they drive a foreign motor? His hands were too cold to grip. Tried a run and jump but got closer to going through than over. His knee stung.

Galabert didn't want to lose sight of the gates in case anyone left and he missed them. Yet he needed to find a better place to scale the wall. Was it likely they'd leave so soon after arriving? No. Who lived in there anyway? The brass plate on the gate had given a name and initial. No profession. Chances were they didn't work. At one time this area was full of lodges and private hunting grounds. Rich nobles escaping Paris for a few days of leisurely killing. Nowadays Paris had spread out to join them and the motor-car meant the centre of the city could be reached in no time. The land still belonged to those ennobled families though.

If Jouvin did leave then fuck him. It was too cold to be arsing about. Galabert tracked the course of the wall until he found a Virginia creeper within reach of his blue and trembling hands.

The girls were back on stage, marcelled waves and kiss curls bounced. Tits wobbled and legs kicked. Some were stone cold drunk. No-one gave a damn. The punters had had a taster, literally, and drooled over what they saw. Philippe wanted to vomit. It didn't normally get to him like this. He could normally stand it. Now everything he'd planned with Maddie had gone to hell. She'd treated him like he had dog shit on his shoes.

Philippe poured drinks, waited the tables. Tried not to look at the stage. Kept himself busy, didn't look over at the girls. If he'd seen her again and she'd snubbed him once more he didn't know what he'd have done..

Sod the bar. His little room was cold though it appeared

to be sweating. The shelves, with rusting tins of paint and empty bottles of booze from the early twenties, creaked along to the music. Philippe eyed the mould around the ceiling and down the corners of the walls. Took a swig from his bottle and flicked a match to life. Smoked a cigarette and thought of burning the place down.

A voice called for service. Philippe reckoned the bulge in his trousers would be hidden by the bar. Stubbed the cigarette out on a shelf where it made a home with its many cousins. Maddie's factory grunt wanted a gin. Philippe glanced down at the man's nicotine stained fingers and thought of where they'd been. Poured a gin and passed it over. Wasn't tempted to spit in it even if he'd gotten the chance. The man was just a man like any other. His job would be shit, his life would be shit. All there was to take his mind off the crushing futility of his existence was this hole and the diseases he'd catch if he actually slept with any of the girls.

The final dance done. Philippe gave the customers the evil eye. They knew he didn't want them lingering. Wasn't supposed to kick them out but he would soon enough. In ten minutes the girls would start leaving. Some hardly got changed, threw on a coat and strutted over to the brothel. Most of the men would follow their scent to the red light and their dingy bedrooms.

Maddie didn't normally go there, although Philippe knew she had done at least once before. Ten more minutes and he'd go and take a look, just to see if she was nearly dressed. Then he'd have it out with her, find out why she'd been behaving like Lady Muck. She had no right to give him the cold shoulder. His feelings oscillated from violence to fear then desire and back again. Maddie's behaviour had hurt him and his instinct was to lash out. That would get him nowhere. But he didn't have the guile to talk girls round. His brother could. Léon was born with the right words in his mouth. Philippe got the leftovers, the words that didn't quite make sense, got taken the wrong way and would be spat back at him. The trick, he decided, was to play it by ear. Think what Léon would do and say anything that came to mind. Who'd care how true it all was.

Galabert made his way between the wall and the trees and bushes which lined the garden. The house was quiet although he could make out cameos of people moving around inside. Those lit windows left him feeling exposed but actually worked in his favour – any casual glance out and they'd see the room reflected back at them. He was concerned because most people would have closed the shutters by now. He had to assume they'd left them open to look out the windows. In which case it wouldn't be casual glances but a face pressed to the glass with hands blocking out the room's light.

From now on he had to be careful. No mistakes. If these people were who he thought they were then they were killers. Powerful, influential, cold-blooded murderers. In their hands his life would be worth nothing. Galabert knew his body would never be found.

There were twenty metres to cover from the bush to the house. Twenty metres of open ground where he'd be vulnerable. Where a man with a rifle in an upstairs window could take his time and aim for the head. And out here, a bullet in the night, who was going to hear or care?

Galabert put his National Service training to use. Where Syria had been hot, here every centimetre would be over cold hard ground. The same principles applied. He got down and crawled on his belly. Best not to over-think these things. Physical exertion gave him something to focus on. Forget about the building, forget about snipers. Think about the pain in his knee, the throb of his elbow as it hit a rock. The cry of an owl over in the forest, the smell of the cold grass. He thought of trivialities, how his pullover would be ruined and that his trousers already were.

A sudden crack and he rolled over three or four times to get away. He lay still wondering if he'd been hit. There were no further sounds. If someone had taken a shot they'd be shouting now. Or they'd have taken another shot. He rolled once more, back to his belly and took a look at the building. A sniper would be at one of the unlit windows. He stared at each of them in turn. Was there a different shade of darkness in that one?

Now he could hear them. Nothing articulate. A background hum of human chatter. Galabert kept perfectly still and continued watching the house. There was a large *porte-fenêtre* in what was probably the ballroom. These tall glass doors would make it easy for someone to come out and catch him.

Back pressed to the wall. Breath condensed around his face. His pulse pounding in his ears drowned out the voices from inside the house. That was the hardest part over. Now he had to get on with what he was there for. He risked a quick glance through the edge of a window into the ballroom. There were men in there, hard to say how many. Someone called out and the murmur of voices died down.

Galabert risked a longer look. The men were all stood up and faced away from him towards a top table where three more men were seated. There didn't seem to be any women. Someone knocked three times on the floor with a staff and the men put on black hoods. It was now Galabert realised they were all in the same outfit. Apart from the hoods they'd modelled themselves on Mussolini's Black Shirts. Black shirts with red armbands, brown trousers and black riding boots. It was close to what he'd expected and it left him feeling sick.

The men at the top table also wore hoods. The man at the front in the middle seemed to be delivering a speech. It went on for a good fifteen minutes. Then he saluted, also like Mussolini with his arm held straight and high. All the other men in the room saluted back.

They removed their hoods. Galabert kept his eye to the window and searched for Jouvin. Didn't see him. He did, however, spot Superintendent Péraud. He was one of the three men who'd sat facing the crowd. Galabert could only conclude that he was one of their leaders. Jouvin must be in there. That didn't seem to matter now that Galabert had seen the other faces, a general, a leading politician, an examining magistrate who was often seen around the Quai des Orfèvres. No doubt there were plenty of other flics and a fair share of army officers. The sort of people who could and would cover up the murder of an Arab boy.

'That's terrible, Phil, I'm so sorry for you. How did it happen?'

Philippe took another swig of gin and tried to look sad though his heart beat like a drum in a parade.

'Hit by a tram. He made it to hospital but died of his injuries later that night. That's why I was so ratty, Maddie. I don't even remember calling you a whore, I was just lashing out.'

'Forget about that, Phil, but you should have told me your brother had died. I would have helped you out.'

If she ever came to the apartment he was going to have to make sure Léon was out or brief him and pretend they'd had a third brother. Léon would play along with that, for about ten minutes then announce that his brother was a liar. Maddie would hate him for lying and then hate him again for calling her a whore. Why had he said it? All he could remember of that night was being in a foul mood.

'Would you like another drink?'

'Go on then, a small one.'

She stood at the bar while Philippe poured a pair of gins. The Bitch had already left. By now she'd be in some cheap restaurant with the part remains of a dead lobster dribbled down her chin. The other girls would be on their backs or at least pulling off their panties. Albert was somewhere about, he could be heard but not seen. He'd be gone soon.

Maddie picked up her glass, took a swig, and looked up at Philippe. Some days he could be quite sweet. Other days he was plain creepy. All the girls knew that he spied on them when they got changed. They didn't care too much: let him look but if he touches charge him double 'cos he should know better.

'I've just got a few things to clear up,' he said.

Philippe walked around the bar with a mop. Cleaned up the spilt beer and cigarette butts. No vomit, thank God. He didn't want to be mopping up sick with Maddie at the bar watching him. The stage and the area away from the bar would be cleaned by the Breton woman tomorrow. He didn't know her name. A broad, ugly, woman who'd normally left long before he arrived.

After mopping the floor Philippe lit a cigarette and put all but one of the lights out.

'I'd best be running along,' Maddie said.

'Not yet,' he said, 'have another.'

Maddie thought about it. Did she want to stay? She'd fucked worse than him and if she stayed that's what he'd want. Those other men had been business. They had to pay to touch her. Phil wouldn't pay, other than with fags and gin. She might get a snack from a bistro but not dinner. She was hungry and if she wanted to eat she'd need cash.

'I better be going,' she said.

He came and stood next to her, loitered behind her right shoulder. The room was dim lit by a small lamp above the bar. The rest of the lights were out. She could feel him next to her, feel his breath on her shoulder.

'Don't go yet,' he said, 'we could have some fun.'

She turned around and leant back on the bar. It felt safer, being able to see him, and it gave them a few centimetres gap. She laughed and said 'give us a fag, will ya?'

He pulled a Gitane from his packet and handed it over. Then he leant in to light it, kept his eyes fixed on her the whole time. She giggled out of nerves.

'Let's have another drink.'

'Best no. I've gotta be going. My friends will be wondering where I am.'

He leant over the bar, almost pinning her, and took hold of the bottle.

'Go on, Maddie, you can have one more with me.'

She didn't want to fight so she gave in. He poured two large ones.

'Here's to us,' he raised his glass and drained half of it.

'Sure, Phil, to us.'

She took a swig then put the glass back on the bar. Phil stared at her, stared straight into her eyes. It unnerved her.

'I've really got to go now,' she said

'You haven't finished your drink.'

'I couldn't drink all that, I'd drown. Besides I've got to ride my bike home and I'll get all wobbly.'

He put his glass beside hers then he put his hand on her waist and pulled her towards him. She could smell his sweat and cigarettes. Onions too, she could smell onions.

She put her hand on his chest to push him away. He didn't let her and pulled her in tighter and put his mouth on her's. She stopped pushing, she'd let him have a kiss and a feel and then she'd leave.

Saturday, November 21st, Morning

'Too many of my weekends start like this,' Belmont said. His eyes bloodshot, his clothes crumpled. He sparked up another cigarette and paced the area at the end of the alleyway. The local flics loitered there too: they'd set up a cordon at the end of the alley and moved on the morbidly curious.

Galabert didn't look much better than Belmont. He'd put on a clean pullover and a new pair of trousers but two hours sleep left him empty. Last night he'd watched the meeting of the black hoods until they all filed out. Saw Jouvin leave. Then he'd scaled the wall and caught a taxi-cab home. Hardly got his head down when he was called out.

In the alleyway, amongst the bins, the Bureau of Identification were at work. A rag picker had called it in. The body of a girl had been folded into a dustbin. Folded being a nice way of saying she'd had her limbs broken and bent at unnatural angles to stuff her in the bin. Rubbish was strewn around the alley, no doubt emptied to make room for the corpse. A motorcycle belonging to a Madeline Legrand was parked four metres away. The girl's handbag identified her as the self-same Madeline.

What made this more interesting than your common or garden Friday night murder were the injuries she'd sustained. The girl had been strangled. Belmont had seen the bruising on her neck where the hands had choked her. Seen that enough in his career not to need a doctor to confirm strangulation. The interesting injuries were to the girl's ears which had been cut off. She'd also been stabbed repeatedly in the right ear hole.

The doctor climbed out of a taxi-cab in front of Belmont.

'What have you got for me, Belmont?'

'Looks like a dead tax payer, Doc.'

'Oh Jesus Christ, not the same MO?'

'Yes and no. I'd like you to take a look before I say anymore. The boys will be finishing soon, they told me ten more minutes and that was fifteen minutes ago.'

A couple of flashes went off as the photographer took his final photographs. The doctor went to work. Belmont and Galabert continued pacing the pavement at the end of the alley like a pair of expectant fathers.

'Last night I followed Jouvin to a meeting.' Galabert whispered so as not to let the local flics overhear.

'We already knew he went to meetings, what of it?'

'In attendance were a cross-section of the Parisian elite, our superintendent, an examining magistrate, all the people you'd need to carry out a cover up.'

Galabert was an intelligent officer, Belmont thought, but if he had any sense he'd pull back from this one. He was going to get his hands burnt. Maybe this girl's murder would re-focus his energies.

Belmont would reassemble the team with the exclusion of Riquet who was wrapping up the Post Office robbery. That would only take another couple of days, then he could come back.

A van pulled up ready to take the corpse away. The doctor carried on examining her as two orderlies got out and waited for the body. Belmont decided to let Galabert's sentence hang in the air as he went to peek over the doctor's shoulder.

Pools of blood lay over the cobblestones. There had been no rain in the night to wash it away. It was mixed with the rubbish which had been tipped from the bin. The pale faced girl had blonde hair, now stained and matted with blood, and looked to be in her early twenties. The doctor unbuttoned her blouse to reveal bruising on her stomach. The stockings were torn and her underwear was missing. Or she didn't wear any. She only had one shoe. Whether she wore pants on not was one thing but shoes came in pairs. Belmont called over one of the local flics.

'Find her shoe and keep an eye out for any knickers.'

'If you do find the pants,' the doctor said, 'don't touch them. I'd like to examine them first.'

The flic began his search.

'What are you thinking, Doc?'

'Like you said, it's the same and it's not the same. She was strangled by hand not by a rope. She was struck in the stomach and there is some bruising around the wrists. He probably held her hands together at one point. She'd had sexual intercourse but I couldn't say how long that was before death. Her legs and arms look to be broken but I suspect that was post-mortem. More than likely so they could fit her in the bin.'

'Rape?'

'That's for you to ascertain, Belmont. The violence indicates she was forced to do something. But evidence of sex isn't evidence of rape. This area's not short of working girls and she isn't dressed like a nun. Maybe she was raped and murdered. Maybe she had sex and an hour later she was raped and murdered. Maybe she had sex and an hour later she was murdered.' The doctor stood up and brushed down his trousers. 'What I can say is this, she has the same kind of knife wounds around the ears that I found on the two dead tramps. It makes me think the same perpetrator was involved. The differences? Again, that's your field. I'm off for a hot chocolate and a croissant. Then an hour in bed before I get up and start this day all over again with an autopsy on our lady friend.'

Belmont ordered two large black coffees. Rolled himself a cigarette. One of the local flics had found the missing shoe but not the knickers. They were now going to start a centimetre by centimetre search of the alley. Belmont had left them strict instructions to report straight to him should they find anything.

'You look done in, Galabert. How much sleep did you get last night?'

'Two hours, Chef. After staking out Jouvin and spying on that Black Shirt crowd it was late. By the time I got home the adrenalin was still pumping and I couldn't sleep. I sat up with a glass of water, then our child woke up and the wife saw me. Blamed me for waking the kid, as if sipping water made that much noise. Then she saw the state I was in, torn trousers, mud all over my pullover and jacket. Well, it's hard to sleep straight after a row and harder still on our sofa.'

'Poor lad, it's hard with a young kid in the house.'

Galabert was about to say something, then remembered. Belmont had lost his son to the Spanish Flu. Made him feel sick to think what it'd be like to lose his own kid.

'I know she's not a child, but that girl's got parents out there somewhere. We can't bring her back but we can find the bastard-'

Belmont reached across the table and put his hand on Galabert's shoulder, 'don't personalise it, it'll only eat you up. You're right, she probably has got family out there who are going to be weeping for the next few days. That's not our business. We're not going after him because he killed that girl or those tramps.'

'But what, why then?'

'We're going after this one because he's not going to stop killing until we've got him. Then, when he's safely locked up, the examining magistrate can take him to task for what he's done here. This one ends with his head in a basket and his blood flowing along the boulevard Arago.'

Galabert looked away, he didn't like to think of the execution that followed the arrest of a murderer.

'Don't get squeamish, Galabert. Murderers get caught and then they get murdered. That's the French way.'

'I know, I'd just rather they went to jail instead.'

'I would too, but I don't lose any sleep over it.'

'What about this girl, Chef, what do you think happened to her? I heard the doctor say he didn't know if she'd been raped.'

'Doc's an intelligent man, but sometimes you don't need that much intelligence. The girl's pants were missing. My guess is, someone ripped them off then fucked her. She started to scream so he wrapped his hands around her throat. He probably didn't set out to kill her in the way he set out to kill the tramps, which is why he didn't use the rope. Once it was done he reverted to type and went at her with that knife of his.'

Galabert watched Belmont's smoke rise to the ceiling. 'You say he reverted to type. The other bodies had been left where he killed them. This one was put in the bin like he was hiding it.'

'Good point, but what does it mean?'

'I don't know, Chef.'

'Neither do I. When we catch the bastard perhaps we can ask him.'

Saturday, November 21st, Afternoon/Evening

Galabert looked shattered. Belmont didn't feel much better himself, an hour's kip at his desk didn't cut it anymore. Jouvin, however, looked fresh, this despite a night dressed up like one of Mussolini's thugs.

The Notre Dame murder files had been retrieved from the archive and Belmont had re-pinned the photographs to the wall. They were joined by pictures of the Legrand girl. Images of her contorted body looked down on the men tasked with finding her killer. Not one of them wanted to meet her gaze.

'The Montmartre flics are in the process of going from building to building. Most of these places are bars, nightclubs, bals musette. Which means we won't get many answers until this evening. From what I hear, the people in the upper apartments are all playing dumb. Didn't recognise the girl in the photograph, hadn't seen a thing. They're probably lying but if you live above a nightclub you learn to ignore a lot of what goes on.

'I visited the victim's apartment. She lived down in Montparnasse. The concierge told me that Legrand worked in a Montmartre nightclub. So that narrows it down for us.'

There was a groan from the assembled officers. How many times had they heard lines like that – she worked in a nightclub, he worked in a café in Montparnasse or he worked on the railways. Worse still, "worked in a nightclub" either meant she worked in a nightclub or she walked the streets. Which could also mean she worked in a brothel or a bordello.

'Alright, it's not that bad. I took her photograph over to vice and nobody recognised her. We can't rule it out for certain but she probably wasn't a street walker. She's not on their register of working girls, not under the name Madeline Legrand anyway.

'Caillou, you take Jouvin and go through the sex joints in Montmartre and Pigalle. We found a photograph of the girl in her apartment. I've managed to get some copies made up,' he nodded at the table behind them. 'Take one each and don't get too distracted, boys. I don't want you coming back with any diseases you didn't leave here with.

'Which brings me back to our girl. The doc says she was clean. So she's either lucky, new, or not a whore.

'Tabaraut, you take Galabert and go house to house for two streets around the alley where her body was found. There are plenty of places to park a motorbike but she chose that spot. It wasn't anything special so she must have chosen it for convenience. Start with the revue bars and nightclubs, she just might have worked in one after all. Go and get some kip now and approach it fresh and open minded. If anyone gets funny with you, bring them down here and we'll see how long the joke lasts.

'Gracianette, you get down to Montparnasse and go through her apartment for letters and anything else you can find. I had a brief look this morning and found her photograph. You go through everything. I want to know: did she have a lover? Ask the neighbours – the concierge was useless. Was she Parisian? I've a feeling she wasn't. If not, you'll need to get the provincial police to break the news to her family. I also want a list of everyone she knew in Paris and then I want them in this building answering questions.

'On second thoughts, Gracianette, I'll ride with you, I want a proper look through that girl's belongings.'

Gracianette woke Belmont as they pulled up in a down and out Montparnasse side street. A uniformed flic stood outside the apartment building. Belmont managed to wake up and start rolling a cigarette in one easy, free flowing, movement. Wiped the dribble from his chin as he licked the cigarette paper.

'We'll make our own way back, Charles,' he said.

The driver left them at the curb side.

'You're not going to suggest walking, Chef? I nearly died when you made us walk back from that robbery in the Gobelins. My feet felt like two rhinos stuck in an elevator.'

'It's not so far from here, Gracianette. Besides, it'd help you to lose a kilo or two.'

'I don't want to lose a kilo or two. They're mine and I earned them. All that giving up food and running about walking places, it's not natural in the age of the motor-car.'

They approached the uniformed flic. 'Any news?' Belmont asked.

'None, Chef. The concierge keeps giving me filthy looks and grumbles every time I ask for a coffee. Other than that, nothing.'

'Good lad. I'm here now, so take yourself off for half-an-hour and get yourself a nip of something to keep the cold out.'

Gracianette and Belmont climbed the stairs to Legrand's apartment. Dirty walls with peeling paint. Banisters with broken or missing balusters. Communal lavatories at the end of each hallway. From the courtyard could be heard the sound of two washer women singing. Gracianette mopped his brow with a handkerchief. Belmont pushed open the apartment door. The same emptiness he'd felt on the morning visit.

'You have a nose through the drawers in that bureau,' Belmont said, 'and I'll take a general look around.'

There wasn't much to look around. Two adjoining rooms – the living room and the bedroom. She'd rigged up a Sterno stove in a corner of the living room. It rested on a piece of slate which she might have dragged in from somewhere or inherited from the previous occupant. A coffee pot sat on top. Probably contravened building rules, although only the concierge would care. Near the window, on the floor, sat a saucepan. Above it, on the ceiling, a brown stain. A plain white door separated the living room from the bedroom.

The bedroom smelt feminine. Of her, Belmont thought. It was pleasant, floral. He sat on the bed with its crocheted cover lain over moth-eaten blankets. It wasn't much to look at. Beside the bed was a dressing table, seen better days, littered with make-up, brushes, powders. A bedside table with some photographs and a book. A wardrobe. A threadbare rag rug covered part of the floor. Unpainted walls decorated at the head of the bed with pictures cut from fashion magazines. Vogue models in fur coats or sleek black dresses. The same magazines his wife reads.

The bed was top and tailed with iron work. An array of stockings hung over the end. All in need of repair. She obviously had a habit of tearing them. Which meant the pair she was found in might have been torn before the attack. Belmont picked one up and held it in his hand. Thought he might get a sense of the girl by touching something personal. He didn't.

Belmont got up and opened the dressing table drawer. She owned knickers anyway, he thought. He pulled them out to check if anything was hidden beneath the lining of the drawer. Nothing. The wardrobe held dresses, shoes, some hats and scarves. Nothing special.

There were two photographs. A house on the coast, probably Brittany, with a middle-aged couple stood out front. The other, a young man of similar age to Legrand staring straight into the camera. The hint of a smile on his lips. Her brother? Her lover?

'Anything?' Belmont took a seat in the living room and watched Gracianette rummage through a pile of papers.

'Too much, Chef. The girl was a hoarder. Bills, shopping lists, a bunch of letters. She's from Deauville, Normandy. Her maman was alive and well last week when she wrote this.' Gracianette held up a letter. 'Her father's been ill but is back at work again. Someone called Paul-Henri has been a great help. She wants to know if Madeline will be coming home for Christmas.'

'I guess she will. Better get someone to go and break the news. Unless you fancy a trip up north. If you do, ask the usual questions but go easy on the family.'

'You don't think someone up there had anything to do with this, do you, Chef? It all looks like it was the same mad man who's been doing-in the vagabonds and he's one of this city's colourful characters.'

'No, I don't think it was someone from up there. I'm happy for the local boys to cover that end. Just thought you might like another break by the sea. You enjoyed Marseilles from what I hear. And you could go for some early morning swims and a run along the beach.'

'I wouldn't run along the beach if the sand was on fire. Let the local boys cover it.'

Jouvin saw it as a night on the tiles. Why not? Two down and out nobodies and one dead whore, who cared? Nobody was sat at home weeping over them and he sure as hell wasn't going to start.

'Go on then,' he said. 'Just a small one.'

The madam poured Jouvin a glass of whiskey. Only his third that night but he'd decided to let go now. They'd been to nine of these places. It was getting close to 10 o'clock. No reason why they shouldn't slow down, take their time, enjoy the sights.

Caillou was sat on a small sofa with a girl on each arm, ruffling his hair, blowing in his ears. One of them let her finger trace the scar which ran down Caillou's forehead. He liked to let on it was a shrapnel wound. Falling out of a tree as a kid didn't sound so heroic. Jouvin wasn't worried about girls. Had declined the offer to have someone take care of him. In the back of his mind he'd always thought of his uncle, dead from syphilis. Belmont had been joking about picking up diseases but there was a lot of truth to it. Last thing Jouvin wanted was to be washing his cock with mercury three times a day.

'Why don't you take them upstairs, Caillou, you can question them in more detail up there.'

'It's on the house for you, Sergeant, we always like to keep on the right side of the law.' The madam smiled and topped Jouvin's glass to the brim.

Caillou answered by virtually carrying both girls, giggling, out the room. He came down later with his face covered by that silly grin of his.

'You got everything you need, Caillou?' Jouvin said.

'Everything and a bit more. That's the secret to a happy marriage. The wife is for company and the occasional ride. The real appetites should be satisfied away from the home.'

Galabert stood in the dim light of the nightclub doorway holding a photograph in front of the doorman's nose.

'Do you recognise her?'

'No.'

'Take a good look. Ever seen her around? Ever worked here?'

'She in trouble?'

'That's for St. Peter to decide.'

Same answers at every bar, café, nightclub and revue bar. One waiter thought he recognised her. Said she might have been in once. Had a coffee or a gin, if it was her. Couldn't be sure.

'Come on, Galabert, let's go get a drink. Give ourselves a break. Then we'll get back and check the places that were shut the first time around.'

Tabaraut's feet ached and he longed for a sit down. He could see Galabert was driven. The young lad could probably do two more laps. Maybe ten. It wasn't youthfulness, it was obsession. Galabert was the sort who wouldn't let go. The sort who'd crack. If you couldn't let go you ended up carrying all the crap that didn't work out. Not healthy. This was a job, it wasn't personal.

'This'll do,' Tabaraut said. It was the first café he'd seen since suggesting a drink. Galabert didn't respond – the rudeness of a distracted mind. Tabaraut put his arm over Galabert's shoulder and guided him into the café. 'Two beers.'

Galabert took a sip before realising what he was doing. 'Oh, I was going to have coffee.'

'Don't worry, son, I was going to do a whole pile of things that never got done.'

Tabaraut took out his pipe. Spent a moment poking and fiddling with it before stuffing the bowl with tobacco. A minute later a cloud covered the table and Tabaraut leant back in his chair, looked content.

'This is the life, Galabert. A pipe and a beer some place warm. Times like this I think of all the ice cold nights I spent walking the beat. Six years plodding over in Belleville. Breaking up street fights. Shaking down the local hoods. Sex attacks in the park. Those were the days.'

Galabert had done two years out in Versailles. They had their problems, even a murder. It didn't come with the hard-nosed experience of a working-class district. There were no slums in Versailles. No gangs of Apaches roaming the streets. People got robbed, people got raped, houses got broken into. Most of the time it was pleasant. You didn't have to worry some yob was going to stick a knife in your belly just because you were a flic. It was policing but not the kind he'd been after. He'd been keen. Put in extra hours. Tagged after the big boys when they came down to investigate the murder. Solved a few crimes, got promoted then got his transfer. The days in Versailles were too close on the heel to get sentimental over. Those weren't the days, these were the days.

Tabaraut seemed to spend an age scraping the embers from his pipe. Then he tapped it endlessly before sticking it in his jacket pocket. Obviously didn't want to leave the warm. Galabert waited outside. Wouldn't be party to Tabaraut's stalling.

'We should go back the way we came,' Galabert said,

'picking on the clubs that were closed earlier. What do you think about the ones we've covered so far? Any of them strike you as suspicious, any we should revisit?'

'None of them struck me as suspicious, Galabert. They were worried they might get the girl in trouble. Look at her,' he held up his copy of the photograph, 'she's not bad looking. They think if they do her a favour they'll be in with a chance. Problem is, they didn't actually know who she was. I can tell these things. That's why I got you to do all the talking, so I could observe.'

Galabert wasn't convinced of either – that they were all telling the truth or that Tabaraut was observing. Was more like he couldn't be arsed with the whole thing and wanted to spend the night drinking beer.

'Hello, hello,' Tabaraut said.

'Evening, Tabaraut,' Jouvin replied. 'Your maman know you're out this late, Bébé?'

'You leave my maman out of it, Jouvin.'

'Whoa there, hit a nerve have I? Wouldn't want to offend your dear old maman, not when she's produced such a lovely baby.'

Galabert's heart raced, he'd had enough of Jouvin. All those jibes and snide remarks were like an ulcer about to burst in his gut. It was time to take Jouvin down a peg or two and this was as good a place as any to do it. He squared up to Jouvin on the street outside Kiki's bar.

'What's with you, Jouvin? You've been needling me ever since I arrived. Well I'm sick of it.'

'I couldn't give a toss what you are, Bébé. What will you do about it, that's what I'd like to know?'

'I'll give you a damn good hiding.'

'Hold on, son,' Tabaraut said. 'We can't have police fighting out in the street.'

'Don't worry, Tabaraut, Bébé is all talk. He's not the type to actually put up a fight.'

'Any place any time, Jouvin, you just name it.'

'OK, Bébé, I name now as the time and round that back

of this bar as the place.'

'Jouvin, you're crazy. You two can't start fighting, you're on duty,' Tabaraut said.

'This one's been brewing for a while, Tabaraut,' Caillou said. 'Best we let them slug it out. You and I can make sure it doesn't go too far. And we can move on any sightseers.'

'If they agree,' Tabaraut said, 'that if we say stop you stop. You two agree?'

'Yes,' Jouvin said.

Galabert was shaking, kept his eyes fixed on Jouvin, 'yes'.

The street at the back of the bar was a dark alley. Not much space to fight. Caillou stood between the two men. Tabaraut held their coats and jackets. Jouvin and Galabert stood facing each other, shirt sleeves rolled to the elbows, fists up, oblivious to the cold.

'When I say stop, you stop,' Caillou said. 'If not I'll wade in and so will Tabaraut. Right, let's get this over with.'

They circled each other cautiously. Galabert kept his fists up, his face serious. Jouvin tilted his head to one side and grinned. Thought he'd give Galabert a beating then head off for another round of free drinks, this looked to be turning into a pretty good evening. He was confident of his street fighting abilities. Unlike Lady Versailles he'd spent time in the tough neighbourhoods, because they were the streets he'd been raised on. If you didn't know how to throw a punch you didn't survive.

The first blow hit him on the right hand side of the mouth. The second and third came in quick succession and hit the same spot. The fourth struck him below the left eye. Sent him staggering back a few steps. Galabert kept his guard up and circled his opponent. Jouvin tried to get his bearings and stepped forward. Two more jabs hit him on the mouth and the third struck his nose. His eyes stung. Galabert moved slowly, watched Jouvin, ready to defend, ready to attack.

Jouvin edged back, let his guard down but got it up as Galabert took a step forward. Galabert seemed to sway, the top half of his body moved right, he feinted, moved left. Back to centre then left again. Jouvin tried to line up a punch but wasn't sure where to land it. Heard a crack and blood poured into his mouth. His nose felt dead. Then his right eyebrow took a blow, started to burn and sting from sweat and blood. He couldn't see properly.

Something struck him on the chin. His fall backwards stopped by the wall. He got his fists up but couldn't see. Swung wildly and lost his balance. Could hear talking but not sure who. Saw a shadow move towards him and swung again. Heard that voice once more. Sounded like it was coming from the bottom of a well. Staggered to his right and found himself against the wall. A pair of arms gripped him from behind, heard the voice, closer, clearer.

'It's over. We need to get you patched up.'

Caillou took out a handkerchief and wiped the blood from Jouvin's eye. It'd be sealed up soon and he wouldn't be able to see out of it. Galabert had whipped him good and proper. Not what they'd expected, if only he'd run a book on it. Caillou had thought Galabert would swing a few air punches before Jouvin went to work. He'd fully expected to have to pull Jouvin off at some point and send Galabert home. But Jouvin hadn't been in it at all, not landed a single punch. Galabert was a boxer, you didn't get that style, that grace, without spending hours in the ring. Who knows where he picked that up. Tabaraut would be asking him about it now. Caillou had sent him off to buy Galabert a drink. Meantime, he'd take Jouvin to the local hospital and get him stitched up.

Tabaraut ordered beer, a towel, and plenty of ice. Wrapped the ice in the towel and placed it over Galabert's right hand. The left needed it too but not so bad.

'Where'd you learn to do all that, son?'

'My dad taught me and I kept it up at university.'

'But boxers have misshaped noses and cauliflower ears.'

'The ones that get hit do.'

Galabert smiled. His hands throbbed. The adrenalin

flowing through his body caused him to tremble. Didn't get like that for a bout. Then this wasn't a bout, it was as street fight. It felt good. Tabaraut now treated him with respect. He'd always been kind, in a fatherly way. Now he treated him like an equal. Didn't matter how many years you put in, if you could stand up for yourself, if you could fight, then you were alright.

He thought too of Jouvin. If ever a bastard had earned a thumping it was him. Maybe he'd lay off the Bébé crap, maybe not. Didn't matter now. He'd been beaten and there had been witnesses.

What would Belmont say? One of them was bound to mention it. And Jouvin couldn't hide those bruises. Should have stuck to body blows.

An hour passed and the shaking subsided. Tabaraut looked happy, half-asleep with his pipe and beer. Galabert had ordered more ice and stuck it over his left hand. He chewed on a bonbon. Wanted to get back out there and finish off the questioning. Tabaraut had vetoed it. Said their minds wouldn't be on the job. They'd finish up tomorrow night. Galabert wasn't inclined to argue.

Saturday, November 21st, Night

'Well, you're late, Phil, that's not like you.' Albert clapped his hands together and blew on them. Stomped his feet to get the feeling back in his toes. Most hours of most nights were spent performing this ritual dance against the cold.

Philippe ignored him and brushed past into the bar. The Breton woman had finished her cleaning, she left behind the faint smell of fish soup. The stage was empty. From the back dressing room came the sound of female chatter. The noise was always the same and it wouldn't be too surprising to find their conversations were the same too.

'All they do,' Albert said, 'is chatter and show their legs. Get me a whiskey, Phil, there's a good man.'

He'd followed Philippe into the club and taken a seat at the bar. Philippe ducked into his room. Removed his jacket, hung it on a peg and pulled on his bar coat. His hands trembled. He sparked up a cigarette and took his place behind the counter. Albert stood at the bar and sipped the drink Philippe passed him. Philippe poured one for himself.

'On the hard stuff tonight?' Albert said. 'Good for you.'

Philippe drank at work but not often at the bar until after closing. He gulped down the rest of his whiskey and wiped the back of his hand across his mouth.

'I actually like this place when it's empty,' Albert said.

'It's not bad,' Philippe replied.

Not bad! He felt like shitting himself. Every creak of a floorboard or shriek of laughter sent his heart racing. Why weren't the police here? It was eighteen hours since he'd murdered Maddie and nobody seemed to have noticed. At least they were pretending not to have noticed. Eighteen hours. He poured himself another drink and sent it down with a quick toss of the wrist, then he poured another and planned to send it the same way.

'I'll join you if you're having another,' Albert pushed his empty glass towards Philippe.

What was he still doing here? Philippe thought. Normally Albert would have a drink then sod off back to the door. What was he after? Was Albert keeping him talking while the police got into position? Were they hiding, listening out for some slip of the tongue that would send him to the guillotine? He let a generous measure fall into Albert's glass. Didn't want the old fool to think he wanted rid of him. This was all wrong. Léon had warned him not to do anything unusual and here he was drinking at the bar with Albert before the club had even opened.

'Make that one your last, Albert,' the boss called out as she made her way over to the bar. 'I want you with a clear head when you're on my door. Same for you, Philippe. Once the wankers know you're on the booze they'll be pulling fast ones all night long. Cute little bastards that they are.'

'Sure thing, boss,' Albert said.

In the half-light of the club she looked like a hideous creature sprung from the disturbed mind of an Ancient Greek poet. Didn't look much better in the full-light. She sent chills down Philippe's spine. He'd have to humour her now, pour her glasses of wine and listen to her moan about every sou she fancied she'd been cheated out of.

'That lazy bitch, Maddie, hasn't shown,' she said. 'Always one of the ungrateful bitches lets me down. I wish I could whip them, like in the old days! I'll be able to soon. I get more girls knocking on my door looking for work than I do dirty old bastards come to leer at them.'

Philippe tried to smile. A painful attempt. The woman didn't notice. Nobody noticed. They didn't talk to Philippe because they liked him. They talked because he was the barman and he was there to listen. So he listened and what he heard was the sound of his heart beating like the fists of a jilted man on his lovers' door. She went on moaning about the girls and money and the same things she always moaned about. But he kept hearing Maddie's name and, had she accused him?

'Well?' she said.

'Well, what, Boss?'

'Well, where's my wine, Philippe? If I paid you to stand around looking handsome I'd be asking for my money back. I pay you to pour drinks so get bloody pouring.'

Philippe poured a glass of white and tried to fake an interest in her complaining, remonstrating and berating monologue. For the briefest of moments he envisioned taking a small hammer to her face and ending this headache once and for all. The fleeting pleasure he gained from such imagining was caught short by the remembrance of sweet Maddie's face. Her eyes had penetrated straight into his soul and asked so many questions. Then they were blank voids filled with red and staring the infinite stare of death. He poured himself another drink. His boss was speaking at him - ordering, snarling, bossing - he didn't give a damn. If she wanted he'd pay for the drink and if she didn't like that she could take his job and stick it up her constipated arse.

She left to chivvy the girls. Philippe watched her go without taking it in. He sweated heavily, drink did that to him. So did nerves. He kept seeing Maddie out the corner of his eye. Sometimes there was someone there, scurrying along the edge of the stage or fastening a stocking in the corridor. Other times, no-one. He recalled ghost stories he'd heard as a kid. The ones where the victim came back to haunt their killer until he either went mad or simply topped himself.

Two old men played backgammon at the window. Woollen scarves wrapped around their necks. Cigarette smoke dissipated above their heads. Dice clicked on the board. They sipped mint tea, sweet and hot.

Ferhat sat in the far corner of the café. He ached.

Occasional spurts of pain shot through his body. The broken nose hadn't healed, made breathing difficult. One eye was partially shut. His good eye kept returning to the door. Even with a crowd in the café and people sat at his table he was afraid the door would burst open again. That they'd drag him outside and leave him dead on the pavement. As that flic had said, they'd been after him, not Ahmed.

'They won't come today, Ferhat,' Hakim said. 'Be not afraid.'

'And if they do come.' Omar pulled back his jacket to reveal a revolver.

These men were old comrades from The Party. None of them felt safe. Ahmed's had been the first death, it wouldn't be the last. If these thugs were able to beat them without recourse it was only a matter of time before the next funeral.

'How can we fight back when we don't know who did it?' Ferhat said.

'We strike back as they strike at us,' Omar said. 'We pick a café and drag out a Frenchman.'

'No,' Ferhat said. 'We must not use the innocent as pawns. We must not become like them.'

'There are no innocent Frenchmen. They are either active in our oppression or they turn a blind eye and allow it to continue.'

'No, Omar,' Hakim said. 'That would trigger reprisals. Every Frenchman would have a reason to hate us. Our people would be driven from the city.'

'Then what? Sit back and take it? Accept that we can be dragged into the street at any time?'

'What about the police?' Ferhat said. 'The one who came to my apartment seemed to believe me. He is going to investigate.'

'He believed you until he got back to Police Headquarters and they told him to drop it,' Hakim said.

'We don't know that.'

'Has he arrested anyone? Has the hit and run story been changed? No, no. He might have started out with good intentions but they evaporated under the heat of police corruption,' Omar said.

'On this, Omar and I are in agreement,' Hakim said. 'So long as that man Chiappe is in charge of the police we are on our own.'

'Then what?'

'We take action against a symbol,' Hakim said.

'Symbol, what do you mean?'

'We blow up Jeanne d'Arc.'

Ferhat stared at Hakim, tried to fathom the purpose of such an act. The Jeanne d'Arc statue stood on a plinth in place des Pyramides, pretty much in the middle of the road. What could they possibly gain from blowing it up? How would it stop the attacks on their old party brothers?

'How will it stop them?' Ferhat asked.

Omar also waited for Hakim's reply. He liked the idea of a bomb but would rather see it thrown into a crowded picture house. Or Police Headquarters. Somewhere it could do real damage. Kill people.

'Once they know we are prepared to strike back they will leave us alone. The bomb will be a threat. A message will be sent to the press, this time we chose a statue, next time...'

'Shit, shit, and shit again. I can't even get a glass of wine.' The boss strutted up and down in front of the girls. Most of them were leant against the wall weeping. They smoked and tried not to catch anyone's eye. If they did they knew they'd lose it. Some girls were hated, some tolerated and a rare few - Maddie - were liked.

Philippe sat at a table with Albert. He wished he could get out of there. Felt like he was choking. Albert wouldn't stop jabbering. Philippe no longer pretended to respond. Stared at the table. Any moment he'd surely puke all over it. He wanted to jump up and shout, 'it was me, God damn it, it was me.' Anything to put an end to this self-tormenting hell.

'Nothing, Chef.'

'Once more, then we'll call it quits.'

Belmont rolled a cigarette. If they found the girl's knickers he'd have this club closed down while they took it apart. Without them there was nothing. Nothing other than that lot up against the wall. They'd be taken in for questioning as soon as the vans arrived.

They would be questioned tonight, despite what that hideous over made-up woman had said. Threatened to ruin his career. Said she had contacts and so on. All bluff. You don't stand on top of a shit heap like this, crow about your influential contacts and expect to be taken seriously. All she'd achieved was an engendering of contempt in Belmont and a desire to inconvenience her as much as possible.

An officer came to report the vans were outside. Belmont dropped his cigarette and ground it into the dirty floor. 'May as well get that lot down to the Quai then.'

A couple of officers escorted the staff outside. There were no punters. Galabert had shown Albert the photograph of Maddie before the club opened. As soon as Albert had said, 'yes, Maddie, she works here,' Galabert had called in re-enforcements and had the place closed off. Belmont arrived in a taxi-cab twenty minutes later.

Gracianette spat his drink back in the glass, 'watered down piss!'

The search was over. They'd found three pairs of knickers. None belonged to Madeline Legrand. These girls were so used to taking them off they'd sewn their names in them.

Belmont assembled the team in the briefing room before commencing the interviews. Jouvin, who'd not made it to the club, turned up with a swollen eye and bruising all over his face. Someone had obviously taken him to town and it couldn't have happened to a more deserving chap. Belmont had noticed the red marks on Galabert's knuckles but couldn't picture him giving Jouvin a thrashing. Not without receiving a punch or two in reply and Galabert's face was spotless.

'Right, we've got our work cut out tonight. Last week it was vagrants, tonight it's exotic dancers.'

Caillou nudged Tabaraut. 'How'll we divide them up, Chef? I'd like the blondes. Tabaraut here can take the boss and Riquet can have the men, after all he's late to the party.'

'Late to the party!' Riquet said. 'I was here at the get-go, so to speak. Just happens I had to solve a post office robbery in the meantime. Besides, I outrank you. The inspectors should get the good looking ones, you sergeants can fight over the rest.'

'Alright, you two,' Belmont said. 'I admit the prospect of spending time with these girls is more appealing than another round with the vagabonds. But let's not forget were investigating the murder of a young woman. Could be that one of this lot killed her.'

'You don't believe that do you, Chef?' Caillou asked. 'I mean we've got the link to the girl but what about a link to the tramps?'

'I've thought about that one, Caillou, and I don't know that we should link the cases.'

'But, Chef,' Galabert said. 'the method of killing is so unusual and we didn't let the press know about the ear mutilations. In fact the press have hardly covered the killings at all. Whoever killed her must have been the same person who killed the tramps.'

'That's very assumptive. The second tramp was found in front of Notre Dame. Plenty of people saw him lying there. One of those people could have been the second killer. Think about it, he forces himself on Mademoiselle Legrand, she struggles and he strangles her. It's not uncommon. Now he's got a dead body and begins to panic. He remembers the dead tramp. Takes out his knife and has a go at her ears. Now he's got you lot thinking it was the tramp killer and he gets a free pass.'

Galabert was about to speak but couldn't find the words. It seemed improbable yet it fitted the scenario better than if it were the same man. After all, there were as many differences as there were similarities between the killings.

'So, Chef,' Jouvin said, 'as our victim was raped do we just interview the men?'

'My God, Jouvin,' Gracianette said, 'what's happened to your face?'

'I got into an argument.'

'You shouldn't argue with brick walls, you'll never win.'

'It ain't over yet, Gracianette.' Jouvin turned to look straight at Galabert. Galabert kept eye contact until Belmont spoke.

'Good point, Jouvin, but she may not have been raped. Imagine one of those girls catches our Mademoiselle Legrand *in flagrante delicto* with her boyfriend. She strangles her. The boyfriend may have even helped dump the body.

One or other of them comes up with the ear mutilation because they saw or heard about our tramp. I'm not saying that's what happened I'm just telling you to treat them all as suspects. As for dividing them up – there are enough girls to go round. However, Galabert, you and I will take the two men. And,' Belmont raised his hands to keep everyone in their seats as they were about to get up and leave, 'we also want a list of regular clients. It's as likely to have been one of the men whose laps she wriggled about on as anyone else.'

Albert sat at the table and stared straight ahead. He sat erect, didn't smoke the cigarettes he had in his jacket pocket. Left his cap on the table. He'd been sat like that for ten minutes as Belmont watched him through the glass in the door. Albert never once turned his head in Belmont's direction. Most suspects spent the time before an interview staring at that small portal to the outside world. Not Albert Oboeuf.

Belmont burst into the room to surprise Albert. It worked. Albert jumped in his seat and looked flustered.

'Your name is Oboeuf, correct?' Belmont hadn't reached the table yet.

'Correct, sir, that's my name.'

Belmont was reading from a file. He sat down and continued to read, didn't look at Albert. Flicked through the pages then put it face down on the table.

'You were in the army, Oboeuf?'

'Yes, sir.'

'You made it to corporal then you were busted back down to private. Why was that?'

Albert shifted uncomfortably in his seat, lost some of the ramrod posture. 'Well, sir, it's difficult to explain exactly.'

'Says here,' Belmont lifted the file and dropped it back down on the table, 'that you were caught stealing.'

'Well, not stealing exactly, sir, more like borrowing.'

'I see, you asked if you could take the items and the owner said yes. How did that lose you your stripes?'

'Well, sir, I didn't exactly ask, I was just intending to

return them later.'

Belmont picked up the file again and flicked through the pages. He paused at one and said, 'you were intending to return four bottles of white wine, three-hundred cigarettes and a side of beef?'

'Well, it wouldn't have been the same ones-'

'But you would have returned them?'

'Yes, sir.'

'When did you plan on returning these items?'

'Well, I didn't have an exact date in mind, sir, I was just planning to return them.'

'And have you?'

'Have I what, sir?'

'Returned them?'

'Well, no, sir. I thought the demotion meant I didn't have to.'

Belmont dropped the file back down on the desk. 'I'll tell you something, I don't care about sides of beef, bottles of wine or packets of cigarettes. I do care about young women getting murdered by dirty old men who should know better. You work at that club to ogle the girls, don't you, Oboeuf?'

'No, sir, it's just-'

'Don't lie to me. You thought by working at the club you'd get yourself something on the side. Thought the young women would be throwing themselves at a big strong man like you. Only they didn't, did they?'

'No, sir, I mean –'

'It's because you're too old for them. Too old, despite being a big strong war veteran who fought at Verdun. And what have those girls ever done? Nothing but chitter-chatter about make-up and movie stars. Did they laugh at you, when you made advances?'

'No, I mean they didn't, I didn't, they were-'

'What did you want that side of beef for, Oboeuf?'

'The beef? Well, I thought I might sell it on, I –'

'You were going to sell it on, even though you'd only borrowed it?'

'I would have got some cheaper and then I could have replaced it.'

'Did the girls kiss you on the cheek, like you were some old uncle? Did they treat you like some sexless eunuch? Is that why you got angry?'

'I didn't get angry, they were nice to me.'

'Nice to you! Giving you pecks on the cheek! Did their breasts rub up against you as they went up on their tippy-toes to plant those pecks on your cheek? They knew what they were doing, didn't they? Those girls know all about arousing men. They didn't rub their breasts against you by accident, did they?'

'I don't know, I can't remember, sometimes that happened.'

'A goodnight kiss for big strong Albert who spends all night making sure none of the grubby men grab them. But all he gets is a peck on the cheek and a nipple rubbed against his chest. And when you wanted a little bit more, what happened? Did she laugh at you? Is that why?'

Albert slumped on the table, his head buried in his arms.

'Tell me, can you still hear her laughing?'

Belmont stood up and walked around the table. Took a clump of Albert's hair and pulled his head back so he was leaning awkwardly in his chair. Then he put his mouth to Albert's ear, 'can you still hear her laughter, Oboeuf? Is she still laughing at you?'

Albert's voice came in gasps as he fought back the tears. 'It wasn't like that, sir. She didn't laugh much. I only wanted a proper kiss to warm me up, she didn't need to get all funny about it. I didn't mean to hurt her, I promise, sir, I didn't.'

Belmont let go the hair and returned to his seat. Took out his tobacco and rolled himself a cigarette. Lit it and blew smoke at Albert Oboeuf.

'Didn't mean to hurt her, did you,?'

'No, sir, that's right. I didn't mean to hurt her.'

'Just like you meant to return those cigarettes, that wine and the side of beef.'

'That's right, sir.'

Belmont slammed his hand down on the desk and shouted, 'you're a liar. You stole those items because you thought you were smarter than the army. And when Maddie Legrand laughed at you, you snapped. What right had she to laugh at you, Albert Oboeuf, veteran of Verdun? You thought you'd teach her to respect you. So you pulled her into that alley and you put your hands–'

'No, sir, it's-'

'And she started to scream. The laughter turned to screams and you didn't know what to do, you had to shut her up. So you put your hands over her mouth but still she screamed so you put your hands on her throat.'

'No, sir, it wasn't her, sir, it wasn't Maddie. It was Renée. She laughed at me and I grabbed her wrist and twisted it a bit. She slapped my face and I let her go. I didn't mean to grab her wrist, sir, I just did it. But I didn't touch Maddie, sir, honest, sir, it was Renée. Go ask her.'

'Evening, Tabaraut, Gracianette, mind if I join you?'

'Help yourself, Boss,' Tabaraut said.

Gracianette stood up and held his chair out for Belmont.

'No, no, Gracianette, I'm not staying long, you sit yourself back down.'

Gracianette didn't wait for Belmont to change his mind. He'd begun to regret offering his seat before he was fully stood up.

'And you, young lady, must be Renée Guillaume.'

'Sure,' she said.

'Who do you think killed young Maddie?'

'I wouldn't know, officer, but I'd bet it was one of the creeps?'

'You get many creeps around the club, Renée?'

'Many, ha! The whole club's full of them.'

'Well, then it's a good job you have a man like Albert Oboeuf around in case the creeps get out of hand.'

'Albert? Albert's alright but he gets carried away at times. I had to slap his face for him just last night.'

'You had to slap his face, Renée, why was that?'

'He got a bit over excited, that's all. They're both like it, him and Philippe. Phil's always taking a peep in the dressing room when we're getting changed.'

'Well, I suppose we can't blame a man for that.'

Renée smiled, 'no, least I don't. If they go a bit too far they get a slap in the chops and if they go any further I'll send my Florian round to give them what for.'

'Your Florian?'

'My brother. Haven't had to use him yet though.'

'You're a smart girl, Renée, you can look after yourself all right, I can see that.'

'That's right, officer, I know my way around.' She reached out and put her hand on Belmont's thigh. He took a step back.

'How about your friend, Maddie, was she a smart girl?'

'No, she was a darling. Sweet kid. Damn it! Ain't any of you got a cigarette?'

Renée's eyes filled with tears and Belmont gave her a moment as Gracianette lit her a cigarette.

'What's happening now, Chef? Do you still want me to interview with you?'

Galabert was stood outside the interview room drinking coffee. Belmont had sent him to fetch one then gone and interviewed Albert Oboeuf alone. After that he'd disappeared to interview Renée with Tabaraut and Gracianette. Galabert was afraid he'd been left out on purpose. He looked through the window at Albert who was slumped over the table, his shoulders rocked as if he were sobbing.

'Did you fetch that coffee I asked for?'

'Yes, Chef, but it'll be cold now.'

'That's no use, Galabert, I don't want cold coffee. Fetch us another and meet me in my office. You,' Belmont accosted a passing officer, 'stand guard on this room until I get back. Keep an eye on the mug inside. He's more likely to top himself than escape and I don't want him doing either.'

'Yes, Chef.'

Galabert brought in the coffee, pleased to see that Belmont was at his desk and not off interviewing the other guy from the club.

'Good man, Galabert, sit down.'

The room was warming up. Belmont must have stoked the stove. Kept that thing going night and day. Galabert watched his boss roll a cigarette and wondered what they were doing in the office instead of the interview rooms.

'What's going on, Chef?'

'Good question. We're letting him stew.'

'Oboeuf? Looked like he was sobbing more than stewing.'

'I've a nasty feeling about that one,' Belmont said. 'A really nasty feeling. I'm going to let him stew then we're going to pay him another visit. After that I'll get Caillou and Gracianette to have a word.'

'Caillou and Gracianette, Chef? Surely we can get as much out of him as they can.'

'Caillou and Gracianette are past masters at dishing it out, Galabert. Been doing it since you were in short pants. If they don't get a confession we'll go in again. In the meantime, the others can process the girls. I've arranged for a van to take them back to the club when were done – can't have young ladies roaming the streets at night, they'll get reputations.' Belmont laughed and took a sip of his coffee.

'What about the other one, Philippe Bodescot? The barman.'

'We'll get to him, Galabert. When Caillou and Gracianette are having a go at Oboeuf.'

'Do you really think it's him, Chef?'

'I think it likely. He's sneaky and weak and that makes him dangerous. I've got a request in with the Bureau of Identification. They'll match his fingerprints and anthropomorphic records against any known sex attackers in France from the last ten years. Could be he's gone by names other than Oboeuf.'

'But his army record was in the name Oboeuf.'

'True, Galabert, but he's had a number of years in between to have used an alias. Doing who knows what. He's been at that club two years, leaving a decade unaccounted for.'

'And if it is him, Chef, what do we do about the murders by the Seine?'

'I don't think he'll have been responsible for those. We'll see what he has to say when Caillou and Gracianette have had their talk with him.'

'Chef.'

'Galabert.'

'I was going to use this weekend to finish gathering evidence for the Arab boy's murder.'

'Not murder, Galabert, hit and run. And no, you can't drop this to go rooting out cover ups.'

'Not drop this, but can I have two more days when I'm not needed here? I'd like to stake out that house to see if anything else is going on there.'

'Look, Galabert, you're keen and that's all well and good but that case is poison. Imagine you're right. Just say Jouvin killed the Arab lad and Péraud covered it up. You get concrete proof, the sort that would bring a conviction. What then? You'll be the flic who busted a flic. Your name will be mud. Nobody will want to work with you, nobody will drink with you. I'll try to look out for you, but all in all your life as a judiciary flic will be shit. The Sûreté wouldn't want you either. If you wanted to keep on as a flic you'd have to get posted somewhere out in the sticks and hope they don't read the newspapers.'

'Are you telling me to drop it, Chef?'

'I'm not telling you, I'm advising you. I doubt that will make much difference. If you do turn anything up, bring it to me, don't go public. Maybe I can use it to force Jouvin to quit.'

'But, Chef, this is a murder we're talking about. It

wouldn't be right to let him get away with just quitting. It would be an injustice and I became a flic to fight injustice.'

'How many of those vagabonds did you interview, Galabert? Didn't that teach you that life isn't fair or just? One day you're at work, you've got a family and a home. The next you lose your job, lose your home, lose your family. All because some Americans wanted to play cowboy with the banks. The best result you can hope for is to cost Jouvin his job while keeping yours. That's if Jouvin had anything to do with it, which I suspect he didn't.

'Now, if I can draw your attention to the case at hand, there's the small matter of Albert Oboeuf. I've already ridden roughshod over him so you can be the nice guy. Every now and then I want you to chip in and say something positive. Make him think you're on his side. Meanwhile I'll try and break him down.'

Albert had stopped sobbing. He was sat up and staring at the wall. Less like a soldier more like the inmate from a faraway asylum. Even rocked back and forth in his chair. Belmont rolled a cigarette and watched Albert through the window, Galabert stood beside him.

'What do you make of it, Chef?'

'That we've got the girl's killer in there and another nutcase on the loose killing tramps.'

Belmont took a seat opposite Albert. Galabert closed the door and sat next to Belmont. Albert didn't acknowledge their arrival. Kept up his rocking and his fixed stare at the wall opposite.

'Oboeuf.' Belmont clicked his fingers in front of Albert's face. No response. He clicked again. Then he got up and left the room, called to Tabaraut who was taking a break between interviews, 'Tabaraut, fetch me a bucket of cold water. Then I want you to go wake the magistrate. Tell him to draw up an arrest warrant.'

'Christ, Boss, he confess?'

'Not yet but he's going to, now fetch me that bucket.'

Belmont tipped the water over Albert's head. Albert jumped up and slipped. Fell on the chair and toppled over. Swore and for a moment looked as if he might attack Belmont. Thought better of it and climbed back in his seat.

'I'm going to give you a chance, Oboeuf. You tell me and the good Sergeant Galabert here all about it and I'll see to it that you get some nice dry clothes and a lovely warm spot to spend the night.'

'Well, I already did tell you all about it, sir. I mean there's not much left.'

'What you told me, was a big steaming pile of shit. Do I look like a man who wants a steaming pile of shit, Oboeuf?'

'No, sir.'

'Indeed not. What I want is a fine cognac. Why don't you give me some of that.'

'I just don't know what you mean, sir. I've told you the truth of –'

'Don't talk to me about the truth, Oboeuf. You're a born liar. You lie so much you don't know when you've started. Stealing from the army and still trying to con me that you only borrowed those items. Renée's got a large bruise on her wrists from where you grabbed her. And what about poor Maddie Legrand?'

'I never laid a finger on her, sir, never touched her.'

'Perhaps,' Galabert said, 'he's telling the truth this time, Chef.'

'The truth! Him! You're soft in the head, Sergeant.'

'Couldn't we give him the benefit of the doubt, Chef, just this once?'

'This is a murder, Sergeant, not pinching an apple. He'll go to the guillotine. Public execution outside La Santé prison. All his former workmates will be there. All the girls lined up to watch him die. They won't be can-canning for you, Oboeuf. They'll be screaming for the blade to drop.'

'I suppose so, Chef, he just seems like a good sort that's all. Maybe he didn't mean to kill her. You didn't mean to kill her did you, Albert?'

'No, sir, I mean –'

'There you are, Chef. He didn't mean to kill her.'

'He'd have to convince a jury of that, Sergeant, and I'm not so sure he can. He doesn't convince me. If he didn't mean to do it you'd think he'd start by saying sorry and helping us clean up this whole affair. No, no, Sergeant, this one's going right to the execution block, I can see it.'

'But he is sorry, Chef, I'm sure of it. You are sorry aren't you, Albert?'

'No. I mean, yes. But no, I didn't do anything.'

'There he goes again, Sergeant. I've had enough of it.' Belmont stood up and leant across the table towards Albert. 'I'm going to send in two officers who are expert at making men like Albert Oboeuf talk. Come, Sergeant, it's over to them now.'

'You did well in there, Galabert.'

'Thanks, Chef. But not well enough to save him from this,' Galabert indicated the arrival of Caillou and Gracianette.

'They won't hurt him too much and if it helps take a killer off the streets then so be it.'

'We're ready, Chef,' Caillou said.

'Good man, Caillou. No broken bones please.'

'We'll do our best, Chef.'

'Come on, Galabert, let's go see what this barman chap's about.'

Albert backed away into the corner of the room. One of them was huge. The other looked mean, like an old army drill sergeant.

'Come here, you,' Caillou said.

Albert kept to the corner, shivered in his wet clothes. Caillou pulled a small cosh from his jacket pocket, slipped the strap around his wrist. He did it without looking, so used to slipping it over his wrist it was second nature to him.

'Don't make me fetch you,' Caillou said.

Albert slumped to the floor, wrapped his arms around his legs and buried his face into his knees. He blubbed like a kid. Caillou approached, swung the cosh, catching it in his left hand. It made a smacking noise as it hit his palm.

'Get over here and sit at the table.'

Albert ignored him.

'OK, Gracianette, give me a hand.'

Gracianette joined Caillou. They each took hold of a shoulder and lifted him. Ran him at the table and threw him into it. The table jumped under his weight and Albert collapsed to the ground. He rolled around a bit until Caillou's boot caught him full swing in the gut. Albert doubled up and whimpered.

'You gonna sit yourself in that chair or am I going to sit you in it?'

Tears fell down Albert's cheeks as he cried without restraint. Gracianette and Caillou lifted him up and dumped him in the seat. Then Gracianette took Albert's left wrist, twisted it and stretched out his arm behind his back. He grabbed a handful of Albert's hair and forced his face into the table. Caillou made himself comfortable in the seat opposite Albert.

'I don't care if you didn't do it, Oboeuf, do you know why? Because I don't like you. I don't like you so I'm going to hurt you. My friend there, Sergeant Gracianette, he doesn't like you either. Do you, Sergeant Gracianette?'

'Can't stand him, Sergeant Caillou. If you weren't in the room I'd tear him apart.' Gracianette put a little extra weight into Albert's face.

'Well, I might just leave and let you to do that, Sergeant Gracianette. But first I'm going to hurt him. Know why I'm going to hurt you, Oboeuf?'

Albert sniffled rather than speaking.

'What was that, Oboeuf? Did you say it's because you're a miserable slug? You're right, it's because you're a miserable slug. In ten seconds I'm going to come around there and teach you a lesson. The only thing that'll stop me is you confessing what you did to that poor innocent girl.'

'But I-'

Gracianette twisted Albert's arm which killed the sentence. Caillou rounded the table and swung his cosh straight at Albert's kidneys. Took three or four swings as he was never certain exactly where the kidneys were. Then he nodded at Gracianette who changed his hold. Got his arm around Albert's neck and held him up in the chair. Albert's feet began to flail about as Gracianette exerted pressure on his throat. Caillou swung and crouched in one easy movement. The cosh struck Albert across the shin of his right leg. Albert yelped but the sound hardly escaped him. Caillou did it again, this time hitting the left shin. Then again hitting the right kneecap. This time Albert's scream managed to escape. Caillou pocketed his cosh and slapped Albert across the face, 'quit screaming you filthy bastard.'

November 23rd, Early

That flic had been watching him the whole time. It was nearing one in the morning, he'd been there almost four hours. Philippe was the last. He'd seen the girls called one-by-one. The boss, who'd waited silently, saving her wrath for the unfortunate flic who had to interview her, was the last of the others to go. Albert had been among the first. Why had they saved him until last? There could only be one reason and it wrenched his gut to think of it.

Philippe got up and paced the room. The flic glanced over, eyed him for a moment, then resumed his blank stare. What would Léon do if he were here? Not much he could do, either sit down and wait or pace and wait.

They'd soon call him out as they had the others. Ask him when he'd last seen Maddie, what was his relationship with her. One stupid act, one wrong word, and he'd never know freedom again. Léon warned him to stay silent, only answer with the minimum.

The room felt empty. He wished the boss was still there. Wished he wasn't alone with that flic. Then he saw her, sat on the bench, picking at a hole in her stockings where they'd laddered.

'Got a cigarette, Phil?'

He choked. Stole a furtive glance at the flic who'd kept up his fixed stare at the opposite wall. She wasn't there, else the flic would have said something. Yet, there she was, one leg crossed over the other and bobbing up and down. Her garter showing. She held an unlit cigarette to her mouth.

'Got a light, Phil?'

Don't answer, look away. He stopped pacing and focused on the furthest corner of the room. How long before the flic got suspicious? Or was this a ploy? Had she been sent in to test his reaction? But she was dead. At least he thought she was dead.

He was inside her when she'd decided to scream. Before that she'd been telling him no, asking him to stop, pushing at his chest as he lifted her skirt. It had felt like a game until the scream. Stuck a hand over her mouth, then it wasn't so bad. After he'd finished he'd told her to keep quiet. But when he removed his hand she'd screamed again. Why? She wasn't a virgin and he was already out of her. She could have gotten on that bike and ridden away. Instead she'd screamed and he'd gripped her throat to silence her. She slipped to the floor. It had felt like she was dead when he'd dragged her behind the bins. Then he'd gone home. Gone home and told Léon what he'd done. And Léon went out to find her. When he got back, Léon said that she was dead.

Maddie screamed. Her cigarette fell to the floor and rolled away. Philippe covered his ears and looked at the flic. The flic frowned. Philippe forced himself to take his hands away from his ears. She screamed again, louder than before. He sat on the opposite bench and looked on as spit dribbled from Maddie's mouth and her eyes turned red. Her scream ate into his soul. Tears of blood trickled down her pale cheeks. Didn't think he could take any more. Wanted to scream back or reach over and put his hand across her mouth.

'It's been a long night, Monsieur Bodescot,' Belmont said.

Philippe wasn't sure if that was a question. He'd been escorted into this room and the two flics were already sat across the table. They hadn't said a word until now. Five long minutes of silence. The taller one had rolled a cigarette and the younger one picked at his nails. Then they led with this ambiguous question that might not be a question. He nodded his head.

'It'll be over soon,' Belmont said.

Philippe forced a smile.

'How long had Mademoiselle Legrand been working at the club?' Belmont asked.

Philippe looked up at the ceiling. How long? Felt like forever.

'About ten or eleven months.'

'Ten or eleven months,' Belmont said. 'How long have you been working with us Sergeant Galabert?'

'Me, Chef? About two months.'

'Only two months, really? I would have wagered it was longer, maybe four or five. So, Legrand started around January time?'

'Yes, end of January.'

'How can you be so sure?'

'I'm not so sure. You should ask the boss, she'll know when she started paying her wages.'

'Good idea, Monsieur Bodescot. Could you describe Legrand to me? I have seen her, of course, as has Sergeant Galabert. But not alive. To us she was just a dead body pulled from a rubbish bin.'

The flicker of a grimace had flashed across Philippe's face.

'I… that's horrible, the bins?'

'Yes, yes, murder is horrible, that's why we have to get involved. Can you tell me what was she like prior to being killed and stuffed into a bin?'

'She was lovely, I mean she was a nice kid.'

'She was lovely, Sergeant Galabert.'

'I mean compared to the other girls,' Phillipe said. 'She wasn't so crude, you know, brazen.'

'Not crude or brazen, she does sound lovely. What did she do when the other girls were, what was that thing called, Sergeant?'

Galabert flicked through his notebook and read it out loud, 'mingling, Chef.'

'That's right, mingling. I think that's when customers stick their fingers up the girls' private parts. Or grope their breasts while slipping five francs into their brassieres. What did she do during mingle time, Monsieur Bodescot?'

'Same as the other girls, but that's not what I meant. She didn't go to the brothel after hours.'

'Instead of going to the whore house, did she sometimes stay behind for a drink?'

'Sometimes, yes.'

'Just the two of you in that dimly-lit club. Didn't you sit with her when she had this drink?'

'No, I wiped down the surfaces, mopped up the puke, locked up the bar, that sort of thing.'

'And she sat alone at one of the tables?'

'Yes, or on a stool at the bar. She liked the quiet of it all.'

'I see, and what about you? Did you ever pay a visit to the brothel after hours?'

'What do you mean?'

'I mean, when you'd finished wiping the surfaces, mopping up the puke and locking up the bar, did you ever go to the brothel?'

'No, I went home.'

'You spent the night serving drinks and wiping up after others, then you pulled on your jacket and caught a taxi-cab straight home?'

'Not a taxi-cab.'

'But straight home?'

'No, not every night. Sometimes I went for a drink on the way. You know, Les Halles or some all-night bar in Montparnasse.'

'Never the brothel?'

'No, just a drink.'

'But you do like girls?'

'I'm no queer.'

'You needn't get upset about it. You have a perfect right to be a homosexual if you wish to be.'

'I'm not a homosexual, it's disgusting.'

'I see. I didn't think you were. I know, for example, that you like to take a look at the girls when they're getting undressed. Isn't that right?'

'I might have, once or twice, accidentally looked in while they were changing.'

'Once or twice accidentally. And how many times on purpose?'

'I, I didn't, that is, I had to go back that way and they often left the door open a bit. I couldn't help it. You'd have done the same.'

'I'm sure I would have. All those naked and semi-naked young ladies. Good looking girls too, some of them. I've seen them remember, they've all been here tonight. All except one that is. Which was your favourite?'

'I don't have a favourite. They're all too crude.'

'Come, come, Monsieur Bodescot, you're no queer, you said so yourself, there was nothing platonic about your peeking. You were looking because you like to see naked women. So do I. So do the men who buy postcards from the hawkers at the Gare du Nord. And we all have favourites. How about you, Sergeant Galabert, I know you have a wife but supposing you cast an eye into a room full of naked women, wouldn't you focus on one particular girl, a favourite?'

'If I did look in, Chef, and if my wife asks I never would, but if I did, then I'd be drawn to any red-headed girls. Do any of them have red hair, Monsieur Bodescot?'

'Yes,' Philippe said, 'one of them does.'

'Then, Chef, I would have favoured her.'

'See, Sergeant Galabert would have favoured the red-head. I can't say which one I would have favoured but I do like bobs, like Louise Brooks. And I like girls that aren't too big but not too skinny either. Which one was your favourite, Monsieur Bodescot?'

'I suppose it's Renée.'

'Ah, yes, I remember her, a charming girl. She might have been my favourite too. Were you never tempted to visit that brothel to see if Renée was working there? I'm sure she would have been.'

'No, I couldn't do that with a girl from the club.'

'Really, you couldn't fuck a girl because she dances topless in a nightclub? Even after you've been spying on her getting dressed.'

'I have to work with them, it'd be awkward.'

'Do you find sex distasteful?

'No, I like sex.'

'When was the last time you had sex?'

'Friday night.'

Philippe thought he was going to throw up. Why the hell did he say Friday? Might as well go the whole hog and tell them it was with Maddie. Shit, shit, shit.

'Friday night, who with?'

'It was a street walker on the boulevard Edgar-Quinet. Called herself Mimi.'

'What time was this?'

'About six-thirty. Before I went to work.'

'I don't get it, Chef. Why did we let Bodescot go but keep Oboeuf?'

Belmont sighed and poured two glasses of cognac. Outside the early risers would be wiping sleep from their eyes, but Belmont hadn't been to bed yet, to him it was late.

'A flic's instinct, Galabert. Oboeuf's just the type to strangle a girl after raping her. Bodescot is a fool but not a killer. Did you notice the way he grimaced when I mentioned the bins?'

'But all that stuff about the other girls being brazen and then claiming Renée was his favourite. She was the most brazen of them all.'

'I know, Galabert, he was lying. His favourite was Maddie. He didn't want to say so because she was the one murdered. Lying isn't the best move when you're that easy to read but it's understandable.'

Galabert decided to drop it. He didn't believe either Oboeuf or Bodescot were the killer. Unlike Belmont, Galabert's flic instinct told him the killing was directly related to the tramp murders.

'What did the magistrate say?'

'Said we could hold Oboeuf for longer but we don't have enough to arrest him yet. He's given us a warrant to search the man's apartment. In the meantime, I recommend we get some sleep. Oboeuf is in the cells. The rest of the squad have gone home. I've got men ready to go on a perv hunt with the Montmartre boys. They'll round up the club's customers we've got addresses for. The rest will be picked up if and when they enter the club. There were two in particular who favoured Legrand. If we can get hold of them then you and I will drill them.

'I've got someone scheduled to be at the club the moment it opens. He'll have a fun night watching girls can-can waiting for the boss to point out the men we're after.

'By the way, Galabert, I was impressed by your style during that interrogation. It's difficult to know when to keep quiet and when to pipe up but you did both to perfection. And the questions you asked were spot on. Are there any red-heads? Fantastic.'

Monday, November 23rd, Morning

Church bells chimed for five am. That gave him at least two hours until daylight. Galabert needed the darkness and tonight he'd be bogged down interrogating the nightclub clientèle and preparing the case against Oboeuf. There was no telling how long all that would drag on. If he wanted to do this then it had to be now.

He found a taxi-cab at the rank on the rue de Rivoli. Hadn't wanted to catch one near the Quai des Orfèvres, didn't want the driver knowing he was a flic. He kept an eye on the road while shamming drunkenness. They drove west to Galabert's slurred directions. When they got within a kilometre of the house he tapped on the driver's shoulder and said, 'this'll do, mate.'

The rear of the house was in darkness. Shutters blocked out all but a trace of light. Because of this darkness Galabert didn't feel the need to crawl on his belly across the lawn. His clothes were dark and the sky cloudy. No sniper good enough to hit him under these conditions would be working night shifts as a glorified gamekeeper. Still, no need to take unnecessary risks, Galabert went down on his haunches as he scampered across the garden. Then he made his way to the front of the house, ducked windows as he went.

Round the front a porch light lit up most of the courtyard. This was interlaced with a weaker light from the street lamps. The courtyard itself was covered with gravel, every footstep would crunch and echo off the boundary walls. Two garages faced each other across the courtyard about twenty metres from the house. Twenty metres of gravel and light.

Galabert bit his lip and considered the options. There was the wall he'd climbed to enter the garden. It ran around the whole property, interrupted only by the iron courtyard gates. He could climb that wall and drop down on the far side of the garage. He was a good climber, the risk of falling was slight. However, he'd been over that wall, the risk of a brick coming lose and crashing down was high. No, the wall was out and that left nothing but a sprint across the gravel.

Galabert took off his shoes, tied the laces together and hung the shoes round his neck. Stones cut into his feet as he darted across the courtyard like a fakir over hot coals. Headed for the far side of the right-hand garage. He felt exposed as he passed through a section lit by a street lamp. Expected to hear those dreaded words, 'stop or I'll shoot.'

Behind the garage. They'd need to leave the house to see him now. Would they be that curious? They would if he made any more noise. For a good five minutes he stood stock still and listened to his heart beating. A cold and sticky sweat formed on his brow. His feet were numb. He crouched down and quietly pulled his shoes over torn and bloodied socks. He felt more nervous now than when he'd watched them in their Black Shirt regalia. That time he knew where they were. The fear had been of a hidden sniper, but really, why would they have a sniper? This time he couldn't see them. But they were there, in that dark house, listening.

The garage had three doors in total. Two large green wooden doors which would swing out and allow vehicles to pass through. Inside the left-hand door there was a smaller, man-sized door which had the garage's only window. A window so filthy with black grime that it acted as a mirror. Galabert could just make out a motor vehicle. Couldn't be certain but it was most likely the Rolls. He put his ear to the glass and listened, wanted to make sure the chauffeur wasn't kipping in the auto. Didn't hear a thing. He was all too aware that, from where he was standing in front of the garage, he could be seen from the house. He tried the door handle, locked. He retreated out of sight to give himself time to think.

He'd always known the doors would be locked and had planned for it. To this end a jemmy weighed down his satchel. A bit of force would see those doors open in seconds. There'd be some noise but nothing louder than the sound of his walking on the gravel. So it wasn't from fear of waking anyone that he didn't use the jemmy, it was the stupidity of the plan. If he forced the lock they'd know they'd been broken into. Any evidence would be inadmissible. Not only now but later too, for if they could prove Galabert had broken into their garages then they could cast aspersions on any evidence he presented. And with their money, their resources, they'd walk free while Galabert would be put on a charge.

Galabert's father had an old shed which he'd kept locked. Aged 12 Galabert had worked out how to get in. It was simple. He'd turn the handle of the door then lean back. His weight would pull both the door and the lock forward until the door sprang free. It was harder to close again afterwards but he could use the jemmy for that, it would act like a shoehorn for the lock and not cause any damage. The plan was clean but involved a lot of noise. If anyone heard him he'd scale the gate and hope they were a lousy shot.

The house was dark and silent. Galabert stepped gingerly over the gravel to the garage door and took hold of the handle. He leant back and pulled. The door stayed shut but he could feel some give and he could see the outer door bow where the lock was. He tugged at the handle with a series of jerks until, just like his father's shed, the door sprang open. Galabert went sprawling over the gravel. He lay there looking at the house. The noise had been tremendous. Might as well have fired a cannon at the damned door.

Cannon or not, no-one had woken up. Galabert slipped into the garage. He switched on his torch and pointed it into the dark corners. Most of the space was taken up by the Rolls-Royce. Alongside the motor-car there was a shelf with oil, tools, dirty rags, nothing out of the ordinary. The street was probably lined with garages like this, each containing its own luxury automobile and shelves full of bric-a-brac.

Galabert climbed in back of the Rolls and rested on the cold leather seat. The smell of leather mingled with old cigar smoke and a hint of booze. A walnut cabinet sat below a glass screen which separated the driver from his passengers. The cabinet was divided into three sections, Galabert flicked the doors open. The left and right-hand sections held bottles of booze. The centre revealed an array of glasses. Elasticated straps held them all in place. A nice life for some, being driven around the city with a personal drinks cabinet in situ.

Galabert sat back, considered taking a nip of something and cursed. He wasn't sure what he'd hoped to find but he supposed it'd be something that would force Belmont to leave his overheated office, get a warrant and come down here to arrest someone. That, he knew, would have required a hell of a lot of luck on his part and a great deal of stupidity on theirs. He freed a bottle from its elastic constraints and poured a healthy measure down his throat.

With the help of his jemmy, Galabert eased the door shut. It looked good, you'd never know anyone had been in there. And if the senator was in the habit of marking his bottles then it was tough luck for the chauffeur.

With his shoes on this time, he walked nonchalantly across to the other garage. If they hadn't heard him rolling about on the floor earlier then they weren't likely to hear him now. This time the door took more pulling and when it opened he stumbled back across the driveway and shouted in surprise as he thought he was going to fall. He eyed the house, all nonchalance gone, certain that someone must have heard him. Every muscle was taught, ready to spring at the gates and scramble over. Eventually his muscles began to ache. Once he'd accepted nobody was coming he walked back to the second garage and entered.

A large white baker's van crowded the garage. A perfect match for the van Ferhat's attackers had used to drive to and from the murder of Djaout. To and from those other beatings which, by luck, didn't end with a death. Galabert was no longer in any doubt that these people had murdered Ahmed Djaout. And these people, whoever else they might be, included Superintendent Péraud, Inspector Cruchon and Sergeant Jouvin. Jouvin who'd arrived at work with bruising on his cheek the day after the attack. Jouvin with his hatred of Arabs, who'd warned Galabert off this investigation. He thought of Ahmed, the young man in the photograph on his brother's sideboard, the one draped in black crepe. The photograph showed a young man looking out to the future unaware it would be two or three years and not the fifty or sixty he might have expected.

The van was locked, front and back. Galabert had just tried the rear doors for a second time when someone called out, 'who's there?' Galabert froze. He'd left the garage door open, they'd have no doubt he was inside. There was nowhere to hide, it was difficult even to move. 'Come out whoever you are.' If they had a gun his best chance would be to stay in the garage. Movement was restricted. They wouldn't be able to take proper aim. Not that he could spend the night circling the van. Whoever was out there would call for help. They'd drive the van out. He heard the jangling of keys then the sound of the large outer doors opening.

'I said come out.' The voice came from a man stood at the entrance to the garage. He carried a torch in one hand and a shotgun in the other. The shotgun was trained on the floor, the torch pointed into the garage. The man had to decide, should he wait outside or enter? He couldn't fit alongside the van and shoulder the gun. He'd also have to ditch the torch if he wanted to fire the thing.

The man decided to place the torch on the ground. Then he got down on his hands and knees and took a look under the van. Nothing, no feet to be seen, nobody hiding under the van. He took the shotgun and moved sideways along the gap between the van and wall. If he had to fire it would be a mess. Might even get hit by a ricochet. So be it. He couldn't risk going in there unarmed and there was no time to go back for his pistol. The man edged along one side of the van. Stopped to listen then pushed on when he didn't hear anything. He reached the rear, nothing. Tried the doors, locked. There was a window which he peered through. It was hard to say for certain in the darkness but it looked empty. He completed his circuit and returned to the front. Tried the cab door. Locked. Got down on his knees with his torch and shone it across the garage floor. Still nothing. The garage door hadn't blown open, he'd better take a look around the grounds. First he locked up the garage.

Monday, November 23rd, Afternoon

'If we leak details of this girl's death to the press it'll be me they take to task, not Belmont. Besides, Belmont looks like he's caught someone. He's been strutting in and out of the examining magistrate's office most of the morning.'

'That's not the point, sir. If we leak the story and an arrest is made -'

'They'll make a hero of Belmont.'

'Until it gets out about the tramps. I've questioned Belmont's suspect, Oboeuf. He was at work when the first murder took place - plenty of witnesses. We'll let the press know about the girl. Belmont will formally arrest Oboeuf. Then, as you say, they will call Belmont a hero. Let him lap it up because I'll be having a drink with a journalist friend. Of course he'll have to drag it out of me but I'll let slip about the tramp murders. Without wanting to go into details I'll insinuate that the murders are linked. And, I'm afraid, Oboeuf had a solid alibi for the first of those killings, probably the second too. His paper will run with it in the morning, the rest will jump all over it for the evening editions. It'll be obvious Belmont has the wrong man. I can see the Bumbling Belmont headlines now.'

Péraud pushed aside his plate, gave his fingers a wipe on a napkin and took a quick look around the brasserie. Belmont had friends and he didn't want to continue this discussion if any of them were sat alongside him. Nobody seemed to be paying them undue attention.

'Go on.'

'The press will up the ante. Belmont will be blundering

around with this Oboeuf chap, going over his alibi for the first murder. I'll suggest to the commie press that Belmont's wealth makes him a dilettante. That he doesn't care about the homeless. That Belmont picked on Oboeuf because he didn't want to get his hands dirty with a real investigation, that he as good as ignored the first death.'

'But that was me, Jouvin, I told him not to waste resources on the first murder.'

'The press don't know that, sir. Soon as they print the story about the other killings and Oboeuf's alibi, you'll be ready with a statement for the evening papers. It'll look like you're defending Belmont when in reality you'll be casting him adrift. Something like: I trust my officers to make the right decisions. Chief Inspector Belmont is a good and loyal officer who has given many years of valuable service. That way, if he tries to blame you for holding back on the initial investigation he'll look like an ungrateful runt. If this plays out you could be rid of him once and for all.'

The superintendent grinned. Began to see Jouvin as a protégé. Began to see him as inspector material.

'Do it, Jouvin, but co-ordinate with me. First make it known that the murder of the girl was violent, that she'd been raped and mutilated. No details about where she worked or what she did. Don't want the public knowing she was a slut who got what she deserved.'

'Tits or arse?'

'Arse.'

Belmont rolled a cigarette and leant back in his chair. The man opposite puffed away on a Gauloise. He looked, given the fact he was being interviewed at the Quai des Orfèvres, quite content.

'Blonde or brunette?'

'Blonde, provided she's got a nice arse else brunette. I don't really care that much about hair colour.'

Caillou sat silent with arms folded. Watched his boss question the suspect. He knew the chef was going easy.

Knew why too: Belmont still had Albert Oboeuf pegged as the killer. So far that particular weasel was keeping quiet. Another round of questioning and Caillou figured he'd crack, one way or the other.

'And which girl from the club was your favourite?'

'Maddie.'

'She was brunette wasn't she?'

'Yes but she had a fantastic rump. Besides, she was good. Made a man think he was *her* favourite, that she didn't care about the money. Sweet kid. Pity.'

'Pity, indeed. Where did you go after the club closed?'

'Me? Usual routine. Went for a drink in the bar across the road. Downed a couple to keep warm. Walked home. Stopped to get a wank from a street girl on the way. One-eyed Bella did it for me.'

'And One-eyed Bella, would she vouch for you if we brought her in?'

'Sure she would, I'm a regular.'

'Can you give us an approximate time you were with her?'

'I weren't with her long, I'd gotten worked up at the club and the extra pair of drinks set my juices flowing. Couldn't say exactly when I saw her but it was two o'clock when I came. I remember hearing church bells at the critical moment. Then I buttoned up, paid up, and went straight home.'

Unlike Galabert, Caillou enjoyed the heat of Belmont's office. He slouched in a chair while Belmont talked on the telephone. Caillou sat up when Belmont put the receiver down.

'He's not been home. She thought he was here. He's in for an earful from me and he'll get double from her when he finally shows.'

'Maybe he stopped off to see One-eyed Bella, Chef.'

Belmont laughed and got out the cognac.

'I've got a feeling I know where he is and, if I'm right, he'll be on shit shovelling duty the rest of the week. I explicitly told him the Legrand case comes first.'

'What case is he putting first, Chef?'

'Never you mind, Caillou.'

'When do you want us to question Oboeuf again? Are you going to join us this time?'

'Let Oboeuf have lunch then take Gracianette and have another word with him. I'll leave him to you two, for now. I'm going to visit one of my informers, see if any pervs have gone A.W.O.L. in the last couple of days. If they have we might let Oboeuf go. If not, unless you get a confession, it'll be for the magistrate to decide what we do next.'

There was a knock at the door. Galabert entered. Looked rough. Unshaven, crumpled clothes, dead on his feet.

'Alright, Caillou, hop it. And thanks for filling in on the interviews. To make up for his disappearing act, Galabert will be polishing your boots at the start of each shift for the next week. That alright with you, Galabert?'

'What, Chef?'

Caillou left. Galabert took his seat.

'Stand up, Sergeant. I didn't tell you to sit.'

Galabert leapt from the seat and stood to attention.

'That's better. Let's try to remember that I'm The Chef. That means I give the orders. And when I say report back here at one o'clock you get here at five-to-one and wait. Do you understand?'

'Yes, Chef'

'Good. Now sit down and tell me why it's appropriate for you to turn up late for work looking like you've slept in a ditch. You been going undercover with the tramps?'

'I got a lead, Chef.'

'A lead on what?'

'The Arab. I went back to the big house and had a nose in their garages. They've got a baker's van in there, Chef. A baker's van!'

'And?'

'And, Chef? It ties them to the killing.'

'What did it look like?'

'It looked like a white baker's van, Chef. Just like the victim's brother described.'

Galabert had imagined, by this stage, that Belmont would be patting him on the back. The van was a coup. If they raided the property now the murder would be wrapped up in no time.

'How big were the dents?'

'What dents?'

'The dents in the front of the van.'

'There were no dents, Chef.'

'Then it's not likely to have been involved in a recent hit and run.'

'I don't buy the hit and run story. I think the brother was telling the truth about the gang of attackers.'

'You'll need to prove it wasn't a hit and run before we can act. That'll require more than a van without dents.'

'But, Chef, I have a witness. The brother. Where did this hit and run story come from anyway?'

'From the superintendent. I'm your boss, he's my boss. He says hit and run, I say hit and run, you say hit and run unless you can prove otherwise. The brother, remember, was responsible for knocking the victim into the road. He has a motive for lying, to ease his guilt.'

'How can we say that? Nobody saw them fighting.'

'Listen to me, Galabert, and listen good. Witnesses don't mean a damn thing. If you push your witness forward then at least three new witnesses will pop-up having seen the whole thing - the brothers fighting, the van hitting one of them. The magistrate will drop the case without a second thought. Then whoever's orchestrating all this will turn their attention to you. Do you understand what I'm saying? This case is poison, stop drinking it.'

'I can't, Chef.'

'Those garages you were creeping about in belong to a senator. You put one finger out of place and you'll lose your job. They could get you jailed. Is this case worth risking your job for, risking your freedom? Who'll look after your kid when you're inside explaining to your cell mate that you used to be a flic?'

'I won't put a finger out of place.'

'How did you find out about the van?'

'I climbed the wall again, then-'

'Show me the warrant.'

'There wasn't one, Chef, I did it undercover. I thought we could get a warrant and go back now, while the van's still there.'

'You don't think searching a senator's property without a warrant might be a finger out of place? As for me, I'd be better off writing my resignation than making a request to search that house. Now, tell me, can you be certain that nobody saw you there?'

'Yes, Chef. It was close but I hid on the roof of the van. I was stuck up there for over three hours before I could get away. When I got back I was exhausted. I over slept. That's why I was so late.'

'Go careful, Galabert. I advise you to drop the whole thing. If you can't, bring me something cast iron and I'll see what we can do about it. Just don't do anything stupid.'

Monday, November 23rd, Evening

Early evening. Already pretty dark although the street lights hid it well. Belmont slipped out of the Quai des Orfèvres and into a taxi-cab. His informant was in Montmartre. A greasy runt who called himself Blue-Fingered Pierre. Pickpocket and occasional break-and-entry man. Belmont had caught him at it two years ago. Took one look at his record and got a banishment order drawn up. Didn't mess around, laid it on the table and said, 'snitch for me or fuck off out of Paris for the next five years.'

Pierre was sat in the corner of an anonymous bar-tabac off the rue Lepic. Not his usual haunt. This was the place he used for meeting Belmont. Didn't want anyone asking him questions about the tall gent with the expensive coat. Not that they'd ask questions. They'd just mark him down as a snitch and ostracise him.

Belmont ordered two beers. Pierre fumbled about for cigarettes, matches, fiddled with a napkin, cast furtive glances at the door.

'Don't get me wrong, I like skirt. Don't mind watching the odd strip show either. But pervs aren't my crowd.'

Belmont took out his tobacco and rolled a cigarette, took a sip of beer. Made Pierre wait a good five minutes before he spoke. 'Let's not waste too much time with idle chit-chat, Pierre. I don't want to be here and I'm sure you'd rather not be seen with me. You've had twenty-four hours to ask around. Crowd or no crowd, anyone skip town?'

'There was someone, but he wasn't a perv. It was Maurice the Tadpole. He got in bad with The Marseillais gang. From what I hear, he owes five grand. Anyway, Maurice likes boys, not skirt.'

Chief Inspector Belmont left the bar-tabac and walked to the Blvd de Clichy. He stood for a moment in the shadow of the Moulin Rouge. The sound of black American jazz leaked onto the streets around him. A taxi-cab pulled up and Belmont climbed in. The cyclist, who'd been at the curb on the junction with rue Lepic, moved out into the traffic and followed the taxi.

In a city as busy as Paris a cyclist can tail a taxi with relative ease. There are stretches of open road where the taxi will pull away. Then there are patches of congestion, junctions, stop signs and passing trams which allow the cyclist to regain position.

Belmont's taxi drove out to Passy. Léon panted cold air in and out of his lungs. He was used to cycling but six kilometres paced by a taxi took it out of him. His cheekbones hurt from the cold, his ears burnt. Felt as if he'd lost sensation in his fingers. Now the sweat on his back was turning to ice. It had been easier following Belmont from Police HQ to Montmartre. All uphill but the roads were busy and the traffic slow. Coming out here meant long flat out stretches.

Belmont was in a restaurant and Léon was left out in the cold. There was a café-bar within sight of the restaurant. Léon sat on the terrace, despite the chill, and ordered a beer, despite the price. The other customers were well-to-do. Men, mostly, whose waistcoats cost more than Léon's entire outfit including the bike.

The chatter from the bar was loud and punctuated with laughter. Léon felt sure they were laughing at him: the scruffy man sat outside on a winter's night.

The sky hung heavy above him, an eternal black void. The door to the bar opened and the warmth hit him, followed by a wave of beer, tobacco and eau de cologne. Up the street he could see a flic. Léon felt conspicuous, trapped outside with nowhere to hide.

The cold chilled his bones. He lit a cigarette and held the glowing tip beneath his fingers to warm them. His coat was too thin, good for early autumn, not for winter. Cycling had warmed his body, let him forget his clothes weren't suited to this weather. That heat had long since gone and he'd started shaking. The obvious cure was less than a metre away, the heat of the bar. It would also remove him from the prying eyes of passing flics. The thought of Belmont slipping away unseen kept him outside.

What had possessed Philippe to kill that bloody girl? There must have been five hundred whores between their apartment and his club. Why couldn't he have dipped his wick in one of them?

'I didn't want a whore, Léon, I wanted her.'

Léon had slapped him. Then he'd gone up there, hoping Philippe had been wrong. Hoping the girl had crawled away. But there she was, lying behind the dustbins, just as Philippe had described. Léon dragged her out by the ankles and tried to force her into one of the bins. Tried three times but she wouldn't go. Anger got the better of him and he'd cut her ears off and stabbed the side of her head until he'd calmed a little. After that he broke her legs and forced her inside the bin.

Blood ran down Albert's face. His head span. They wouldn't let him be. At times he felt as if he were away from there. But those times took him back to the war. The fear was the same - that of an unknown act of violence which could strike at any moment. Knowing only the lucky ones made it out alive.

Gracianette dabbed his forehead with a handkerchief. He'd worn himself out lifting and shoving. Watched Caillou lean over Oboeuf and shout in his ear. He felt good, like the old days.

'What did you say?'

'I did it, I confess.'

'Say it loud, you worm, so Sergeant Gracianette over there can hear you.'

Tears washed some of the blood away and mingled with snot. Albert's words seemed to drown in the mixture. 'I did it,' he said again. 'I killed Madeline Legrand.'

Belmont looked across the table at her. Hard to take his eyes away. He was still lost in the early days of infatuation. One day, he knew, these desires would turn to boredom. That day had to be an eternity away. He couldn't remember his previous infatuations being this strong. This vibrant. He burnt with lust, wanted to eat her, right now in the restaurant, on that table.

'So what else do you like, apart from frottage in the Métro?'

'Oh, I don't know,' Belmont said, 'frottage on an auto-bus or frottage on a tram.'

'How about the elevator to the top of the Eiffel Tower?' Her foot hooked his leg then stroked it. 'Would you last until the top?'

'I'm not sure I would but I'd be willing to try.'

She laughed and lit a cigarette. Relationships like this didn't last. Were never meant to last. So she'd have fun. She couldn't even say what it was she liked about Belmont. But she did like him and she knew it would hurt in the end.

Léon had finished his beer and didn't have the money for another, now the waiter was giving him the evil eye through the steamed up café windows. Didn't want a scruff sat out front like a gargoyle scaring away the customers.

His hands shook violently as he tried to light a cigarette. Ten minutes more, he decided, then he'd quit. Next time he'd bring a knapsack with a spare pullover and gloves.

Five minutes later Belmont emerged, a woman clung to his arm. She stumbled like a drunk. Belmont lifted a hand to hail a taxi-cab. Léon was already on his bike.

They lost him on the Avenue de Tokio but he caught

them in the slow moving traffic crossing the river. He weaved between the autos as they made their way through the 7th arrondissement. Confident, Léon drew alongside the taxi-cab. Belmont was looking out the opposite window at Haussmann's grey six and seven storey buildings. She was stretched across the seats, almost on the floor, behaving like a prostitute.

Léon gave up following Belmont after he'd dropped his slut companion off on the rue Bonaparte. She'd gone up to her apartment and Belmont had climbed back into the taxi.

It had been while watching them kiss goodnight that Léon realised the enormity of the mistake he'd made. By cutting the ears off Philippe's girl he'd linked that crime with his. There were differences of course. She'd been raped, she was a woman, she'd been strangled by hand and she wasn't a destitute. But that link remained and it would give the flics a route via Philippe to him.

Philippe had been questioned over her death and subsequently released. Suspiciously quick Léon felt. Philippe claimed it had all been fine, they weren't interested in him. That worried Léon. Made him cycle to the Quai des Orfèvres to find out who he was up against. That they'd let Philippe go so quickly proved they were after him. Some dirty flic would tail Philippe until he fucked up. And that would happen, Philippe was a born fuck-up. This time his silly mistakes would cost both their heads.

Following Belmont had revealed nothing of interest other than his mistress. Which might be of interest - knowing her address and what she looked like gave Léon an edge. For now though he thought it best to avoid any battle with Belmont and instead he'd throw suspicion elsewhere. He'd do that by giving the flics something compelling to separate Philippe from the murder.

Inevitably he'd have to kill a woman the same way he'd killed the tramps. A distasteful idea but he'd have to swallow it. For now another tramp would do. This one he'd kill like the woman. Strangle him by hand.

Philippe would be at work for another two hours or more. As well as the witnesses in the club there would also be the testimony of whichever flic was following him. Léon rode the rest of the way up rue Bonaparte to the river.

Tuesday, November 24th into Wednesday 25th

Belmont sat at his desk slowly picking apart the cigarette he'd just rolled. Strands of tobacco littered his trousers. His eyes scanned the headlines of the various newspapers scattered across his desk: Horrific Murder in Montmartre, Paris Ripper at Large, Mad Man Strikes in Montmartre. The anger he felt at such sensationalist headlines was tempered by the knowledge that the killer was in custody. Albert Oboeuf had been formally charged late last night and was now on remand at La Santé prison.

In the meantime Superintendent Péraud instructed Belmont to prepare a statement for the evening editions. The killer had confessed, the so-called ripper was behind bars. People could sleep safe again tonight. A coup, Péraud had said. And that worried Belmont. Any other breakthrough and Péraud would call a press conference himself. After the golden light of glory had shone on him for long enough, he'd magnanimously give some credit to his team of officers who worked so tirelessly etc. There was no way he'd permit Belmont to jump in before taking the cream of the credit for himself.

Belmont handed the statement to Galabert who took it to the superintendent. Once alone again, Belmont sat and stared at the stove. Watched orange sparks of flame through the black metal casing. It looked how his brain felt. A confusion of thoughts leaping about within an iron cage.

The Legrand murder had been an unpleasant distraction. Putting Oboeuf away would rid the streets of one lunatic. It still left another running free. At least that one didn't rape his victims. Belmont held on to that small consolation.

Belmont sat in the Scarlet K surrounded by the sound of raucous laughter. He'd contributed a couple of bottles of champagne to the celebration. Although he felt languid, in no mood to celebrate, he recognised that a good job had been done. The city was that bit safer thanks to the efforts of these men who were dancing about the café smoking, drinking and slapping each other on the back. Even Jouvin and Galabert seemed to have put aside their differences, Belmont wasn't naïve enough to think that would be a long term truce.

The evening newspapers had led with the news of Oboeuf's arrest. One or two rolled out an old photograph of Belmont and his wife attending a gallery opening. He was dressed in a black tuxedo with bow-tie and she in a Chanel dress with a diamond necklace. He didn't like the photograph associated with the crime, it felt out of context. He also felt uneasy about the way the papers portrayed him as a hero. Uneasy because he knew that not feeling pride didn't mean he'd escape the fall.

The faint early morning light was supplemented by an arc lamp. The doctor was already at work. Belmont had been delayed by the suicide, he arrived in a stinking mood. He'd left the Scarlet K having drunk too much champagne. Been asleep less than an hour when he got called out again. Was still at La Santé when they'd called him here.

Belmont picked his way between the muddy puddles of the riverbank to the corpse. The doctor stood up, wiped his fingers on a handkerchief.

'Evening, Belmont.'

'Doc.'

'I hear your man Oboeuf managed to rip up enough sheets to fashion himself a noose.'

'At least he did it at La Santé and not in my cells. The paperwork for suicide is a bitch. And he's saved the state the cost of a trial even if he's deprived the press of a spectacle.'

'Well I don't know how this sits with all that but it rather points towards his innocence.'

'What?'

'We've got a tramp. Strangled by hand. This one's soiled himself. Ears removed, right hole attacked in the same fashion as all the others, including the girl. I can't say a lot more until I perform the autopsy but I'd estimate his death at approximately twenty to twenty-four hours ago. Late Monday night.'

Belmont looked at the body, lain close to the water. The smell of shit and the buzz of flies couldn't distract from the horrific look on the dead man's face. He was covered in dried blood. Both ears had been removed. Bits of hair, brain and skull were scattered to the side of his head. His right eyeball had been punctured by the frantic stabbing of the right ear hole. There was bruising on the man's neck but hard to see through the grime.

The body would have been easily visible from across the river, where he'd have looked like a tramp sleeping off a bottle of rough red wine. On this side he was down the slope a little out of sight. The delay in discovering his body meant it'd be harder to get witnesses and their statements would be less reliable.

It couldn't have been Oboeuf. He was under lock and key twenty-four hours ago. They'd have to check on all the other suspects from the club, the barman, the regulars. This killing, however, probably had nothing to do with them. The hand strangulation provided a strong crossover with Legrand, looked like she was killed by the same lunatic who did this. The one lunatic.

Belmont had managed to keep the other tramp killings out of the papers. Madeline Legrand's murder was different. She had family and friends who could have blabbed.

Galabert arrived looking done in. Seemed to have adopted the pasty-faced look these days. Walked over to the body. Took in the riverbank, the bridges, the silhouette of Notre

Dame downstream across the river. This killing was about 800 metres away from the first murder. Maybe the killer hadn't been able to find a suitable victim or maybe the tramps were staying in groups forcing whoever did this to go further afield to find a target.

'Well, Chef, what do we do now?'

'Same as always, Galabert, we do the basics. Find out who he was, find out who knew him. Check the Bureau of Identification to see if he had a record. Is there anything to link him to the other two killings or to Legrand? Did anyone see anything? Put a witness appeal in the press but don't give away any details. We don't want it leaking out that the Paris Ripper is still at large.'

'Paris Ripper, Chef?'

'Paris Ripper, Mad Man of Montmartre, whatever it is they're calling him to scare the citizens of this city and sell their rags. It looks like I made a mistake with Oboeuf. I know you were never sold on him.'

'I wasn't, Chef, until he confessed. I'd like to know what the barman, Bodescot, was doing last night.'

'Pick him up at the club and find out. Take Gracianette with you. And be wary. Oboeuf's still guilty as far as they know, I don't want you letting them think otherwise.'

Galabert and Gracianette arrived half an hour before the club opened. The new doorman was out on the street smoking a cigarette. Younger and tougher looking than Albert. Spent his time running a comb through his hair and eyeing Galabert as if expecting a fight. Kept them out in the cold until the owner turned up to usher them inside.

She escorted them through the club to a large messy room which she called her office. Remembering her from last time, both flics had been expecting an earful. Instead she was compliant and hospitable. Offered them both drinks. Not one word about flics putting off her customers. But then she didn't know about the recent murder. Didn't know her rapist murdering doorman was actually innocent.

Gracianette had told Galabert that he'd handle things. Galabert agreed. He wanted the barman for another round of questioning. Beyond that his mind was full of conspiracies, baker's vans and secret fascist societies.

'We're concerned Albert Oboeuf may not have acted alone,' Gracianette said.

'Sweet Jesus Christ.' She crossed herself like a virgin in a melodrama. 'Who would help do something like that?'

'That's what we'd like to know. Has anyone been missing from work or quit since your trip to Police HQ?'

'No, I have all the same staff as before, with the exception of Stefan. He's in to replace Albert. Stefan's my nephew.'

'Has anyone missed work?'

'No-one at all. Phil was ill for a couple of days but they were quiet nights and he's back in now.'

'Which days was he ill?'

'Sunday and Monday.'

'Thank you, Madame, we won't take any more of your time. However, we will need Philippe Bodescot to accompany us for some further questioning.'

'Oh, I don't know. We're opening soon and he runs the bar.'

'Forgive me, Madame, but I wasn't asking permission.'

'I was ill. Spent most of the time in bed. The rest was spent with my head over the shit hole puking.'

Belmont had chosen Caillou to assist with the interview. Galabert had been up early with the murder and was losing his spark. He'd be OK for the next round of interrogations in the morning. In fact, Belmont liked having the combination of Caillou and Galabert at his disposal. The others were good but none of them knew how to play along like Galabert or had the natural menace of Caillou.

'Anyone see you?' Belmont asked.

'My brother.'

Philippe bit his lip. Léon was good at playing along but they'd come at him cold, he wouldn't even know he was supposed to be covering. Why had he even said any of that? He hadn't been sick and plenty of people had seen him.

Sunday evening had been spent at the picture house. He'd chatted up the usherette. She'd slapped his face, and was bound to remember that.

Monday night he'd been in a drinking mood. Got into a fight with an American black on rue Fontaine. That was after another fight in a bar near the Saint-Lazare station. The guy from the bar might not want to remember. He'd looked at Philippe the wrong way. Philippe smashed his face into the wall before kicking shit out of him, left him in a crumpled heap on the lavatory floor.

The American had been in the street on rue Fontaine shouting up at an apartment window. Philippe told him to get out the way, called him a nigger, suggested he go do his shouting in the jungle. He wasn't certain what happened next but he came to in an alley with a swollen eye and bruising over his chest and back.

'How'd you get those cuts on your hands?' Belmont asked.

Philippe looked at his hands. They were scraped and cut. The ones around the knuckles were from punches. Wasn't sure about the rest.

'I got in a fight.'

'With who, your brother?'

'A drunk on the way home.'

'The way home from where?' Belmont asked.

'I get the feeling we're being lied to, Chef,' Caillou said.

'Do you, Sergeant? I do too. It's an uneasy, dirty, sort of feeling.'

'Makes me angry, Chef. Like seeing someone kicking a kitten. I haven't lied to him, why should he lie to me?'

'Ask him, Sergeant.'

'Why are you lying to us, Monsieur Bodescot?'

'I'm not lying.'

'You said you were sick in bed. Then you say you got into a scrap on the way home. One of those was a lie. Which one?'

She was leant against the wall. Pale blue skin showed off her necklace of bruises. She paid them no attention, smoked a cigarette and gazed absent-mindedly at the door.

'I was in bed but I went out to get some medicine.'

'There you are, Sergeant, he went to get some medicine.'

'I don't know, Chef. I still smell the stink of lies.'

'It wasn't a lie, was it?'

'No.'

'There you are, not a lie. Where did you buy this medicine?'

'At the pharmacy on the corner of rue Gracieuse and rue Lacépède.'

'How much did it cost?'

'Two francs.'

'Fantastic. What more proof could you want, Sergeant?'

'I'd like to speak with the pharmacist, see if they can remember Monsieur Bodescot buying any two franc medicine.'

'Quite right, Sergeant. I'll have someone check that out in the morning. No point waking the pharmacist at this hour to talk about fictitious medicinal purchases.'

Philippe wasn't listening to Belmont. Maddie was talking and she had all his attention.

'They're gonna get you now, Phil. You forgot what your brother told you, say nothing.'

'Right,' Belmont said, 'you can spend the night in the cells. Tomorrow morning we'll have another chat. That'll be after we've visited your brother and the pharmacist.'

Galabert hid in the bushes and watched the house. Over the last few days he'd spent much of his spare time watching the senator's house. Did it at the expense of sleeping, at the expense of eating. Most days he was fuelled by a jittery energy which came from cognac, caffeine, adrenaline and sleep deprivation. Now he needed to get inside and find the evidence Belmont wanted.

The study, he reckoned, looked out at the gates. He'd seen

an old man, late fifties, going grey, sat in there typing. That was almost certainly the senator. Walked with the unnaturally erect posture of an ex-soldier or a snooty homosexual shopkeeper. An hour earlier that same man had been driven away in his Rolls-Royce. Since then the downstairs lights had been extinguished, except the one in the porch and another inside, probably the hall light. Galabert had given it thirty minutes from lights out before scaling the wall. He'd have liked to have left it longer, let them fall into a deep sleep, but the senator might return. It was time to get inside and scratch that itch once and for all.

The windows were locked. It was winter, he'd expected that. Galabert rummaged through his satchel. Pulled out a thin metal ruler, thirty centimetres long. The shutters were easy, lifted his metal ruler between them and unfastened the catch. The windows were different, he had to push the ruler against the catch between the top and bottom panes. The lock had been twisted tight, there was no slack to move it all. Still Galabert pushed with as much strength as he could put into it before giving up. Then he closed the shutter and tried the next window. Same result.

The lights of a motor-car lit the driveway. Galabert crouched, ready to run. Tried to think of the best route back through the garden. Perhaps if he stayed still they wouldn't notice him and he could escape when they parked. He'd only need to get round the corner of the house to be out of sight. He peered at the road, afraid that by looking at them they would see him. The vehicle turned. A moment later it drove back up the road.

Galabert dashed past the front door. For a matter of seconds he was lit by the porch light. He stood in the shadows, back to the wall, and faced the gates and the road beyond. This time he watched the surface of the road, tried to spot the early signs of oncoming headlights. There were none. He counted to twenty, opened the shutter and had a go at the window lock.

The lock sprang back and Galabert lifted the bottom

window. It made an unbearable screeching noise. He waited for someone to come, ready to run for the gates. No-one came. There were no excuses now. If he was caught inside the house he was done for. There was a good chance they'd shoot him and claim he was a burglar. Being a senator's house they were more likely to call the police. And, as Belmont had said, Galabert would become the ex-flic in jail. He'd be lucky to see out the prison term. One way or the other, if he was caught, his wife would be burying him.

He pulled the window down and sat beneath it on the cold gravel driveway. It wasn't worth it. Whoever those people were and whatever it was they were doing, they'd slip up. They'd forget to pay off a witness. Or get caught red-handed. Or one of their lackies would cut a deal. And when that happened Galabert would be ready. For now it was time to go home and get some sleep.

Then he thought of the Arab boy. The dead body covered in bruises. His swollen face. He thought of Ferhat breaking down during their interview. He thought of Jouvin and his Black Shirt friends. Could picture them beating poor Ahmed. Could picture them marching through Paris in the same way Mussolini's thugs marched through Rome. If he turned away now he'd be handing his daughter's future to men like them.

The window didn't seem so noisy the second time. Galabert slipped into the house like a practised cat burglar. This was the drawing room. A few easy chairs, a magazine and newspapers on the coffee table, a ladies writing desk against the wall. A gramophone in the far corner. The dim half-light revealed dark red wallpaper and the portraits of self-righteous looking gentlemen.

Galabert crept along the parquet floor of the hallway. The dead eyes of a stag's head watched him from the wall. The light was on and the hall was overlooked by a gallery above the staircase. There'd be no mistaking the intruder. He prayed nobody got up for a glass of water.

The study door opened with a click. During his surveillance he'd not seen any dogs. Now he fancied a

Terrier or some other yappy creature bounding along the hall and waking up the household. He closed the door behind him and took a moment to allow his eyes to adjust to the dark.

A large wooden desk and the smell of cigars dominated the room. Galabert sat himself down at the desk and pulled at the drawers. All but one were locked and that contained a jar of ink and three glass paperweights.

Footsteps from the room above. Galabert froze with his hand on the part-closed drawer. There was a cough followed by the sound of bedsprings. Still Galabert didn't move. The room was filled by the regular beat of a carriage clock ticking out the seconds. It ticked for a full three minutes before Galabert returned to life.

The drawers didn't give to a strenuous pull. No keys in the obvious places, under the plant pot or typewriter. Galabert produced a set of lock picks from his satchel. He'd brought them knowing he'd have to use them while hoping he wouldn't need to. Picking locks was not something he found easy and, despite the greater good he was sure would come of it, it left him feeling seedy.

He inserted the rake and began applying pressure with the wrench. The best part of five minutes went by as Galabert silently swore at the lock, applied pressure to the wrench and moved the rake in and out. He had a chisel in his bag and the thought of opening the desk the easy way passed through his mind. At that point he didn't care they'd know someone had been inside, he wasn't planning a return trip. Then it opened, as easily as if he'd used the key.

The drawer revealed a pile of correspondence between the senator and a friend. He skimmed through the letters, originals from the friend and carbon copies from the senator. The friend's son had been accused of raping a village girl near his army base. The senator was going to see to it that the dishonourable discharge was changed to medical discharge. It was important as the friend had political ambitions for his son. The last letter, confirming the medical discharge, had been sent to the senator's friend the previous day.

That was the top right drawer. The bottom right was deeper and took longer to open. Inside was a bottle of calvados and a set of files. Galabert salivated at the sight of the bottle. He could use a shot of something to keep him going. Didn't wait to be asked. Popped out the cork and took a couple of swigs straight from the bottle. The pungent smell of the booze reminded him of Belmont's office and the purpose of his visit.

The files mostly related to personal and household matters. Requests to attend functions, a receipt for the purchase of a nymph statue – one Galabert had seen in the garden. There was even a brochure from Rolls-Royce Motor Cars with a picture of the senator's motor. Nothing in the drawer about that baker's van in the other garage.

The top middle drawer opened more easily. The first thing Galabert noticed was a sleek black folder with a silver ibex insignia over the top. Also in silver, written above the ibex, were the words: *Les Cagoule Noir.* He pulled it out and opened it. Found a typed sheet with a list of names. Top centre was the senator's. Lower and to the left was Superintendent Péraud's. To the right at the same level as the superintendent was a Doctor Jaccard. These three names were written in a large bold font. Below them was a list, in four even columns, containing about another hundred names. The top two names in each column were in bold and all the rest were in normal font. It looked like a war memorial with it's neat rows and the occasional duplicated surname. Brothers? Father and son, coincidence? Galabert scanned the rest of the list only stopping to rest his finger beneath Jouvin's name.

The folder contained a letter from Italy. High quality paper with a gold embossed address at the top, sent from an Italian ministry. Galabert understood the odd word. Whatever it said it was obvious the senator considered it important. If he had time he'd copy it out and get it translated.

The folder also revealed photographs of the senator dressed in his Black Shirt regalia minus the hood. One, a head and shoulders profile. Another on a white horse in a street somewhere down South. Another giving a speech and framed to look like a French Mussolini.

Galabert went back to the drawer and pulled out a khaki folder. Plain and battered. Out fell a newspaper clipping. The report of an Arab man beaten-up near the Panthéon. Galabert tipped out the contents of the folder. More clippings. Arab man attacked, Arab beaten, Arab man badly beaten. Fifteen in all. Then there was the article from L'Humanité, the one Galabert had shown to Belmont.

Galabert wanted to go running straight to Belmont. Almost did. But it was as if he could hear his chef talking in the room, 'what of it, Galabert, the man collects newspaper cuttings.' And although it was obvious the senator had played some part in these attacks there was no damning evidence. Maybe if he weren't a member of the French Senate but a street sweeper, then maybe they'd progress. Bring him in and grill him. Get a warrant and turn this place upside down. Not for the senator. His house had to be searched illicitly, the evidence insurmountable.

Then Galabert found a second list of names. Members of the North African Star Party. Every person mentioned in the press clippings was on the list, except Ahmed Djaout who had never been a party member. Each victim, including Ferhat, had a star in red ink drawn next to his name.

Again Galabert could hear Belmont, 'a morbid fascination with the crime, Sergeant. He may have been playing amateur sleuth, trying to prove a link between the attacks and the party members. Remember, Galabert, this man will come armed with the most expensive advocate money can buy.'

'But surely,' Galabert said to the typewriter, 'this must prove that Ferhat was right. That he was also targeted and beaten. His name has a red star even though he wasn't mentioned in the newspaper report, his brother was.'

In his mind he saw Belmont give him that one. He'd be allowed to investigate the case, perhaps even call it a murder inquiry. He sat in the chair behind the senator's desk and stared up at the ceiling rose and fancy lampshade. The light was off. The room was lit by the combined efforts of the porch and street lights. Belmont was right. The case would die within days. The superintendent and the senator would starve it of oxygen. The examining magistrate would dismiss it out of hand. Best result – the case left unsolved as murder by person or persons unknown. Ferhat would be shown to have played no part in the death of his brother. The rest of Galabert's career would be a walk through quick sand.

What were these bastards up to anyway? The North African Star Party had disbanded two years ago. The fight for Algerian independence had been reduced to a few radicals in Africa. It had no wide spread support. Of course, having been disbanded the party was no longer a unified whole. These Ibex could beat up the ex-members one-by-one. But why? Pure spite? It hardly seemed worthwhile. Whatever their reasons, someone else could fathom them. Galabert was taking himself off the case.

Galabert yawned, he needed sleep. He needed to kiss his daughter's forehead and hope the world she'd grow up in wouldn't be as dark as the one he saw coming. He stood up to leave, as he did he heard the click of the opening door.

Wednesday, November 25th

Belmont fought his way through the reporters gathered outside Police Headquarters. The second murder was all over the morning rags. L'Humanité had a photograph of Albert Oboeuf, innocent man driven to suicide by the brutal judiciary police. They ran a photograph of Belmont too, labelled it Decadent, Dilettante, Detective. He hadn't failed to notice it was the same photograph they'd run the day before where it had been labelled saviour.

Asides from the headlines most papers had run editorials on the killings. They all questioned Belmont's suitability in one way or another. The Left leaning press blamed him for Oboeuf's death. Said he had an innocent man's blood on his hands. The Right ignored Oboeuf and focused on Belmont's incompetence and the rise of violent crime. Their ink was spilt attacking the weak government which allowed criminals to run amok on the streets of Paris and Inspectors, like Belmont, who failed to bring them to heel.

Belmont knew he'd fallen into the middle of a political mudslinging contest. He'd guessed it was coming the day before but was helpless to stop it. The papers were grinding political axes and his head was on the chopping block. The only way out, as ever, was to find out who was committing these murders and haul them in.

So he elbowed his way through the throng of reporters. Ignored calls for an interview. Held his hat in front of his face to prevent them taking photographs. And burst into the Police HQ.

'Get those vultures off my doorstep.'

Six officers stepped outside and shoved the press back. It wasn't easy and in the end they gave up and came back inside.

Belmont was intercepted and told to report to the superintendent. No point rushing. He rolled a cigarette and told a passing officer to fetch him some coffee. Then he took a deep breath and wished this morning had never happened.

Caillou and Tabaraut ate brioche with pâté and stared idly at the photographs on the wall. The first two tramps pinned up alongside Legrand. The success of the Legrand case had been so short-lived nobody had taken her pictures down. Someone had stuck up a single image of the latest victim. Oboeuf was there too, under the section labelled suspects. He could come down.

Belmont stood at the back of the room. His ears still burnt from the meeting with Superintendent Péraud. Péraud had had a go, got all red faced and talked of ministers asking questions. The smarmy bastard was going to release his own statement to the press. Something saying Belmont still had Péraud's complete confidence. But no more fuck-ups.

'Anyone seen Galabert?'

'No, Chef.'

'I'm getting sick of his antics. When he gets back tell him to see me. He's going on a charge this time. Caillou you can join me again for the Bodescot interview. We may have to lean on him. First, Tabaraut, you take Jouvin, if you can find him, and go interview the pharmacist and Léon Bodescot. Have you read the interview notes from last night?'

'Yes, Boss. And Jouvin's about, I've seen him.'

'Don't take too long, I want to get at Bodescot soon and I want his lies exposed before we go in.'

The pharmacist stroked his moustache. Said he thought he might remember a man of that description buying some medicine for two francs. But he couldn't say when, not for certain.

They traipsed a few dirty streets to the Bodescot apartment. It was in a narrow alley sided by five storey apartment blocks. The sound of arguments emanated from more than one building. Kids played in the gutter, dirty faced and dirty clothed. A man with a thick drooping moustache took one look at Tabaraut and Jouvin, spat on the floor and said, 'fucking flics.' Tabaraut twitched, ready to lay the man out. Jouvin was up ahead reading the building numbers. Further along the road, in front of a café, some women were singing, their voices echoed along the street. Jouvin disappeared into an apartment building.

Tabaraut had hoped to find an elevator. The apartment was on the top floor. Jouvin didn't bother to look, headed straight up the stone stairs. Tabaraut followed after having searched in vain for his elevator. Five flights of stairs and two cigarettes later he joined Jouvin in banging on the Bodescot door.

No-one answered. Jouvin gave the door another hammering then stuck his ear to it.

'Nothing,' he said.

'Well, he's probably at work,' Tabaraut said.

There was another apartment on this floor. It sat at the end of the hallway near the communal latrine. Jouvin knocked and called out, 'police.' This time he was answered by a cough belonging to an old man who peered round the door at them. Jouvin held out his police identification.

'We're looking for Léon Bodescot,' Jouvin thumbed over his shoulder at the Bodescot door.

'He'll be at work, his brother may be in. Give it a knock.'

'Do you know where Léon Bodescot works?'

'Some hotel.'

'Which one.'

'No idea. I don't really like them Bodescots. Always throwing their weight around. What do you want them for anyway?'

'That's between us and them. Anyone in the building who

might know the name of the hotel?'

'The concierge.'

'And do you know where she is?'

'If she ain't in her rooms she'll be at the grocers having a drink.'

The greengrocers had a simple bar setup. Two women drank wine while a third groped an onion. The grocer hefted boxes about. They all stopped to stare at the two flics stood in the doorway.

'Anyone here work at number six?' Tabaraut said.

One of the women put her glass down, 'me. Who's asking?'

'I'm Inspector Tabaraut and this is Sergeant Jouvin. We're looking for Léon Bodescot.'

'Léon Bodescot? Don't surprise me. The man's a pig and a bully.'

'You know where he works?'

'Today he'll be at the Hotel Bordeaux. It's on the Quai de Bourbon. He works some other place too but it's the Bordeaux on Wednesdays.'

The hotel manager hovered around the two flics, keen to escort them out the lobby. Tabaraut stood his ground. Didn't like the look of the place. There were a couple of girls, obviously hookers, talking to men who looked like they were up from the sticks.

There wasn't much to see. A veneer of respectability over the slum of reality. Lower-middle class clientèle who'd make a fuss if they got a dirty glass or their breakfast was late.

Tabaraut felt like being awkward. But he acquiesced to the manager's squirming and sat in the bar. Both he and Jouvin took coffee not wine. By this time the porter, who'd been dispatched to fetch Bodescot, had returned with a dirty looking thug.

'You Léon Bodescot?'

'Who's asking?'

'I'm asking,' Tabaraut said. Then he took a sip of his

coffee and stared over the cup at Léon. The hotel manager started to fidget. 'You can go now.' Tabaraut indicated the manager and porter. The porter was out of sight in an instant. The manager loitered by the bar door.

'So are you Léon Bodescot or do I have to put you in the cells for six hours before I ask you again?'

'Yeah, I'm Léon Bodescot.'

'Where were you on Monday night?'

'At home.'

'Got any witnesses?'

'What's all this about? I haven't done anything.'

'Then answer the question. Can anyone vouch for your whereabouts?'

'The concierge saw me come home, about six. My brother got home at two. He works in a nightclub so he gets in late.'

'And he'll vouch for you from two in the morning?'

'Yeah.'

'Are you sure?'

'I heard him arrive at the same time I heard the bells ring. I said hello to him. So, yeah, he'll vouch for me but only from two.'

'We can't afford any scandal, Bodescot, this is a respectable hotel.'

Léon threw a dirty wash rag at the manager's feet. Then he picked it up again, walked past the manager and back downstairs. How the fuck had they gotten onto him? Once they'd ruled Philippe out of the investigation that should have cut the chain to him. Instead they seem to have sniffed him out. At least his alibi should hold. Nobody had noticed him slip out in the evening and nobody had seen him return just after one. They needn't know he'd not been to work, that he'd spent the day following Belmont.

He went back to the dirty plates. Everyone knew the flics had been in for him. So what? Half the staff had criminal records. And, despite what the manager claimed, this was not a respectable hotel. Even as he scrubbed a plate clean he knew that was the point. The scandal to be avoided wasn't Léon and the flics, it was the flics paying too much attention to the residents. Having the sordid sex lives of their guests splashed over the papers would see this hotel's bookings drop like the dead of Verdun.

Léon's face was white, a fixed stare at the wall beyond the basin. He scrubbed and shifted his way through the dishes. All the time his mind raced. He had to throw them off his track. Maybe kill a girl, take something of hers and plant it somewhere. Let some other sap take the heat for a while.

The press had been onto Chief Inspector Belmont. The Oboeuf arrest was a fuck up. Maybe a letter to L'Humanité mentioning Belmont's mistress. The timing was only out by a matter of hours. And if all that hit the news kiosks at the same time as another killing. Another dead girl. Maybe Belmont would head out on another false trail.

What if Léon was that false trail? They were onto him, that's for sure. One more murder and they might place him under arrest. Not that he'd be taking the coward's way out like Oboeuf. Although once they had him inside there'd be nobody doing any killings to exonerate him. He'd go to jail and that would be the end of it. Because this time they'd have the right man.

It took twenty minutes before Léon realised Philippe could do it. If they arrested him, Philippe could go out and strangle someone. Male or female, it wouldn't matter. So long as he used Léon's knife and cut off their ears. Where the hell was Philippe anyway? He hadn't come home last night.

'Nice work, Tabaraut.'

'Thank you, Jouvin. The idiot didn't even know I was playing him.'

Tabaraut and Jouvin met Belmont and Caillou in the briefing room. Belmont paced the floor, smoked a cigarette and chewed his nails. Caillou sat on one of the chairs looking much like he had at the whore house when he'd had a woman on each arm. His scar glistened under the electric light. Tabaraut let them know there was no alibi, pharmacists, inconclusive. Brother, definite.

Caillou went in first, alone. Sat opposite Philippe and lit a cigarette, blew smoke at the yellow ceiling. A sardonic grin on his otherwise expressionless face.

Philippe fidgeted in his seat. He'd spent a long night in the cells. Maddie had kept on at him until he'd passed out. Constant taunts, she took a lot pleasure in Philippe's predicament. Now this barbaric flic was glaring at him from across the desk. He looked mean, merciless. The sort who'd burn the wings off flies and drop their bodies in a spider's web.

This was the flic who'd called him a liar. Straight out said it even though he had no way to know that Philippe had been lying. And all the while he looked as if he wanted to grind Philippe's face into the dirt.

The room, which had been so cold yesterday, felt hot. Stifled him. Left him short of breath. If he could only run somewhere, anywhere and keep on running. Don't get scared, Philippe, remember you can take it. Whatever they throw at you, you can take it. All those beatings from Léon had taught him to toughen up. Before that his father had been the one to beat him. One, then the other. At least Léon had been predictable. He'd lash out after an argument or because Philippe had screwed up. Their father wasn't predictable. He lashed out because he was a mean bastard.

Belmont came in and sat alongside Caillou.

'We've been checking on you, Bodescot, just like you suggested,' Belmont said. 'Your boss confirms you weren't at work on the night in question. We believe her, why wouldn't we, after all it tallies with what you told us, that you were ill. Despite us believing her she produced her books and showed how she'd paid for a relief barman. That's settled then, you weren't at work. And yet, here's a puzzle, your brother, Léon, seems to think you were. He told us you came home from work at two A.M. Maybe he's lying but he has no reason to, does he?'

'You're headed for the guillotine, Phil. What a tragedy to die so young.' Maddie laughed then struck a match on the wall and lit a cigarette. Philippe stared straight past Belmont, directly at her.

'We've given him a chance, Chef. Let's deal with him the old fashioned way.'

'OK, Sergeant, why not.'

They got up at the same time and came round the table at him, one from each side. Maddie was gone, leaving just the two flics who yanked him from his seat. Before he even thought about struggling he'd been cuffed to the radiator.

He looked up to see what was going on. What was going on was a fist travelling straight at his eye. That was the thin one they called Chef. The mean one was stood back, baring his teeth in a terrible snarl.

Three or four kicks caught him straight in the gut. He doubled up with his cuffed arm stretched out to the radiator. The Chef took his free arm, pulled and twisted it. The mean one moved out of sight. Philippe felt a boot strike him in the back.

Pain shot through his body and he thought he might have pissed himself. The Chef twisted his arm again then did something to his fingers. Felt like each muscle, each tendon, was being torn.

The attack was nothing like his brother's beatings. Except that first punch. What they did to his hand was torture. And he knew now that he had pissed himself. They'd left him on the floor, still chained to the radiator. Maddie came back and he realised he was crying.

Philippe didn't know how long he'd been left on the floor. The door swung open and the same two flics marched back inside. A bucket of water was tipped over him. The cold caused him to jump which twisted his arm and wrist. The mean looking one, who'd kicked him in the back, undid the handcuffs. The two flics lifted him and stuck him in a chair.

'You'd pissed yourself so we had to wash you,' Belmont said.

The cold of the room clawed at him. Shivers came and seemed to overtake him. Yet Maddie wore her skirt short, a thin blouse which he knew smelt of lavender, torn stockings and she didn't shiver. But she was pale blue.

'As I said earlier, Bodescot, we talked with your brother. He didn't say a word about you being sick. In fact he said you were at work. We'd already talked with your boss who said you'd been off ill. We're stuck on that one, Bodescot. Are you going to answer us truthfully this time or are we going to have to restrain you again?' Belmont said.

Say nothing. That phrase ran threw his head like a prayer. Say nothing. Maddie echoed it from the corner of the room. 'Say nothing, Phil.' His heart seemed to beat it out, boom boom, say nothing, boom boom.

But he couldn't take the cold and he couldn't take another beating. His insides hurt. Felt as if his liver had been kicked out his throat. He couldn't fully open or close his hand. All across his face were pin pricks of pain, bruises, cuts, scrapes. Dried blood clung to his skin and his right eye kept closing on its own accord.

'Cuff the little bastard,' Belmont said.

'Yes, Chef.'

The mean one stood up. Philippe tried to back away. He fell off his chair and crawled towards the door. The flic's steps were slow and precise. He locked eyes with Philippe. Maddie laughed hysterically. 'They're going to kill you, Phil. You're going to die and I'm going to watch just like you watched me. And when you die, Phil, that's when you'll get what's coming to you. Do you hear me, Phil, that's when you'll get what's coming to you.' She laughed again, a screeching laugh which ripped at his heart and tore at his eyes.

'Please, please, I'll talk.'

Wednesday, November 25th, Night

Léon rode hard from the hotel towards Montmartre. Philippe ought to be at the club by now. Had the police got to him? Had Philippe confirmed his alibi? There was no reason for him not to but Philippe was an idiot.

The lower slopes of Montmartre took the panic away. As the sweat of exertion replaced the sweat of panic Léon realised he was in the clear. The flics had been focusing on his alibi from two. They weren't interested in what he'd done between six in the evening and two in the morning and that was when the murder took place. They'd gotten the timings wrong. The tramp was already cold by two.

The hills didn't bother him so much anymore. He still sweated and grunted but he could handle it. The days spent tracking Belmont around the city had firmed up his leg muscles. And now, as he freewheeled past a jazz club towards the boulevard de Clichy, he fancied a beer.

Two sips in. There was a bit of a crowd. A group of English were shouting in one corner. A drug dealer peddled his dope to street girls who queued at his table. And life felt good. The last tramp had been killed to get Philippe off the hook. And the flics were after him, not Philippe. So it had worked. Until now that focus had spooked him. But his alibi was water tight and so was Philippe's because they had been in the apartment together.

A first sip of the second demi. Why weren't they after Philippe? The whole point of his alibi was that he'd be at work. At two A.M. he wasn't at work. He was at home. So why were they asking after him and not Philippe?

The rest of the beer was left undrunk. Léon ran alongside his bike before jumping on and heading straight up the rue Lepic. There were Montmartre tourists all over the road. Groups of five or six, doing circuits of the night spots. Stepping into the road like dumb lemmings. If he'd had any saliva left in his mouth he'd have spat at them.

The guy on the club door was a greasy weasel. Eyed himself in a bit of polished metal and combed his hair.

'You ain't a member,' Stefan said.

For a moment Léon was ready to strike. It was his default argument, a punch in the face his opening gambit. He'd always been like that, it kept him ready, alert. And after a while people learnt to drop the shit and steer clear. Until he moved to Paris. He was anonymous here. Too many people. No-one knew who he was. Everybody gave him shit.

'I'm Philippe's brother, come to see him.'

'Philippe who?'

'Bodescot, the barman.'

'Oh, him. He ain't in.'

'What do you mean, he ain't in?'

'He left with the flics last night.'

'What?'

'They turned up and took him off, last night.'

Léon pushed past into the club. Stefan on his tail. The place was medium full. It had the nightclub stink of sweat, booze and tobacco smoke. There was a short guy behind the bar. Looked about sixty. A line of girls on the stage kicked their legs and flashed their cunts. Someone put their hand on Léon's shoulder. Léon swung round and laid Stefan out cold. A couple of punters stood up and backed away from the scene. The music continued, the dancing kept up. Stefan let out a groan and began to move. Léon leant over to take a look at him. Stefan rubbed his chin where a bruise was forming. Then Léon was spread-eagled on top of him. A moment of stunned silence before Léon rolled over and off of Stefan. Saw the old barman holding a cosh and preparing to use it again.

'Hold up,' Léon said.

'You can get out,' the old man said.

Léon crawled towards the door. His head felt heavy. The floor stuck to his hands. As he tried to get to his feet someone kicked him in the thigh. He went down. Stefan stood over him. Was about to kick out again, the barman prevented him.

Rue Lepic swayed in time to the pulsations of his head. Léon steadied himself against a wall. Thoughts of vengeance flooded his mind. Stomping on that barman's face, cutting off that doorman's ears. He pushed the growing rage back down.

The incline carried him down to the boulevard without his having to pedal. It was as he was about to pull out, as he looked to his right and saw the red sails of the Moulin Rouge, that it struck him. The flics had never been interested in him. Philippe wasn't his alibi, he was Philippe's. And he'd blown it.

There had been a rainstorm. Run off from the Black Mountains transformed the timid unassumingly lazy river into a bullish drunk rampaging through the countryside. It called to Léon, it called to Philippe. Or rather, they had no place else to go so they always made for the river.

They darted through the shadowy medieval streets, out through the place Gambetta to the bridge. Léon, confident he was out of sight, sparked up a cigarette. Philippe gasped, if Léon got caught smoking he'd be in for a beating.

'You shouldn't.'

'It don't matter, Philippe. I realised it last night. When was the last time you went a whole day without a beating?'

'Um.'

'Except when he was at war, never. So I get a beating for smoking. If not I get a beating for being untidy or cheeky or ungrateful. And as for you, the bastard beats you each morning for wetting the bed and each evening just for breathing.'

Léon looked at his brother. An eleven year-old sprat with big innocent eyes and short dark hair. Beneath that shirt his chest and back were covered in welts from their father's belt.

He didn't remember it always being that way. When he stretched his memory back, long before the war, he couldn't remember any beatings. But they came and didn't stop. He remembered the joy they'd felt when papa was called away to fight. They'd prayed he'd never return, not articulating a desire that he be killed just that he wouldn't return. 1915 was a glorious year, 'til the old man got shot in the leg and they sent him home.

If he really thought about it, the violence began when Léon was eight and his brother two. That would have been late 1910. Philippe had learnt to toddle about. Léon could remember him reaching for his papa. At first the old bastard would get up and walk away. Later he started pushing him over. Philippe would sit there and cry. Léon would run to him. Called his papa names. Around that same time papa started flying into rages, sometimes disappearing for days.

Nine years had passed. The war was over. Léon was nearly eighteen. Philippe eleven. They stood on the bridge and Léon smoked his cigarette. It was true, what he'd said to Philippe, but it wasn't the whole truth. Léon had been fighting back for a few years. He didn't feel the hurt of the blows anymore he only felt anger. Now he'd had enough. He'd been holding back out of a perverse filial respect. Not no more. If he touched him again Léon would let fly.

Philippe went down to the river. Threw stones in the water. Léon watched him. Philippe was tough enough, for his age. Tough but stupid. Twice Léon had had to fish him out of that river. And how many times had he stood between Philippe and papa because Philippe hadn't seen it coming? The daft kid was still toddling up to the old man for cuddles.

It was as the light began to fade. A dark velvet sky. Cicadas shouting from every bush. Léon lay on his back near the river watching stars arrive in the sky. Philippe scampered about on the rocks, threw more stones. They often stayed out late like this because the river bank, and not that hovel back in town, was their home.

There'd been a mumbled shout from the bridge. The alcoholic wreck came stumbling towards them. Called them names as he came. And Philippe froze. Léon tossed his fag into the river and sat up. Their father's left arm clouted Philippe and the kid went down.

'That's enough of that.' Léon marched towards them.

His father's glazed eyes tried to focus on Léon. Then he came at him with a bull's bellow of a roar. Léon put up his fists. His papa hit him in the stomach so hard Léon thought he'd die. He crumpled to the ground and squealed for breath. None came. He wheezed and rolled around in the dirt, a doubled up heap. Eventually some air fought its way through and Léon tried to remember where he was.

Philippe's cries rose above the insect calls and the splash of the river against rocks. Léon looked over to see his brother cowering beneath blows from their papa's belt.

This time Léon ran at him. Screamed as he went and their father spun around to greet his son with a fist in the face. Léon went scattering down, face first into the river. Took a mouth and nose full of water. Blood flowed where his father's wedding ring had cut his cheek. Dazed he watched the pink water head off towards the sea. His eyes stung, his nose burnt and his hands shook.

Papa was still whipping Philippe. He ought to have stopped by now. The kid's shirt was torn and red gashes coloured his back. Philippe's sobs had become groans and above them came his father's shouts, 'dirty bastard son of a whore.'

Léon came quiet this time, from behind, rock in hand. The first swing stopped the old man raining his blows down on Philippe, his arms hung limp by his side. The second swing made a loud crack and caused blood to run down the back of his father's head. The old man collapsed in a heap. Léon didn't check for a pulse or breath. He grabbed his father's legs and dragged him down to the river. Then he rolled him over and kicked him in. The body drifted for a few metres, hit some rocks and went under.

Later, the police said their old man had been drinking most of the day. Must have fallen off the bridge and hit his head. They found his body a hundred metres downstream. The night of the killing Philippe had lain in his cot bed and cried. Léon stroked his brother's hair and sang old Catalan songs until those tears turned to snores. And that night, for the first time in his life, Philippe didn't wet the bed.

Thursday, November 26th

Belmont never read the newspapers at home and seldom read them anywhere else. These last few days, however, he'd taken to glancing at the headlines, to see how badly he'd been mauled. It was pride, he knew, but he felt angered by the press. Why should he, a man who was actively pursuing the killer, be getting all this aggravation? What good did they think it achieved? Of course, he knew the answer to that. Could hear the paper boys shouting, 'killer on the prowl!' and could guess how many extra copies they were shifting.

To add to Belmont's general annoyance, two or three reporters had taken up residence on his front door step. They pestered him from the moment he set foot outside.

Again he had to elbow his way through the press pack outside HQ. And his reward was a summons to the superintendent's office. Three chief inspectors from the Paris Police and a superintendent from the Sûreté were already there. Until he'd seen them Belmont had expected another dressing down. They'd become a regular ritual since the murders hit the news kiosks. Péraud had released his own statement which the papers lapped up, the whole thing being nothing more than a poorly disguised kick in the balls for Belmont. And now the obnoxious oaf was constantly asking for situation updates. Each one followed by the line: 'it's not good enough, Belmont.'

'Ah, Belmont, glad you've deigned to join us,' Péraud said. 'You already know the others so let's not fuss.'

Belmont ignored his boss and finished shaking the hands

of his colleagues. Then he took a seat, pulled out his tobacco and papers and rolled himself a cigarette.

'We are under attack, gentlemen,' Péraud said. 'Those very people who turned to France for her beneficent protection have chosen to rape her. Yes, gentlemen, I say our beloved France is being raped. And by whom?'

The superintendent looked around the room at each man in turn. He was pulling off a second rate impersonation of Mussolini or Chiappe. Belmont wanted to slap his face.

'Charlot Chaplin?'

'This is neither the time nor the place for your flippancy, Belmont.'

'It's not the place for political hyperbole either. What's all this actually about and what do you want us to do about it?'

'If you looked at anything other than yourself in the morning papers, Belmont, you'd have noticed that a bomb was detonated in the centre of Paris last night.'

'I saw that, a few stone chips blown off Jeanne d'Arc's plinth. She's been through worse.'

'In the days of the anarchists this city was engulfed in terror,' Péraud said. 'And these Arab radicals must be stamped out in the same way those anarchists scum were. There shall be no mercy. We will go after them, after their families, after their friends, after their associates, after anyone who so much as says "good day" to them. And we will keep going, if necessary, until every brown face has been driven from this city.'

Belmont shifted uncomfortably in his seat. The temptation to simply walk out had to be resisted. If he left now the super would suspend him and bring one of his odious 'yes' men in to replace him. Inspector Cruchon most likely.

When Galabert got back, after putting him on a charge, Belmont decided he'd support his investigation. If Péraud really was involved in some conspiracy then this might be an opportunity to bring him down. At the moment he didn't know exactly how. Péraud would be protected, the whole thing could blow up in their faces. It was a risk, he knew that, but Péraud's 'brown faces' spiel made the risk worth taking.

'I want every available officer focused on this. It's going to be run as a joint operation with the Sûreté. We'll start by going after the newspaper that printed this,' he held up a copy of L'Humanité. 'Find out who wrote this letter. Get the original to The Bureau for examination.'

Péraud dropped the paper to his desk, Belmont snatched it up. It was folded to show an open letter from a group calling itself The Arabian Brotherhood. The letter drew attention to a series of attacks on Arabs in Paris including the recent death. The Brotherhood wanted justice for these beatings. If not they would step up their bombing campaign. No doubt Péraud intended to use the letter as an excuse to make life difficult for the publishers of L'Humanité. Being a communist press they were always in the fascist firing line.

'Are we going to investigate these attacks?' Belmont asked.

'Certainly not! I forbid it!' Péraud said. 'We will not give in to blackmail."

'We wouldn't be giving in to anything. We'd be investigating a possible link between a series of crimes.'

'All of those so-called beatings have already been investigated. The last was a straight forward hit and run. No further time or resources shall be spent on any of this rubbish. All available manpower will be directed at these mad dogs and their dynamite. '

'It was trinitrotoluene rather than dynamite,' the Sûreté man said.

She virtually pounced on Belmont as he entered his office.

'Where is he?'

She looked terrible. Dark bags under red eyes which fixated somewhere a kilometre behind Belmont's head. Her make-up was smudged and her hair, although stylish, was bedraggled as if she'd spent her time waiting in his office worrying it. It took Belmont a moment to recognise her as

Mme. Galabert.

'I was going to ask that of you. Sergeant Galabert hasn't been into work since Tuesday. I sent him home to get some rest and expected him back Wednesday morning.'

The woman slumped into the chair Belmont offered her and started bawling, 'something terrible has happened to him.'

Belmont produced his cognac, poured them both a glass. He sat on his desk to be closer to her.

'Did he say anything to you about where he might be?' Belmont asked

'No. Except he said he was working on two cases.'

Her tears had stopped but she still sobbed intermittently.

'I'll get my men to look out for him. We'll call the hospitals just in case.'

'The hospitals, you don't think?'

'I don't think anything, Mme Galabert. We call the hospitals to make sure he's not there.'

Belmont smiled and she half-smiled back. She looked sweet if overly jumpy. Belmont would have helped her for her own sake. But in this case it didn't matter how sweet the wife was, Belmont knew Galabert could be in trouble. Last time he'd gone A.W.O.L. he'd nearly been caught breaking into the senator's garage. A senator with connections to an underground organisation which, according to Galabert, had beaten a man to death.

The briefing room felt empty without Galabert. No, it felt empty knowing Galabert was missing. Galabert had skipped these briefings before and Belmont had hardly noticed. He only missed him during interviews or when he needed someone to discuss the case with. He missed the spark of Galabert's intelligence. The rest of his men were solid, experienced and reliable but they weren't smart. Jouvin was smart but he wasn't solid or reliable which meant Belmont would never talk things over with him. Besides, Belmont didn't consider Jouvin to be one of his men. Jouvin lived in the superintendent's pocket.

'Riquet is working on the Post Office case,' Belmont said. 'They've got their man but loose ends and all that. Galabert, however, is missing.'

Belmont kept an eye on Jouvin, who'd simply glanced across the row of seats as if to confirm Galabert's absence.

'Do we know where?' Caillou asked.

'No, Caillou. I've had his wife in asking after him. His description has been circulated to all the police stations in Paris and to the Sûreté. Caillou, you and I will go search for the lad after this briefing. In the meantime, the murders…'

Belmont let them know that Bodescot had been released an hour earlier. His new alibi had checked out. They couldn't find the black American from the rue Fontaine or the victim of Bodescot's attack in the café. However, the toilet attendant had seen Philippe and recalled him beating up some queer in the bogs. Beaten up a queer and didn't leave a tip, that's what the man had said. Belmont's bad mood had kept Bodescot in the cells longer than necessary. That and the fact he hadn't asked for legal counsel. Two officers had been assigned to follow him, each working a twelve hour shift. They'd been instructed to call in whenever Bodescot changed location so HQ would always know his whereabouts. Belmont ordered Jouvin to join them, reducing their shift rotation to eight hours a man. Jouvin should take over at nine that night, when Bodescot would be starting at the club.

Tabaraut and Gracianette were given the task of reviewing all the old interview records. Check for anything which might have been missed, possible links between the testimonies. Anything. They groaned, they had a right to. But Belmont knew they wouldn't shirk it.

An officer knocked on the briefing room door with a message for Belmont, 'your wife called, Chef, can you fetch an apple tart on your way home.'

Belmont and Caillou stood before the iron gates of the

mansion house. Belmont rolled himself a cigarette. Caillou spat on the pavement. They both knew the next ten minutes could land them in it deep.

'You ready?'

'Yes, Chef, let's get this over with.'

They remained in front of the gates. What kept them? Belmont cast an eye along the wall and tried to imagine Galabert climbing over. He remembered Galabert saying he'd found a way in via some creepers at the side of the house.

'Come with me.'

Belmont led Caillou along the wall until they reached the Virginia creeper. There were footprints in the mud at the bottom of the wall. Belmont already knew Galabert had been over the wall, these footprints signified nothing but they helped firm up Belmont's resolve.

'Is this what you expected, Chef?'

'Yes, Caillou, it's how Galabert got over the wall. I suppose I wanted to see the spot for myself.'

They arrived back at the gates and Belmont took in the opposing garages on each side of the driveway. One had contained a Rolls-Royce and the other a baker's van. If they got the opportunity they'd have to take a look inside.

That was why Belmont was hesitant. He realised it now. They had no search warrant. Not even bothered to try and get one. There was no chance anyone would sign one off. Not without a great deal of persuading. He didn't try persuading as he doubted Galabert would be anywhere near the place. Even if harm had come to him in this house they wouldn't be stupid enough to leave him there.

'Time to blow your whistle and lead us over the top, Chef.'

'It feels like that.'

Belmont pushed at the gates which refused to budge. Caillou tried his luck. It worked. Then again Caillou's luck carried a few extra kilos of bulk. The left-hand gate sprang open, almost screamed as it went. If there was anybody in they'd certainly have heard them coming.

The two men crunched across the drive to the porch. Belmont tugged at the bell-pull. He looked back at the two garages. Both were closed, although Galabert had told him how he'd opened them up. The gate had bounced back halfway to closing again. Footsteps echoed from beyond the door.

'Yes?'

The man was in his late middle-age with grey hair and a wrinkled face. He wore a liveried butler's uniform of blue and red. Shoes shone like an old soldier's. Nice crisp crease in the trousers.

'Chief Inspector Belmont, Judiciary Police,' Belmont lifted his hat then placed it back on his head, 'and this is Sergeant Caillou.'

'How may I help you gentlemen?'

'We are making enquiries about a missing officer, one Sergeant Galabert. This was his last known whereabouts.'

'There is no Sergeant Galabert here, Inspector.'

'Would you mind if we came in and took a look around?'

'I don't think-'

Belmont stepped into the doorway, 'it'll only take a minute.'

The butler asked to see Belmont's identification. Belmont showed it. With that the butler stepped to one side and let them enter. It meant the master was out. If he weren't the butler would have asked them to wait and gone to fetch him. Then they'd have been sent away with a flea in their ear. It also meant the butler didn't know he was meant to be covering anything up.

Belmont and Caillou took a few steps along the hall, 'can you tell me what this room is?' Belmont pointed at a closed door.

'It's the withdrawing room, sir.'

Belmont opened the door and took a look inside. 'Caillou, you take a look along the hall, I'm going to give this room a quick once over.' Belmont knew Caillou would catch on -

ask the butler questions to give Belmont a chance to search unobserved.

Stuffed chairs faced each other over a coffee table on which old newspapers and magazines were gathering dust. A lady's writing desk was setup under an electric light on the far wall. Belmont took a look but saw nothing of interest; blotting paper, ink pot and pen. There was a gramophone in the corner with a cleared space in front. Belmont could imagine the senator's young nephews and nieces dancing in that corner. Over the walls were some, mostly atrocious, paintings of aristocratic men. Belmont tried to look at them dispassionately, but failed. He hated that formal style, the stiff lifelessness of the poses.

Gossamer curtains fluttered, drew Belmont's attention away from the portraits. There were four sets of sashed windows, he examined them carefully. It was when he reached the window nearest the front door that he thought he saw something. He produced a magnifying glass and examined the window seat. Thought he could make out the traces of a footprint beneath a cushion. With one hand he swept the cushions off the wooden seat. There was something. Enough to convince him that Galabert had entered the house through this window. Belmont lifted the catch. It was loose, easy to pry open from outside with a piece of metal forced between the wooden frames.

Belmont scanned the room again. It would have been late, it would have been dark. Galabert had just broken into the house, what did he do next? Belmont walked slowly towards the door and opened it. He saw Caillou pointing up at a stag's head on the wall, the butler humouring him by looking up at the dead beast. Galabert would have been drawn that way. The other direction led away from the heart of the house towards the kitchens.

'What's behind that door?' Belmont asked.

'That's the master's study, sir, but I can't allow you in there.'

Belmont opened the door and stepped in anyway.

'Sir, I must insist that you leave that room at once.'

There was a large wooden desk, bookshelves, wood panelled walls. The room was about a quarter the size of the drawing room. It smelt of smoke, whiskey, camphor wood. Belmont felt the butler's hand on his shoulder.

'I must ask that you leave now, sir. I cannot permit anyone to enter that room in my master's absence. If you would care to call back this evening…'

It crossed Belmont's mind to carry on but he thought better of it. Galabert wouldn't be there, there was nowhere to hide him. Belmont stepped back and closed the door, 'sorry, I don't mean to be intrusive. I wouldn't like someone poking around in my study when I'm not home.'

The butler looked appeased although he manoeuvred himself between Belmont and the study door. He didn't say a word but he seemed to be willing them out the house.

'Thank you, you've been most helpful,' Belmont said. 'Before we go, would you mind if we took a quick peep in those garages?'

He hadn't gone in, didn't think he'd be welcome and didn't want to stir things up. He'd wanted to be certain Philippe went to work and he'd arrived thirty minutes earlier. Léon had been sat in a café, keeping an eye on the club's entrance, for over an hour. Once he'd seen Philippe enter he'd ordered another beer. Took his time over it to make sure Philippe didn't decide to leave again. He didn't, so Léon settled up with the woman at the cash register. He had work to do. Some low down dirty work.

As he crossed the river, Léon hopped off his bike and stuck it against the embankment wall. Over on his left, Notre Dame filled the night sky like a beacon. A repulsive beacon which shouted its ugliness across the city. Still, even at night, there were tourists detouring to point and coo at this monstrosity. Not two streets away was Sainte-Chapelle. That was a nice church, beautiful. The only thing wrong with Sainte-Chapelle was the location, halfway up the collective arse of Police HQ and the City Courts.

Léon needed to plan his next move. There was nothing pleasant about the situation. For a start, he didn't feel like killing. And it would have to be a girl. He'd done a tramp like the woman from Philippe's club. Now he had to do a woman, like the tramps. Maybe with something extra to confuse things. That idea, though, was losing its appeal. It'd complicate matters and when things got complicated the flics would revert to type and haul Philippe back in again.

A violent surge of electricity ran through his body and he retched over the railings into the river. Nothing but a frothy spit came out. All triggered by the remembrance of how Philippe had looked when he'd gotten home. Those rotten bastards had given him a right going over. Léon fed him bread and watered down wine until he got some strength back. Has to be said though, the kid held out and Léon felt proud of him for that. Some people would have cracked and confessed, people like that stupid old duffer Albert Oboeuf. According to Philippe, Belmont had been the lead man. Léon wished he'd been there to protect his brother. Hammered his fist down on the railing and gritted his teeth. Then an idea came to him.

Léon was whistling as he crossed the river to the Left Bank. A tune from back home, *Muntanyes del Canigó*, and his mind was looking out across the Pyrenees. The music carried him. Carried him along the boulevard and then up the rue Bonaparte. It played over as he took his bicycle and placed it in a side alley. And it played again as he pressed the buzzer.

He didn't know exactly what he'd say when she answered the door. Or if he'd say anything. There wasn't much need for talking. The only problem would come if other people saw him and could then identify him. But there weren't too many people about. Still, he pulled his cap down to cover a bit more of his face and pressed the buzzer again.

After five minutes he gave up. Belmont's slut was probably on her back under some stranger. She'd keep. Time was pressing on and Léon had to make certain that this crime was committed and discovered while Philippe was still at work. He couldn't afford for the flics to mess up the timings again. Which meant he'd need to be finished by midnight at the latest and it was already pushing ten-thirty.

He peddled slowly back alongside the river. There was no music in his head now. He felt like a hawk circling in the sky and the women of the city nothing but rabbits. There weren't that many of them. It was cold, people were using taxis or maybe not even going out. Whenever he did spot a woman she'd be on the arm of a man or in a group. He turned right, away from the river, into the Latin Quarter. The streets were narrow, he liked the medieval feel. Halos from café lights glowed across the pavements. Students sang songs fuelled by cheap wine. Political arguments raged under electric light bulbs. Léon watched and heard it all. Every footstep caught his ear. The flat thud of a man's boot, the faster clipping of a woman's heel, their separation.

Léon picked up the pace and turned quickly into the next street. He saw a figure up ahead. She lingered a moment before disappearing into the rue des Trois-Portes. A short narrow street. Léon went full pelt to turn into the street just after her. She didn't look round to see him as he entered the street. Instead she walked up to a door in one of the buildings.

There was nowhere to leave his bike but he didn't care. Dumped it against a wall and ran. She turned her head to see him running towards her. Her key already in the lock. There was no chance he'd reach her before she got inside. He called out, 'excuse me, mademoiselle'.

Friday, November 27th, Morning

The motor dropped Belmont off at the end of the street. It was too narrow and too busy to try and drive up there. He rubbed his eyes, 2 A.M, He wasn't likely to get any sleep now.

Since leaving the senator's house the problem of Galabert had been gnawing at him. The empty garages exacerbated his concern. They'd been exactly as Galabert had described, minus the vehicles. The roller was easy to explain, the senator was out and it was his motor. The van was different. What was it doing there in the first place? And if you had a body you wanted to dispose of, what better vehicle?

Up the street he saw a uniformed flic put a hand against the wall and throw up. Not a young recruit either, he looked to be pushing forty. Belmont took out his tobacco and rolled a cigarette as he walked towards the crowd of uniforms. They snapped to attention when they saw him approach. Tabaraut stepped out of the front door.

'Morning, Boss.'

'Morning, Tabaraut, what have we got here?'

'It's ugly, Boss. Can't remember the last time a corpse made me vomit but this one did. Half the men here have been sick. It's like something out of a horror story.'

Belmont cast an eye around the men. They all looked pretty peaky. And despite the fact there were five of them nobody was talking, no jokes being bandied about. Tabaraut too, who must have seen a thousand dead bodies both here and in the trenches, looked as if he could do with a lie down. Belmont tossed his cigarette into the gutter and rolled another.

'So what have we got in there, Tabaraut?'

'A girl, probably early twenties. Throat's been cut and they've ripped her open. It's not pretty, Boss, not pretty at all. Even Doc had to leave the room after he stepped in there the first time. Took a minute to brace himself before he went back in. He's gone for a drink round the corner, says he'll wait for you there. The café was shut but one of the boys persuaded the proprietor to open up for us. The specialists are on their way but I made sure you were called first, because of the ears.'

Tabaraut looked down at his shoes.

'Don't tell me that, Tabaraut, don't tell me she's had her ears cut off.'

Tabaraut didn't say anything, just kept looking at his shoes like he'd be happy to do that now for the rest of the day.

Upstairs, outside the apartment, a uniformed officer stood with his eyes fixed on the wall across the hall. From as far as the stairs Belmont could see the man was shaking. He stood to attention when he noticed Belmont but he didn't make eye contact or attempt to speak. The door to the apartment was open. Belmont entered and made straight for the bedroom, it was the only door off the living room. He wanted to get this part over with.

He couldn't say which image hit him first. The wallpaper, pale blue with lilies and songbirds, upon which, above the bed, written in blood, was his own name. Each letter half-a-metre high. All capitals. Or was it the grotesque toothless smile which had been carved into her neck? Or the dressing table with powders and creams, her rouge and perfumes, hair brushes and mirror, all decorated with the innards which had been pulled from her stomach and thrown across the room? His eyes kept returning to his name, not from vanity but to avoid looking at the girl whose name he didn't know.

All that was taken in from the threshold of the bedroom. And like each of his colleagues before him, Belmont felt like puking. Like Tabaraut, he'd seen hundreds of dead bodies.

Yet even the men who'd been blown to bits by artillery didn't disturb him like this. Maybe because in war you hardened yourself. Maybe because this was a girl. Maybe because so many years had passed since those days he'd forgotten some of what it had felt like. But he knew she was like them. She wasn't the victim of an everyday Parisian murderer but the victim of war. The victim of a crime so grotesque it could almost be mechanical and so hideous that it begged for another name to define it.

Belmont didn't puke. He didn't look to the heavens and ask why. He didn't bow his head and cross himself. He took off is hat, entered the room, stood at the foot of her bed and silently wept.

The tears didn't last long. They were wiped away with his handkerchief as he moved closer towards the dead body. Belmont was conscious that the room hadn't been photographed or thoroughly examined yet. So he stepped carefully as he went. The entrails had been thrown from the bed across to the right, so he approached from the left.

The smell of blood was strong. She hadn't been dead long enough to add the scent of putrefaction.

This was a two roomed apartment. The bedroom and the living room. No kitchen no bathroom. Communal toilet in the hallway. Belmont's eyes had flitted around the living room. A small coffee table with a magazine beside an ashtray. A chair tipped over and a smashed glass in the middle of the floor. A flower in a pot on the window sill. A cardigan, folded and placed on the settee. A plate with some biscuits resting on the arm of the settee. Near the bedroom door a picture had been knocked from the wall. And there were blood stains. The first drops could be seen at the entrance to the apartment. More in the centre of the room near the broken glass. And Belmont had noticed blood stained fingerprints on the bedroom door frame. On the bedroom floor was a bloody hand print which had been smudged as if she'd been dragged face down by the feet.

From what he could make out, Belmont guessed she'd been carried to the bedroom and dragged from the doorway.

He couldn't say what had caused the blood outside the bedroom. A quick glance at the woman showed cuts on her head and a blood encrusted nose. Perhaps her assailant had punched her in the face causing a nose bleed. Maybe he'd struck her on the head. Whatever it was it hadn't been enough to subdue her.

Belmont spotted her ears by the wall on the left. It was a guess, but looking at some of the flecks of blood along the wall, he'd say they'd been cut off and thrown over there. Thrown as opposed to placed or dropped. These weren't the sort of details that'd help catch or convict the killer but they helped Belmont understand what had happened.

He looked at her and saw how it must have played out. She, lain on the bed, and he sat up at the other end probably resting on her legs. No, her legs were spread. There were deep cuts along her thighs. Veins and arteries hung from the open wounds. Belmont noticed that she still wore her pants. Her blouse, vest and bra had been cut open. The garments still attached to her. He looked around and saw a blood soaked skirt lying near the door. That must have been pulled off and the killer then cast it behind him, perhaps throwing it over his shoulder. The stomach had been sliced open, left to right or right to left. The doc would be able to tell and from that he'd know if the killer was left or right handed. After slicing the belly open he'd forced his hands in and pulled out what he could. That mess had been thrown over to his right, landing on the dressing table. And, at some point, he'd cut her throat. Almost decapitated her.

And this madman, this Paris Ripper who now seemed to be living up to his press bestowed epithet, had scrawled the word 'Belmont' on the wall above the bed. Belmont took a look at the dark stains on the bed and saw footprints. So he'd stood over her body as he wrote, used her blood as an inkwell. The lunatic must have been covered in it. The records guys from the bureau of investigations would tell him what size shoes the killer wore. If they were lucky they'd find a match for the fingerprints too.

There was no point hanging round in there any longer. Before he left he forced himself to take a good look at her face. She was young, early twenties. It was hard to tell from the body how she might have looked. Her eyes and nose seemed large, her physique, slight. Her hair, shoulder length, black. It was matted now with blood and difficult to say what style she'd have worn it in. Her eyes looked back at him and Belmont lent forward to close them.

He sat on her sofa and looked again at the floor. There were no bloody footprints leading to the apartment door. Yet the killers shoes would have been soaked in blood. Belmont didn't feel like puzzling this out. He needed some sleep before he could think. All he could think of was the attack that had taken place in the next room, the scene of the most brutal murder he'd ever been involved with. What's more it was probably the same killer who'd already seen off four or five other souls. He pulled himself up and left the apartment. Time for a drink and a quick chat with the doc. Then a trip to the baths to scrub himself clean. And after all that he still had a murdering bastard to catch.

The café was small, the proprietor half asleep by the cash register. One table was taken up by three uniformed flics. They were fortifying themselves before returning to their respective beats. The doc was on his own, looking over his notes and pouring more water into his Pernod. Belmont sat down in the chair opposite, called out to the proprietor and ordered a cognac.

'What do you make of it, Doc?'

Doc's eyes looked weary, beyond tired. He had the look of a man who was contemplating retirement for the first time and deciding it might be a good idea.

'I'd say she died this evening. Despite the tremendous loss of blood the body held some warmth. Then again, you'd know that already. Tabaraut told me the front door was left wide open as was the door to her apartment. Makes me think the killer wanted her to be discovered. Also, from what I can gather, he hadn't forced his way in. Maybe he knew this victim or else he knocked on the door and tricked his way in.'

'I haven't really spoken to Tabaraut yet. He'll be here shortly though. All I know is what I saw in that room.'

'Your name scrawled on the wall, Belmont, that gave me a chill.'

'Me too, Doc. I guess my name's been in the press a lot recently. Do you think it's the same killer who did the tramps?'

'The tramps, the girl from the nightclub, quite probably. The ears had been cut off and he'd stabbed her in the right ear hole. I couldn't tell if she'd been strangled because of the gash in her neck. Once I do a proper examination I'll know. There were spots of blood in her eyes which indicates strangulation. I'd say all the killings are related in some way. They have the same motif.'

'If it's the same person then were in trouble. We had the tramps, killed a week or so apart. Then the girl where he'd moved on to rape. Then another tramp and now this. They don't normally go back. Every time the violence escalates it stays on that level or rises again. Although the last tramp killing was much like the earlier ones. As for my name, I guess he thinks that's funny. Disturbing though, that in the midst of his killing frenzy he took the time to taunt me.'

The bell above the door jangled and Tabaraut walked in.

'Boss, Doc. The technicians are there now with their photographers and what not.'

As Tabaraut ordered himself a whisky the doc got up, shook their hands and left. He now had the unpleasant task of autopsying her.

'I've never seen anything like that, Boss,' Tabaraut said. 'Not in the force, not in the army.'

'There were photographs in the living room,' Belmont said. 'She had a simple country-girl complexion with large, alert, eyes. Not a head turner, the kind of girl you'd want your son to bring home when he's ready to settle down. She was standing with her parents. They looked like they had money, not rolling in it but well-to-do. I guess she was studying at the Sorbonne, must have been approaching her final year. One moment.'

Belmont got up and walked over to the proprietor.

'You got a telephone?'

The man went behind the bar and came back with a telephone which he set on the counter. Belmont picked up the receiver.

'Yes…Police HQ. Good, yes, Chief Inspector Belmont. We've been tracking a man, Philippe Bodescot. That's right. Locations tonight from nine. Home, OK, Then the club…what time? Eight-thirty. And what time did he leave? Two-thirty, that's fifteen minutes ago. OK, thank you.'

Belmont sat back down, 'we can rule Bodescot out. He was at the club until recently. Besides, we've had a man on his tail since his release. Every minute accounted for.'

'Where does that leave us, Boss?'

'Back at square one, Tabaraut, that's where it leaves us.'

Friday, November 27th

Belmont could hardly bring himself to look at the men sat in front of him. It was the usual crew along with Riquet who'd been recalled to the squad. After leaving the crime scene café, Belmont had gone straight to HQ. Made a few notes on his impressions of the scene and gave orders that the others be summoned to the office by seven. After that he put his head down on his desk and stole a couple of hours of fitful sleep.

Tabaraut hadn't been home either. Since being called out to the murder he'd kept on working. At some point Belmont would give him a few hours to grab some sleep. For now Tabaraut was the one who knew the most about the case so he'd have to stick around.

Then there was Galabert. Still missing with no leads as to his whereabouts. Belmont had a half-formed idea he might follow Galabert's tracks. Go out and interview the Arab lad's brother. Take it from there. If nothing came of it, well, he knew how Galabert had gotten into that house.

Belmont reached into a buff coloured folder and fished out a series of photographs. Took some tacks and pinned them up in front of the men. He'd waited for them all to arrive, wanted the shock he'd felt on seeing the body to resonate with them. It worked. The chat stopped as each man found his gaze drawn to the mutilated girl Belmont was pinning to the wall.

'Jesus Christ,' Gracianette said, 'glad I wasn't called out for that one.'

'No,' Tabaraut said, 'it was me and I wouldn't have wished

it on any of you.'

'Her name was Lorène Lochet, aged twenty, studying at the Sorbonne,' Belmont said, turning to face the men. 'The attack was frenzied. Her body sliced up. Entrails torn out and thrown around the room. In the middle of all that, the killer managed to find time to write my name on the wall. And do the usual with her ears. We think this is the same perpetrator. Only he seems to have upped the scale of craziness. And this means we don't have much time to catch him, we can't afford a series of corpses like this on our hands.' Belmont pinned up a final picture, a copy of the one he'd found in her apartment. A sweet, bright, young woman with her doting parents. Something to show she hadn't always been a piece of butchered meat.

'Was she, I mean had he?' Gracianette said.

'She's with the doc now. There wasn't a lot he could ascertain at the scene as she'd been cut up too badly. He thinks she was strangled but will confirm that later. She had her pants on, so maybe not, Gracianette. Again, the doc will confirm that after his examination. In the meantime we have nothing. Jouvin, I called in about Bodescot, they said he'd been at the club. That correct?'

'Yes, Chef. I took over surveillance at nine, I had him under observation until relieved at four. He arrived at work about eight-thirty in the evening and left at two-thirty in the morning. He went straight home. And, by the way, I'd only had two hours sleep when they called me in for this.'

'Alright, Jouvin, I appreciate your efforts, you and Tabaraut can get some kip after this briefing. Tabaraut, Gracianette, you went over the evidence again yesterday. Find anything?'

'There isn't anything, Boss,' Tabaraut said. 'Most of the regional police came back with nothing, as did International Criminal Police Commission.'

'That's right, Chef,' Gracianette said. 'We re-read every statement and every note in the file. There just isn't anything to go on.'

'The English couple from the Notre Dame killing, did they say anything that didn't appear relevant at the time but is now? Did we miss anything at all?'

'They didn't say enough for us to miss anything,' Tabaraut said. 'Average height white male. Then there was the vagrant Galabert interviewed. He confirmed the height but described the complexion as swarthy. That's about it.'

Belmont rolled and lit a cigarette. 'Bodescot has dark skin, anyone notice?'

'Yes, Chef,' Caillou said. 'I noticed when we interviewed him. He's from Carcassonne. He's got that permanent tan all southerners have.'

'But he was under observation all day, Chef,' Jouvin said. 'And there's no way he could have left that club while I was watching him. Whenever anyone entered the place the door would open wide enough to show the bar. At least three times I saw him stood there. If you want I can go back and interview his boss, find out if he went missing any time during the night.'

'Do that, Jouvin. They don't know we've got him under observation so just enquire. Her address is on record, go wake her up. Don't bother coming back, telephone to let someone here know what she said. Then go get some sleep. I want you to take up your post again tonight, I'm not ready to let Bodescot out of our sights just yet.'

'There were good quality fingerprints at the murder scene,' Tabaraut said, 'the records boys told me.'

'That's fantastic. We've got Bodescot's prints from his recent visit. Check if they're a match. This could be our first break. Go do that now, please, and come straight back down with the results.'

Belmont watched Tabaraut leave. The records office was at the top of the building. It shouldn't take too long for them to match prints from the scene against the Bodescot set. Hopefully the young woman hadn't had too many visitors back to her apartment, leaving their prints all over the place.

'Then there was your psychiatrist's report,' Gracianette

said. 'You'd made notes about the suspect.' Gracianette flipped open his own notepad and read, 'a foreigner or a non-Parisian Frenchman, works at the bottom of a hierarchy.'

'Non-Parisian ropes Bodescot back in. But he's not at the bottom of a hierarchy. There's just him and that boss of his. Mind you, from what I remember of her, an overbearing boss like that might have the same effect. I don't like the way everything's pointing at Bodescot when he has a tight alibi. And, alibi or not, he did stand up to some strenuous questioning from Caillou and myself.'

'His boss will confirm if he was there or not, Chef,' Gracianette said. 'And Tabaraut will be back with the fingerprint details any minute.'

It was only five minutes more before Tabaraut returned.

'They had six sets of prints in total. One set was everywhere and they think they're hers. That'll be confirmed later as they've got a man waiting to take her prints the moment Doc's finished with her. There was another set which was in the blood, implies they were made after the killing, we're assuming they belonged to the killer. However, none of the six sets of prints matched Philippe Bodescot's. They're now making a comparison of his prints against all the other prints they have on record. Give them a few hours, if there's a match, they should have found it.'

Belmont crossed Bodescot's name off the list of suspects, sighed then swore three times in quick succession. He decided he'd pay another visit to Dr. Frappier later that day. After that Doc's autopsy report should be ready.

'Gracianette, you go and join the local flics. Take charge of the interviews, the girl's neighbours, relatives, the usual. Let me know if anything comes up that matches anything we've already got. I'm tying this murder in with the others but keep an open mind. There are enough differences for me not to be certain.'

'In which case, Chef,' Caillou said, 'You've crossed Bodescot's name out, but he only has an alibi for this killing.'

'Thanks, Caillou.'

Belmont wrote Bodescot's name back on the wall and as he did it he imagined the killer writing 'Belmont' on the wall above his victim. Was it a taunt or a call for help even?

Belmont had to get away from the Quai. It was still early, not yet nine. The number of reporters crowding the street outside had reduced but there were still enough to get up Belmont's nose. He strode off towards the Métro. Two reporters followed him until Belmont made it clear what would happen if they didn't back off. They took the hint and he journeyed alone the rest of the way.

He recognised the café from Galabert's description. A line of five men stood at the counter drinking coffee. Belmont regarded them through the window. Then he looked up and down the street. Not too busy. A slight drizzle encouraged people not to linger. The clothing of the passers-by was close enough to French to fit in, different enough to be noticeable. One or two of the men wore Fez hats. A woman walked past wearing a veil over her mouth like a character from the Arabian Nights.

According to Galabert's report, a van had been parked across the road. The elder brother, Ferhat Djaout, had been dragged from the café and beaten up in the street. Belmont looked at the café door, tried to imagine the shouts as Djaout struggled to free himself. And who was waiting for him in the road? They couldn't have all gone in to get him. And they would have needed backup. Two or three men wouldn't be enough to risk it. They could easily have been overwhelmed by a couple of passing good Samaritans. There had to be enough men involved to feel confident about snatching Ferhat from the café and dealing with any passers-by. And to deal with anyone like the brother, Ahmed, who came running from the café to his brother's defence.

The autopsy had been carried out by a Doctor Jaccard on the other side of the city. A doctor Belmont didn't come across often. Jaccard had described the wounds as being consistent with someone being struck by a motor vehicle. Belmont would have felt better about that had Doc done the autopsy. Maybe he could arrange an exhumation and another examination.

Belmont walked up the street towards the Djaout apartment. Three elderly men sat on the steps of the apartment building. They smoked and talked with each other and anybody passing. Belmont drew curious glances. He knew they were now talking about him but couldn't understand what they were saying. He smiled, said 'good morning' and climbed up the steps.

The door to the building was open so he let himself in. The men gave up watching him and went back to their conversation. How long now before Superintendent Péraud dispatched a squad to drag those old chaps off the steps for interrogation? And what was Belmont doing here? He'd wanted to get away from HQ, give himself some space to think after the murder of Lorène Lochet. There was nothing he could do about that for now except wait. By coming here he hoped he'd get some clue as to where Galabert might be. Even then he knew it was unlikely. Retracing Galabert's footsteps really meant breaking into the senator's house and hoping for a bit of luck.

He stopped on the stairs and rested his back against the wall. Sank to his feet and sat on the cold stone step. He knew that Galabert had to be in serious danger. If he'd been discovered in that house and they hadn't simply called the police then they'd either already killed him or intended to kill him. And that baker's van wasn't in the garage. He'd get a man to watch the place. The moment the van came back Belmont would be over there, officially or unofficially, to give it a going over.

The smell of coffee drifted down the stairwell and brought him back to himself. Belmont climbed the last flight of stairs and knocked on Ferhat's door. A woman answered. After he'd explained he was there for Ferhat, she disappeared back inside the apartment and a man of about thirty-five appeared in her place.

'What happened to the other one?' Ferhat asked as he led Belmont into their apartment. Belmont was led into a drawing room which, from the look of the cot bed in the corner, also doubled as a bedroom. The woman must have retreated into the main bedroom. Belmont thought he could hear a small child's laughter.

Some photographs had been lined up on the sideboard. A recent one had black crepe draped over it. It showed a young lad. Must be Ahmed, the one they killed. The others looked older, a father and maybe a grandfather. There was also a picture of a baby.

Ferhat himself looked bad. His nose bent out of shape. Scabs on his face. His ear partly mangled. Walked with a limp and obviously found moving difficult.

'Have you discovered anything?' Ferhat asked.

'What do you know about the bomb on Wednesday night, the one under the statue?'

Ferhat looked shocked then glanced over at the photograph of his brother. It was enough for Belmont to know he'd struck gold.

'Nothing at all.'

Any other case, any other suspect, and they'd have finished this conversation down at the Quai. But Belmont was too weary. He didn't want Péraud patting him on the back. Didn't want this man's family being brought in. Didn't want to add to their loss. What he did want was to find Galabert.

'Did you think a bomb would go unnoticed? And that letter in the papers, Djaout, you might as well have signed it.'

Ferhat hung his head and buried his face in his hands. There was no fight in him. Belmont would have to stop him confessing. If he confessed, Belmont would be duty bound to arrest him.

'Look, I'm not here about the bomb. There was no harm done. Just make sure it was the last because if there's another explosion I'll be back with a team of men and you, sir, will never see your wife and child again. Do you understand that?'

Ferhat looked at Belmont, hope returning to his face as he realised he wasn't going to be arrested.

'The officer who was here before, Sergeant Galabert, has gone missing,' Belmont held up his hand, 'don't worry, I don't suspect you.' And in that instant he realised he should have suspected him. However, the man's face was an open book and it was clear he'd been shocked to hear Galabert was missing and afraid he'd be blamed. If only everyone were this easy to read. 'I want to know what you two talked about.'

'I just told him about the attack. I was dragged from the café, my brother came to help. I can't say what happened next, I was confused by the beating, unsure what was going on. The attackers fled leaving Ahmed dying on the road.'

'You previously mentioned a van. Could you describe it for me?'

'It was a white van. There was a picture like a bit of wheat and also a loaf. There was writing on the side but I couldn't focus to read it.'

'What kind of a loaf? A traditional stick or a rounded country loaf?'

'It was a baguette and the wheat was sprouting from it. The bread underlined the writing.'

'Good. And were there any other vehicles?'

'I think so but I don't know for sure. I was beaten up and my brother-'

'Since then you must have talked about it. Did anyone else see anything?'

'No. It was late. The café nearly empty. People here go to bed early to be up for morning prayers and work. I have spoken to friends and nobody saw a thing. It is possible someone in the apartments above the shops saw but nobody has told me.'

Belmont stood up and put his hat back on. 'Thank you, M. Djaout. And remember, no more bombs.'

Belmont nodded to the men on the steps then walked back towards the Métro. He stopped to use a telephone. Got a man sent over to the senator's house to watch out for the van. Then he ordered two men to go house to house around the Arab quarter, in case anyone had seen anything that night.

There wouldn't be any news on the murder yet. Belmont rode the Métro aimlessly for thirty minutes then decided to call on her. Stood in the rain on rue Bonaparte feeling like a naughty schoolboy. Responsibilities were mounting and yet here he was calling on his lover.

They walked beneath her umbrella, hand in hand, to the Deux Magots. Took a seat near the window. It was nearing lunch so they ordered something light to eat. The conversation had been scant, Belmont answering with a yes, no or a nod of the head. He'd felt happy to be with her but his mind was drawn to a darker place.

'So, Monsieur Chief Inspector, are you going to tell me what's on your mind or shall I ditch you and go shopping?'

Belmont managed a smile which quickly faded.

'One of my officers is missing. Galabert. I told you about him.'

'Oh Christ!' Her mocking expression replaced in an instant with one of concern. She leant forward and took hold of Belmont's hand. 'What happened?'

'I don't know. He was working a case on his own. I knew it was dangerous and warned him off it. But I knew he'd keep on and I was curious to see what he'd find. Now he's disappeared and I don't know where to start looking for him.'

'Do you know where he might have gone?'

'I've a good idea that he broke into the house of a powerful and influential man. Proving that will be difficult. If he's not turned up by this time tomorrow I'm going to call in some favours and get a warrant to search that place. It's a move that could cost me my job. I'd do it now only I'm not sure what it would prove and I'll have to fight to get anything progressed. There'll be internal sabotage.'

'Internal? You mean other flics?'

Belmont didn't answer, just gave her that same empty smile once more.

'There's more,' he said. 'Another murder. This time a female student and she was killed in her own apartment. The things he did to her. It was hideous. I've got a lunatic killer out there and next to nothing to go on. I keep going over it all in my head. There has to be something I've missed. This is where I need Galabert. He's only worked for me on this one case and already I've come to depend on him. Guess that's why he got promoted so rapidly.'

'At least the press seem to be losing interest in you. With a bit of luck another government scandal will break and you won't be in the papers at all. They're about due another scandal too, it's been all of two weeks since the last one.'

'The heat will be right back on me when they find out about this girl.'

Belmont finished his drink and paid up. They held hands and, as they stepped out onto the boulevard Saint-Germain, Belmont pulled her close and they kissed. He didn't want to let her go. A motor-car was parked straight outside. The rear door opened. A magnesium flash lit up the rain sending a thousand rainbows towards the café. The engine roared and the motor-car was gone.

Belmont sat in his office with Caillou. Doc had sent over his findings. The girl had been strangled. Impossible to say if it was by hand or rope. Not sexually violated. The knife used was the same simple design used in the previous killings. The ears had been removed in the same way too. The damage to the skull through the right ear hole was similar, deep wounds with extensive fracturing to the skull. He'd cut the belly left to right. From the angle of the wound it would appear he'd been sitting at the end of the bed facing her. That probably meant he was right handed, the fact the entrails had been thrown to the right pointed to right handedness too. The mutilations, thankfully, had been carried out post-mortem. She was already dead when he went to work with the blade.

The doc signed off his report with two words: find him.

The bureau had also prepared a summary of their findings. The blood near the apartment door was hers. The blood in the middle of the living room was hers. Belmont scanned the report, all the blood was hers. They detailed where the killer had stood. Estimated his height and shoe size from the footprints, both average. There were some clear photographs of the bloodied footprints. No special markings, a few nics here and there. They wouldn't find him from that but once they had him they could compare the prints with his shoes. Might help secure a conviction. Belmont scanned the rest of the report.

'Anything, Chef?' Caillou asked.

'I'd say he followed her into the building. Maybe invited, maybe he simply caught the door before it closed. Tailed her up to the apartment at which point he jumped her. First off he punched her in the face, bloodying her nose, then bashed her head into the wall near the door. She broke away and moved into the middle of the room. Then he pushed her or grabbed and threw her. Either way she went tumbling over a chair, breaking a glass on the way down. Maybe she cut herself on that glass or maybe the blood was from her nosebleed. He picked her up and carried her to the bedroom. She grabbed the door frame with her right hand, there were a set of prints at the right height for her to have been carried over his shoulder. Once in the bedroom he dropped her and dragged her to the bed. I don't know why, I guess she wriggled off his shoulder. Once he got her on the bed he strangled her. Then he cut off her ears and stabbed her in the ear hole.

'Until now, with the exception of them being in her apartment, things are much as they were for the other killings. At this point things change. He has a go at cutting off her head. Found it too difficult so he gutted her and threw the entrails across the room. Those last two events could have happened the other way around but I think it was that way, throat then guts. After that he cut up other parts of her body, slit the insides of her thighs open and put lots of little slices across her arms. Finally, he picked up her silk scarf, daubed it in the blood and wrote my name on the wall.'

'Sounds like a man I'd like to interview,' Caillou said then cracked his knuckles.

'So would I. But what comes next is less clear. I suspect he wore an overcoat which he'd removed at the beginning of the attack. He put this back on to cover his blood-stained clothes. Put his shoes in the coat pockets and walked home barefooted.'

'Barefooted, the ground was icy last night, he would have been freezing.'

'Which makes me think he may not have had that far to walk. Still, we can make some enquiries, did anyone see a man without shoes between ten at night and one in the morning.'

There was a knock at the door. A junior officer entered. 'You may want to see these, Chef, afternoon editions. Just hitting the news kiosks.' He dropped a pile of newspapers on Belmont's desk then retreated.

Belmont glanced down at the headlines: Ripper strikes again, woman attacked in own home, city at the mercy of blood-thirsty killer. There were photographs of the apartment building and the police stood out front. They'd printed details of the woman's life alongside an interview with a fellow student. Belmont's heart sank. They hadn't been able to get in touch with the girl's parents yet and here she was being named in the press.

Caillou leant over and picked up a paper. Both men sat and read in silence.

'Makes you feel sick, all this,' Caillou said. 'We see it on the briefing room wall, the city map with one more red pin, the photographs, the suspects' names, but you read it here and you realise she could have been anyone. Any girl could have been targeted. Or man come to that. Anyone who happens to be on their own at night.'

Caillou shook his head and carried on reading. For Belmont the papers meant being summoned by the superintendent once more.

Actually Belmont didn't give a rat's arse if the superintendent called him in again. He could pull him off the case if he wanted. It was no matter. If someone else could do better, let them. Only Belmont knew there wouldn't be any doing better. It would just be a starting over and a losing of valuable time.

Jouvin arrived at the Brasserie Lipp feeling crap with sore eyes and a dry mouth. He'd had two hours sleep before Péraud had called him up and told him to get over to the brasserie.

The superintendent had finished a late lunch. A frothy glass of beer was sat to one side of his plate. The afternoon edition of Figaro on the other. Jouvin said hello and took a seat without waiting to be asked.

'You seen this, Jouvin?'

'Not seen any papers this afternoon, sir, I'm on night work.'

The superintendent picked at his teeth and ignored the implication of Jouvin's answer.

'Well, take a look.' He turned the paper around for Jouvin to read. 'What do you think? Time to give Belmont the push? Make a big show of removing him so everybody knows he's failed and that I'm taking control? I ask as you seem to have a nose for these things.'

Jouvin ordered a lemonade. He'd have gone for wine but that always woke him up and he wanted to get some more sleep after this meeting.

'If you make a big fuss about replacing Belmont the focus will be on you not his replacement. I don't like the man, he doesn't put France first and that makes him a traitor in my book. However, when it comes to tracking down a killer, Belmont must be the best we've got. That means the case will be stuck and without a quick conviction it'll be you the press pillory and someone higher up the food chain will have to decide if they want to let you go.

'Besides, we don't need this case anymore. And now the killer's branched out from vagabonds and whores, he needs taking off the streets. Leave it to Belmont and if he does fail,' Jouvin shrugged, 'the press will call for his head. The politicians will echo the press. If you cave into their pressure you won't be held responsible for any of his replacement's failures.'

'Well put, I'll leave it for now. Give him enough rope and all that. And you're right, we don't need this case anymore. Our other plan worked far better than expected.'

'Certainly did, sir. I thought we were going to have to up the ante to get a reaction. That one dying probably did the trick. I couldn't believe it when they set off that bomb. Felt like I'd broken the bank at Monte Carlo. Those idiots couldn't have played it better.'

'Very true, Jouvin. However, there is something I need you to take care of. Can you drive?'

Péraud told his driver to catch the Métro back to HQ and wait there for him. Jouvin took the keys and climbed in behind the wheel. The super sat up front for a change.

'There's a delicate matter you need to take care of, Jouvin. You play this right and I'll see to it that you're promoted. That's at work and within Ibex. First, I need you to re-swear your Ibex oath of loyalty, just to remind yourself of the part about absolute secrecy.'

Jouvin's mind raced. A promotion was something he'd dreamed off. To be recognised in both work and Ibex was something special. He didn't need to think twice about re-swearing his oath. Those words were the code by which he lived his life. And he'd rather pull out his tongue than betray Ibex.

Saturday, November 28th

The night was well into the morning when Belmont arrived home. His wife was in bed, her coat draped over a wicker chair in the drawing room and a half-finished glass of martini sat on the table. There were no other coats, no second glass, so he assumed she was alone and crawled into bed beside her.

She didn't wake, just swung an arm over her husband's shoulder and snuggled into his back. Belmont lay on his side with his eyes open, fixed on his wife's dressing table. Perfumes, powders, brushes and creams. A velvet stool. Three mirrors reflected back the shadows of the darkened bedroom. A necklace lay there too, dangling over the edge. It all looked so normal. And it filled Belmont with absolute terror.

At some point he must have passed out. Woke himself with a loud snore. Came to with a start. Mme. Belmont had rolled over to her own side of the bed. A street light shone through a crack in the shutters. The distant sounds of motor-cars could be heard. One or two tearing up the Grand Boulevards. At one point a taxi-cab dropped someone off outside. Belmont could hear them talk but not what they were saying. Then he was a sleep again.

'I've brought you some coffee.'

Mme. Belmont put the cup down on Belmont's bedside table. She opened the shutters. They didn't normally do that. The shutters were left shut morning and night. But then Mme. Belmont wasn't normally up before her husband and she didn't normally make coffee, the maid did that. But this was Saturday and the maid was late.

He thanked her as the memory of his dream slipped away. There had been a chase and some sand. Just that fragment remained and he was no longer sure about the sand. He swung his legs out the bed and sat up to drink the coffee. Took a swig then stood up and pulled on his dressing gown. Took a bleary-eyed look out the window, a low fog had settled across the city. He heard the maid arrive and his wife greet her. She pretended to tell her off for being late, then flopped down on the sofa to read the newspaper. The maid brought Mme. Belmont a daily newspaper and, on Saturdays, a magazine.

Belmont was pulling on his slippers when he heard her calling his name. Probably reading about that murder. The morning press would have sensationalised it to the point of absurdity. He walked slowly through to the living room. His wife was sat with the newspaper in her hand. 'This is terrible, what shall we do?' She held up the paper so Belmont could see. He took it from her and collapsed into an easy chair.

'Bastards.' He couldn't think, felt as if his brain had rusted to a standstill. The paper had a photograph of the kiss outside the Deux Magots. The headline was simple: Chief Inspector Belmont and *not* his wife. The first paragraph summed it up: yesterday afternoon, while the rest of Paris was reeling from the horrific murder of young Lorène Lochet, Chief Inspector Belmont, head of the murder investigation team, was living it up with his mistress in a Left Bank Bistro.

'It's no good,' said Mme. Belmont, 'I'm sorry, dear, but you'll have to move out. For forms sake. For a short while. You go to work and when you get back I'll have a suitcase packed and ready for you. I'm sorry. Give it a week, maybe two, and I'll take you back. OK?' She kissed him on the forehead and almost skipped out the room. Belmont scrunched up the newspaper and threw it at the wall.

The atmosphere at the Quai des Orfèvres was electric. The

murder investigation had people buzzing about. The fact they'd all seen the photograph of Belmont added to the charge. And, as the atmospheric pressure built, so came the impending storm. Belmont was summoned to see the superintendent.

'Any reason why I shouldn't suspend you, Belmont?'

'What for, sir?'

'For this.' He jumped up, snatched the newspaper from his desk and flung it at Belmont. Belmont let the paper hit him and fall to the ground.

'As you know, sir, I'm investigating a series of brutal murders. They are taking most of my time and energy. Having said that, I still need to eat so I stopped for lunch with a friend. And who I eat with is really nobody's business but mine. It certainly has no place in the news and the implication that I'm neglecting my duty is spurious.'

'It makes us look bad, Belmont. Can't you see that? The citizens of Paris have a right to trust us and you're spitting in their eye.'

'I'm sorry, sir. If you can provide me with a list of all the citizens of Paris who haven't had an affair I'll apologise to them personally.'

'There you are once more, flippant! This is a serious matter.'

'No, sir, this is a trivial matter. The murder of Lorène Lochet, however, is a serious matter and I'm treating it seriously.'

'I hear you had some men going door-to-door in the Arab quarter. Asking questions about the hit and run.'

'Correct.'

'Correct!' Péraud's shouts had reached the point of becoming screams. His face turned a dark red and it looked as if he was about to burst a blood vessel or two. 'Didn't I, in this very office, forbid you from investigating the matter?'

'I think it's linked to the bomb, sir. That's why I sent them out.'

Belmont took out his tobacco pouch and started rolling a

cigarette.

'You may not smoke, Belmont.'

Belmont finished rolling his cigarette then tucked it in his breast pocket. Put the tobacco away and said, 'anything else, sir?'

'Get out of my office, Belmont. And watch yourself. I may not be able to defend your position for very much longer.'

An hour passed as Belmont read the report from the house-to-house in the Arab Quarter. One of those bastard officers was a snitch for Péraud. Belmont made a note of their names.

As for the report itself: nobody had seen anything useful. Some people had heard shouting. One person had noticed a white van parked in the road. They couldn't describe it in any further detail. Belmont stopped reading and allowed the files to slip from his hands back to the desk.

He let the silence grow heavy. There was work going on along the corridor but his office door shut most of that out. The windows were closed. They let out into a courtyard. Some days there was an incessant shouting out there. Today it was quiet. The only sound to be heard was the occasional crackle of burning wood from the stove.

Tonight he'd check into a hotel. It annoyed him but he didn't blame his wife for it. She was already the subject of enough gossip. This way she'd get some sympathy and support. He considered sleeping over at rue Bonaparte. Dismissed the idea. The press would catch on and then she'd be hounded too. The telephone rang.

Belmont dropped the receiver back in the cradle, picked it up again and called for a driver to meet him out front. The colour drained from his face. For a moment he could hear the pulse beating in his temples, the blood rushing through his ears. He grabbed his hat and coat and dashed out the office.

A police motor-car drove him at breakneck speed through

the city. Belmont watched it all in a trance. Until it stopped. And there he was. Sergeant Galabert. Dead like a dog in the street. What would Galabert have been doing in this anonymous Parisian suburb?

The flic who'd called Belmont was stood at the side of the road, said it was a hit and run. The vehicle must have carried him along the road for a few metres before he fell off. Hit his head on the curb. Belmont scanned the road. There were no tyre marks. No sign of a vehicle coming to an abrupt halt.

'Doctor Jaccard is on his way, Chef.'

Belmont said no. Insisted he call Jaccard back, tell him not to come, then send for Doc. If anyone else touched the body, Belmont said, he'd personally cuff them to a lamppost and leave them there to rot.

Belmont knelt down beside his dead colleague. Put his hand on Galabert's cold forehead.

'When was he found?'

'Thirty-five minutes ago. I found his police identification and called you straight away, Chef. Besides, I recognised him from the photograph and description we've got up at the station house.'

'Who discovered the body?'

'That woman.' The flic pointed at a woman who was talking to another flic.

'What'd she say?'

'She was on her way back from posting a letter. Saw the body and called us.'

The woman was middle-aged. Nice clothes, respectable looking.

'Where do you live, Madame?'

'Over there.' She pointed up the road at a house. 'Number seven.'

'And you found the body on your way back from posting a letter?'

'That's right. It gave me quite a turn. You don't expect-'

'What else had you been doing?'

'Nothing else, I just popped out to post a letter to my

sister in Nantes.'

'Where did you post it?'

'Round the corner at the end of the road.'

'How long was it from the time you passed here, on your way to the post box, until you returned?

'Not long. Five, maybe ten minutes.'

'Did you hear or see anything at all?'

'I did see a white baker's van earlier but it was driving up the road in the opposite direction.'

'Thank you, Madame. The officer here will need to take a full statement. You've been very helpful.'

Belmont smiled and bowed before he left. Her opinion of him transformed from impertinent oaf to charming fellow.

'You.' Belmont pointed at the original flic. 'You been here the whole time?'

'Yes, Chef.'

A doctor arrived, Doctor Jaccard. Pulled up in a swish new Citroën. Climbed out and sauntered over smoking a cigar. 'Afternoon.'

'You are not required,' Belmont said, 'I've got another doctor coming.'

'I couldn't give a fig who you have coming, Chief Inspector, I've been called out and this is my district.'

'You take one more step towards this body and I'll have you arrested.'

'What for?'

'For long enough.'

The doctor eyed Belmont and realised he'd lose any confrontation. He snorted and tossed his head back like a horse.

'You'll be hearing more about this, Chief Inspector. I shall be filing an official complaint about your outrageous behaviour.'

He still didn't leave until Belmont took out his cuffs and stepped towards him.

Five awkward minutes passed as the flic and Belmont waited in silence. Then the doctor arrived.

'Doc.'

'Belmont.'

'He's cold, Doc. This was supposed to have happened less than sixty minutes ago. How can he be cold?'

The doc knelt down and felt Galabert's cheek. Unfastened Galabert's shirt and examined his chest then looked at his head.

'He's cold because he's been dead for over twenty-four hours. He's already lost the rigour mortis. I'd say he's been kept in cold storage from the time he died until very recently. Look at these markings.' He lifted one of Galabert's hands. 'You can see his wrists have been bound. Soon as The Bureau have done their work I'll take him back for a full autopsy.'

'Fuck The Bureau, Doc. You.' Belmont nodded at the flic. 'Help me carry him to my motor-car.'

The doctor objected, saw Belmont meant business and decided to give him a hand. Belmont's driver watched them approach and decided he'd help out too. They laid Galabert's body on the back seat of the motor-car.

Saturday, November 28th, Late

The men sat and stared blankly at Belmont. They'd been summoned at short notice. Tabaraut and Jouvin in from home. Gracianette had recently returned from interviewing Lochet's neighbours. Belmont reflected their stares, not certain what to say. Wary too because Jouvin was there. He had to be there, Belmont had decided. For a long while he'd considered excluding him but that would be one step away from accusing and Belmont wasn't ready to point any fingers. Not yet.

'Galabert's been found dead.'

There was an audible gasp. Belmont let his gaze rest on Jouvin. This time he didn't look innocently along the seats, he glanced down at his shoes then up at the wall behind Belmont. Belmont resisted the urge to leap at him. He stuffed his hands into his jacket pockets where they formed tight fists. Teeth clenched and beginning to grind. He'd planned on giving a speech. Meant to say a few words about the funeral. Instead he simply said, 'I've got to go now and tell his wife.' With that he picked up his hat and left the briefing room.

Caillou caught up with him in the hall. 'I'll drive you, Chef.'

Belmont looked at his sergeant. The two had been through hell together. Belmont had briefed Caillou under fire in the trenches. Ordered him to form raiding parties, told him to prepare the men for assault after assault over the top. Crawled over no-man's-land with him. Belmont had been promoted, reaching captain as superior officers dropped dead around them. All the way through Caillou had been his sergeant. They'd been de-mobbed three months apart. Caillou joined the police first, serving years in a local force. When Belmont made it to inspector at the Judiciary he'd had Caillou transferred over. There wasn't a man alive he trusted more than this one. Still he didn't want him coming to Galabert's apartment. Didn't want to put checks on his feelings of anger and sorrow.

'Thanks, Caillou, no. I want you here to keep an eye on things. Especially on Jouvin. Let me know if he slips off to the superintendent.'

'Will do, Chef.'

Belmont didn't have to explain. Caillou knew the deal with Jouvin.

Belmont was certain Galabert had been killed because of his investigation into the hit and run. That meant there were men, sitting behind desks in the Quai, who had played a part in a colleague's death. Who could he count on? The dressing down over the house to house showed that Péraud had snitches all over the place. Asides from Caillou, there was Gracianette, he'd walked the beat with Caillou for years and he'd proved himself on many occasions. Tabaraut was solid, Belmont had saved his life in '17. Once established in the police Tabaraut had requested a transfer to serve under Belmont. Was always covering his back. Riquet was different. He was a flic with no particular loyalty to anyone. He'd never go behind Belmont's back. Nor would he disobey a direct order from Péraud. Chances were he'd tell Belmont about it first. No special loyalty. He just wasn't the type to shit where he ate. Jouvin, however, was the superintendent's man. A spy in their midst. Most days he was a good flic. Most days you'd pick Jouvin to cover your back. Some days, though, you wouldn't want Jouvin standing behind you.

Belmont nearly went for a reporter who'd door-stepped him on the way out. Shoved him aside and marched off. Caught a taxi-cab, told the driver he'd pay double if he put his foot down. Belmont kept a watch out the rear window as he gave the driver directions. Sent him on a weaving route through the city in the opposite direction to Galabert's place. Got dropped off at a tram stop and caught a tram back into the city and out again to the Galabert apartment.

Belmont stood outside the apartment. He gave the door a rap. Mme. Galabert looked pale. Her hair was neater than last time they'd met but she hadn't done anything to it. It simply fell lank down the sides of her face. She wore no make-up and she'd been crying. The kid, she said, was with the grandparents. She just wasn't able to look after her with the worry. In the time it took to escort Belmont to the living room she'd rattled off what felt like a thousand questions. Half of them she'd answered herself. Belmont's head span.

'Please sit down, Mme. Galabert.'

'I can't. I can't keep still. I feel I should be doing something. Last night I walked the streets until four in the morning searching for him. I can't tell you how many people sleep on the streets of Paris. And they weren't too friendly. Please, Chief Inspector, find him for me, bring him back home.'

'I have found him, Mme Galabert. But I'm afraid your husband is dead.'

She didn't say or do anything for a full thirty seconds. Then she let out a scream like a wild banshee. Stood there, stock still, mouth wide open, screaming. Belmont wanted to cover his ears, wanted to run. It was like something from a fairy tale, a demon spirit returning to the netherworld. Just as he thought he couldn't stand it any longer she fell, silent, to her knees and began pulling at her hair. First he thought he should go for a doctor, get her a sedative. Instead he dropped to his knees and took her in his arms, let her bury her snotty face in his shoulder.

They stayed like that for a long time. She was quiet, her chest heaved and fell with silent sobs. It wasn't too long before Belmont joined her. His tears felt like the most honest thing he'd done that day. He couldn't say he was crying for Galabert, just as he couldn't say his tears in her apartment had been for Lorène Lochet. All he knew was a great sadness had descended and the tears helped him to shake it off. Twice in two days he'd wept. Twice in two days and twice in ten years.

Eventually he stopped. And eventually she stopped too. She sat back on the floor, away from Belmont, and looked at him through red rimmed eyes and said, 'I want to see him.'

'You can't just yet. He's with the doctor. He's got to finish the autopsy.'

He knew it was wrong. That she should have identified the body first and he should never have mentioned the autopsy.

'Who did it to him?'

'They say it was a hit and run, the driver didn't stop.'

'They said that about the Arab. But Dédé didn't believe them. Do you believe them, Chief Inspector?'

'No, Mme. Galabert. I don't believe them.'

She sniffed and Belmont handed her his handkerchief. 'Call me Michelle,' she said. 'He looked up to you. Said you were the best Chef in the department. That you were on his side even though the higher ups were trying to shut down the case.'

'It's true, I guess.'

'Then will you find out what really happened to him?'

Belmont already had a good idea what had happened to him but didn't want to tell her just now. 'I will.'

She shuffled over and put a trembling hand to his cheek, looked straight into his eyes and said, 'I want the bastards to suffer.'

Before he could reply she'd put her lips against his and moved her hand around the back of his head.

Sunday, November 29th

Belmont rode the Métro to the office. His shirt felt grubby. Pulled his collar and tie off and stuffed them in his coat pocket. Later he'd pop home and pick up some clean clothes. Then he'd find a hotel.

Last night had been a mistake. A mistake that brought a rare smile to his face. He hoped he'd been of some comfort to Mme. Galabert. She'd been ferocious. Once they'd worn each other out, she'd calmed down and slept the night in his arms. Come the morning she made breakfast as if it were perfectly natural that he be there. Made small talk and sipped coffee. Behaved as if Belmont were a family friend who'd slept on the couch. Until she passed by with bread and jam. He'd grabbed her round the waist, pulled her onto his lap. She wriggled, tried to turn her face away as he kissed her lips. So he kissed her neck. The wriggling ended. She threw herself into the kiss. Clothes strewn across the floor. She pushed Belmont backwards on to the kitchen table. He smiled at the remembrance of her climbing on top of him. Maybe he'd pay her another visit before finding a hotel.

Two sergeants intercepted him before he'd made it ten paces into headquarters. The superintendent wanted to see him immediately. They pretty much frogmarched him to Péraud's office.

'I don't know what you think you're playing at, Belmont, but you've gone too far.'

'Too far, sir, in which direction?'

'Yesterday you sent the official doctor away from a crime scene. You moved a corpse before The Bureau had completed their investigations. No doubt you have destroyed much evidence. One of our officers killed and you've ruined our best chance of catching the driver.'

'I doubt very much that the driver did anything more than dump Galabert's body at the side of the road. I wanted my sergeant to be seen by a doctor I trust. Without his examination we stand little chance of catching the killers.'

'We don't play favourites between the medical examiners. They have designated arrondissements and it's not your business to rearrange them.'

'I don't trust that other-'

'Silence! I'm not interested in your paranoiac suspicions. As of this second you are suspended from all duties. Hand in your identification and your weapon and get out. There will be a hearing shortly where we'll decide what to do with you.'

Belmont was going to object but knew he'd be pissing against the wind. His gun was in his desk, Péraud could fetch that himself. He pulled out his police ID and dropped it on the super's desk. Then he stood to attention, saluted, about-turned and left the room.

Before leaving the building he paid a quick visit to the sergeants' room near his office. Caillou was alone in there, smoking a cigarette whilst admiring some recent vice squad photographic confiscations.

'I've been suspended.'

Caillou looked worried. 'Why, Chef?'

'I can't talk here. Can you and Tabaraut meet me later for a drink? Not the Scarlet K. Somewhere like the Flore, upstairs. Shall we say five?'

'We'll see you there, Chef.'

'Keep it between us, Caillou. Only let Tabaraut in on it.'

The knock-on effects of the American stock market crash were now hitting France. People were losing all their assets. Companies going bankrupt. Once wealthy families were finding themselves selling off country estates or pied-à-terres. Those families without pied-à-terres were finding themselves on the streets. Yet Belmont's money was safe. His family's wealth came from vineyards in Bordeaux. He had millions of francs hanging on the walls of his apartment. It wouldn't matter financially if he lost his job, he didn't need to work. Didn't need to yet he always had. And if he chucked it in it would be on his terms. If needs be he'd burn his entire fortune fighting to get reinstated. And finding out who'd killed Galabert - nobody nowhere was going to take out one of his men and walk away from it.

He rode a taxi over to that apartment with the millions of francs worth of paintings. His wife ought to be in. Sunday morning and early afternoon she normally spent in bed. Saturday nights, she'd claim, are rather taxing.

Ernst's half-human bird seemed to be screeching, an ear piercing squawk to go with the evil eye it gave him. There was a man's coat hanging on the stand. Not one of his and it was accompanied by a white scarf. There were voices echoing through the hallway. Belmont called out, 'hello,' to no reply.

Clusters of discarded clothing lay outside the bedroom door. They were in there, giggling. Belmont went to the drawing room and helped himself to a cognac. There was no ice in the apartment so he took it neat, just like he did at work. His suitcase was over by the mini-grand. He trusted his wife to have packed it well. Actually, he trusted his wife to have told the maid to make sure everything was in there. His shaving kit, his toothbrush, comb and hair oil. Shirts, vests, underwear. A copy of that Zola book he kept starting and never finishing.

The door opened and a young man entered, stark naked.

'Oh,' he said, 'I didn't realise you were here.'

Belmont recognised him as the sculptor, Séraphin. Guess this meant the naked statue of Mme Belmont would soon be finished.

'The drinks cabinet is here.' Belmont stood to one side. 'She likes a martini after sex.'

'I know,' the man said. 'I mean, I know where the cabinet

is.'

At least he had the decency to blush. And to lie. Belmont had no doubt M. Séraphin had fixed Mme. Belmont quite a number of martinis.

'There are cigars in that desk over there.' Belmont gestured with his glass over at his desk. 'Help yourself. I'll down this, then I'll be off. Tell her I stopped by. I'll leave my key on the table by the front door. And I'll call round in the week to pick up some more clothes.'

'I will,' he said and proceeded to mix a pair of martinis and carry them off to the bedroom.

Belmont finished his drink. Left the key on the table and took his suitcase to the Hotel Welcome on the boulevard Saint-Germain.

Caillou and Tabaraut were already waiting at Café Flore when Belmont arrived. They'd taken a table in the corner. They both stood to shake Belmont's hand. Tabaraut pointed to a glass of cognac. 'We ordered you something, Boss.'

'Good man. Who have they got in to replace me?'

'Superintendent Péraud's taking personal charge for now, Boss' Tabaraut said. 'Which means nobody's in charge. He sits in his office issuing proclamations which get delivered to us third hand.'

'Funny thing is,' Caillou said, 'even Jouvin doesn't seem too pleased about it. I'd never have pegged him for a fan of yours, Chef.'

'He isn't. If he's sulking it's for some other reason. Which is interesting as the only other reason I can think of right now is Galabert.'

'You can't believe Jouvin played a part in that, can you, Boss?'

'I can, Tabaraut, but I'd guess it wasn't a direct part. When I announced that Galabert was missing I paid close attention to Sergeant Jouvin. He was as surprised as any of you by the news. However, when I announced that Galabert had been found dead, Jouvin didn't look in the least bit perturbed. I certainly don't think he played a part in the killing but he played a hand afterwards.'

'Christ, Chef, do you really mean that?' Caillou said. 'You're talking about a fellow officer. Jouvin may be a prick who had it in for Galabert but would he really cross the line?'

'There are two Jouvins. One is the flic who had it in for Galabert. And no, that Jouvin wouldn't cross the line. Then there is another Jouvin, the one who's in the superintendent's pocket. I used to think it was because he was smarming up to him for a promotion. Recently I've had cause to re-think that position.

'Galabert was working another case, an Arab lad who died after a hit and run. Galabert thought there was more to it. Interviewed the lad's brother who claimed they'd been attacked. Galabert followed Jouvin. Thought he had something to do with it. I don't know whether that was a hunch or he straight up didn't like Jouvin. Either way he ended up at the house of a senator, that same house we were at the other day. There he saw Jouvin and Péraud attend a meeting of some fascist group. All dressed up like Black Shirts but wearing hoods like the American Klu Klux Klan. Call themselves the black-hoods or Ibex, Galabert wasn't clear which. Later Galabert broke into the garages of that house and found a white van. A van very similar to the one the Arab described his attackers using.

'There wasn't enough to go on, not when the suspects include a senator and a superintendent. When Caillou and I paid that house a visit there was no van but I did find evidence that Galabert had broken in. I suspect he was caught. That they held him for a day or two then killed him. That other Jouvin, that Ibex Jouvin, is more than capable of covering up Galabert's death.'

They sat staring at each other in silence. They all knew what was coming next and none of them liked it. Belmont knew he was going to have to suggest it and they knew they'd have to agree. For now though they were hoping it would all go away. That Galabert would walk in and join them. That they could finish their drinks and return to the Quai des Orfèvres, all together.

'Well, there's no way anyone is going to sanction an official investigation. But as I'm off the books at the moment,' Belmont said, 'I might as well begin an unofficial one. I'll try to keep you out of it but I may need to call on you at times.'

'Whenever you like, Chef,' Caillou said.

'I'm with you every step, Boss. You can count on me,' Tabaraut said.

They didn't like to mention that Galabert's investigation had led to his death. That Belmont was going to have to break into that same house. That whatever had happened to Galabert could easily befall him.

'In the meantime,' Belmont said, 'any news on the Ripper killing? I'm about a day behind.'

'There's not much going on,' Tabaraut said. 'We interviewed the other residents from the victim's apartment building. They're all pretty spooked, didn't give us anything pertinent. The downstairs door ought to spring shut. We took a look at it and the spring works fine. The upstairs neighbour thought he heard a shout and a glass break but put the two together and ignored them. That was at half-eleven. We're interviewing the poor girl's family and friends although I doubt they had anything to do with it.'

'Did she have a lover?'

'She did but he'd gone back home to his parents. His grandfather had recently died. There are plenty of witnesses who saw him there, the murder was on the night of the wake and that went on until midnight. It's over two hundred kilometres away, he wouldn't have been able to leave after midnight and reach Paris in time to have killed her. Besides, we also think that shout and the glass breaking the neighbour heard was the killer at work, in which case she'd have been dead a bit before twelve.'

'I imagine it's the work of the same man who killed the others,' Belmont said. 'I just didn't want to close off other avenues before we began. I don't suppose you know if Jouvin's kept up his tail on Bodescot?'

'He has and Bodescot's been going to work and home as normal. No change to his routine at all.'

'OK, what are you two doing later tonight?'

Chief Inspector Belmont had spent nearly an hour in the Café Flore. Léon had never once set foot in there. It was a place intellectuals went to watch their coffee grow cold while discussing the meaning of a pebble. Léon preferred to drink with real people who had blood pulsing through their veins.

Léon felt sick as he thought of that girl. Of her blood. The electrical surges had been strong with her, perhaps that was due to the confined space. Even yesterday he'd felt them. They'd come back, of a sudden, as he stood at the wash basin. The room, full of shouts and clashing pans, fell silent. He squeezed a coffee cup so hard it cracked in his hand. Then it all came back in an immediate rush and all those suspended sounds hit him at once. His finger had bled into the dish water.

Later, a waiter had kicked his ankle as he stepped back from the sink. Must have been the tenth, the twentieth, kick that day. But this kick came as the sound once more hung suspended in the air. Then he was watching the white face of the waiter whose mouth was opening and closing and whose arms were gesticulating. The sound came back and Léon heard his own name. The waiter was abusing him, the old woman at the next basin had frozen with her hands in the water. The waiter stormed off and she came back to life, chuckling to herself, 'he deserved that alright but they'll give you hell now.' And all afternoon every waiter had kicked him every time they passed.

Man, Léon thought, was made rat by work. The fear of losing a wage, it enfeebled the mind and left a man emasculated. And that's how they wanted us, with no fight and willing to feed on whatever shit they wanted us to eat. So hang them all. He wouldn't go back to take their kicks and their miserable sou. No more second fiddle. No more any fiddle! Léon would be the conductor, the maestro of his own future. He would spit in the eye of fate and if fate wanted to make something of it, so be it!

The nausea abated.

Belmont was probably the maestro of his own future too. Under the surface. When he wanted a woman he just took her. And if his wife didn't like it he upped sticks and moved into a hotel. If life had dealt them different cards, Léon and Belmont would have been fast friends. That was why he'd been so pleased to spot Belmont, almost by accident, an hour earlier. Belmont looked as if he'd just stepped out from the Hotel Welcome. Léon couldn't be certain of that. Belmont might have been adjusting his flies or turned to sneeze. Most likely though, he'd been leaving the Welcome. Léon laughed and rubbed his hands together for warmth.

The laughter ended when he recalled that afternoon's newspaper. Belmont had been suspended. After all the effort Léon had put into getting to know him. All the time he'd spent following him and thinking about him. Well, they might have taken Belmont off the case. But Léon hadn't.

The doc was in his office. Belmont knocked and entered.

'Doc.'

'Belmont. Sit down.' He indicated a seat which Belmont took. The room had an interesting fragrance, tobacco smoke, wood polish, formaldehyde. The doc had his glasses pushed up on his forehead as he wrote in some ledger. 'I'll just be ten seconds.'

Eventually he put down his pen, pulled his glasses over his eyes and looked up at Belmont. 'You landed me right in it with young Sergeant Galabert's body, Belmont, do you know that?'

'Sorry, Doc, they suspended me for it.'

'Can't say I'm surprised. However, I've worked with you long enough to know that wasn't like you. And Galabert wasn't the first officer you've lost. So what was it all about, can you tell me?'

'I can tell you some, Doc. I doubt you'd want to hear it all.'

'Proceed.'

'I suspect the results of the autopsy will tell us that Galabert was killed in a hit and run where we found him.'

'But that would mean-'

'That's exactly what it means, Doc. That's why I wanted you in on it and it's one of the reasons I'm here.'

'One of the reasons?'

'I want to know if you got a chance to examine him, before they took his body away.'

'I did carry out a cursory examination. Enough to know that he was killed by a blow to the back of the head by a blunt object. There is a remote possibility that he could have been struck by a vehicle and hit his head on the curb. But there is no chance that it happened where and when we found him. I would also say that he had been bound both wrist and ankle for a long period before he died. And there certainly was enough evidence to suggest he'd been stored on ice after death.'

'Was there anything to indicate where they might have held him?'

'I'm sorry, Belmont. If there was I didn't have enough time to find it. If they do file an autopsy report which states that Galabert was killed by a hit and run driver, then I shall challenge it. I saw more than enough to indicate foul play. If needs be I'll-'

'No, Doc,' Belmont said, 'that would be inadvisable. The people who killed Galabert are ruthless and they've got connections. You start issuing challenges and you'll become a target, maybe there'll be a real hit and run and it'll be your body left dying in the road.'

'What? I won't give in to those sorts of threats. If that's how they want to play it, then I'll-'

'It's not play, Doc. I've already lost one good man. I don't want to lose two. You write up your report then hide it. Give it to your notary. When the time comes I may have need of it. For now, keep it under your hat. If anyone asks, you tell them that you never got time to examine the body. Tell them you don't know what all the fuss was about. You only did it as a favour to me because you thought Jaccard was unavailable. And then, for good measure, make it known that you're displeased that I've put you in such a position.'

'If you say so, Belmont, although I can't help feeling this is the coward's part.'

'It's tactical, Doc. You'll be no use to anyone squashed on the road.'

Sunday, November 29th, Night

Earlier that day Belmont had had the feeling he was being followed. After leaving the Flore he'd ducked in to the Saint-Germain Métro station. Climbed on a train and hopped off at the next stop. Then he ran full pelt up to the street and jumped on a tram. On arrival at the medico-legal institute, to see Doc, he'd taken up a covered position in a doorway and scanned the roads. He'd lost them. Even so, it didn't feel good knowing Ibex were already on to him.

Belmont took a good grip of the creeper and hauled himself up onto the wall. He lay on the top, like a leopard, and listened. Not a sound. On the other side of the wall there were bushes and trees. Galabert had described this route - in along the garden between the vegetation and the wall. Enough cover until he reached the house. Then things would get tricky.

The senator had left the building two hours earlier. Belmont had waited for the downstairs lights go out. Watched them one by one, except the one in the porch and what could be the one in the hallway. On this side the house was in near darkness, with just the faint hint of light from the hall shining through to the garden.

This would be as good a time as any. Galabert must have thought the same thing. That didn't stop it being true, Galabert had been unlucky. For all his impatience he was nobody's fool. He would have waited for the right moment and gone in quiet. Some piece of bad luck occurred and they caught him.

Belmont stalked across the end of the lawn to the house.

Pressed himself up against the building and stuck to the shadows. He ducked under windows and made his way around to the front of the house. There he paused, looking at the porch with its light spilling out over the gravel of the driveway. There was no getting around this. His footsteps would crunch and the light would make him visible.

He decided speed was the best policy and darted across the front of the door. Made it to the drawing room window and paused. Silence both from the street and house. He used his knife to open the shutter then put his ear to the window and listened. Nothing. Not the slightest vibration.

A thin strip of metal pushed up between the wooden frames and against the catch was all it took to open the window. It screeched as he lifted it up. Then he climbed through. This was his Rubicon, a suspended flic caught breaking into a senator's house, they'd throw the book at him. His suspension would become dismissal. There'd be criminal charges. Belmont had enough years of good service, enough commendations and war medals to keep him out of jail. Plus he had contacts who could pull strings. Although, if incarceration were the threat he wouldn't have been there. He'd have been at home instructing his advocate to get Galabert off a charge of breaking and entering. No, it wasn't jail he needed to be afraid of. It was a blow to the back of the head and a van ride out to some quiet residential street followed by a falsified autopsy.

The drawing room looked much the same as it had in the daytime. Except long shadows clung to the wall where light from outside shone through the windows. Curtains floated gently up in the breeze. Belmont pulled the shutters closed but left the window unlocked. He scanned the room again, this time looking for places he might hide. Hiding places were scant but there was one spot where he could take cover. It wouldn't withstand a serious search but it would see him through a casual glance around.

The hall light glared at him. He'd been in the half-light of outside for long enough that his eyes had adjusted to the darkness. Now they were being hit full force by an electric bulb.

Belmont's heart beat *doppio movimento.* There'd be no bluffing his way out of this one. If confronted he'd run for it. Back to the window and out. Then straight over those iron gates. If anyone tried to pull him down they'd get a kick in the chops. And if they came after him with a gun? Fear could be crippling and deadly, sometimes it was best to stop thinking and to act instead.

He crept along the hall to the study. Slipped inside and closed the door behind him. There was an almost welcoming aroma of cigar smoke. The room was pitch black. In the darkness he could imagine the senator puffing away, watching him. Belmont switched on his torch and flashed it round the room. Bookshelves, a table, a large rug over a parquet floor. Nothing of interest except that huge walnut desk.

The drawers were locked. Belmont had brought along a sturdy screwdriver which he used to prise open the first drawer. He discovered notes on household expenditure. He went for the top middle drawer. Wedged the screwdriver in and put his weight into it. This drawer, like the previous one, cracked open. Two drawers with splintered wood around the locks, they'd know they'd been broken into. After tonight there'd be no coming back. The window locks would be replaced and they might even hire a night watchman. Either that or a pair of guard dogs.

The drawer contained a brochure folder with a silver ibex embossed on the front. He dumped the folder's content on to the desk. First thing he saw was a picture of the senator dressed in his Black Shirt kit addressing a rally from the saddle of a grey stallion. Second thing he noticed was a list of names. All ex-members of the North African Star Party. There were asterisks besides some, including Ferhat Djaout's. Then Belmont spotted another list. Right at the top was the senator. Beneath that, Superintendent Péraud and alongside him, Doctor Jaccard who was now performing

Galabert's autopsy. There were columns of names beneath these. The top two names in each column were in bold, as were the senator's, the doctor's and the superintendent's. Belmont folded the list and tucked it into his back trouser pocket. Once he'd scanned the rest of the contents he stuffed it all back into place and closed the drawer. He'd seen enough to convince him that Galabert had been right. Dead right.

Belmont had just wedged the screwdriver into the next drawer when he heard the click of the door opening.

The silhouette of a tall, broad, man framed the doorway. His features were indistinct. The gun wasn't. Belmont turned to look at the windows. Even if they'd been wide open the shutters would have blocked his escape. Belmont ducked under the desk.

'Get out from there,' the man said.

Belmont kept quiet. Despite having been seen he hoped to create some doubt in the interloper's mind. It didn't work.

'I said get out from there or I start putting bullets through the wood.'

Belmont took a look at the desk above him. Thick and sturdy but no shield from a bullet. There was no way out. He'd have to give himself up and hope he'd get an opportunity to escape. No doubt that was the same hope Galabert clung to. The man flicked the study lights on.

'OK, I'm coming out.' Belmont put his hands up above the desk then stood up slowly. The man was clearly visible now and he'd taken up a position in the middle of the room. He stood at least one metre eighty tall. Looked tough, cauliflower ear, nose bent from a break, a cut on his forehead which had recently healed over, muscular. Had some weight on him. The sort of weight that would add to his momentum rather than slow him down.

'I'm a police officer,' Belmont said.

'Yeah, and I'm Nefertiti's sister. Now step around that desk and don't try nothing or I'll shoot your knees out.'

Belmont was about to protest when he remembered he no longer had any police ID. Wouldn't have made any difference if he had else Galabert would still be alive.

He skirted round the desk maintaining constant eye contact. This bruiser never once looked away. No doubt he'd done this a hundred times before. Belmont to him was no different than a pig to the slaughter man.

Belmont's knife was in his jacket pocket. If he got half a chance he'd stab the man, get him in the leg so he wouldn't be able to give chase. Belmont stared hard at him. If push came to shove he'd stick it straight in the bastard's neck.

'Now turn around and get on your knees.'

'I'm telling you right now that I'm a chief inspector with the Paris Judiciary Police. My men are waiting outside these gates. If they hear one shot or if I don't leave this building in five minutes they'll raid it. And you will be in it up to your neck.'

'I said turn around and get on your knees, Chief Inspector, else you'll make me angry and if I get angry I'll do something that you'll regret.'

Belmont thought about bluffing some more, feeding him some line. It would have been a waste of breath. Instead he turned around and got on his knees, hands still in the air. The man walked up behind him.

Belmont was on the floor, face down. Felt groggy, wasn't sure where he was. His arm was stuck. He struggled, couldn't move his arms. Then he realised his feet were stuck too. Couldn't work out what was going on and began to thrash about. As he struggled he got a fuzzy vision of the room he was in, realised he wasn't at home. Then the pain in the back of his head kicked in and he felt sick. At that moment it came back to him and he realised he was still in the senator's study.

'You have a nice sleep?'

A hazy figure peered down at him. That bastard must have knocked him out then trussed him up. How long had he been out for? And now he really was in Galabert's shoes. They'd keep him somewhere for a day or two then kill him. Belmont began to fight desperately against the bindings. His efforts earnt him a kick in the guts. It knocked the wind out of him, left him gasping for breath.

'Try not to struggle or I'll have to kick you to death before the boss gets home. That'll upset him. He likes to look into the eyes of the condemned before they die. Tells them a bit about the world we're creating. The better place they'll never see.'

Belmont lay on his side. Air began to find its way back and forth to his lungs. He'd landed in the shit and had no idea how to get out of it.

'By the way, I found a screwdriver and a knife in your pockets. Hope you don't mind but I'm going to keep them. Of course, I should send them to your next of kin. Sure they won't mind though, it's only a screwdriver and a pocket knife, hardly going to see them destitute.'

'You bastard.' Belmont spat the words out between choked breaths, he still wasn't able to take on enough oxygen.

'Well, if you feel like that about it, I guess I could post them back to your wife or whoever inherits your estate.'

Belmont closed his eyes. Had a vision of the naked sculptor strutting around his apartment, sizing up the paintings, deciding which he'd keep and which he'd sell. Adrienne in their bedroom, giggling and drinking martini after martini. The vision of his wife and her lover grew faint. A greater darkness came. And through it he could hear someone calling, 'papa, papa.' He looked down at a cot bed, a thin blanket and his boy. Hair dripping with sweat. Big black eyes in such a pale face. He hugged his son and kissed his forehead. Held him so close. Heard the rasping of his breath until the rasping grew faint and stopped. His baby was gone. All that remained was the void, the twin infinities of time and space. The vastness which turned all to nothingness.

Caillou was sweating. Tabaraut was calm. They were both smoking, and looking out the windscreen at the iron gates of the senator's house. Belmont had been gone too long. They both knew that. Caillou wanted to go in and check. Tabaraut didn't want to blow Belmont's cover. Gave Caillou a hit from his hip flask, 'give it ten more minutes. He won't thank us for bungling in and blowing it all.'

'And he won't thank us if we don't, Tabaraut, because he'll be dead.'

'Don't panic. Ten more minutes then we knock on the door and search the place top to bottom.'

'We don't have a warrant.'

'Your fists will be our warrant. Anyone gives us any shit you lay them out. I'm the inspector, I've got rank over you, so I'll take the heat. If it means getting Belmont out alive I don't care if I have to spend a couple of years in La Santé.'

'I don't like it, he's been in there too long. If we hadn't already lost Galabert then-'

Tabaraut held up his hand to stop him. 'We'd already lost Galabert when we agreed the timings. You know it's important to stick to the plan. That's why we make it beforehand, when we've got cool heads. So at moments like now, when we're getting worried, we don't have to think about it. We just rely on the plan. Nothing out of the ordinary has happened that we need to start ad-libbing.'

Caillou's leg was jigging up and down causing the whole motor to shake. 'We weren't cool headed though. We were planning to break into a senator's house because we think he killed a flic. It's too personal to be cool headed.'

'Can you stop juddering the car, I can't think properly with all that shaking.'

Caillou steadied his leg. Lit a cigarette off the one he was smoking. 'What was that?'

'What?'

'I heard something.' Caillou wound down his window. 'Listen.'

There was silence. Then a creaking followed by the sound

of a van door slamming. Tabaraut didn't need to think, turned the key in the ignition and set the motor idling.

Caillou opened his door and slipped out the motor-car. All nerves gone. Behind him he heard Tabaraut give the motor a gentle rev as he released the handbrake. Caillou made it to the gates. A large white van was parked in the middle of the courtyard. He signalled to Tabaraut then crossed the gates to get a look past the van to the front of the house.

A big man stumbled out the front door with a Belmont shaped burlap sack over his shoulders. He loaded the sack into the back of the van. Caillou held his right arm high with his fist clenched. That signalled to Tabaraut that Belmont was in danger. They couldn't act yet, not with the gates locked, it'd mean trying to scramble over as someone put a bullet in Belmont's head.

The man went back and closed the front door. Then he approached the gates. Caillou pressed himself against the wall so he couldn't be seen. The gates swung open into the courtyard. When they were both open Caillou held his right arm out horizontally from his body. Heard Tabaraut gun the engine of the motor. Caillou ran in through the gates and jumped the man.

They rolled around on the gravel. The back of the man's head cracked into Caillou's face. He could taste blood as his lip split open. His front teeth felt numb as if they'd been deadened. He moved his face out the way as the man's head jerked back again. This time Caillou worked his arm round the man's neck and started to choke him. The man managed to roll over and broke free of Caillou's grip, scrambled to his feet. Caillou stood up with his back to the van. He could hear the sound of Tabaraut getting out the motor. Caillou called out, 'check the back of the van. Make sure the chef's OK.'

The man swung at Caillou who attempted a dodge but the fist caught him on the chin. Then the man lurched forward, swung another punch, Caillou weaved right and came back at him with a couple of left-handed jabs. The man dropped his guard and Caillou followed up with a right upper cut. Got the man reeling so Caillou jabbed twice with his right, straight at the bloke's nose. Swung in with the left and caught him just above the eye. Then the man jumped at Caillou, grabbed him by the lapels of his coat and head-butted him in the face.

Caillou's head spun. Blood flowed from a deep cut above his left eye. Blurred his vision. The man sprang forward again. Caillou stood his ground, hit him in the solar plexus. He doubled up and fell to the floor. Caillou was blinded, used his sleeve to wipe the blood from his eyes. When the man got back to his feet he had a gun pointed straight at Caillou's guts.

'You can drop that right now or I'll put a bullet in your back,' Tabaraut had a gun trained on the man.

'You try anything, you flic bastard, and your friend-'

Tabaraut didn't hit the back. Instead he shot him in the arse. The second shot hit his thigh. Caillou dived to one side as the man let off a round which passed through the van door. He collapsed, dropping the gun, as Tabaraut jumped in and cuffed him. After that Tabaraut helped Caillou to his feet.

'I'll say one thing, Caillou, you're a tough bastard. I always knew you were a bastard but I didn't realise you were quite so tough.'

Caillou laughed and spat blood on the floor. 'That's right, Tabaraut, you wouldn't want to get in a fight with me.'

'I don't know about that. My fights are gun fights and I've won them all so far.'

Belmont leant against the back of the van, tried to focus on the scene in front of him, couldn't and gave up. 'Which one of you lovebirds is going to untie me?'

'What now, Chef?' Caillou said. 'I mean, if we take him in he's going to blab about the break in, he could land us in some stinky shit.' Caillou was holding a blood soaked hanky to his eye. It did little to stem the flow of blood.

'I see it like this: if we take him in the senator hires the best advocate in town, gets his Ibex magistrate friend to take the case and our man in the van walks free with our apologies echoing in his ears. And yes, we land in the shit - maybe get put on a charge or demoted or fired. To be honest, I couldn't give a rat's arse about any of that right now. Can either of you two drive a van?'

They tied a tourniquet round the man's leg and patched up his arse cheek with some old rags. Then they bundled him, handcuffed, into the back of the van and locked the door. Should they get separated, a rendezvous point in the north of the parc de Bagatelle was agreed. A discreet location near the lake.

Tabaraut and Belmont rode in the van. Caillou kept close behind in the motor. From Bagatelle they hit a trail into the Bois des Boulogne. Kept going until the trees got thick. They pulled over and Belmont and Tabaraut went and joined Caillou in the motor.

'What we going to do, Chef?'

'Question him. That man played a part in Galabert's death. Might not have given the order but I'd be happy to bet he carried out the execution. And, let's face it, without executioners there are no executions.'

'I say we kill the bastard,' Tabaraut said, 'an eye for an eye and all that. Find a ditch, put a bullet in his head, drop him in and cover him up with a branch or two and some leaves.'

'I can't deny that isn't tempting, Tabaraut, but he's small fry. Someone gave him the order to kill and he's the one I want.'

'We know who that was, it was that son-of-a-whore senator. He owns the house, hosts those Black Shirt meetings and gives out the orders. We should kill him then go put some lead into the senator's brain.'

'I'm not going to give you a load of moralising spiel,' Belmont said, 'not going to sell you any phooey about us being better than them. If I thought we could walk away from it then I'd do it. But that senator isn't some no-mark we can drive out to the woods. There'll be an investigation and the Ibex group already know I'm on to them. I don't want to go to the guillotine for them.'

'So what then, Boss?'

'I want that thug to tell me who did what, where and when. And I want to know who was giving the orders. Yes, I think it was the senator but let him confirm it. I also want to know what Ibex are up to. What are these Arab attacks about? Then we let him go, let him go crawling back to his boss and blub about us being mean to him.'

'What if he doesn't talk, Chef,' Caillou said.

'We make him talk. If not, we play it by ear. Like I said, we aren't going to kill him but at the moment he's losing blood through that leg wound. If we don't get him to a hospital he'll drop dead anyway.'

Caillou and Tabaraut dragged their captive from the van. You could see his grimace of pain from a hundred metres. His face was bruised and his left eye swollen. Belmont went through his pockets, found some identification.

'Jacques Delfour, pleased to meet you,' Belmont said.

Delfour said nothing. Belmont gripped his chin and lifted his head up. They were almost nose to nose. Belmont kicked the bullet wound on Delfour's thigh. Delfour let out a cry of pain.

'Where were you planning on taking me?' Belmont asked.

Delfour said nothing. Belmont let go his chin and Delfour dropped to his knees. Belmont reckoned he was faking, exaggerating the extent of his injuries so as not to cooperate fully.

'Do you know who we are?'

'You're flics, I know that much.'

'That's right, Jacques, we're flics. Any idea why we brought you here rather than back to Police HQ? After-all HQ is much warmer.'

Delfour took in the scene, seemed to be comprehending that he wasn't in a police interview room. Looked up at

Caillou's bloodied and bruised face. Then at Tabaraut who was staring back at him while lighting his pipe. He met Belmont's eyes, intelligent and bright with a hint of cruelty. These men looked like they'd dug graves in this wood before. Looked like they'd kill and bury him then go home and eat a hearty dinner. The ground had a frost on it, felt hard and cold beneath his knees. They wouldn't be able to dig too deep.

'Maybe you brought me here because you queers like the woods.'

'What did he just call me?' Caillou lurched forward, blood soaked handkerchief clenched tight in his fist.

'He called all of us queer,' Belmont said. 'Some people are queer and some people aren't. He just got us marked wrong, that's all, it's nothing to cry over.'

Belmont took out his tobacco pouch and a cigarette paper. Turned to look at Caillou who realised he'd fallen into the trap of getting riled. Belmont understood. It's easy to get riled by someone who's twice smashed his head into your face.

'Now then, Jacques, I'd like to know where it was you were planning to take me in that van of yours.'

'Go fuck your maman,' Delfour spat at Belmont but the spittle didn't travel much further than his own chin.

Belmont lit his cigarette, 'I'm afraid my maman's been dead for a number of years, Jacques. How about your maman, perhaps I can fuck her instead?'

'You leave my maman out of it, you son-of-a-whore.'

'I'm sorry, Jacques, didn't mean to offend you.' Belmont addressed Tabaraut, 'how long do you think it'd take to get an address for Mme. Delfour?'

'Depends if our man here has a police record,' Tabaraut said. 'If he does his prints will be on file. Should be able to get an address from that. If he hasn't moved around too much we should find her in a day. Might take two.'

'Would you like us to look up your maman, Jacques? Think she'd be interested to know that her son killed a flic?'

'You can't prove that.'

'Who would I want to prove it too, Jacques? Anyone here need me to prove that Jacques killed Sergeant Galabert?'

'No,' came the chorus reply.

'Hear that, Jacques, nobody needs me to prove anything. We already know you did it. And, you see, Sergeant Galabert was one of us and we look after our own. There's no need to get magistrates and judges and executioners involved, they *would* want proof *and* make a lot of fuss. Not worth it when we can deal with all that right here, right now. It'll save a lot of time and trouble. Tomorrow morning, instead of writing up a report for the examining magistrate, explaining all the naughty things you've done, I can spend a couple of hours relaxing over a coffee or two. That's so much nicer and so much more satisfying. There'll be no worrying that your senator friend will pull strings and get you off. No concerns that the president might decide to grant you a last minute pardon. There'll just be you, me and your own gun. Then there'll just be me. Unless, of course, you want to start talking.'

'I'm not talking to you, you flic bastard.'

'Come on, Jacques, my colleague here made it sound easy. It's not easy. To find your maman we'll have to fill out a pile of forms, ask a load of questions and go travelling about knocking on doors looking for her. Don't make us go through all of that.'

Delfour looked worried. Belmont could see he wanted to talk. To help him make his mind up, Belmont took hold of his shot leg and gave it a heavy handed squeeze. Delfour yelped and squirmed away.

'Sorry, Jacques, was just taking a look at that wound. I'd say it needs treatment. Can't say for sure but I fancy it's going septic. I remember once, during the war, a soldier in my unit got shot in the leg. Wasn't much more than a flesh wound. Problem was, we were under bombardment so we couldn't get him out to the ambulances. Instead he had to lay on a stretcher for a day and night. The wound got infected and by the time he reached the hospital it was gangrenous. The doctors amputated it there and then. Still, on the bright side, that was him out the war. Last I heard he'd committed suicide. You wouldn't commit suicide over a lost leg, would you, Jacques?'

Belmont squeezed hard on the leg. He moved in close, squatting down so he was at Delfour's height. Suddenly Tabaraut and Caillou were squatting on either side of Belmont. The four men were so close they shared each other's breath.

'You've got to decide if tonight's the night you put a bullet in your head. Your gun is in my pocket. I'll wipe it clean of all prints then reapply yours. Your body will be found in a couple of days by one of us, out for an innocent stroll in the woods.'

Belmont drew Delfour's gun, pulled back the hammer and pushed the muzzle against Delfour's forehead. Looked him straight in the eye and said, 'you a good catholic boy, Delfour? They won't look kindly on you as a suicide. Some cemeteries won't permit your burial. Maybe you'll have to get cremated.'

'I wouldn't like that,' Caillou said. 'I haven't stepped foot inside a church for years, but when I die I want to be buried properly. Don't want no protestant burning. May as well buy a one way tram ticket to hell.'

Belmont pushed the gun a little harder against Delfour's forehead. 'Maybe our Jacques isn't worried about all that. What about your maman, Jacques, will she be OK with you committing suicide and having to be cremated? She a modern woman?'

'I told you to leave her out of this,' Delfour said, the menace gone from his voice. He sounded old and weary. Kept trying to look at the gun pressing against his head.

'We can't leave her out of this,' Tabaraut said. 'She'll need to identify your corpse. I once had a woman, about sixty she was, had to identify her son's body, he'd shot himself in the head, and she had a heart attack. Imagine that, the son's suicide caused his maman to drop dead. It was as if the son had murdered his own maman. Your maman got a good heart, Delfour?'

'My maman's got a good heart,' Caillou said, 'but it'd break if she thought I'd committed suicide and had to be cremated. Then she lives in a small village. Everyone in the congregation would know her son had committed a mortal sin.'

'Come now, gentlemen,' Belmont said. 'Take a look at our Jacques. Doesn't he look like a man who fornicates and masturbates?'

'He looks like a right fornicator,' Tabaraut said.

'I think he's a masturbator,' Caillou said.

'Exactly,' Belmont said, 'two mortal sins already. Then there's his other mortal sin, the murder of Sergeant Galabert. I doubt that he's too bothered about mortal sins.'

'I won't be the one sinning,' Delfour said, 'you will, if you kill me.'

'Good point,' Belmont said. 'This'll be a sin he hasn't committed. So when he comes to meet his maker that one won't be on the books. But he'll still be dead and everybody in this realm will believe him to be a suicide. And I guess that's the difference, isn't it, gentlemen, that this is the sin his maman will hear about. She might suspect that he fornicates and masturbates. She won't have guessed about the murder. But this one sin will be public. This one will cause her priest to avoid eye-contact. This one will have her neighbours gossiping. This will be the one she gets down on her knees in front of the altar and prays to the Virgin Mother over. This mortal sin will be the one that keeps her up all night worrying about her son's soul and wondering how a boy who loved his maman could ever do such a thing to her.'

Belmont eased the gun away from Delfour's head. 'Seems a shame but we can't wait around here all night for him to change his mind. Budge over you two I'll need to do this from the side. First I better give the thing a clean.' Belmont took out his handkerchief and busied himself wiping the gun.

Delfour stared at Belmont who was concentrating on getting all the prints off the gun.

'OK, OK, What do you want to know?'

A slight drizzle began to fall. They dragged Delfour through the dirt to a tree and dumped him against it. Tabaraut stood off to the right, hands placed firmly in his coat pockets, one of them holding a revolver. Caillou stood back, near the van. The blows he'd taken were beginning to tell. Left him feeling sluggish.

Belmont crouched down in front of Delfour. He wanted to be all this man could see. Deep down Belmont agreed with Tabaraut. He wanted to kill Delfour and dump him in a ditch. Wanted cold-blooded revenge for what had happened to Galabert. And Michelle Galabert's words echoed in his head, 'I want the bastards to suffer.' No doubt Delfour thought he was suffering. Belmont had worked that bullet wound in his leg. But that wasn't suffering, that was pain. A shot of morphine and it would all be gone. Suffering isn't so easily appeased.

Belmont bit his lip. They weren't there to enact a personal revenge. As much as he might like the idea of emptying a few rounds into Delfour's hands. Or crippling him and leaving him to crawl home. They weren't things Belmont could do. Not tonight. Delfour, even with Galabert's blood on his hands, was a small cog. Get rid of him and another yob with a gun would take his place. What Belmont wanted was something to tie in the higher ranks of Ibex. Something on the senator, the superintendent, that crummy doctor. They might not be able to take out the group as a whole but they could have a go at knocking the leadership off their perch.

'Start by telling me about Galabert. What happened to him?'

'You know what happened to him. He died.'

'Give me the details and don't spare my feelings.' Belmont

sneered at Delfour, his hatred barely concealed.

'I caught him in the boss' study, just like I caught you.'

'Then what?'

'Same thing. I put him in the van. The boss has a hunting lodge out in the Meudon Forest. I drove him out there and chained him to a metal ring by the fireplace. Went back each day and fed him, gave him some water. Let him take a shit. That kind of thing.'

'So you left him chained up in an empty lodge in the woods in the middle of winter and gave him some food and water once a day?'

'That's about it.'

'Where is this lodge, what's the address?'

'There isn't an address.' Delfour described how to find it.

'What happened next?'

'I don't know what happened but they told me I had to kill him.'

'And you did what they told you?'

'Yeah. They said I had to kill him by hitting him over the back of his head. I used the poker from the fireplace. I gave him his food and when he turned to eat it I picked up the poker and that was that. Out like a light.'

'Your boss give you a bonus for such great work?'

'It's not like that. I didn't want to kill him. Didn't even know him. If he hadn't been snooping round the boss' study he'd still be alive. Anyway, I was just doing what I was told. It's the same for you.'

'Same for me is it? You think someone told me to take you out to the woods and kill you?'

Delfour looked up with a start, 'you said you weren't going to kill me, you said-'

'You just keep answering my questions and you'll live. What did you do with him after hitting him over the head?'

'I brought him back in the van, I don't know why. I don't know why they wanted me to kill him a certain way. I don't know why they didn't just have me bury him in the woods or dump him in the river.'

'You bury many people out in those woods?'

'No, but you could, couldn't you, if you wanted.'

'You brought him back, then what?'

'Then nothing. There was another man with the boss when I got home. He owns a fish place, a warehouse by the river. I gave him the keys and he took the van.'

'And that was the last you heard of it?'

'I know a day or two later they moved his body. Left it somewhere to look like he'd been run over.'

'The man you keep calling the boss, that's the senator, correct?'

'Correct. He's my boss. I live in the house and keep an eye on things.'

'You in this Ibex group too?'

Delfour turned away. Didn't want to talk about Ibex. That only served to inflame Belmont. He'd sat there the last ten minutes trying not to pick up a rock and dash this bastard's brains out. Hearing him talk about Galabert, chained like a dog, growing weaker each day until they decided to murder him, made him sick. Made him angry. Instead of picking up a rock he slapped Delfour across the face with his open hand. Delfour looked up and Belmont slapped him again.

'Don't get coy with me, Delfour, the only thing stopping me from blowing your brains out is the sound of your voice.'

'Yes, I'm a member of Ibex. That's how I got the job at the house.'

'While the senator was thinking about killing Galabert did he have any meetings with anyone? Someone he might have been talking it over with?'

'Yes.' Delfour left the sentence hanging. It wasn't just a reluctance to talk, he was losing blood and growing weak.

'Who with?'

'With Superintendent Péraud and Doctor Jaccard. They're his Ibex deputies.'

At this point Delfour slumped forward. Belmont lifted his head by the hair. His face pale, no expression in his eyes.

'Get him in the motor and turn it around,' Belmont said.

'I'll take care of the van. Wait for me a hundred metres up the road.'

Tabaraut kept the engine running. Caillou sat in the back with Delfour who was now conscious again and mumbling to himself. Caillou looked out the rear window to see Belmont running towards them. They left the woods to the dancing light of a burning van.

Tabaraut put his foot down, the motor sped out of the woods and straight over the river bridge. Delfour was talking but not making any sense. They pulled up outside a private clinic. Belmont and Caillou got out and dragged Delfour to the doorway, rang the bell a couple of times and dumped him.

'So long, Delfour,' Caillou said, 'give my regards to your maman.'

The three of them sat in near silence for ten minutes. They'd ordered drinks, lit cigarettes and Tabaraut his pipe, shifted about in their seats, eyed the two other customers, but didn't say a word.

'I'm sorry I got you involved in all this,' Belmont said, breaking the silence.

'Were not babies,' Tabaraut replied.

'I liked Galabert,' Caillou said, 'he had spirit. You should have seen him tear a strip of Jouvin. No joke, he took him to pieces. Jouvin didn't put a glove on him.'

'Jouvin had that coming,' Tabaraut said. 'I was beginning to think Galabert wouldn't make it. The amount of abuse Jouvin gave him without doing a thing about it. I even tried to talk him out of the fight, thought he'd get a thrashing. Boy was I wrong, that lad knew what he was about. He'd have made a fortune in the ring.'

'He was a good officer,' Belmont said. 'Could have been a real star in the department.'

'Anyway,' Tabaraut said, 'that's why you don't need to be saying sorry, Boss. Galabert was one of us and you don't fuck with us and walk away with a smirk on your face.'

'Here's to that,' Caillou said. He downed his whiskey and called for another. 'What do we do now, Chef?'

'There's the problem. What can we do? All the information we gathered this evening is no good in court. For a start I'd broken into that house. That on its own made everything that followed legally impermissible. It's why we took him to the woods instead of getting you to take him to the Quai. We know who did what and it means nothing. We'll never get one of them to confess. Can you imagine bringing in the senator or trying to arrest the super? Even if we brought the doctor in he'd have an advocate by his side in seconds. Those Ibex, they've got judges and all sorts on their lists. Jouvin's one of them. I spotted Inspector Cruchon's name too. In fact,' Belmont reached into his back pocket and pulled out a sheet of paper, 'I've still got the list here'

The three men peered at the piece of paper, pointing at names they recognised. Five judiciary flics. At least two from the Sûreté.

'This is a list of actual Ibex members. It doesn't include all the people who make a profession of toadying up to men like Superintendent Péraud. He's got all sorts in his pocket, not just at the Judiciary but in the local police. And this one's the senator, this one's an examining magistrate, this one's a medical examiner, this one's an arrondissement mayor. Think about their sympathetic associates. Our very own head of police, the Prefect of Paris, Chiappe, is a right wing zealot. No doubt he knows all about Péraud and his Ibex group. Then there'll be the financiers, the industrialists and bankers who fund Ibex and God knows who else. We get too close and they'll be pulling strings right across the country. I can't see how we can take them down.'

'Then what is there, Chef?'

'Not much. We can't go on doing what we did tonight. They'll have us out to Devil's Island in the blink of an eye. That's if they don't cut our heads off. All we can do is wait. We know who they are so be guarded. Give me a bit of time to think about it. For now there's a certain hunting lodge out in the Meudon Forest that ought to be dust and ashes. Anyone fancy another trip to the woods?'

Monday, November 30th

Three hours of sleep. Belmont found himself outside Mme. Galabert's apartment. Hadn't even considered a visit to rue Bonaparte, which was only round the corner from his hotel. Another faded infatuation.

She took her time answering the door. He'd woken her. It rarely occurred to Belmont that other people might be sleeping while he was awake. He followed her to the kitchen. She sat herself at the wooden table, eyes half open, and lit a cigarette.

'Coffee,' she said.

'Please,' Belmont replied.

'I'm telling you to make some coffee not asking if you want a cup. It's the least you can do after waking me so early.'

Belmont looked at his wristwatch. Nearly eight. He'd fallen into bed at four. Woke at seven. Didn't care much for what had happened in-between - a fitful sleep plagued by harrowing dreams.

Belmont put the coffee on the stove. Rolled himself a cigarette. Wondered what he should tell her.

'This going to be a regular thing?' she said.

'What?'

'You waking me at unholy hours?'

'It could be, if you'd like it to be.'

She squinted up at him. A worried face frowning under an electric light. Tall, handsome, a man her husband had looked up to. Lighting the cigarette he'd just rolled while fixing them coffee.

'I'll get you a key. Don't wake me before eight unless Lilian's around. When she's back any time after six is fine.'

Should he tell her anything? They'd found the hunting lodge, the acrid stink of smoke clung to his coat. There'd been a fireplace with an iron ring stuck in the brick work. A large splodge of dried blood on the hearth. It was easy to imagine Galabert chained to that wall, and to read his thoughts. The shrinking hope that Belmont would save him. It was easy to imagine Delfour picking up the poker that was lying in the fire grate. Had it been over as fast as Delfour claimed?

'Sugar?'

'No thanks.'

Belmont joined her at the kitchen table. They sipped at their coffee. He stubbed out his cigarette. A rain started up and beat against the closed shutters.

'The people who killed Galabert, I mean Dédé, I know who they are.'

She seemed to come to life. Looked up at Belmont rather than down at her cup. Her slow timid movements replaced with an animalistic alertness.

'Who? Where? Are they under arrest? I want to see them.'

'Did Dédé talk to you about the case he was working on?'

'No, not in any detail. An Arab was attacked. He suspected a cover up.'

'That's right, and the people doing the covering up wield a lot of power and influence.'

'And they killed my Dédé?'

'Yes.'

'And you can't arrest them, why?'

'They have the whip hand. I'm talking about power and influence in the police, in the judiciary, in the army, in the government. Any investigation would be snuffed out the moment it got started. Besides, currently, I'm suspended, I can't even try to investigate.'

'Tell me who they are.'

Belmont would find her at the senator's house, a smoking

gun or bloodied dagger in her hand. 'No, I'll make sure they pay. You've got the kid. If you go and do something stupid who'll take care of her?'

'Just tell me who they are.'

'I can't, but I will in time.'

'Get the fuck out of my house.' She stood up and pointed at the door. Belmont didn't move. 'Out!' She pretty much screamed it. Belmont went and stood in the rain.

The rain began to soak through his thin coat. The cold was getting to him. A bit of shuffling and foot stomping helped. Ten more minutes, twenty at a push, that's all he'd give her. Then he'd quit. Quit to a hot toddy in the corner of a crowded bar.

Léon blew into his cupped hands then stuffed them back into his trouser pockets. About an hour earlier he'd taken up a sentry position on the rue Bonaparte. A light had flickered on after twenty minutes. It showed through the slats in her shutters. That was enough to keep Léon waiting.

Either she'd gotten up to go out or she'd spend the day lounging in her apartment. It was tempting to break in there right now. But she'd already become something different. A sport. A contest between himself and Chief Inspector Belmont. Of course, there was no doubt, he'd win. Belmont would lose.

Five more minutes ticked by. Léon rubbed his wrists. Ran his fingers over the scratches and cuts from her vicious nails. What was her name? Leoine, or something like that. They itched now rather than hurt. Served him as a reminder. Don't strangle with your hands from the front. Use the knotted rope and do it from behind. Still, life is all about experience and these last weeks he'd learnt to accept change.

Phillipe had instigated the changes with his silly girl from the club. Poor Phillipe. It was all at an end for him now. For all Léon's work to shake the police off his tail. For all he'd done to keep himself out of the police investigations. For all that, nothing. Blown out the water. By poor simple Phillipe.

Léon didn't know how long they had left, only that time was short.

First Léon had ignored it. Thought it was an affectation. A rather strange affectation. Next day he'd grown concerned. Phillipe had been in the kitchen. The coffee pot began to boil. Phillipe had said, 'you want one or not?' 'Yeah,' Léon replied. Phillipe turned, startled, 'didn't see you there, Léon.'

In the evening, through the bedroom wall, Léon could hear Phillipe talking. Kept saying, 'you're a malicious bitch.' Yesterday he called her Maddie, it had been like a punch in the guts. If that babbling simpleton was talking to Madeline Legrand they were done for.

At first there'd been panic. Phillipe went off to work. Léon ensconced himself in the window seat. Looked out over the grey city roof tops lit by the dull moonlight. He'd fretted. Hours passed before he first thought of killing him. He'd be kind, smother him in his sleep.

But what would be the point? Phillipe was as much his son as his brother. All his life Léon had looked out for him, taught him everything he knew. Sure he'd been rough in his teaching. Life was rough. He'd have sold him short had he been gentle. And now he was thinking of killing him. And realising he'd rather die than do that.

Early, when the sky was at its blackest and the moon long since hidden by rain clouds, Léon had an idea. He needed not wait to get caught. Instead he could raise the stakes. Play at a higher table. Face them head on. It would be romantic, like a duel between two honourable gentlemen from a Dumas novel. Chief Inspector Belmont and Léon Bodescot at fifty paces. Choice of weapon, their wits alone.

That was why he was waiting. You couldn't duel with a man who didn't know anything about it. When he was ready, Léon would send Belmont a pneumatic. He knew for certain that Belmont was staying at the Welcome. It was one of the places Léon had followed him before the chief inspector shook him off. Léon would make sure Belmont was in then send him a message and they'd learn soon enough who was the better man.

Belmont entered the first bar he came to. Sat in the back, in the dark, and ordered a demi. The rain had penetrated his coat as he'd stood outside the Galabert apartment. He felt wretched. If he couldn't pursue Galabert's killers the way he would any other murderer then there really was no decency in the world. He laughed, what right had he to talk of decency? There was no doubt in his mind that he would have killed Delfour out in the woods. If one of his questions had been met with the wrong answer, or if Delfour had managed to spit in Belmont's face rather than dribble down his chin, Belmont would have pulled the trigger. And, sure, yes, he would have regretted it. But how much? Right now he wouldn't be regretting anything.

Belmont took a swig of beer then reached for his tobacco. What right did he have to feel sorry for himself? None at all. He had work to do. And then it hit him, he had no work to do. The Paris Ripper was now someone else's problem. That someone was currently Superintendent Péraud. Péraud and whoever the Ripper ran into next.

He had no work to do but if he wanted to get his job back he needed to keep himself on the case. Caillou and Tabaraut had arranged to meet him each day and brief him. Other than that it was up to Belmont to go over the evidence, which was going to be copied up and sent over to the Welcome by Tabaraut, and dig something up.

As for Galabert, an idea was forming. They'd started out down the vigilante path. Breaking and entering, illegal interrogations, burning the van then the lodge. Now Belmont wanted to take Caillou and Tabaraut out of it. True, their hands were dirtied and both were willing to keep doing as Belmont asked. Shouldn't abuse that loyalty though. Caillou's got a wife and three kids - three that he knows of. Tabaraut's got a wife. If anything happened to them their families would be in dire straits. Belmont had a wife too. A wife with her own money who could survive without him.

Although, if Belmont's idea worked he wouldn't need to get his own hands any dirtier. Or, just a little bit.

The beer left him sleepy. Three hours kip after the day and night he'd had didn't cut it. Besides, his clothes needed drying out. After paying the patron's wife at the cash register, Belmont caught a tram back to the boulevard Saint-Germain. Trudged along to his hotel, picked up the key, climbed the stairs one at a time, and virtually passed out the moment he entered the room. Thought better of it. Undressed, hung his clothes out in front of the radiator to dry. Then collapsed on the bed and fell into a deep sleep.

Six hours passed as Belmont dribbled onto his pillow. There were no haunting dreams, just an oblivious unconsciousness. He woke and pulled on his now dry clothing. Reminded himself to pop by the apartment to pick up more of his stuff. Also, this room was too small for a long term prospect. He'd needed to find another hotel, one that had suites.

He sat on the bed and scratched his stubble covered chin. Rummaged through his pockets for tobacco. Rolled a cigarette and gazed out the window. Need this be a long term prospect? Hadn't his wife said it was only until the fuss in the press died down. In fact, having had his head, the press hadn't mentioned him these last couple of days. Even so, she'd need two weeks, perhaps a month, before she could accept him back. Then he'd have to act suitably contrite. Not everywhere though. The people at most of the parties they attended knew the status of their relationship.

Belmont knew, though, that he wasn't going back anytime soon. Adrienne kicking him out had little to do with it. Their relationship was over. Had been for the best part of a decade. They loved each other. But with the death of their son something had died between them. And that something contained the crucial ingredient for their happiness.

Belmont had met Adrienne before the war. They were young. They'd married in 1913. Belmont a vibrant eighteen year old. His wife six months his senior. The new Mme.

Belmont quickly fell pregnant. Their son was born three months before the outbreak of war. They had six months together before Belmont was called up. He left for the front as a young lieutenant and settled into the routine of war. Got back to Paris whenever he could, which wasn't often. Doted on his boy and loved his wife. Wrote her long passionate letters from the front. After the armistice, whenever he got leave they went for long family walks in the parks of Paris, talked about the places they'd go and the cities they'd like to see. They shared all the usual ambitions for a happily married bourgeois couple. He was de-mobbed in mid-1919 and two months later the boy was dead. Died of the flu while Belmont and his wife never even got ill.

War had stolen the most precious years of Belmont's life, the years his son was alive. Adrienne started drinking. Belmont joined the police. Six months later he came home one night to find her in bed with another man. Rather than start a fight or call his wife names and kick up a fuss, Belmont had gone to the drawing room. Lit a cigar and poured himself a drink. And once the initial shock had diminished he realised he wasn't angry or jealous. And so they settled into this new life. A life where they searched for that missing element in the bodies of others. The constant thrill of new relationships coupled with the stability of a long term one. It had become habit as much as anything.

Five P.M. The hotel room was growing dark, Belmont was fastening the buttons of his shirt and thinking about food when a knock came at the door.

'Inspector Belmont, sir, you have pneumatic.'

Belmont opened the door and took the note from the porter, gave him a coin, then closed the door and read the message. Short and simple, 'I'm coming for your slut, Belmont.'

Belmont used the hotel telephone to call Caillou. Told him get round to Galabert's apartment, *tout de suite*, no delay. Then he dashed down to the tram stop. Jumped on board the tram as it was moving away. He couldn't keep still, paced the carriage urging it to move faster. Leapt off before it came to a stop and struggled to keep his balance as he ran down the street.

It took a full minute of hammering before she opened the door.

'Thank Christ you're alright. I've got to get you out of here.'

There were protests as she wriggled free from Belmont's grip. He'd gotten her in a bear hug and was almost crying with relief. She'd thought he was drunk. Drunk and dangerous. Eventually the explanation came out. She didn't waste time. Grabbed a few items of overnight clothing and stuffed them in a bag.

Outside a police motor screeched round the corner, bells ringing and drawing stares from everyone on the street. Caillou and Tabaraut leapt out. Belmont spoke to the driver. Take her to pick up the kid then on to a hotel somewhere out of the city. Make sure she has a police guard, round the clock, understand? Good. He bundled Mme. Galabert into the motor. The three of them watched her drive off.

'May I see the note, Boss?' Tabaraut held out his hand and Belmont passed it to him. 'And she's your slut?'

'Jesus, Chef, you move faster than me,' Caillou said. 'When did that start?'

'That's not important now. Let's get a drink.'

There was a café overlooking the entrance to the Galabert apartment building. The three men took a table by the window. Belmont facing out and across, although it was dark now and not so easy to see outside.

'It's a worrying progression,' Belmont said. 'He wrote my name on the last victim's wall. Then this note. He's singled me out. The question is whether this was a real threat or a perverse joke.'

'At least she's safe for now, Chef, but we've got to catch him before she'll be permanently safe. And we've still got nothing to go on.'

'I fear this was some form of test,' Tabaraut said. 'He takes up a position, like this, where he can see the apartment. Then he sends you the note and watches.'

'What for?' Belmont said.

'To prove he has power over you. He sends you a note and you come running. Who knows what he's got up his sleeve. The man is insane, we know that, but in some respects he must have his normal faculties else he'd stand out like a sore thumb. And that makes him doubly dangerous.'

'Is Jouvin still keeping tabs on Bodescot?'

'Yes, although today's the last day of it. You know he's being promoted, it's Inspector Bloody Jouvin these days.'

'On the superintendent's orders no doubt. That means, if I ever get my position back, you'll have to accept the promotion I keep trying to foist on you, Caillou. We can't have Jouvin outranking you.'

'Maybe, Chef, although, as I've always said, I'm happy being a sergeant.'

'Is it possible that Bodescot sneaks out the back of the club then returns when his shift finishes?'

'It's possible,' Tabaraut said, 'in that anything is possible. That last murder, Jouvin said the door opened a number of times and he saw Bodescot at the bar. To make certain he questioned the boss. She confirmed he never left the club and she's the sort of woman who'd dock his pay if he did. You can't be at the oven and at the mill, Boss, there's no way he committed the last crime.'

'I don't like it, Tabaraut. He fits so neatly. He's suspicious, there's no doubt in my mind that he's hiding something. He's got that dark southern skin. The English couple and the tramp Galabert hauled in described the killer as being dark. Then there's the psychiatrist's opinion that he might be a foreigner or non-Parisian. Also, that he worked at the bottom of a hierarchy and resented it. Who wouldn't resent taking orders from his boss? He fits the bill and there he is working with one of the victims.'

'Most of that would be true of his brother, wouldn't it?

Except he didn't work with any of the victims.'

'What are you talking about, Tabaraut?'

'Remember, Phillipe Bodescot gave his brother as an alibi. Didn't work out though as I asked him in such a way that he thought he was providing an alibi for himself.'

'Yes, yes, Tabaraut, I remember. But what of it?'

'Well, he's southern. In fact his skin's slightly darker than Philippe's. They're both from Carcassonne, I think, so he's not Parisian. He works as a washer-upper in a flea-pit hotel. The boss there is a real pain in the arse. And, when it comes to it, he couldn't provide his brother with an alibi because they weren't together. In fact, he was on his own in the apartment from six in the evening until two in the morning.'

Belmont hadn't waited for the end of Tabaraut's sentence. He'd thrown a ten franc note on the café table, enough to pay for their drinks five times over, and was pulling on his coat and heading out the door while Tabaraut was still talking to his empty chair. Then he and Caillou jumped up and ran after Belmont.

'Where does he work?'

'Hotel Bordeaux.'

They ran to the main road and flagged down a taxi. Ten minutes later all three were outside the Bordeaux. The manager looked nervous. 'Bodescot, no, he hasn't been in for the last couple of days. In fact, if you see him, you can tell him from me not to bother coming back. He's fired.'

They'd kept the taxi waiting. Tabaraut rang the office, got Bodescot's address, rue de Pot de Fer. A seedy address. Tabaraut remembered it now from his first visit with Jouvin. The concierge who'd rather be in the greengrocer's drinking than at her post. The old man who'd hidden behind his door and said he didn't like the Bodescot's, that they were trouble. Most of all he remembered the lack of an elevator.

They ran up the stairs, Caillou and Belmont keeping even pace, Tabaraut bringing up the rear. 'It was the top floor, door on the right,' Tabaraut called as he began to lose sight of the other two.

There were only two doors. Belmont hammered on the one of on the right, 'open up, police.'

Caillou unbuttoned his holster.

Phillipe Bodescot opened the apartment door as Belmont was preparing to kick it in. He wore pyjama bottoms and a dressing gown. It was seven P.M. Belmont didn't have any identification so Caillou flashed his, 'police.' They barged past Bodescot without waiting to be invited in. Tabaraut arrived, panting, a minute later. Phillipe simply held the door open for them all.

'I don't know,' Phillipe said.

'Don't know what?' Tabaraut asked.

Bodescot frowned and shut the door. Tabaraut accompanied him to the living room. They were after his brother, Léon, but that didn't mean this one wasn't dangerous. 'You sit there.' Tabaraut pointed at a chair.

The apartment was small, two bedrooms, a living room and a large cupboard which had been converted into a rudimentary kitchen. Not much to search and nowhere to hide.

'He's not here,' Belmont said.

'Yes, I am,' Phillipe said.

'Are what?'

'I am here, can't you see me?'

'We're not looking for you,' Belmont said.

'Never the less, you have found me.'

'Where's your brother?'

Phillipe looked over at the corner of the room as if his brother might be standing there, 'no I won't,' he said.

'Won't what?' Belmont asked.

'I wasn't talking to you. What do you want my brother for?'

'We want a word with him.'

'Well, he's not here, I'll tell him you called.' Phillipe stood up and took a step towards the door.

'Sit down, Bodescot,' Belmont said. Phillipe did as he was

told. Belmont came and stood over him. 'Where's your brother, he's not a work.'

'No I won't, I simply won't, so you can shut your stupid bitch mouth.'

Belmont grabbed Philippe by his dressing gown and yanked him out of the seat. 'Look, you, I'm not in the mood for games. You tell me where your brother is right now.'

'Why should I, you stupid bitch? All this is your fault. If you hadn't led me on none of this would have happened. You're a prick tease, that's what you are.'

Belmont glanced over at Tabaraut who was rotating a finger by his temple, nuts. Was Bodescot play acting? It didn't feel like it. Bodescot hadn't shown the least sign of recognising him or Caillou and they'd all spent hours in a small interview room together. And why did he keep peering over to the corner?

'Who's over there, Bodescot?'

'Over where?'

'Over in the corner, who is it?'

'You can see her?' A frantic smile appeared on his face. He looked at Belmont with pleading eyes.

'Yes, but I don't know her. Who is it?'

'Maddie.'

'Madeline Legrand?' Tabaraut asked.

'That's right, Maddie. She's been following me about ever since it happened. She says the most awful things to me.'

'Why do you think she's picked on you?'

'She's a vindictive bitch.' Suddenly he turned his attention to the corner of the room again. 'No I won't, you devil, they'll take my head.'

'What did you do to her, Phillipe,' Belmont sounded calm. Soothing.

'I didn't mean to, it just happened. I was after a kiss, that's all. I didn't try anything the other men haven't done. It's not like I was breaking new ground. But she laughed at me, said 'if you want to behave like a punter, Phil, you best put some money on the table.' I thought we were friends. I grabbed her, just to show I wasn't like them. I kissed her with passion.' He looked over at the corner of the room again, 'she struggled but I knew she liked it. Don't try to deny it, you wanted me to take control.'

'Then what happened?'

'I don't know. My hands were on her neck.' Again to the corner, 'I never meant to hurt her. You know, I think I loved her. That's what was eating me up. Seeing those other men stick their hands up her skirt. I couldn't stand it. And then she rejected me. Yes you did, you rejected me. I was being gentle. No. You were, you were teasing me like I was trash. Leading me on. I deserved more respect than that. No. No, I didn't.' Philippe wept. 'I never meant to hurt you. I wanted us to be together. To quit that stinking club. Maybe move down south, get a bit of land and grow tomatoes.'

'Tabaraut, he'll need to be taken back to the Quai and formally charged with the murder of Madeline Legrand. Caillou, go call for a police motor and come get us when it's arrived.'

Phillipe wiped his nose on the sleeve of his dressing gown. Tabaraut cuffed him.

'You better get him some clothes, Tabaraut, I'll watch him.'

Tabaraut left to pick clothes from the piles on Philippe's bedroom floor. Belmont sat on the coffee table and rolled a cigarette. Sat there and watched Phillipe sobbing. He'd given up talking to the ghost in the corner of the room. The psychiatrists would have to work that one out. What they had to say would be the difference between him going to the guillotine or the asylum.

Tabaraut came back with a pair of trousers, a pullover and a shirt. He removed the handcuffs and helped Phillipe dress. 'Still puzzles me,' he said to Belmont. 'We know he can't have killed the last one. Jouvin had him under observation.'

'We've still got to find his brother, Tabaraut. Problem is, this one's not in any state to help us.'

Belmont gave up watching Phillipe dress and picked up the newspaper from the coffee table. It was an old edition with the front page photograph of himself and her outside the Deux Magots. He smiled. That photograph had seemed catastrophic at the time. Now he felt as if it had helped him. Helped him realise he was stuck in a rut, that he needed to move on with his life. He decided that he wouldn't look for a hotel suite. Instead he'd get an apartment, somewhere near the old one. That way he could still lunch with his wife as they led their separate lives. He looked at the photograph again. Only a week ago his passion for her had seemed inexhaustible. Now he hardly thought of her. She'd have moved on too. That is to say, Belmont was not the only man, or woman, in her life. He'd have hardly left a vacuum to be filled with pity or regret.

'Oh, fuck, fuck, fuck.'

'What is it,' Tabaraut said.

Belmont held up the newspaper, 'she's my slut, Tabaraut, not Mme. Galabert. Call the office and have them send men to rue Bonaparte. And get there yourself. Have Caillou drop you off. Léon's gone after her,' he patted the picture then let the paper fall to the floor. By the time it hit the ground Belmont was out the room.

Belmont had seen death as a kid. His grandfather lying in his coffin, laid out in his best suit. Pale but made-up to look less pale. Eyes closed. Arms folded over his chest, hands resting on opposing shoulders. The hint of a smile. He'd felt sad because he liked the man and was going to miss him. Not sad because his grandfather was old and ill and had died a peaceful death.

Then came war. After the parting tears, Belmont spent months in basic training. And he enjoyed it. Once you accepted the routine it was fun. Transferred to the trenches he saw more death. Not the peaceful sleepy death of his grandfather. These were healthy and fit young men, eyes open, futures stolen.

Then there'd been his son.

The same emptiness, aloneness, hit him again as he rode a tram to the rue Bonaparte.

Everyone else carried on as normal. People stopped and looked then crossed the road. Men and women walked arm in arm seeking the right bistro or restaurant for their evening meals. Laughter, shouts and music emanated from the bars and cafés. The moon shone through gaps in the clouds. Street lamps lit the pavements. The world conspired to pretend that everything was as it should be.

The door was locked. Belmont beat upon it. Pressed every buzzer.

'Who's this?'

'Police, open up.'

He took the stairs three at a time. Leaping more than running. He had no gun, felt vulnerable. Tabaraut would arrive soon with backup. But Belmont couldn't wait for them. He'd have to face him, Léon Bodescot, the Paris Ripper, alone and unarmed.

Her door was wide open. He burst into the apartment. No caution or delay. A wireless played. He knew she kept it in the drawing room.

Empty. He stared at the wireless set as if it might tell him where to look. Then he switched it off and listened to the silence. Trembled as he walked towards the bedroom which was off the drawing room. He put one hand on the door and gave it a gentle push. The shutters were closed. The room dark. A flick of the switch and the room was lit. Nothing. He'd feared seeing his name scrawled above her bed. Feared seeing her body lain upon it. No sign of her. No sign of him.

He went back and scanned the hallway.

At first he wasn't sure what he was looking at. Near the storage space where she hung her coats. On the floor. Four drops of blood.

He knelt down to examine them. Touched one drop with his finger. It was still wet. Then he noticed some scuff marks. On their own insignificant. Could they represent a woman being dragged?

Belmont opened the store cupboard door. Coats lay on the floor. More blood. His guts wrenched and twisted in his body like they wanted to escape from him. She must have answered the door then run to this cupboard in fear and confusion. Into this tiny cupboard which didn't even have a lock. A clump of hair lay on the coats and one of her shoes besides them. But she wasn't here and neither was he. So where?

The man who'd let him in appeared in the doorway.

'You see or hear anything?'

'No, like what, what's happened?'

'Come with me. The police are on their way, I want you to stand at the front door and let them in. Tell them the hallway needs a technical exam. And the cupboard, they need to look in the cupboard.'

The man followed Belmont down the stairs. Belmont's mind ran wild. Jumped through the evidence, everything related to the case. All mixed together with images of her, their first meeting in his kitchen. Their first taxi ride together. Her touch. Their first night together. Murder scenes, the Ripper's victims. The map of Paris with the red pins marking the location of each killing. Conversations with Galabert. Notre Dame. The girls from the club lined up against the wall. Albert Oboeuf and his suicide. He remembered Galabert, their walk from the cathedral over the river to the bridge.

'When they get here,' Belmont said, 'tell them Belmont's gone to the river. The pont de l'Archevêché. And tell them to come with weapons drawn.'

Belmont ran straight up the rue Bonaparte to the river. The pont de l'Archevêché was four bridges away. And here it was busy. There were people walking. Motor-cars by the dozen. Cyclists. How would he bring her here? Was he carrying her? Did he hold a knife to her back? Maybe he took a different route. Cut through from rue Bonaparte to the rue de Seine. Then kept to the quiet streets until they came out facing the Île de la Cité.

Bells sounded for eight-thirty. Belmont sprinted up the road, paused for breath as he neared pont Neuf. He slipped down the stairway to the river's edge. Headed under the low arch of the bridge and along the wet and slippery cobbles. Up ahead on his left, over the water, he could see the Quai des Orfèvres. Police Headquarters. He wanted to shout, wave his arms, draw their attention. But it would be useless, too dark, nobody inside the building would be able to see him. He kept on past bridge after bridge. Notre Dame loomed up before him, seemed to lean across the river and reach for him. Up ahead was the pont de l'Archevêché.

The embankment was wide. Normally the vagabonds would be lined up along here. Was it too early for them? He approached the bridge. No longer ran. He crept along by the wall, moving around the trees, afraid of what he might find. The city fell silent.

He edged along the foot of the bridge which rested on the embankment and reached the beginning of an arch which allowed people to pass under. He waited and listened. Sprang round as if to catch someone by surprise. Nothing. No trace of them. He looked back along the river. Had he taken her to Notre Dame? Or further upstream like the third victim, murdered under the pont de la Tournelle?

There would be too many people at Notre Dame. Belmont stalked through the archway. A wooden cart, one wheel broken, rested against the wall. Planks of wood were piled up and covered with tarpaulin. Two barges moored on the river's edge. And over by the lockups, a single shoe to match the one Belmont had found in her apartment.

Belmont lifted her shoe. Sniffed it as if trying to pick up her scent. There was no need, no other place they could have gone.

The doors were black. Paint peeling, large bands of rusted iron over the wood. Belmont pulled one back. It was dark. The street lamps from the road didn't penetrate this far.

Most of these lock-ups had fallen into disrepair. At one time they'd been used as stores for produce coming in off the river. They weren't much more than cellars under the road, convenient for water traffic. Larger warehouses and motorised transport had left them all but redundant. Belmont stepped inside and hit his shin on a piece of metal. He pulled out his torch and shone it around the room.

A dumping ground for junk. Old furniture, smashed up and left to decay. Iron bed frames, wooden chairs with no seats, two perambulator frames. Other items broken beyond recognition. There was a narrow pathway through the furniture. A path which lead on to another door at the far side of the room. A door half-opened emitting a low feminine groan.

Belmont switched off the torch and allowed his eyes to adjust to the darkness. Then he picked his way along the path to the door. Shadows were cast on the floor in front of him, spilling away from the door where a shimmering light marked his destination.

A rat scurried across his path. Belmont stood transfixed, alert, ready to pounce. Now he could hear someone moving about. The sound of a man talking. The sound of a woman making frantic inarticulate noises, not words at all.

He pressed his body against the far wall beside the door. The man was still talking, moving about, his words unclear. Belmont risked a quick glance through the door. Candles flickered. A mattress on the floor. And on the mattress, two legs bound together. He couldn't see the rest of the body. Didn't have to see it. He knew those legs, had kissed his way along them. A sudden moan, more of a choked scream, escaped from the room. Belmont had to act. He knew he shouldn't go in without backup. At least not without knowing exactly where Bodescot was and what he was doing. But Belmont did know what Bodescot was doing. He was torturing her.

He counted to three and sprang round and through the doorway. Scanned the room quickly. Except for the mattress on the floor it appeared to be empty. She was bound hand and foot with a gag across her mouth. Stockings, laddered with large holes in the heels.

Belmont turned to his left. Only a shadow. The wood swept down. For a moment he stared straight into the face of Léon Bodescot. Then he dropped to his knees and toppled face forward to the floor.

Belmont came-to unsure where he was. Certain of the throbbing pain he felt in his head. His eyes, unable to focus, registered vague indistinct objects. Tried to move his hand. Felt a tearing excruciating pain. Panicked, he began to struggle but the pain was intense and only abated when he kept absolutely still. A sweat broke out all over his body.

'You back with us, Inspector Belmont?'

The dark room moved in and out of focus. Candles cast dancing shadows over the walls. He saw her, bound and gagged, dumped on a mattress in the middle of the floor. Wide eyed, staring at Belmont with a look of imploring horror. Then him, Léon Bodescot, a smug grin stuck on his face. Eyes alert, lock knife in hand, blade exposed. He looked proud like an arrogant toddler showing off to a doting parent. Over on the floor, a long, thick piece of wood, bloodied at one end.

Belmont tried to touch the wound on his forehead. Pain shot through his hand and ran up his arm. Felt as if he were being ripped apart. Looked down his arm to see his hand nailed to the wall. Then, quickly, across at his other hand. Léon had crucified him to the wooden support beams in the wall. Blood ran from his hands down his arms, it soaked through his shirt and jacket before dripping to the floor. Now that he could see them, the pain in his hands intensified. He gasped for air, suddenly finding it difficult to breathe.

Léon was laughing. 'What do you reckon? Funny, hey? Don't worry, they won't think you did it. After all, you could hardly cut up this girl then nail yourself to the wall. One hand, perhaps, but not the second. Actually, I've given you the perfect alibi. You ought to thank me.'

'I'll watch you die, Bodescot.'

'No, you thank me.'

Léon punched Belmont in the stomach. It tore at his hands as his arms moved in reflex. Blood from his head wound trickled down between his eyes and along his nose.

'Thank me then.'

'Fuck you.'

Another punch. The pain so great he thought he'd pass out again. Belmont's head slumped forward. Léon reached out his index finger to Belmont's forehead and pushed his head back up.

'Thank me, Chief Inspector.'

'Thanks.' Belmont spat it out no louder than a whisper.

'Too quiet but I'll take it. After all I've won our duel. You did well to find us, although you did little to rescue your slut. Up close, by the way, she's a real looker.'

He took the knife in his right hand and cut her cheek just below the eye.

Tears mingled with the blood. Her eyes flicked to Belmont nailed to the wall, unable to help. This was how it would end, in a damp and dirty cellar, raped and murdered by a mad man.

In one swift movement Belmont wrenched both hands free from the nails pinning them to the wall. Pain surged through his body. His hands a bloody mess of exposed bone and tendon. His agony was channelled into a scream which seemed to erupt from the roots of the Earth. Belmont launched himself at Bodescot.

The weight of Belmont's body pulled Léon away from her. They collapsed on the floor beyond the mattress. Belmont scrambled to his feet. Léon didn't know what had hit him, took a moment to realise that Belmont had torn himself away from the wall. He looked down at his right hand, then at the mattress where he'd dropped the knife. Belmont was going to step back and grab the knife when

Léon picked up a short piece of lead piping and swung at him.

Belmont backed off. Léon pressed forward. He put too much into the next swing. Belmont side-stepped him, then, as the follow through left Léon off balance, Belmont moved in and delivered an upper cut to the face. The punch struck Léon in the mouth, opening up his lower lip. Belmont screamed again, it felt as if his hand had collapsed in on itself. He wouldn't be able to throw another punch. Not if he wanted to keep his hands. A river of blood flowed down his arm. Léon turned, bloody mouthed, ready to come at him again.

They'd skirted the mattress and were now back by the wall where Belmont had been nailed. Léon kicked over the candles as he past them. The room grew darker. Belmont found it difficult to focus. The earlier blow from the wooden strut had already left his head spinning. The loss of blood and the pain in his hands meant he couldn't concentrate. Léon swung again. Belmont dodged but the pipe caught him on the left shoulder. His knees buckled and he went down.

He saw the wood, grabbed it and rolled onto his back in time to parry a blow coming straight for his head. The wood, held like a staff between both hands, absorbed most of the force. It hurt his hands but he could take this level of pain. Léon swung down again and again. Belmont blocked each blow with the wood. Léon kicked out at Belmont's legs. Belmont swung the wood, striking Léon in the arm. Léon roared in fury and rained blows at Belmont. The pipe struck the centre of the wood. There was a ripping tearing noise as it began to splinter under the ferocity of Léon's blows. A second and third strike hit at the same spot and the wood broke in two.

Belmont couldn't defend himself from the next blow. Léon had switched targets and swung down at Belmont's shin. Belmont screamed. Tried to jab at Léon with the broken wood. Léon struck him across the arm and that half of the wood was dropped. Léon hit the arm again to the snap of a breaking bone. Léon struck once more. Belmont tried to crawl away. Léon laughed. 'It's over, Belmont. I never intended to kill you but I shall. Then I'll kill your slut.'

Léon, still laughing, turned to look at her on the mattress. She wasn't there. Before he could wonder where she was the knife entered his thigh. This time it was Léon's turn to scream. He dropped the piping and fell to the floor. She pulled the knife out. Blood squirted from his leg. He pressed his hands to the wound to stem the flow.

Léon thrashed about on the floor holding his leg. Belmont caught her wrist as the knife was about to enter Léon's back. She struggled against his grip before dropping the weapon and collapsing in a crying heap on the ground. Belmont could hardly move. His left arm hung limp at his side. He reached for her with his right hand which bled profusely.

'Get out of here,' Belmont said. He sat down beside her. I think he's out of action for now but who knows how long that will last. You get out of here, go for help. My men should be on the riverside.'

Blood ran from the wound on her cheek. For what seemed like an age she didn't move. Her body began shaking as she crawled towards the door. She picked up one of the candles. As she got to the door she used its frame to help climb to her feet. Léon was silent now. Belmont watched him, wondered what would make a man do the things Léon had done.

Monday, December 14th

The morning felt like early spring, crisp and cold. Belmont lounged in a wicker chair, blanket over his lap. Smoked a pipe. Earlier he'd tried rolling a cigarette. His fingers unable to manipulate the paper, tobacco had fallen all over his blanket. Then the papers, the tobacco and his lighter were thrown on the lawn. A table which had been set out beside him was kicked over, breaking a water jug. He was content now with his pipe.

According to the nurse he'd been there two weeks. Last night he'd woken and, for the first time, been aware of his surroundings. The night nurse explained he'd had a fever, brought on by an infection in his left hand. At one point the doctor had talked of amputation. All was well now, she said, although he might never have the same dexterity as before.

Belmont had then fallen into an exhausted sleep and woke early.

'Morning, Boss.'

Tabaraut peered down at Belmont.

'There are more of these chairs inside, Tabaraut, go grab one.'

Tabaraut disappeared and returned with another chair. 'I asked them to telephone when you were able to talk.'

'It's good to see you, Tabaraut. I don't really remember much of what happened. I know I went after the Ripper and I think I caught him.'

'Both correct, Boss. We were on the embankment when your lady friend emerged from one of the cellars screaming and shouting. We couldn't get much sense out of her but it was obvious where she'd come from. I was there with Caillou. Can you remember us arresting Phillipe Bodescot?'

'Not quite, I do recall going to his apartment.'

'That's right, the three of us found him talking to Maddie Legrand. Then he confessed to killing her. Anyway, you went running off and we had to get Bodescot to headquarters. I decided to have the motor drop both myself and Caillou off at rue Bonaparte. Told the driver to take Bodescot in, HQ's only a five minutes' drive from there. I instructed the driver to send reinforcements. Outside the apartment there was a chap who told us you'd gone down to the river ten minutes earlier. By the time we'd gotten there and had a look around another ten minutes had past. Then we heard her upstream from us.

'Caillou stayed with the girl. We couldn't leave her. Don't worry, Boss, after a couple of days rest she was right as rain. He hadn't hurt her, just a few bruises and a cut on the cheek.'

'Some of it's coming back to me, Tabaraut. He did do something to her. I remember him leaning over her.'

'Yes, she's told us what happened. He'd gone to her apartment and attacked her. Marched her through the streets. Kept her close to him with a knife pressed against her back. Soon as he got her into that cellar room he bound her and threw her on the mattress. She can't say how long they were there but it was over an hour. She had no idea why they were waiting, until you turned up. I don't know what you recall so I'll just fill you in. Soon as you poked your head round the door he whacked it with a piece of wood and you went down. If it weren't for your injuries I'd hardly believe the next part. Seems he nailed you to the wall. I can't get over it, Boss, that must have been horrendous.'

'It was no picnic, Tabaraut. Most times something bad happens I can always shrug and say I've been through worse. Not this time, that was the worst. Felt like my hands were being pulled inside out. I feel sick thinking about it.'

'Do you want me to stop, Boss, we could talk about

something else?'

'No, Tabaraut, I want to know what happened.'

'Well you were out for a couple of minutes as he nailed you to the wall. Then Bodescot taunted you, made you thank him for crucifying you. Said he was going to cut the girl up. Then he cut her cheek with his knife, that was her only real wound, needed two stitches. She couldn't see you then but you must have wrenched yourself off the wall and jumped him. There was a fight and as it went on she used Bodescot's knife to cut herself free and stabbed him in the leg. While he was on the floor she went for help, which is where we started.'

'What of that bastard Bodescot, where's he being held?'

'We've buried him, Boss. That knife in the leg severed an artery. When I arrived you were unconscious and, to be frank, I don't give a fuck about Bodescot, so I attended to you. By the time I got to him he was dead. He may have been dead the whole time, I really don't care.'

'Thanks for getting me out of there, Tabaraut.'

'No problem, Boss, but I didn't do anything. You and the girl had already taken care of him. By the way, Péraud has been all over the newspapers telling them what a hero you are. You're up for a commendation. I wouldn't be surprised if they gave you the Legion d'honneur. Of course, you've been reinstated. The newspapers themselves are all feting you too. You wouldn't think you'd recently been villain number one in most of them.'

'And Phillipe Bodescot, what's happening with him?'

'The magistrate attributed all the murders to Léon except the Legrand killing. Philippe's been charged with that one. A panel of psychiatric experts carried out an evaluation and found him perfectly sane. They must be nuts themselves to think that. He'll be going to trial sometime after the New Year most likely in the spring. Then, I guess, it's the guillotine.

'By the way, Boss, at one point your girl asked Léon Bodescot why he did it. Do you know what he said?'

'No idea, Tabaraut, what?'

'He said he was spitting out some of the shit he's had to swallow. Murdering people is spitting out the shit, I have to say it's a new one on me.'

'Sounds like he was spitting out some more shit when he said that, Tabaraut.'

Belmont puffed on his pipe and gazed across the lawn. None of this felt like it made any difference to him. Léon was dead and if he wasn't they'd have him queued up for execution. Phillipe ought to be going to the nut house but he'd go to the guillotine instead. Being reinstated, what difference would that make? Péraud would suspend him just as quick if the press got at him again. For people like Superintendent Péraud the Judiciary Police was a political tool. This case closed, that one opened, this one ignored, that one prosecuted. And then there was this Ibex business. Péraud exploited his position to shield any number of Ibex crimes. And when Belmont returned he'd be sucked into it all once more. Maybe it was time to step away, dedicate the rest of his life to art dealing. Spend his days looking at beautiful paintings rather than at his own name scrawled in blood on bedroom walls.

Tabaraut mumbled something then stood up to leave. 'If it's alright I'll tell the others they can pop in. They've all been down here once or twice. Even Jouvin, although I suspect he only came because he knew you were unconscious. There was one other thing, Boss.'

'Yes?'

'Galabert's funeral was held a couple of days after you came in here. I thought I should tell you, I know you'd have wanted to be there.'

'How did it go?'

'All well, Boss, we gave him a good send off.'

'And how was his wife?'

'She held up well. The kid was good too. She'd spent the night you caught Bodescot in a hotel with police protection, so she knows she was in danger. But she doesn't know about the note you got. What it said, I mean.'

'Thanks, Tabaraut.'

'I'll be off. The press might try and bug you now you're up and about. You might want to have a session with them and get it over with.'

'They can go to hell, Tabaraut.'

Belmont's next visitor arrived an hour after Tabaraut's departure. Barely enough time for Belmont to have picked open his bandages to take a look at the wound on his left hand, be scolded by a nurse and have the bandage replaced. The nurse had let him take a good look, a scabbed over stigmata, before she put the bandage back on. Despite the scolding, the way she spoke indicated to Belmont that he held some credit with the staff.

The kid, Lilian, sat on the lawn with a drawing book. Mme. Galabert took the chair Tabaraut had brought out.

'We've buried him.'

'I heard. I'm sorry I couldn't have been there.'

'He would have wanted you here, getting fixed up. When I heard what had happened to you I felt sick to the stomach. I thought every man I ever touched was going to wind up dead. I came straight here but they wouldn't let me see you, said your condition was unstable. I spoke to Tabaraut at the funeral. He telephoned to let me know you were up and about. Anyway, listen, I've had time to think. I realise you can't do any more about what happened to Dédé. Not with the people involved being who they are. I wanted revenge, now I just want you safe. If you like, I can still give you that key.'

The kid came over to Belmont, gave him the picture she'd drawn. A cat, colourful, a touch of the fauvist.

'Thank you, young lady,' he said, holding the picture up to fully examine it, 'it's lovely, quite beautiful.'

The kid smiled coyly. He ruffled her hair. She went and hid behind her maman, peeping out at him from around her chair.

'I would like it,' he said, 'if you've a spare key.'

He had time to get a coffee, spill it because his hand wasn't strong enough to hold the cup, get reprimanded for using bad language, get changed and have a nurse make him some more coffee and bring it to him outside, before the next visitor arrived.

'I'm leaving,' she said. 'I would have gone by now but I wanted to see you before I left. To say goodbye.'

'Where you going?'

'America. Start a new life and all that. A life away from France, away from Paris. I may go to Los Angeles. I've always fancied a go at acting.'

'I'm sorry, for what happened.'

She picked up his hand and stroked it gently.

'Don't be. You saved me from a pretty horrible death.'

'You saved me too.'

'But now we must part,' she said. 'I'd ask you to come with me but…'

'But I'd remind you of what you are leaving. But I'd never leave Paris. But you don't want a lover moping about while you're trying to break into movies.'

She kissed his fingers. He stroked her hair with his free hand.

'I'll watch out for you,' he said. 'If you appear in a movie I'll watch every showing.'

'No you won't, but try to watch them at least once. And don't think of what happened in that cellar. Think of what happened before, when there was a passion between us. Remember our meeting in your kitchen, remember our first kiss.'

She kissed him on the forehead, next to the scar that was forming there, and then she was gone.

His wife woke him. Despite the cold they'd let him stay out in the chair. They said it was because he'd been inside so long. He knew it was because they were favouring him. The nurse who'd brought his dinner had said, 'we all sleep a bit easier because of you, Chief Inspector.'

'You can come home,' she said, 'when you're well enough to leave this place.'

He looked at her, the dying winter sun lighting her hair and illuminating her face. She was as beautiful as when they'd first met.

'Things will need to change,' he said.

'What things?'

'Us. I don't want to carry on as before, looking for the magic in strangers we can't find in ourselves.'

'I don't know. I love you but I need more than just you.'

'I do too. But what we're getting isn't what we need. We're not too old. We could try again.'

She looked away, picked at the wicker strands in her chair. When she looked back there were tears in her eyes.

'I can't, darling. I can't just replace him like that. It cut too deep, it'd kill me if that happened again.'

She took his hand and squeezed it, then fussed because she'd hurt him.

'I'm going to look for an apartment,' he said.

'Get one near-by, I like having you around, Monsieur Belmont.'

He wanted to say he'd go back with her. Those tears were breaking his heart. He couldn't. That life was a terminal cancer.

'I will,' he said, 'keep an eye out for me. They say I'll be in here for at least another week.'

December 21st into January

Belmont was happy to be back living in a dingy hotel room especially now the plaster had been removed from his left arm.

He blew smoke at the window pane, watched it drift up to the ice patterns in the corners of the glass. Early evening and already pitch black outside. Now that he was free Belmont realised his prickliness wasn't all about being cooped up in hospital. It was about wanting to do things he wouldn't be able to do. He opened and closed his right hand. Formed a fist with difficulty. The pain was almost gone but the tendons fought against his hand closing.

A week went by. Christmas Eve spent with his wife, exchanged presents and pleasantries. Just the two of them. They'd enjoyed themselves while knowing it would be their last Christmas spent alone together. The apartment had felt alien to him. His paintings hung on the walls but his scent had faded. Over by the dining room window was the naked statue of his wife. He stared it as he ate. She was bending over backwards to the point where she'd have fallen if she weren't made of bronze.

By the New Year Belmont had fallen into a routine. The routine of a man with no work and no demands on his time. He spent hours in galleries, read books, smoked his pipe. Coffees in the morning, wine in the afternoon and spirits in the evening. Two more days and Belmont could return to work. Light duties.

There was an apartment two streets from his wife. It would be vacated at the end of the month. Belmont knew the owner. All it took to secure the place was a handshake and a tedious retelling of the Ripper case. Belmont took it in good spirit. The case itself was over. Léon Bodescot was dead. Phillipe Bodescot was to go on trial in April. He'd confessed so it was a matter of execution, banishment or confinement. In fact, Belmont felt good. For the first time since being kicked out of his apartment, he walked with a spring in his step.

That spring took him out for a late-night stroll along the river. Puddles of ice where that morning's rain had frozen. A chill wind ripped up the Seine and cut right through you. Vagrants slept, huddled together under the bridges. They were safe from The Ripper now, if from nothing else. Belmont tip-toed past, trying not to wake them. Made his way up to the quayside warehouses. Then he took a circular route back through the city, along the Rivoli then down past the Quai des Orfèvres.

Light duties involved shaking hands with every employee in the building. The females kissed him on both cheeks. Some of the males kissed him on both cheeks. Many patted him on the back, including Péraud who didn't waste the opportunity to give an impromptu yet overly rehearsed speech. Belmont was a hero, a great officer, and so on and so forth. Belmont disliked the fuss but he sucked it up, they'd lost one officer and had nearly lost him. They'd taken two murderers off the streets and, for the time being, people weren't knocking the department. So he let them revel in it. What's more, the smell of the building was a tonic to him. Felt healthier just breathing in that heady mix of tobacco smoke, dusty old files, coffee and sweat. The odour of the Quai des Orfèvres, they ought to have brought it to him at the hospital. It was in his blood.

'Hey, Chef, good to have you back,' Gracianette said. 'I've had the stove in your room burning these last two hours. The room's toasty. I have to say, without you this place has been like a statueless plinth.'

'Thanks, Gracianette, any chance of getting some coffee sent up?'

With all the handshaking and backslapping, it had taken Belmont over an hour to reach his office and it told more than he'd expected. He was exhausted. He eased himself into his chair and stuck his feet up on the desk. Rooted his cognac bottle out from the bottom drawer. Poured a glass as the lad from the café arrived so he tipped some booze in the coffee and drank that.

Gracianette was right, the room was toasty. The desk dusty. Papers had been shifted around. That could have been Tabaraut bringing him copies of the Ripper case files. Or Péraud taking the papers for himself. He had an idea he might clear his desk completely, sort through his notes and get them archived. Start the year off with a nice neat office, or at least a nice neat desk.

'How do, Boss.' Tabaraut sauntered in looking pretty pleased with himself. He took a seat opposite Belmont and stared at the cognac bottle like a puppy dog. Belmont poured him a snifter.

'OK, Tabaraut, give me the low down, what we got on the books?'

Tabaraut pulled out his notebook and flicked through the pages. 'We've got a murder, nothing special. Some drunk idiot clobbered his wife with a brick. He'd brought the brick back from work in his coat pocket. Anyway, not much doing on that one as it's already with the magistrate. Caillou wrapped it up for us. By the way, The Post Office robbers were sent down, that's a feather in Riquet's cap. In the last three weeks there have been four rapes in the Jardin du Luxembourg. One of the victims thinks the attacker has red hair, although he wore a cap pulled over his head and a scarf covered most of his face. Gracianette's working that one. *Inspector* Jouvin is looking at a series of street robberies. The attacker whacks the victim over the back of the head. They collapse and he steals their wallets, watches, whatever else they've got. The latest victim is still in hospital. Then there's one I picked for myself. A river warehouse burnt down. This is the only one Péraud's been interested in. I'll tell you now, I don't know how much longer I could have stuck having him running the squad. And why is he so interested in this case?'

'Seems mysterious, what sort of a place is it?'

'A building loaded with ice. People bring in dead things, fish, and keep them on ice until they're ready to dump them on the street, markets and what-not. Why would anybody want to burn down a place like that, Boss?'

'That must be what Superintendent Péraud was thinking, Tabaraut, he's obviously got a good nose for a case. And it certainly smells fishy,' Belmont grinned, 'like an insurance job. Go over all the owner's financial dealings. Have someone check the books and, of course, the insurance policy. Find out what other dealings the owner had. In short, rake over this man's life and look for anything at all suspicious. Then we'll haul him in for questioning. Teach the little shit what happens when he uses his buildings to store flics rather than fish.'

'It'll be a pleasure, Boss.'

'And Tabaraut, have Gracianette bring me the file on those Luxembourg rapes.'

After work, Belmont took an evening stroll. This time to the Arab Quarter. Stopped at a café. Two old men played backgammon by the window. Their reflected selves playing out in the street. The men wore thick jumpers, berets pulled down over their heads, scarves. Gloved hands rolled dice and moved counters. Belmont didn't blame them for wrapping up. Despite the brazier burning in the middle of the café, it was freezing.

After a thick Turkish style coffee Belmont meandered along the streets to the Djaout apartment. It was too cold for the men to be out chatting on the front steps. Mme. Djaout opened the door to him. From the bedroom crawled a small chubby kid who dribbled and gurgled then stopped to appraise the stranger at the door. He raised one hand towards Belmont and seemed to smile. Belmont got down on his haunches and made cooing noises. The kid sat up and waved both hands at him. Belmont winked and stood back up.

'Ferhat,' she called to her husband, 'it's the policeman from the newspapers.'

This time she didn't immediately retreat to the bedroom. Instead she picked up her child and stood in the hallway. The kid carried on waving and the mother pretended to attend to him while casting sly glances at Belmont. Eventually she said, 'you must be very brave.'

Ferhat escorted Belmont to the dining room. Belmont sat himself down in the seat that was offered and asked if he could smoke his pipe. Ferhat didn't object.

'I saw in the newspapers that you'd been in hospital.'

'I'm out now though,' Belmont said. 'And I noticed there were no stories about bombs in those newspapers.'

'We haven't planted any but the police have been trying to intimidate us. Rounding up Arabs and taking us in. Beating us. I can't promise that there won't be more trouble. No, don't look at me like that. I'm not talking about myself or my brothers from the party. I'm talking about others. There are young men being made to feel weak. Made to feel shame. They're likely to do something reckless. We counsel calm but offer no solution. Why are they being picked on, they ask. And all we can say is, because you are Arab. Might just as well spit in their eye. So, of course, they are angry.'

'I think that's the point,' Belmont said. 'The people instigating this intimidation are the same people behind the earlier attacks. The attack on you and your brother. I realise now they were doing it to get a response and you gave it to them with that bomb.'

Ferhat pulled a packet of cigarettes from his jacket pocket. Belmont didn't recognise the brand. The writing on the pack was in Arabic.

'So we fell into their trap?'

'It was a provocation rather than a trap. What they're

doing now is moving to the next stage. They just need one more bomb, or a demonstration which they'll poke and prod until it becomes a riot, and then they'll crack down further. This time they'll instigate changes in the law. Make life for an Arab in France so unpleasant that you'll be forced to leave.'

'You talk as if you know who they are. Have you found anything out?'

'The official investigation started and ended with the hit and run. Case closed due to a shortage of evidence. My sergeant, Galabert, he continued unofficially and got killed for his trouble. I picked up where he left off. And I found a list of names.' Belmont produced a sheet of paper where he'd copied some of the Ibex names. The senator, the doctor, the names that had been written in bold across the top of each column. A list of the Ibex leadership. An incomplete list. Belmont had not written Superintendent Péraud's name down. He didn't know why. Perhaps he didn't want to betray a fellow flic. Perhaps he was saving Péraud for a personal vengeance.

Ferhat's hands shook as he read the list of names.

'These are the men who killed my brother?'

'I doubt it, they wouldn't have gotten their hands dirty. Maybe they were at the scene, overseeing the attack. But they wouldn't have thrown any punches.'

'They are the generals who oversee the battle. Without them there is no war.'

'There are many ingredients to war, M. Djaout. Without the generals, no war. Without the foot soldiers, no war. Without the prejudice, the greed, the hatred, the fear, no war. But these men oversaw your brother's death.'

'And why do you give this list to me?'

'Because I've no power to touch them. They have put themselves outside the law and so they need to be dealt with outside the law. They killed your brother, Ahmed. They killed my brother officer, Galabert.'

Ferhat folded the paper neatly and tucked it in his pocket. Then he saw Belmont to the door. The wife and the kid had retreated to the bedroom. Little shrieks of laughter came from behind the door. Belmont could imagine the kid being tickled. He shook Ferhat's hand.

'And what do you recommend we do about this list?'

'I'm not going to recommend anything. But I hope you make them suffer.'

THE END

Acknowledgements

This book was originally published by 280 Steps, who unfortunately folded. I'd like to thank Fahrenheit Press for pulling a few of us 280 Steps authors from the wreckage. Also thanks to Eva Dolan, Nick Quantrill and Paul D. Brazill for providing me with helpful feedback while the text was still in development. And also Isla, for putting up with a writer in the house.

About the author

Born and brought up in the West of England, Seth has also lived in Carcassonne, Zurich and the Isle of Man. With two daughters, his writing time is the period spent in cafés as the girls do gym, dance, drama lessons. Previous novels include Salazar and A Dead American in Paris.

More books from Fahrenheit Press

If you enjoyed this book by Seth Lynch you might also like these other Fahrenheit titles from his 3rd Republic series

A Citizen Of Nowhere (Vol 1)

A Dead American In Paris (Vol 2)

Veronique (Vol 4)

Printed in Great
Britain
by Amazon